Colleen —

Remembrances of
things that are dear, is,
indeed, food for the soul.
I remember you —

Dean

THE PIGEON MAN'S DREAM

by

Dean Davis

authorHOUSE®

AuthorHouse™
1663 Liberty Drive, Suite 200
Bloomington, IN 47403
www.authorhouse.com
Phone: 1-800-839-8640

First published by AuthorHouse 6/27/2007

ISBN: 978-1-4343-2019-3 (sc)

Library of Congress Control Number: 2007904252

Printed in the United States of America
Bloomington, Indiana

This book is printed on acid-free paper.

To Trout
For The Memories

PROLOGUE

"I am lying on the bottom of a crystal clear pond. There are large wings growing from my shoulders. My body is covered with silt and mud. I look up and see fish swimming near the top. The sun is reflecting off their scales casting a multi-colored prism that, at times, blinds me. I see my father peering into the water beckoning me to rise to the top. I struggle to free myself from the muddy bottom, but I can't. Trout feeding on bugs near the surface are snapping and breaking water, which distorts my father's face. He looks like a reflection from "The House Of Mirrors" at the carnival, twisted and unreal. I try to move my arms and the wings that are attached to them, but to no avail. The mud that is covering me is too heavy. The trout are in a feeding frenzy and the splashing is slowly erasing the image of my father. I am losing my breath and suffocating. I open my mouth to scream, but no words come. He cannot help me. I am drowning. That is when I awaken."

"How long have you been having this dream?" the therapist asked.

"For as long as I can remember. Ever since I was a kid. What do you think it means?"

"I don't know. Maybe you should write about it, you might find an answer."

CHAPTER 1

The telephone rang in the middle of June. It was the week summer had arrived. I remember it well, because the days started to get hot around ten in the morning instead of noon, and if I recall, the last call I'd gotten was at the end of May, three weeks before.

That was a call from Helga, my ex-girl friend, a vicious tirade that burned my ears so bad I ripped the phone's plug from the wall. After that call I looked at that little plastic machine as some kind of instrument of torture to be used only to call your mother on Sunday, or to dial 911. Since nobody called me anyway it didn't matter much whether the phone was working or not. Figuring it was time to rejoin the real world; however, that very morning I had turned the machine back on. A half hour after plugging it in I got a call.

Summer's arrival on that warm June morning, and the change of seasons that went with it really didn't much matter to me. There could have been a Force Ten hurricane outside and it still wouldn't have altered the state of mind I'd been in since the day Helga left. In the agricultural world they would call it vegetating, or going to seed. The medical term is probably; "Deep Compost, Depression Syndrome," best cured by placing the barrel of a .44-magnum revolver between your eyebrows and squeezing off a round. In the end it didn't matter what it was called. I just knew that my mind had turned into an emotional septic tank, and I had wasted weeks lying on a leaky inner tube floating around in the middle of it.

Helga packed her bags and left for the "Fatherland" the day before my 51st birthday. After she was gone, I realized she not only took all her things, but she also walked off with the wrapped presents that were hidden behind the dirty laundry on the closet floor.

An apt definition of Helga's mind would be the attitude, "Take no prisoners." Walking off with the gifts was just an extension of her battlefield mentality. I can see this short, fat, Nazi colonel running around inside her head, arm held straight out, shouting, "Give no quarter; leave nothing behind the enemy can use!"

She was about as close to mean as I'd ever seen. There was no waiting around for the sun to go down before she would draw blood. For all she cared, it could have been high noon on the hottest day in July because she knew there wasn't a silver bullet or crucifix made that could keep her away from your emotional throat.

A friend once said that she reminded him of Frankenstein's bride in the midst of your worst PMS nightmare, wired on some bad "crank."

I would spend hours asking myself the unanswerable Zen question of how is it that there exists something that doesn't hold six bullets, or isn't shiny with a sharp point that could cause so much pain?

I was slowly drowning in a deep pool of existential sewage, listening to the sound of my heart shrinking, when the phone's ring bounced off the hardwood floor. It ricocheted over the carpet into the living room, landing on the couch next to me where I had been sitting since noon the day before.

The ring had some importance to it, a seriousness hard to ignore. It wasn't one where you pick up the receiver and some lady asks if you take the Sunday paper, and if not would you like a lifetime subscription at half off, or the guy who says we're taking a poll and would like to know if you have a vacuum cleaner in the house.

This ring was different. It had a Tibetan gong quality to it, maybe even a karmic clang. It was definitely doing something to me. I found myself springing off the couch, spilling my third beer of the morning. Anything that could do that had to have some magic in it.

Fully expecting to have the Dalai Lama on the other end, I picked it up. With the deepest and most spiritual voice I could conjure, I said, "Hello?"

At the other end of the line the soft voice of a young woman said, "Hi."

It sure as hell isn't the "Enlightened One." And I don't know any young women, (not lately anyway), except for my daughter, and she never calls. And I know it isn't the high school girl who called last month asking for donations to help send the cheerleading team to Wisconsin for the national finals; not after I philosophically, (and very drunkenly), told her it's really not very cool to be a cheerleader anymore, that it's about as close to being a campus whore as there is.

The silence was becoming deadly. If I didn't say something soon the person on the other end would think that hello was the only word I knew and hang up.

Thinking I'd better say something quick or I would be talking to a dial tone, I uttered a profound, "Who's there?"

"Hey, it's me, Trout."

It knocked me back a step. Trout? I hadn't heard from her in months. The last time I talked to her she was up in Oregon in the middle of her second year of college. She was having a tough time dealing with it emotionally.

Calls from Trout were usually made when she was stressed out or on the verge of losing it, and wanted to drop out of school and out of everything else.

The calls usually caught me off guard. We hadn't had much contact over the past few years and I had a tendency to visualize her as the teenager she was the last time I saw her. I never knew what to say, except to try to give her some fatherly advice or to lend a philosophical ear, which was hard to do. I always had this gut feeling that she knew more about life and its trials than I did. After hanging up I often felt like a Charlatan who had done his best trying to fake his maturity. It was clear to me that I didn't want to be fifty years old with her. I would have been real happy to have been a child of eight, with her giving me enlightening advice. As a matter of fact, I did believe that I was eight most of the time, stuck somewhere back in 1950, and the last 43 years were just a drill to prepare me for the age of nine.

I often wondered what Trout thought of me. There always had been a love between us. A love based on respect, but deep inside my intuitive soul was the feeling that we had something special going on, a Karma-like bond that hadn't yet worked itself to the surface. It floated around in the air each time we met. Every time I saw her it was as if I were meeting my non-identical twin who had been separated from me at birth.

Her father had died suddenly the year before and she had taken the loss hard, falling into that bottomless pit of missing someone so bad you wanted to die too. It was always there in her voice, that hidden message of need, a distress call crying out to the soothing voice of an older man that she trusted.

Maybe that was what this call was about. Whatever the reason, it was nice to hear her voice. It did wonders for my mausoleum mentality, immediately picking up my spirits.

"Trout, what's going on?"

She answered almost apologetically, "I'm in Santa Cruz at my sister's. I wanted to know if I could come up and stay at your place for a few weeks. If it's not OK, just say so. I'll understand."

This was the best news I'd heard since Vampira had left. I said, "Yeah, Trout, it's all right. I could use the company. It would be nice to see your face again."

"I don't want to be a burden. I'd probably get in your way. If you really don't want me to come, it's all right."

She was real good at this. What she really wanted to say was, "I want to come up but I know you don't want me. I'm not worth a shit, and I'd be a pain in the ass anyway!"

Not wanting to lose the chance of having someone to talk to, and to help fill the void, I said, "Trout, I'm sitting here ready to pour some Drano in my beer, and if you don't get up here soon you could possibly have one old friend less!"

Well, I thought, that should get her moving. Maybe it will bring out all of her Florence Nightingale qualities and she would have to come up, if not for nothing else than to save me from myself. She knew I was real good at covering up pain with humor, "Having a tough day, huh?" She said.

"Oh no, nothing a loaded .38 wouldn't handle! It's no big deal. It's just that this big black cloud floated in the front door about two months ago. It likes the place so much it doesn't want to leave."

"OK. If you're sure it's all right, I'll leave in a couple of hours. I'll be there sometime this afternoon."

"Do you know how to get here?"

"Yeah, my mom gave me directions."

"I live way out in the country."

"No problem, I'll find it."

"Great, I'll see you sometime this afternoon."

After hanging up I immediately thought, Jesus, I'm going to have a guest. A companion. A buddy. Someone that's bright and poetic. The house will smell of shampoo and earthy perfume. Maybe from time to time there might even be a soft-laced bra hanging like a banner of womanhood in the bathroom. Yes, this could be just what I need to pull me out of this grave of insanity I'd been digging for the past couple of months.

Trout was coming and I didn't even really know her. I'd been around her since she was a baby, simply because she was the daughter of two of my best friends. Her mother was a childhood friend of my ex-wife's. During our marriage I had become very close to her parents, and had remained so. You could say I was sort of like family. My divorce wasn't a tragic separation like many, but rather a falling out of two hearts. I called it a "Legal Operation," a surgical incision that separates two people before the cancer of lies, lack of commitment and loss of passion eats them both up.

Somehow my ex-wife and I had survived the breakup and for the past twenty-one years had remained good friends, a factor that helped to keep Trout and me in touch.

Having a guest arriving meant that I had to get the old farmhouse in order. The last person to sleep in the spare room was me. That had been an act of survival during the last three days of the Amazon's Dynasty. During those last days with Helga, the one thing I knew for sure was that I didn't want to find myself lying next to her after the sun went down.

I spent the next couple of hours putting Trout's room in order, changing the sheets and clearing out the little closet behind the bed. It was a small but beautiful room with windows at eye level that wrapped around two walls. The windows were old and nine-paned, and through them you could see the eighty-year-old water tower setting at the back of the house. Forty years ago

I'm sure the tower was bright yellow, but through time and the harsh Northern California weather the color had faded into aged gray redwood, allowing only hints of light ocher to show through. Directly behind the window growing between the house and the tower was a huge pink Camellia tree; its wax-like leaves a deep green. During late summer and fall the flowers covered the back wooden steps with a rose-colored carpet.

The year before I had refinished a tall antique writing desk and put it in the corner under the windows facing the Camellias. A perfect place, I thought, for Trout to sit and spend her summer days writing all of that poetry I knew was locked up in that wonderful head of hers.

From the ceiling hung two of my sculptures, flying objects that I titled, "Dragon Killers." Poetic, lethal-looking feathered wire objects, each with a crossbow in front armed with a stone-tipped arrow. I believed then, and still do, that these machines are capable of warding off the demons that creep into our rooms at night. The one's that claw through the skin into our unprotected souls.

After checking the room to make sure it was the kind of place that I thought deserving of Trout, I proceeded to check the rest of the house. I walked around looking down at the floor just to make sure there weren't any pieces of my soul scattered around for her to trip over when she came in with her bags.

Trout would be driving north on Highway 101 into the wine country. When she got almost through Santa Rosa she'd head west on Guerneville Road. She couldn't miss the turnoff because on the left was one of those dinosaur shopping centers built in the late 50's, that was now struggling to survive.

About eight years ago the "Suits" from L.A arrived with their designer attaché cases and BMW's. Along with a few D8 Caterpillar tractors they proceeded to rip the hundred-and-twenty-five-year-old heart out of Old Town. In its place they put up one of those red-brick three-story monsters featuring a Macy's, an Emporium, a restaurant area on the upper level offering Styrofoam food from seven different countries, plastic ivy, and one hundred-and-thirty-seven other stores, most of which sell shoes, monogrammed baseball caps, and shops that melt the photo of your favorite grandchild onto a T-shirt.

The dinosaur down the road has struggled ever since. Not even its attempts at "Super Mega Dollar Day Sales," or its "Free Kiddy Circuses" will save it from the extinction already written. When people ask me for directions on how to get here, I say take 101 to the Tar Pits, then turn left.

Keep going straight and you'll pass Circuit City, Good Guys and the last Taco Bell before Honolulu. At that point you are exactly 7.5 miles from the farm.

At the last light before open country, on the right, is The Organic Grocery Store, immediately recognizable by the large amount of VW vans and decades old Volvos, (vegetarians of the auto industry) in the parking lot.

Cattycorner from the Tofu Palace and directly across the street from West America Bank (free checking, free checkbook, free pen, and no slack if you overdraw) is an extinct Flying A station. It's another fossil that advertises "8 by 10 Truck, Move Yourself, Your Next Door Neighbor and Everybody Else On The Block For Only $19.95 A Day."

Across the street from U-Haul is the biggest Supermarket in the world, a monolithic structure about the size of eight covered football fields. A monument to food and anything else you need 24 hours a day. It's so big that on the shopping carts they offer a little computer-like store map and item finder.

For example, if you want an apple you press "A". A read-out of all "A" items pops up on the screen. To find out where they are, you punch in the coded space next to the word. It will read out "aisle 84 section K." Those numbers alone would put any sober brain into reverse. If you need help finding aisle 84 section K, you punch "Store Map" and a detailed floor plan pops up. In my one and only experience in the store I pressed "Map," and this readout comes on the screen that looks like an engineer's diagram for all the electrical lines that run under the Pentagon. After finding out I was on row 3 section C and the walk to Apples was a good twenty minutes away I decided to pack it in and go home. On my way out to the car, empty-handed, this thought ran through my head of an immigrant family from some former East Bloc country on their first visit to the west. The first place their host family takes them is not to Disneyland, but to "The Grocery Store". The second they walk through the doors they know there is enough food in the store to feed half of Poland for a week, and immediately go into a form of culture shock that is as close to cardiac arrest as you can get.

Past the store and still heading west Trout will find herself in the country driving past emerald green fields filled with dairy cows that look like giant dominoes. Lining the road are twenty-acre truck farms that can grow just about any vegetable known to man in the moist, dark brown earth of western Sonoma County.

Heading due west she'll pass Petrini's Sausage Co. and the Willowside Cafe, then continue out through open country towards the river bottom. When she crosses the bridge she'll be three-quarters of a mile from a hilly dirt road running through a fifteen-acre orchard of ninety-year-old Gravenstein apple trees. At the end of the road, nestled in three acres of oak, pine and redwood is a small cream-colored, two-bedroom house that a family of

Portuguese farmers built at the turn of the century. A haven I have called home for a year-and-a-half.

When Trout heads up the grade towards the three white mailboxes that mark the entrance to the farm as the sun begins its descent into sleep she will see nature's answer to the explosion that put half of Hiroshima to sleep forever. A ball of fire crashing through deep purple clouds that either blinds you or puts you into a deep poetic coma. During summer I've seen it catch the vineyards on fire with every shade of red and orange Van Gogh ever used. Wine made from these grapes is a deep reddish purple. While driving home one day I imagined the sun going down, its hues bleeding over the fields. The wine made from the grapes is organic plasma that people, acting like drunken vampires, drink with their meat and pasta.

If Trout were lucky, maybe she would see the setting sun catch the fields on fire today and marvel at the wonder.

The day was slowly coming to an end. I expected Trout to be driving up anytime. It had been months since there had been any activity around here. I had spent the past two months totally alone, believing that I was living in the midst of some terminal eclipse.

There were a number of reasons why people didn't stop by anymore. They all fell under the category of bad vibes. The negative energy emanating from the house and surrounding grove of trees was as thick as a winter bank of fog. I was convinced that any visitor brave enough to navigate the quarter mile of dirt road leading into the shrouded abyss had to be the reincarnated captain of the Titanic.

The place was slowly taking on the charm of a burial pit at Auschwitz. I believed that the thousands of ravens that began to nest in the grove at night were really the souls of cremated gypsies sent to warn me of the emotional holocaust waiting just around the corner.

I peered through the wavy glass window looking for the dust cloud that always signaled a car coming, wondering if Trout in all her innocence was prepared for my mental state.

I would soon find out. I had just seen a cloud of dry brown earth catch wind and erupt over the road four hundred yards away.

Trout was coming, and unbeknownst to me was bringing with her a velvet bag sewn together with the silken web of the magic white spider, decorated with sequined crystal comets, which when emptied over my heart a few weeks later would change my life forever.

As I waited for the car to come into sight an overwhelming tenseness began to move through my gut. There was a twenty-pound cocoon floating between my ribs that would at any second brutally erupt and send an adrenaline filled, blind butterfly crashing against the walls of my chest.

The feeling had taken control of me before. It was as dependable and predictable as a seventy-five-year-old arthritic hand painfully telling you when a storm is on the way. It was a feeling of doubt and fear; a testament to my past chiseled into a 200-pound stone that every morning laid on my chest when I awoke.

The sun was moving slowly to the west. Soon it would touch the low hills marking the edge of the grape infested valley that, in the waning years of his life, Jack London called home. Growing to three or four hundred feet high the hills would begin to roll for twenty miles, changing into uncountable shades of green before they stopped abruptly at the sheer gray cliffs that kept the Pacific from washing over Northern California. The ball of fire was starting its evening ritual, sending laser beams through the 200-year-old oak that set to the right of the front porch. They started at the base of the three-foot trunk and burned their way east over the Vinka Ivy, singed the patch of Aloe Vera and erupted against the huge spiked leaves of the Century plant.

The dirt road changed from yellow-brown to red- orange to burnt sienna. The egg-sized stones filling the field would lose their gray and become crimson embers; earth stars that the dove and the crow used as guides to find their way home.

I squinted my eyes and watched as the car topped the last hill. It was moving fast. I imagined it trying to outrun the apple trees that were exploding from right to left into red-hued, neon-leafed torches.

The car hit the last hundred yards kicking rocks into the burnt umbra field, slowly geared down, brushed against the eucalyptus, and without a sound slipped into the shaded grove.

Moving through the house from window to window I watched as the car rolled to a stop ten yards from the back porch.

The screen door hid me from view. It was like so many other veiled barriers that held me back in life, transparent walls I built around me, walls that allowed me to observe without being seen. The eight-year-old boy in me had constructed them with trembling hands, believing they would make me emotionally invisible, safe from the nightriders trying to lynch my soul whenever I let my guard down.

This afternoon was no different from so many others in my life. Days where my self-worth was down there with the bottom feeders, where anyone with an ounce of intuition could see right through me. The frightened child in me knew that the 19-year-old-girl opening that car door was no fool. Besides jeans, T -shirts and books that she was carrying in her backpack, would be this unforgiving mirror I would be forced to look into a thousand times before the summer was over.

I stood there in the back porch fighting like hell with that eight-year-old child about who was going to greet her. The adult won, but not before the kid assured me he'd be back. A threat I never took lightly.

CHAPTER 2

With the sound of a warped hinge that had never been oiled, the car door swung open. Looking hot and tired, Trout peeled herself from the imitation leather seat. She stood by the door and arched her back, extending her arms above her head. She reminded me of a swan with its wings and neck stretched skyward, after stepping from a warm nest.

She towered over the low-slung import. She seemed taller than the five-nine I remembered. Her hair was tied back tight in a bun exposing a long thin neck that worked its way down to broad white shoulders that were covered by a sleeveless, brown cotton vest. From cut-off jeans two legs emerged. They reminded me of the long sculptured forms that were used to hold up marble tables during the Renaissance.

As I peered through the veiled door I realized Trout was no longer a child. I had about ten seconds to get my shit together or this young woman that was looking up at the water tower would read me like an old book and get back in the car and drive to a safe haven.

Before opening the back door I made a quick check of my appearance. There wasn't much I could do about the unseen ugliness running rampant under my skin, but I could straighten up any 100% cotton wrinkles that were hanging on the outside.

I did all of the usual checks on my list. Was the zipper open? Were there any organic growths hanging from my nose? Did I wipe off all of the shaving cream that had a tendency to run out of my ears, much like gray brain cells that had turned fossil white, falling out of my head because they weren't needed anymore?

The ritualistic act of running fingers through my hair wasn't a possibility anymore. Five years before I had bought an electric barber's clippers and once a week have been cutting it to the bone.

I stepped out unto the front porch praying that she wouldn't see my soul trembling and said, "Trout, you made it!"

She walked towards me. A willowy arm connected to a long fingered hand reached up and removed a pair of small, round framed sunglasses. "Yeah," she said, "you sure have a nice place here. It looks like you're doing well for yourself."

Well? She apparently hasn't figured it out yet. Maybe her X-ray vision was out of whack from the long trip. It would probably start working again after she sat down and rested. Then her lie detector eyes would plug into mine and get a readout that would look like the San Andreas Fault on a bad day.

Descending the stairs I noticed the little girl that used to jump on my back and beat me playfully on the shoulders was history. That child existed only in a photo album stuck somewhere on a shelf at her mother's apartment in San Francisco.

Trout is beautiful and had the figure of a world-class model. Her dark brown hair framed a face almost Roman in structure. Her heavy eyebrows had gotten thicker, giving her gray green eyes an intense, but sensitive definition. Looking into them would make the strongest of men go into an involuntary heart twitch and look for the nearest chair to sink into.

We approached each other smiling. Trout's was genuine; mine was a cross between Howdy Doody, James Dean, and Vincent Van Gogh just before he shot himself.

Around us the setting sun was turning the air into amber light. It reflected off her hair and put a glow to her skin. Skin that could only be described if one were in an Eighteenth Century potter's studio and saw a white porcelain vase being pulled from the oven after its last firing, its surface still reflecting the blushed warmth of the hot coals.

As we got closer I noticed that her mouth still had that sensual semi-pout it'd had as a child. When she was relaxed her lips parted just a bit, a product of heredity and also of throwing away her retainers when she was thirteen. It was definitely a look any woman would pay a plastic surgeon five figures to obtain.

Approaching her nervously I opened my arms, and with reservation gave her the best hug I could pull out of me.

It had been a while since I had been close to a woman and the smell of her hair and skin aroused senses that had been lying dormant. The embrace pressed hormone buttons that sent waves of guilt through me, and had me wishing Trout wasn't the young daughter of close friends. In the coming weeks these feelings occupied my thoughts daily, feelings I would do my best to run away from.

The hug seemed to last for hours instead of a nervous three seconds. Since I'd been running on empty lately I wanted to breathe in all of the soft femininity my tank would hold, forgetting for a brief few moments that this person with her arms around me was the child I had seen grow up and was almost like family to the man lost in the folds of her hair.

Smiling, we stepped back from each other and stood a foot apart studying each other's faces. At twelve inches it was clear she was aging well. There wasn't a line or blemish on her satin ivory skin. At this distance her eyes had such intensity to them that to say they demanded your attention would be an understatement. Her mouth was big with full rose-colored lips. The upper lip swept up from the corners to form a defiant protruding ridge, which supported a strong Romanesque nose. The nose was a gift from her Italian father, which when seen with the mouth reminded me of a brooding Marlon Brando in "Streetcar Named Desire." With her hair piled up the face had a strong-jawed masculinity to it, handsome, but with a hard edge, one that had never seen makeup or tasted lip-gloss. I had a childish impulse to reach over and untie the bundle knotted in the back and watch as the hair fell in brown, feathered waves down her neck, silently splashing against her shoulders.

I felt like I had a Cosmopolitan Cover Girl/Tomboy on my hands that, with a little tender male coaxing might loosen up and unlock that treasure chest of femininity buried deep inside that protected island she'd been stranded on the past nineteen years.

Trout was the boy her father never had. He was a sportsman, a hunter of big American game, and of any bird legal to shoot. He would fish in any deep-water lake or white-water rapids and always bring home the limit. The man was a star athlete and still holds records never broken. In the 50s he took to the skies and mastered the F-86 Saber Jet protecting our shores from the impending Red Horde. With Hollywood good looks he sang on radio and TV and cut a couple of records, which hit the local charts but never made it big. The man was intelligent and looked forward to a brilliant career in education and politics. From any outsider's view he had it all, a "Man's Man" some would say.

He met and married Trout's mother, and at my house on Christmas Eve in 1970 she went into labor and bore their first child, a girl, the next day.

They waited three more years before trying again, and like any father; the "All-American" dad wanted a boy. Instead he got a little minnow of a girl who grew up with a rifle in one hand and a fishing pole in the other, lovingly accompanying her dad on his weekend outings.

She became dad junior, a miniature sports fan dressed in football gear and baseball caps. By the time she was eight Trout could tie a good fly and put a .22 long rifle in the middle of the red circle on a pack of Lucky's at 100 feet. She never owned a doll and wore a dress only to weddings and family funerals. I'm sure when asked what she wanted to be when she grew up; she'd answer either a game warden, or a linebacker for the San Francisco 49'ers.

Trout had fought every rule and norm ever written about what a little girl was supposed to be. At the age of six she'd picked up a pair of cowboy boots that were six sizes too big and wore them daily for months, daring anybody to pull them off. Her left hook to the ribs was hard enough to make you wear an ace bandage for a week, and her leaping attack from the top of the couch was her six-year-old version of a Jap Zero dropping a 2,000-pound bomb on Pearl Harbor.

The Minnow was her own person, never quite figuring out what she wanted to be, but damn well sure of what she didn't want. She didn't want to be like "them," the world of routine, dishonesty and a boring existence surrounded by white picket fences that some call the "American Dream."

Peering from beneath the masculine wing of her father with gifted and sensitive eyes, she viewed her world with a child's confusion that would stick to her like an androgynous mask throughout her formative years; a mask I noticed the minute she stepped out of the car.

The day was slowly coming to an end. My two-and-a-half-months of solitude would cease the minute both of us climbed the steps and passed through the back porch door.

A warm June day had given way to an evening wind chilled by the Pacific and blown east across the viridian hills. The wind would have been given birth four hundred miles out to sea by the laborious left wing beat of an albatross heading south. Iced Alaskan white caps fanned by formations of gray pelicans would help it gain momentum and grow into mountainous blue glass waves exploding like howitzers on driftwood-strewn beaches. Screeching sorcerer gulls would conjure up wet blustery gusts climbing 200-foot vertical cliffs, reaching the top, then blasting through cypress and pine and over Highway One. Like a freight train with invisible cars the wind would roll over stone walls and moss-covered picket fences becoming an avalanche of clear glass, blowing cool against sheep's wool and Raven's quill. The night stalker, naked Indian runner, untiring as it whips through eucalyptus grove and stream-filled gorge becoming the minstrel of darkness singing ebony star tunes to red-barked trees and falling barns. The wind will sneak over Tomales, caress Bodega and command Freestone cows to bow their heads. Moving downhill like a semi-truck it will whistle past running deer on Graton grade, hit highway 116, and bend the stakes on the 420 acres of grapes across the road.

On this summer eve when Trout arrived the wind crossed the road, dropped ten degrees, and like a runaway night express hit the grove. Soft confettied pine needles filled the air, and as the crow and gray dove sang on their way home apple leaves blew down the drive. With the sound of a thousand racing heartbeats a covey of quail leapt into the falling day, as the red-tail screamed on its way to the Monterey Pine.

At the last step Trout paused, and as fingers of the evening breeze played with her hair, looked towards the tall pines. They swayed and whispered tree chants, castanet-like beats in tune with the pink Camellia.

She had tuned into the wind's recital and stared in awe towards the tree's dancing shadows cast on my studio roof.

As her heart beat in slow motion to the symphonic wind poem being played out in the late afternoon theater of oak, redwood and evergreen, I read her mind.

She turned to me with her mouth slightly open. With soft eyes that gave me that Trout look of ancient understanding, the one I would learn to know, love, fear and respect, she tilted her head a bit and smiled, "It's nice here," she said.

"I know. You just heard the sound of the sun going down. You're fortunate; it doesn't do it for everybody. I think it likes you."

She smiled again, a nervous, half-embarrassed, uncertain upward tilt-of-the mouth smile. Trout was probably thinking how could the sun like me? I don't like me. Nobody likes me. When he gets to know me he won't like me either. He'll find out soon enough what I'm really like and ask me to leave. I'm carrying around enough guilt to have a hundred juries send me to the island of self-loathing for life. He's a man of the world, someone who knows. He was 32 years old when I was born. He probably has already seen a thousand worthless people like me. Maybe I should just say hi, have a cup of coffee and leave.

I got to know Trout's attitude real well as the days turned into weeks, and weeks into months. Her body language always gave her away. I looked at the way she moved as her own private Gestalt. The shoulders would gradually slump and drop her height of five-ten-and-a-half down to one of about five-eight. Her lower lip acted like it had a ten-pound-weight clamped to it. She would shuffle, mumbling, Shit! Fuck! God Dammit! Her body at a 45-degree angle. When this mood came on she would head straight to the bedroom and stack as many blankets, sleeping bags and pillows on top of her as she could find, trying to sleep it off. No coaxing, no soothing words or attempts at humor would budge her from her lair.

I learned to let her hide under that fifteen-pounds of blankets and nineteen years of confusion. When she was ready, she would rise, head straight for the bathroom, draw a bath and sit in the tub until the water got cold. When I felt that she was ready to communicate, I would say, "Is everything OK?" Acting like she was dealing with a temperamental transient rash, she'd say, "I'll be all right. It will go away soon."

I got to know what "It" was, and didn't like it. There was already one living at the farm and I wasn't sure another would be welcome. She handled hers differently; a good definition would be borderline catatonic. Mine was kept at bay, (or fueled, you might say), by opening the fridge and grabbing a cold one. If I were in the chips I'd accompany it by a shooter of James Beam.

I'm sure if I had ever ventured into the world of drugs I would have been vein-less by twenty-nine. When I was twenty-seven a therapist advised me never to get involved in the opiates, or hallucinogens, or any chemical that would alter my mind. She said my psyche was definitely too fragile, and for me to "ride the needled horse," or to "sleep with Mary Jane," or stick "Freud's friend" up my nose would be like opening the door and saying hello to insanity. I figured I was half-nuts anyway, and if she would just review her notes from our numerous 55-minute visits she'd realize that my mind had already been altered pretty bad somewhere between 1942 and 1956.

Thinking that I could live with being half-insane, I stayed away from poppies and hemp and sugar cubes. Instead, I stuck with the corn-grained nectar of poets, painters and construction workers.

Trout on the other hand was addicted to bed and blankets and cussing herself out. Better on the liver, but a real drag when you wanted company.

Sometimes I would crack open the door to check on her. I would strain my eyes to see if there was any breath-propelled movement of the two-foot stack of wool, cotton and foam rubber. Never sure there was, I'd cough or push the door to that reliable point where the hinges squeaked and wait for the groan or sigh that signaled she hadn't emotionally suffocated.

In her short life Trout had taken to swimming in dark, murky water. Water full of bad-dream soul-eating serpents and bottom-crawling heart suckers. Her small pond world was kept dark by the heavy oil slicks of society. Early on she had learned not to strike at the hypocritical lures thrown at her, but in turn was starving for lack of a nurturing truth. Being just like her I was fearful I wasn't the one capable of breathing life into her.

We walked through the screen door into the back porch. It was a room of board and batten walls, a worn wooden floor, and a long window covered with a nontransparent, plastic screen.

There was one of those old pantries with grilled wooden shelves and a screened vent to the outside, a propane fed water heater, a white Kenmore washer and dryer, and enough hooks and long nails on the walls to hang winter coats and rain gear for a family of ten. There was a low wooden stool next to the back door where one was supposed to sit and remove wet, knee-high rubber boots and change into house shoes. It was an old country rule that was meant to keep the farm from invading the house. It was called the mudroom, an apt title for the entry into my dark-earthen, loamy world.

I led Trout into the next room, nervously saying, "This is the kitchen." She didn't have to be a genius to figure that out. The garlic smell that permeated the wooden cutting board was enough to tell a blind man that this was where my Spartan meals were prepared.

Ten years ago the young couple that owned the house set out on a quest of total renovation. Starting at the foundation they worked their way up through the rooms into the attic and out the roof.

The lightly stained hardwood floors starting at the back door and working their way out to the front porch gave the kitchen a feeling of warmth and purpose. The wood decor continued up the walls becoming hand-made oak cabinets, paused briefly, changed into off-white counter tops and then back into enough natural wood cupboards to house all the food, dishes and pans a family of four would ever need. To the right of the back door, tucked into a corner, was one of the most beautiful white enameled gas stoves I had ever seen. It was small, with four black cast iron burners and an oven that would hold an 18-pound turkey. Iron legs with three-toed feet that looked like cat's paws supported the 300 pounds of kitchen art. Chrome strips framed the back panel containing a wind-up timer, and an alcove for a box of "Strike Anywhere Matches." Next to the double porcelain sink, under the counter, was an automatic dishwasher I never used. If I filled it with my day's one plate, one coffee cup and one wineglass it would be a reminder of my solitude, a light-wash, energy-saving, closed-door monument to loneliness. The owners had left a new refrigerator that was twenty times too big for the chunk of cheddar, the plastic pot of Nancy's yogurt, the coffee cream, and the six-pack of Sierra Nevada beer. Each had a shelf on which to stay cool.

On the counter to the left, opposite the stove, was a tall light gray and blue ceramic vase filled with a fist full of brown orange, stiff weeds. The weeds shot up out of the Japanese vase like two-foot long Zen toothpicks creating a forest landscape for the colony of mosquito-eating spiders that moved in the day I did.

Next to the vase sat a flea market wok which I had tenderly steel wooled, then replaced the broken wood handle with a new one; hand carved from the heart of redwood. Above the wok next to the spider grove hung a colored poster depicting a Leonardo drawing. It was of a man flapping his arms behind an object of wood, bone, stone, feathers and wood crate. It was a poster from one of the exhibitions I was involved in when I was rising up the ladder becoming reasonably well known in Germany in the early 80's as a sculptor. My name was listed just under Marc Chagall's and about ten up from Rene Magritte, two men who had ascended to the top of that ladder before I was born. To me it was a ladder that was vertical and rung-less. Sometimes in my climb I felt like a naked one-armed blind man attempting to inch my way up the north face of Everest on a stormy winter day.

Trout looked at the poster, gazing intently down the list of names. She said, "Damn Davis, pretty good company."

Stuttering and mumbling like I always did when it came to talking about my work, I said, "Oh, I don't know about that. It was just an exhibition, besides most of those guys are dead and buried." And of late, I thought, me along with them.

Trout quietly turned to the left. The movement of leaves brushing against the picture window over the sink caught her attention. It was a picture postcard view that started with a tree-like bush filled with clustered orange berries. A robin-sized bird with brown feathers and black tipped wings ate the berries for brunch every day. The bird was my morning partner in contemplation. He'd sit on a branch unafraid, snacking and staring as I stood with shoulders hunched, leaning forward, braced by stiff arms over the sink. This position, I'm sure, convinced him I was holding the sink down with all my might, lest it sprout wings itself like a great porcelain bird and fly around the room.

Trout looked through the bird's green cafe at the same beautiful scene I had stared at every day for the last year and a half. It was a grove of trees just across the drive, thirty feet from the window. Lawns of ivy grew over and around stone paths framing a small pond and waterfall. It was a jade delicacy of fern, evergreen, and redwood trees. Moss-covered stones pushed up through blankets of soft-needled earth, and two spiked palms with tops like giant bayonets shot skyward, fighting through the fir and cedar to capture their share of the sun.

The pond and rocked waterfall hadn't tasted fresh well water since 83' when the pipes froze and broke. During the heavy rains sometimes it got half full, just high enough to touch the long fingers of ivy growing over the sides; like leafed snakes thirsting for cold water.

Towering over the pond was a 100-foot redwood tree. Its moving roots periodically cracked the pond's cement bottom and sides. The tree was a 200-year-old voyeur that sprouted and grew at a time when the wood that built the houses and barns hereabouts still grew solid and round in the heart of its brothers up north. During storms, it would sway and moan lamentations, grieving over the loss of its extended family, whose clear-cut graveyards dotted the nearby hills. A visiting owl, which perched on one of its arms, chanting deep-throated Ohm's, consoled it nightly. I got to know them as dark-winged shaman hymns droning through the night, floating past my bedroom window, reminding me just before sleep that I had made it through another day.

On the east side of the pond next to the plum and yucca was a concrete bench smothered with ivy. Weeks later, with a hungry weed eater in hand, I attacked the green tentacles with such a tenacity it would have put any iron-clawed, rainforest-eating machine to shame.

I was fulfilling all of my childhood Peruvian archaeologist fantasies. The small boy in me believed that the stone wall I discovered was really the tip of an Inca temple, and the bench was the sacrificial stone where young, hard-bodied maidens were philosophically slit from just above their virginal gardens to the base of their screaming throats. I uncovered sleeping lizards, which darted and hissed and became 6-foot fanged Iguanas. The garter snake slithering underfoot was transformed into a Pit Viper, with a bite and poison no belt tourniquet or sucking of the wound could cure. I was a Harvard, Ph.D. bone scientist with khaki clothes and floppy hat, a loaded 38 strapped to my side, crushing crickets turned scorpion, and shooting point blank, the charging wild boar-field mouse that lay now, bloody and gasping at my feet.

The eight-year-old had taken over disguised as Indiana Jones. I was Darth Vader, a poet soldier with a neon machete in my hand fighting off hoards of Aztec warriors. If I were captured they would tie me to a rock wall, cut out my liver and eat it raw before my dying eyes.

I became lost in my past. I saw a small boy with his best buddy, dug in deep in their vacant lot dirt fort, holding off waves of bloodthirsty Indians. Multiple wounds bled from our arms and legs. Never dying, and finally standing triumphant, we gazed out over the fantasy battlefield content, a heroic job well done.

Later, after our fantasy battle was over, I would pack up my plastic guns and knives, go home to dinner then crawl into a bed that turned me into the 70-pound trembling coward I really was. A place where no imaginary tank or flame-thrower could ward off the howling night demons that attacked me as I prayed for sleep.

Trout and I walked to the window and stood side-by-side staring through the fading translucent light. She turned her head slightly and caught me off-guard, deep in thought. It was a look of intuition I would get to know well, one where she recognized instantly that I was somewhere other than in the room with her. She would sometimes ask, "What's wrong?" "Where are you?" Most of the time she would just look then blink that slow motion eyelid movement that signaled she knew and understood. I was on a journey of the mind and soul, a journey she often took, and she knew it was a voyage that most often had to be taken alone.

She broke the silence; "It's really beautiful, so quiet."

"Yes, it's a special place. It's a place to sit and think, away from the rest of the world. It has a meditative quality to it. I call it the Zen garden."

"Oh," she said, almost sighing, "That's a nice name for it. What's that gray thing next to the pond?"

She was looking at the other bench set closer to the house near the edge, next to the rock border framing the pond. A heavy slab of granite supported by two stone piers, which gave the garden the feeling of having been visited by Druid pilgrims.

"It's a stone bench, but looks more like an altar. It's the best spot in the garden to sit and think. Tomorrow we'll go for a walk and I'll show it to you, along with everything else."

Trout continued looking through the gauzed light. It was reflecting off the window and gave her skin a warm, opaque white glow.

At the time she didn't know the stone altar she was staring at was going to play such an important role in her young life. In the coming year it would be the subject of poem and verse, and like a serum of truth would be used to bring back memories that, because of time, defied loss. As we stood watching the night slowly cover the garden, I looked at her reflection in the window. At that moment, for the first time, I saw her with my heart, and saw her as a woman. Soon my visions of her as a small child would end much like the predestined act of tonight's sun as it melts into the sea.

Seeing Trout as woman, rather than a girl, made me begin to feel uneasy and nervous. I began to wonder that maybe her coming here wasn't such a good idea after all.

The karmic bond I'd always felt whenever we were together was beginning to define itself, and as we stood with arms touching, just a breath and heartbeat away from one another I found it working itself to the surface. I didn't know exactly what it was, but I was afraid that when it finally grew wings and flew it might be something that could destroy nineteen years of respect and friendship. It was a frightening thought, a solid black glass wind of thought, and one that awakened that sleeping butterfly and sent it into a gut-filled panicked flight.

Quickly stuffing my hands into my pockets I turned away and walked into the next room, guiltily hoping she hadn't read my mind. With Trout following, we stopped just on the other side of the entrance that opened the kitchen up to the rest of the house.

CHAPTER 3

With the exception of the bathroom and Trout's room to our right next to the kitchen, the rest of the house was laid out like a big square. My bedroom was at the top right corner taking up a quarter of the space. The rest of the house was open and airy, much like an "L" with the foot longer than the leg.

From where we stood it was an impressive sight. Facing the front of the house it was easy to see why I felt that re-doing the interior was one of the best pieces of art I had done in a long time.

Starting to our left, the hardwood floors running from the kitchen filled a long horizontal room with a window that looked out onto the same "Garden of Eden" view one sees while standing in front of the kitchen sink. The brown-blond floors stopped at an open passageway and became a soft, white charcoal flecked, wall-to-wall carpet. To our right, setting on polished red brick, was a black cast iron wood stove. When lit with the door open it filled the room with a warm hue, the same colors you would get if a giant peach stuffed with dynamite had rolled through the door, detonated, showering its powdered skin in misty layers on the walls and floor.

Against the far wall, to the right of the stove was my oak desk. It was a huge, dark-stained assortment of drawers, sliding trays, and secret locks. On it sat my phone, a sculpture, and a white desktop calendar that stared up at me with big squares empty of written appointments. The calendar had become a daily reminder of months of stagnation and lack of creative desire. Behind the desk a large framed window looked onto emerald green ivy, five-foot Christmas trees and a wooden picket fence, grayed and bent from years of fogged weather and wet winter abuse.

Trout, with her wide-angle fisheye lens look, took it all in. She peered into the living room at the two natural pine-framed couches and chair, which were filled with ivory colored sailcloth cushions. They sat around a slab of redwood burl I had painted bone white and placed on a low kidney-shaped piece of blue steel. In the corner was a 1930's secondhand floor lamp resting on a base of polished walnut root. The lamp had an extra switch that turned on a bulb hidden underneath the base. It was a marvel of night light ingenuity. Anytime someone new came by I would act like the proud father of some bright incandescent child, turning it on and off until they got bored and walked away.

Trout's attention turned to the brick lined fireplace, sealed up and crumbling, and what hung over it. Her head reached out and tilted to the side, and with a puzzled sideways glance in my direction, she asked, "What's that?"

She had noticed the perfectly preserved skull and black horns of an African wildebeest, a Christmas present from Helga, the alive and well German wildebeest; the one who had packed her bags and returned to Europe two months before.

The Deutsche Frau had seen me marveling at its natural sculptured beauty in an antique shop one day and secretly bought it and gave it to me on that holy eve of 92. In her early years she had spent lots of time in Africa working for the Peace Corps and the German Consul, and being the inquisitive and brilliant woman that Helga is, learned all she could about the culture and ancient traditions of various tribes there. I'm sure along the way she picked up some tips about Black Magic and mind-fucking hexes, because whenever she felt like it, she could conjure up attitudes that would put your head into warp speed meltdown and shift your heart into park. I'm sure she put a curse on the skull because, beyond a doubt, it was the worst Christmas I ever had.

She had talked me into going with her to a midnight candlelight service at the local Protestant church, for, as she put it, some spiritual cleansing. For the sake of harmony, I reluctantly went along. I thought if there was ever a spirit that needed cleansing it was hers, and I wanted to be there and witness "The Miracle", if it occurred.

We sat there amongst a pure white on white Northern California audience and listened about the goodness of man, with me all the while checking her out to see if the "Exorcism" was taking place. On the way back I realized it hadn't, and in the four miles and eight minutes it took us to get home we got into the worst argument the celebrated baby Jesus had ever seen.

It started out as a harmless discussion about the Catholic Church, with her taking pro and me con. I never had much love for the Vatican anyway, and I guess it was starting to show. She kept defending their goodness and charitable work while I was hard at work putting them in the same Italian restaurant holding hands and drinking Chianti with Al Capone. I followed that with the well-known fact of "The Church" turning its holy face while the slaughter of Jews went unanswered during the war in her beloved Deutschland.

The Christmas cheer mood quickly changed. I watched the jaw in her beautiful North German face lock tight. I'd been there before, and once her circuit was pulled there was no Jesus, Santa Claus, or General Patton that could save the day. Her eyes narrowed like the hatch on a Panzer Tank being pulled down just before battle. It was a look that always sent my adrenaline into a deep-welled, turbine-burning-gut-pump, and I thought, I sure hope

I've got some beer at home, because the liquor stores are probably all closed and it looks like it's going to be a long night.

Her night maneuver battle plan was put into gear, and she fired at me from across the car. Her salvos made Field Marshal Rommel look like the commander of a fleet of Ice Cream trucks dinging bells through West L.A.

In German, she screamed every degrading obscenity she had stored in that pretty little head of hers. The final touch, and the one that put me over the edge was the postscript of, "Dumb, unintelligent, idiotic American asshole."

That shouldn't have been enough to do the trick, but it did. It pressed the button with the tag over it that said, "That's it sweetheart, I've finally had enough," and backhanded her with a clenched fist that hit her on the left shoulder with the deepest voodoo drum thud she had ever heard.

She screamed that I was a brutal man, and at that moment she was right. I had never hit a woman before, not that I didn't want to on occasion, but I had always held back knowing it was a line I never wanted to cross. I crossed that line that December eve and sat up the whole night on the couch hanging myself from every available cross that my mind could erect.

The next morning Helga awoke, or to be more specific, the child in her did. The angry woman had tired herself out the night before and would rest through the day; meanwhile, the cute little girl in her would run and bounce around the house acting like nothing had happened, which is exactly what she did on that Christmas morning. It was a form of behavior I had gotten to know well, and one that had played basketball with my emotions ever since the moment we had first met.

The little girl wanted to go to bed and make love, an act that she could do no matter how grim the situation. It was a trick of the heart I had never learned, and one I didn't want to. From that morning on making love with her was a sporadic act, done by me with a lack of tenderness and passion.

The terminally ill relationship was dying. It was just a matter of days before it would turn belly up and heave its last breath. A week later she did leave, but after a month repentantly returned and seductively let me know that she wasn't quite finished with the curse she had bestowed on my soul.

Standing next to Trout looking up at the meatless head over the mantle, the thought ran through my mind of her 6,000 miles away listening to Mozart, all the while sticking rusty pins into a little mustached doll with a shaved head.

Trout waited for my answer. I finally said, "It's the skull of a wildebeest, you know, those African buffalo-like antelope creatures that run around the veldt in herds by the thousands, you know, the Lion's meal of choice."

"Oh yeah, it's beautiful, where did you get it?"

I thought twice before answering, "A present from a friend. I keep it there to remind me of how things shouldn't be. Some day, when the time is right I'll tell you about it."

She accepted my response without question and turned to look at the rest of the house.

My reply marked the first of many that would follow in the coming months. It was the infamous inauguration of me turning my emotional back on her, a welded-to-my-heart defense system that kept me from talking about things which were too painful to replay, or of hearing words that I felt would hurt or disappoint the frightened man/child in me. It was an emotional reaction I had inherited from my father. I had named it, "The pull the switch and shut it down before it blows, reaction." I could best describe it by comparing it to a man driving an overloaded truck up a steep hill, a hill he has driven many times before and knows the dangers of the grade well.

Under the cautious and manipulating hands of the driver the truck strained and groaned over a road it recognized as one it had taken many times before. The truck was scared to death and dreaded the pain and wear it would take before it got to the top.

Because the truck was old and had been damaged by a history of carrying heavy loads, it started to gear down, anticipating the painful last hill that loomed ahead. As it got closer to the moment of truth, and point of no return, the truck became afraid that it was going to blow and scatter its fragile parts all over the road; a critical and exposing breakdown of sensitive internal gears that anyone driving by could easily see. Fearing the worst, the veteran of many such climbs started to shake and sputter and lose power. It lurched forward awkwardly. Anyone standing by the side of the road could easily see that it was in trouble. The driver, sensing a head was about to crack and spill life-sustaining oil all over the road, pulled the truck over to the side, turned off the key and shut it down.

There was a day in the 40's when I became the owner of that Chevy one-and-a-half-ton truck. It was a truck that my father, with me sitting on his lap, taught me how to drive. When it got too hot and I became afraid, he showed me how to turn it off, take it out of gear and shut that emotional motor down. It was an early life lesson I learned well. In the following years wherever I would go I would load that truck down with all my heavy baggage, start it up and take off slowly down the road scared to death to take it out of first gear.

When I moved in I brought that truck with me, opened the front door and drove it into the house. Trout noticed it after the first week she was there, and every time we would get into a situation where it was time for her to talk about her feelings, or expose her inner self, I would get inside, slam the door and roll up the window. Later on it was a routine she would began to dread. In the course of time, during the following months, she would often become, not the driver, but a reluctant passenger in our many travels of the heart and soul.

I realized much later that I should have gotten rid of that old Chevy the minute she first walked through the back door, or at least let her drive once in a while. I'm sure that if I'd had, she would have put it in neutral, and with all my 51 years of heavy load strapped to the back, pushed it off the first cliff she saw.

Trout headed for the open door of my room and hesitantly peeked inside. I have always felt that the bedroom is the most sacred room in the house, and in the way she cautiously approached mine, I got the impression that she did too.

My room was simple, with no dressers, tables or stools. The floor was covered with gray carpet, which pressed up against off-white walls. The walls framed two windows that looked out onto the ivy-wrapped picket fence, and a wild bush of climbing white rose. Over the bed was a wire mesh gray-screened relief, a 5-by-7-foot triptych with three orange brown feathers hanging from the narrow middle panel. It was one of many from a series I had done, titled, "Woman."

In the corner between the two windows was one of my favorite pieces. It was a welded-together, straight-backed steel chair, half wrapped in mahogany pigskin. Growing from the seat was a small forest of model makers pine trees and sandy-colored brush. Leaning against the back were three steel arrows with stone tips. The metal feathers rested against a four-point rack of hand-forged, iron deer antlers, which I had attached at an angle to the top left corner of the chair.

Directly opposite, next to the door, was the best spiritual object I had ever done. It was a group of twelve stone-tipped steel arrows that hung from the ceiling at different levels, suspended invisibly by clear nylon thread. The arrows plunged straight down into a pile of small, river rock set on a piece of flat wood, which I had placed on top a two-and-a-half-foot white pedestal. It was an object that, while lying in bed, I would stare at and contemplate its meaning. It was a 3-dimensional soundless truth that moved through the room at night, telling me as I slept that everything eventually returns to its origins, and as I had been painfully taught, nothing is forever.

In the middle of the room, laying low on a frame of redwood four-by-fours was my bed. It was of late a queen-size, semi-soft 10-year guaranteed memorial of spending too many nights alone.

The bed looked like a Viking altar, and was covered by the skins of ten Australian sheep sewn together, (I wanted to believe), by a family of mystical, high-on-some-kind-of-spiritual-desert-weed, aborigines.

In those cold winter nights when I laid there alone, scared to death of what demons might be waking up in the depths of my mind, I would pull the pelts up high and tight under my chin. Night sweat visions would come as I imagined the Shaman and his kids naked and stoned, chanting dead sheep songs as they prayed and blessed every single stitch that was sewn. If that didn't keep me safe, I would pretend the big heavy robe was really 20 pounds of compressed sacred white powder that the Indians used to use as protection against the .44 caliber rim fires that were about to rip through their bodies.

As a back up, and the "ultimate solution," was a double-barrel, sawed-off 20-gauge shotgun leaning against the wall in my closet, and a .25 caliber automatic palm gun laying on the floor behind my bed; a sure fire, last resort, between-the-eyes explosion to finally get rid of those screaming creatures that were sharpening their claws on the inside of my head.

Between the bed and the windowed wall, was a white, square cubed nightstand. On it set a thin-stemmed crystal glass lamp. I had taken the dried, fully opened wing of a male ring-necked pheasant, hooked two wire clips to the back and clamped it to the bulb. At night the translucent feathered shade cast soft bird shadows over the art and the lamb-scaped bed.

Sometimes I would awaken with heavy eyes, see the fogged morning green floating through the oak outside, and imagine myself a wounded soldier rising from a field of night battled dead. The ivy became a shrouded mound of blue and gray bodies, with vined arms draped over the picket fence.

My bedroom was often my own private field of fire, where I could crawl through the muddied trenches of my past, digging in deep, afraid to look over the edge into the charging, howling attack of the future.

When all was quiet and the beasts were still, the room was like a soft watered pond. It was a place where night tides came and brought with them blue neon-winged fish, which swam on the floor accompanied by the ghost of soft Coltrane tunes. Heart spirits would sit at the foot of the bed, while little ballerinas with crystal glitter falling from their hair danced on their arms.

The bed was like a raft drifting along with the currents of my mind. It would float behind alcohol-induced dream winds, taking any course. It would finally become a Hindu pyre lying on the sand, beached by white water waves. I began to wear that bed like a long winter coat in my sleep, turning my back to the hard, mad winds of night.

Trout, in her quiet and reserved way, seemed impressed with my art and the room. She had no idea what went on when I was alone behind the barricaded door. But if she was as much like me as I thought, then I'm sure she had in her own room an emotional Armageddon almost every night.

We left the bedroom and headed in the direction of the four walls and a bed that she would be soon calling her own. On the way we passed the bathroom. She looked inside. It was small, with gray and white walls and redwood trim. Above the old fashioned sink, with tarnished brass faucets, reading, "HOT" and "COLD" inlaid into porcelain knobs was a hand-carved wooden medicine cabinet. On the light gray linoleum floor were four cast iron lion's feet. The feet were attached to stubby legs supporting a deep water, antique bathtub. There was no indoor shower, just this big white boat that has stood against the wall in dry dock since before "The Big War". The shower was outside under the trees next to a shed. I would make it a point the next day to show it to Trout as I gave her the tour.

We walked into her little alcove and were surrounded by a chill. I had opened the windows to air it out, and the evening had drifted in with its cool glove touching everything in the room. It was the coldest place in the house, built on as an afterthought, probably to accommodate the addition of a new child.

With its windowed walls facing north, whoever slept there had to stack the covers high, something I'm sure would make Trout feel right at home. She liked it, and it showed by her smile. It was Spartan, but comfortable; a place where she could lay and read, and whenever she chose, escape into a private world of her own.

Over her bed, glued to the ceiling, were little glow in the dark stars, the ones that collected light all day, then in the dark glimmered like a view of Las Vegas as seen from 30,000 feet. They were one of those scientific wonders, like television waves and heat-seeking missiles that boggled my mind. They were always next on the list, after the floor lamp, when I gave my guided tours.

She smiled at my boyish enthusiasm when I turned off the lights and pointed to the ceiling. I did it much like Columbus must have done when he aimed his finger towards America for the first time, because I was acting like I had just discovered a new galaxy right there in her room. We laughed and marveled at the silver comets glittering down on our heads, while the eight-year-old looked up thinking the constellation on the ceiling was probably the best welcome-home-from-a-long-trip present he had ever seen.

I showed her the cupboards and desk, and then we went outside to bring in her things. We stepped into the night and unloaded a backpack, a nylon bag full of books and other treasured things, and a big cotton net sack stuffed with all the clothes she owned.

Her mountain bike was strapped to the back of the car in such a way that it looked about ready to fall and unload itself. It was something that we decided could wait for the next day.

Trout stored her things for the time being on the floor, and then went into the gray harbor where the big boat was moored to throw some water on her face. I turned on some music, paced the floors of my mind and tried to figure out what to do for dinner.

CHAPTER 4

I had been broke since March and hadn't had any real savings since I'd unloaded trucks for my dad in 1954. And that was only because he had gone down and opened the account for me himself.

Money and I had always had strange relationships. They were like little love affairs which would come into my life, stay for awhile, give me a few simple pleasures, a lot of mismanaged pain, and then leave because of lack of securities for the future, and all the bad investments of my past.

For the past 25 years I had been making my living solely from my art. A life style that many people envied until it came time for them to collect on the loans that they had given me. Then they blessed the day that they had gotten that B.A. in business and went to work for State Farm, with all its perks and retirement plans.

My life had its advantages they thought, with all of its freedom, romance, and sleep-as-late-as-you-want days. When I tried to tell them that most of the time I felt like some heroin-hooked whore on my knees in front of the rich, social pimps of society, they would just smile and say, "Oh come on, at least you are your own man." Yeah, I was my own man until it came time to pay the rent, or put gas in the car, or food in my mouth. Then I was the sleaziest street walker in town with a piece of sculpture under my arm willing to give it away for 90 percent off to the first Armani shoe-wearing "John" that passed by. Being your "own man" artist was God's way of showing the rest of the world what he meant when he brought the word humility into the vocabulary of man.

It was a life I was tiring of, and one that had been putting me into a slow Kamikaze burnout ever since I realized I was doing it for the simple act of financial survival and not the obsessed dedication of the other painters and sculptors around me.

Over the past 25 years I had learned my craft well. I had gotten to the point where I could take that Mig welder and acetylene torch, and with my eyes closed or half drunk, fabricate a piece that would make any white-walled, white-couched, designer-put-together, new-moneyed, white man-owned living room proud.

The only problem with that cycle of creativity is that somewhere along the line I would have to sit down, always with a glass of expensive French white wine and fulfill all of the new collectors one-on-one fantasy discussions about deep meaning, and, "will it rust?" The only deep meaning moving around on their $4,000 white-marbled Italian table was, "Shut the fuck up, and give me the check!"

I was always so far in debt by the time something sold, that all I wanted to do was head for the nearest bar and drink something that cost a lot. Then I'd try and decide whether I should give it all away paying people I owed, or take a cab to the airport and get on the first flight back to the states. It was a moral dilemma that, after running up a good-sized bar tab, would usually turn me into an immoral man. After the seventh Jack Daniels on the rocks and all of the warped rational my clouded mind could produce, the decision to take the money and run would be as clear to me as the eyes of a 70-year-old Buddhist monk who had never tasted flesh.

Whenever I would have success or fame close enough to touch, that small boy in me would take off and run with all the fear and lack of self worth that he use to have as a Little Leaguer, last at bat, standing at the plate in the bottom of the ninth with three runs down and bases loaded.

I summed it all up in 1974, in a poem I'd written at 25,000 feet flying back from a successful show in Texas. I had done well and had a pocket full of money, but the boy in me kept saying that the success was too easy and just luck, and the home run I had just hit was because the pitcher probably had the flu and threw a directly-over-the-plate, cinch-to-hit, meatball.

I had spent those late Houston nights in a Motel Six, drinking Lone Star beer and reading Brautigan. He was saying things in a way I understood and identified with, words and truths that spoke for the unidentifiable pain I was feeling at the time.

Laying on that "Magic Fingers" bed, I started to write, and for the first time discovered that I could easily put down in 25 words what I had, in a 35-year-long lifetime, tried so hard not to define.

I sat on that plane eating complimentary peanuts, and using a napkin that came with my drink wrote:

I could probably be a great artist
But
I don't have time
Because
I'm too busy
Being
Mediocre.

It was a poetic truth I wrote down, read and believed, and something that over the last 15 years I have miserably tried with not much success to change. Inside my guts I had never grown out of that little shivering bottom-of-the-ninth boy, scared to death of failure and the responsibilities that went hand in hand with success. There was a day in that hot San Joaquin valley town when that little boy opened the door and let fear move in and build a black, swan-filled moat that has circled my mind ever since.

Trout came out of the bathroom just as I had finished counting the money in my wallet. There wasn't much there, four dollars to be exact. Not even enough for a pizza and a six-pack of middle-of-the-road beer.

If I were going to teach Trout anything this summer, it would have to be how to get by on next to nothing, because as far as money was concerned the future looked pretty bleak. I had just gotten together a thousand for the rent and was running behind on everything else. I had started making sculptured steel gates, a release, I thought, from the financial binds of my art. I had sold two over the last five months, and had a contract for another two due in September; a long, dry, three months ahead. My nephew had arranged an exhibition of my sculpture in San Jose in October, and I had another exhibition planned for the same time at a good gallery in San Francisco.

At this moment, however, I was about as broke as I could be. It was a fact of life that wasn't new to me, but one that could possibly be to Trout. She had come from a family that was well off, and she had never had a concern as far as getting the material things in life. She was starving for other things, stuff that "The Green" could never buy. The girl had been on an emotional diet for years, and coming here just might complete the package.

I hoped that my feeling of being a failure wasn't starting to leak from the pores of my skin, and staining the rug. My life of being "The Artist" was, once again, about to catch up with me. I was sure the beast would come to me in the middle of the night and, with fangs glowing, demand some dues not yet paid.

I would wait until tomorrow to tell Trout that my wallet was collecting summer dust. She wasn't the kind that cared about money, and I'm sure she might even find the poverty that I was living in some kind of Bohemian, poetic adventure.

CHAPTER 5

Both Trout and I were raised in the Central Valley of California. It's the area of California that produces 75 percent of the food eaten in America; enough in one year to feed every third world country on the planet until the year 2010. The Central Valley has the kind of economic environment that produces masses of workers whose backs have been tortured and permanently bent by the age forty, and bosses who are a straight boned, All American, select few.

The valley land around Fresno starts just north of Los Angeles, where the Tehacipi Mountains fall sharp; crashing into rich earth that runs a flat six hundred miles up the middle of the state. The farms and ranches are sprawling domains of cotton, tomatoes and peaches. Almonds and corn bend and gasp under the oppressing summer heat, while the hog and Hereford steer eat their way fat and full, headed for the supermarket and a cellophane-wrapped shroud. The land has tradition and heart, and is as fertile as a Mississippi mother of twelve.

Trout was raised by two people bent on having their careers and a future life as secure as the two mountain ranges that run down both sides of the valley. Her parents were both brilliant, and had chosen lives that involved the teaching of others. They would take their M.A.'s and PhD's and climb the ladder about as far up as it would go. Along the way they made the right investments and stashed enough away so their kids would never want for anything.

The two girls were raised in a condo in the north of town, the "New Fig Garden" as it was known in the social pages and in the portfolios of the real estate brokers who wanted to sell a home for over 500 G's. The "Old Fig Garden" was just across the boulevard, and was a green enclave of expensive homes built before the 50's. It was an area of old curb less streets, old palatial homes, and old Fresno money. Where the kids were raised was just like the above, with the exception of new money replacing the word old.

The parents weren't pretentious people, but along the way picked up a circle of friends that had as much, or a lot more money then they did. Trout being the intuitive and observant child she was, took it all in. She saw the men in their sixty-dollar white shirts, new Cadillac's and numerous affairs. She noticed their bored, valium-ridden wives, who never had a job except to work for charitable causes. The women wore designer clothes from "The City," and had their own liaisons, which were so secret that not even a polygraph could have detected them.

Trout grew up thinking that if this is what money bought she didn't want any part of it. She did her best to look and dress in a way that anyone who didn't know her would think she got her wardrobe at Goodwill, and that her folks were third generation welfare. She bucked all the norms the children of her parent's friends considered the "perks" of being rich.

In the four years she attended high school she never went to a dance or any of the other social functions that were necessary to being accepted at a school everybody in town called "Snob High." Trout's friends were a well-chosen few, middle class, and just like her, rebellious to the bone. She had a couple of boyfriends who smoked dope and played the chemical, nose candy game, and Trout and her group of friends, being the adventurous types that they were, sat in and did their share. Her romances were short-lived and unfulfilling, realizing along the way that her 3,000-year-old mind was too much for a boy's of seventeen.

If you were to ask her now who her real friends had been, she would without a doubt, say her teachers. They were the ones who offered her what she needed most, and that was a truth based on intellect, understanding and trust. Trout found in those adults the mentors she so desperately hungered for. They weren't the good father who, if he wasn't asking her to go fish and hunt, was off in Montana doing it himself. It wasn't the devoted mother who was trying to set an example of how smart a woman could really be, and the sky's the limit as far as a career is concerned. Trout saw in those apostles of the written word that there was something else out there. It was an intangible force that if used right would be the tool that could pry open her mind and set free the captured spirit that had been surrounded and bound by the colony of conformity she had known since birth.

Trout had created, in her mind, a world she could seek refuge in. It was a pool containing only a few fish; the Rainbows and Browns up high towards the surface, and the bottom feeders, slow and lethargic, kept at a distance hugging the muddy floor.

The room at home she protectively called her own wasn't hung with rock posters, prom pictures, or the first dried flowers from the sweetheart who broke her heart. It was a chamber stacked with books and the spiritual prints of Georgia O'Keefe. It was a room with function and purpose, a desk and chair, shelves where poets and writers lay, and walls hung with tied-fly talismans. While her friends were listening to Bon Jovi and Sting, Trout was into "Train" and "Bird." She wanted to sleep as close to the surface as possible, so she had her bed raised 5 feet off the floor, thinking if the sun ever did break through and shatter the roof, she would be the first one in the house it would touch.

I always felt intimidated when I visited and walked into her room. Stacks of books surrounded me, and it was plain to me that this young girl had read more in the last year then I had read in a lifetime.

The more I saw of her, the more convinced I was that we had on our hands a writer and poet-to-be. I knew the thoughts that anguished in her head would someday flow through her heart and down her arm, and turn into the truths she so desperately sought.

Of all the people Trout had met, there was one who carried the influential weight she needed to break away from the snarled line and hooks that surrounded her, that kept her from crashing through the hard glassy surface of her bottomless pool.

It was a woman who taught at her school, someone who saw promise and hope for the girl blind to it herself. She became a friend and counselor, and someone that Trout has been close to ever since. Through her guidance and example, the growing Trout decided to go to a respected and expensive school in Portland, Oregon. Trout had decided to become a teacher, an honorable profession that her parents had also taken. And knowing Trout, I believe that once she took the oath, she would be as good a professor as there is. But before she could teach she would have to learn, and what Trout had to learn wasn't something the shrine of higher education could offer. Trout had to stare at that blackboard in her soul. She had to try to figure out the mess of confusing equations written across her psyche with hard, nineteen-year-old chalk. She had to get out a damp rag and erase the riddles of her existence. Trout had to teach herself how to crawl out of the hole life had dug for her, if not, she would just be another unhappy relater of the written word. I knew deep in my guts that she should end up being the one who writes the books, and not the one who tiresomely grades the papers of the eighteen-year-olds that read them.

As I stood there with my emotional four dollars worth of life, I thought if Trout was seeking truth, then the quarter mile of dirt road she just took to get here was probably the rockiest route to the Gospel she had ever taken in her young life. If Trout really did want to become a teacher, she could practice on me, because the longer I stared into her eyes the more I believed if there was anyone who could make me look honestly into myself, it was her.

I popped the question of food, and said, "You hungry?" Hoping to get an answer of, "No!"

"Yeah! What'cha got?"

Shit! What did she have to say that for? Of all the answers available, she comes up with that one. Whatever happened to, "Oh no, not really," or,

"Thanks, but I just ate," or, "Don't bother, I'm fasting." She's got to pull "Yes," on me, and here I stand with the net worth of four hundred pieces of round copper in my pocket.

The little boy in the back of my head starts screaming, *"See, if we would have gone to college and got a real job like mom and dad wanted, you wouldn't be standing in front of this nice girl stuttering and swallowing your tongue!"*

Trout blinks her eyes, and looking like, (I imagine someone who hasn't eaten in a month) says, "What's in the fridge?"

"Oh, just a chunk of cheese and four friends. They're holding a wake for the last of the French bread I ate yesterday."

"Well fuck it!" she says with a smile, "Let's go shop!"

Shop? Isn't that something that people with jobs do? An hour of fun where you push around one of those chrome carts and fill it with over twenty dollars worth of food?

"Come on, Davis, I know you're probably broke. Where's the closest place to buy food?" she said, reaching in her pocket for the car keys.

"Yeah," I said, dropping about an inch in height. "Well, I guess there is. I think there's one down the road somewhere."

Damn! Read me like a book. Did I look broke? How does she know? Maybe she saw the empty garbage can outside. Have I finally found someone I can't lie to? You mean I'm going to have to tell the truth all summer? That thought alone put my left eye into an involuntary twitch that I'm sure she saw.

"Good, come on we'll take my car," Trout said.

We're going to have to, I thought, because mine probably has just enough gas to make it to the mailbox and back. My van hadn't seen a full tank of gas since 1968, and that's when it came off the assembly line in Hamburg.

"OK" I said, "but I've got to tell you, I'm a little short." Short? I thought, man if I was a stack of half-dollars I'd be about an inch tall.

"Who cares," Trout said, walking for the back door, "I've got money. Come on, let's go."

I followed her out to the car. Hell, I sure wasn't qualified to lead. And if I didn't pick up my head soon, as dark as it was, I was sure to crash into something and make a blundering fool out of myself.

We got in the car and I gave her directions. Trout blasted down the road and we headed for the little town of Sebastopol, four miles south. The blue Z whipped into the supermarket parking lot, and as we approached the door I felt like I was about to go shopping with mom.

We entered the store and I said, "How about taking one of these little red baskets here?" Thinking like I always did, that no more than twenty dollars worth of food would fit into one.

"Are you kidding? We're going to shop!" she answered with a glare.

Damn! There's that word "shop" again, the one that sends waves of guilt and inadequacy racing through my veins. I thought, I might just as well jump up into the cart's kiddy seat and get it over with.

The eight-year-old was starting to fuck with me again, and said, *"If you hadn't wasted so much time the last couple of months staring into that bucket of self loathing, then maybe we would have enough to buy some chips and dip and Rocky Road for dessert."*

By the way Trout was ripping stuff off shelves and sticking them in the cart, you would have thought she had a roll of hundreds in her pocket. On top of that, she was getting things I liked and needed. Maybe she really hadn't gone to the bathroom after all back at the house. She probably suspected I was broke and snuck into the kitchen and went through the cupboards and made a mental note of what was needed. Hell! She was buying Skippy Super Chunk, and honey, flour tortillas and salsa, coffee with real half-and-half, and granola with nuts. I felt like I had just won one of those five-minute TV shopping sprees. The topper was when she said, "How about some beer?"

Well, I could feel as guilty as a fornicating priest about the food, but the minute I heard "Beer," I could dig out every ounce of rationale that had ever crawled into my slimy alcoholic soul.

I said, "Sure, why not?" Pointing to a cheap six-pack. "How about this?" It was a beer I would never drink, no matter how broke I was.

Trout looked at me sideways. "Come on Davis, I know you don't drink that shit! Let's get some Anchor Steam, then preceded to pick up two six-packs.

Well, Trout was my kind of a lady, all right. The girl certainly knew how to shop. I was thinking right then, fuck it, let's return all the food, take the money and buy more beer, then go home, get drunk and philosophize the night away. But Trout was intent on her mission, and dragged me around the store until I got tired and suggested that maybe it was time to go.

It wasn't that I was getting tired. My ego had about all it could stand. So we walked up to the check stand, me the whole time never once looking at the total, growing on the register like a malignant tumor. Trout whips out her check book, pays, and we head out to the lot and load the car.

As we drove home, there was a noticeable quiet in the car. I knew where the silence came from, but Trout didn't. I was getting that same creeping fog of deficiency that always attacks my mood when I know I can't cut it. It was that same helpless anger I got when I failed to gather the will to go outside and fire up my torch and began a day's work, or the same enraged, wall-slamming frustration I felt when I couldn't get it up, not knowing the reason why.

Trout looked over and said, "Listen, if you're bummed because I'm here, it's OK, I understand, I can leave."

No, that's not it, damn it, I thought, it's me again, not you. It's that same freight train of fear and self-loathing about ready to derail and send my head into a spiraling, off-the-trestle plunge.

"No Trout, it's not you. Don't worry," I said, staring out the window.

"Really," she said, looking straight ahead, "I knew I shouldn't have come, I'm just going to get in your way. I knew this wasn't a good idea."

She was driving the Z, but I was suddenly behind the wheel of that old Chevy pick-up again. I thought that if I could have just rolled down the window on that old truck and told her what was wrong, we wouldn't be going through all of this right now.

My revulsion at myself was starting to move over to the left and reinforce that of the driver of the car. Trout, as always, felt that any change of mood had to be her fault, and the best way to cure the problem was to leave, preferably by opening the driver's side door and having me kick her head-first out onto the road.

If I could have just fessed up and told her what was going through my head and not pulled up the drawbridge of fear spanning the moat of my mind, the problem would have been solved. But life was pitching me that last-of-the-ninth fastball again, and Trout had become a spectator in the bleachers screaming for me to hit the ball and get this game over with.

I watched the change in her face. It was a concerned look of introspection, and it had taken over. I saw she wasn't driving the car anymore, "It" was.

"Trout, it's not you. I just don't feel very good about you having to buy all this food. This has nothing to do with you, believe me. It's my problem."

She seemed relieved, and at that moment I felt for her. But at that moment I also knew that she hadn't come up here alone. She had brought this family of self-doubt with her, which was going to share the house with mine. I knew I was going to have to pull out the extra beds because it looked like the house was going to be full of unsavory guests this summer.

We pulled into the drive, unloaded the car and carried the bags into the kitchen. The cupboards and fridge said thank you and, I'm sure, began to sing happy food songs.

I still felt like shit. Not wanting to make Trout's first night a bad one, however, I did my best to cover my feelings. It was a walled remedy I was good at, and around people that didn't know me well, usually worked. But with her it was different. It was something that she would later learn to spot immediately. She would laugh and joke along with me, but she knew, she always did. It was my spontaneous, quick-witted suit of armor; a lie of emotions that I had over the years perfected and honed to a razor sharp edge.

It was that comedic, leafy bush I always hid behind whenever I went for walks in that fear filled landscape of my mind.

Trout and I joshed around in the kitchen. She was busy throwing together quesadillas, and for the first time in months I felt relaxed. It felt good to have someone around. Someone who took me as I was, and who didn't criticize every move I made.

I watched her cook, concentrated and intent on what she was doing. I was feeling more and more like I had known her all my life, and maybe a couple of lifetimes before that. There was an ingrained closeness floating between us. It was an inherent understanding that her being there was part of a plan; a predestined mapped-out route that had been laid out and paved as a way for us to travel and to learn from, one that we were to use to discover who we really were.

In writing this, reaching back for memories of the time we spent together, I realize the truth was born on that summer night, a truth that had been hidden deep inside my intrinsic core. It was a reality that had been waiting all this time for someone to come along and set it free.

We ate that evening setting around the seven-foot, clear heart of redwood and blue steel table I had so carefully made. Trout sat on one of the long matching benches on one side, and I on the other. It would become a place where we would, in the future, spend countless hours sitting opposite each other, sometimes talking endlessly, and sometimes having endless conversations without sound.

The table, with its 500-year-old redwood heart, became our hand-rubbed and oiled pulpit. A lime oak stained altar where feelings and poetic thoughts were delicately thrown, and like sacred holy bones, laid before our eyes.

When I finally moved from that house, I dragged and loaded that 250-pound piece of rose-colored, steel rock by myself. If anyone had offered to help, I would have defiantly turned them down, fearing they might tip it the wrong way and let all the memories slide off.

It is stored now in a room next to the white couches, unsold art, and the raft of a bed that used to carry me through those wind blown nights. Sometimes late at night I will set here in my little wood cabin and imagine the stored table setting alone amongst the holy fields of my art.

I see the room taking on a warm glow as the heart of the wood beats, and the memories that are ingrained sprout and grow, becoming a forest of soft green-feathered trees. I see the hope spirits setting around it with a white raven on each of their arms, wings spread and flapping, creating a turquoise wind that blows away any beasts as they try to crawl through the cracks to eat the heart out of that hallowed wooden shrine.

We finished eating that first night, cleared the table and decided it was time to go to bed. I walked with Trout into her room to see if she had everything she needed, and seeing she did, gave her a reserved hug and reassured her I was happy that she came, and to enjoy the galaxy that was shining over her head.

I walked into the living room, quietly turned on the FM to KJAZ, and slipped into bed. As I lay there listening to Miles, I felt myself drifting off into sleep. For the first time in months I was actually looking forward to the start of a new day.

CHAPTER 6

Awakening the next day wasn't exactly what I would call a rebirth, but it was as good as I'd felt in a long time. It was early, about six thirty, and I figured Trout was probably like most young people and would get up around noon.

The morning was alive outside my windows. The house wren was hopping over the dried oak leaves like they were hot coals, and the dominant Jay searched the front porch for any leftovers of cat food the raccoons had forgotten to eat the night before.

A light morning fog had come in, and before it would decide to leave around nine it made sure that it was going to cover everything it could with a clear, crystal wet sheen. Mourning doves flew overhead with their wings whistling, which I always thought was some kind of an agreed upon morning wake up call for the colony of ground squirrels which always seemed to pop out of their holes at about the same time. The red-tail hadn't yet left its perch in the Monterey Pine. He knew there was plenty of daylight left, enough to snack all he wanted on the rodent-infested apple field down below. A lone crow landed in the big oak and was having some kind of an obscene conversation with the blue jay, who felt like he had a deeded right to the front porch. The pair of gray squirrels that nested in the pine over my studio roof was, no doubt, still asleep waiting for the warmth of day to dry out their acorn breakfast, which hung like little brown torpedoes just outside the front door. I always wanted to be a witness to the destruction of the nasty blue-feathered creature that was arguing with the crow outside. And in my morning fantasies, I would imagine the tree as some great-limbed U boat, zeroing in, and firing one of those acorn torpedoes, hitting that loud-mouthed bird in the back of the head.

I poured myself out of bed, dressed and headed for the kitchen to start some coffee. Figuring Trout was still asleep, I tried to be as noiseless as possible, thinking if she awoke and was confronted with a disheveled, 51-year-old bald man hanging over the sink; she just might turn around frightened, and dive back into bed.

The morning trip to the bathroom was always the ultimate test to see how bad the night had really been, and if I really was actually alive. If a beat-looking stranger stared back at me from the mirror, I knew that I had been fighting the dragons again. And my day would probably begin sometime later on in the afternoon after I had come to terms with the old man that had taken up residence on the surface of my skin. If there were any resemblance to the man who I thought was me, then the day would have as close to a start of being normal as possible. Of course, normal to me was a bad day in hell for anyone else. But I decided that today I was going to give it a shot, pull myself together, and try to show the girl a good day on the farm.

Trout surprised me and woke up half an hour later, and like all people nineteen-years-old looked like she had slept standing up, because there wasn't a mark or sign of sleep on her face.

While she was in the bathroom I drove out to the road and picked up the morning paper. It was a VW bus, loud-muffler ritual that always drove the neighbors on the road crazy.

They never came right out and told me they couldn't stand it. They would, instead, corner me about once a month, and ask me, "why I didn't jog, or at least walk the quarter of a mile to the box? Saying, it was healthy and good for the heart." I would answer, "if I jogged to get the paper, I would never make it back alive to read it, and besides, had they ever tried to run with a bottle of beer in their hands, and if so, how did they keep from spilling half of it all over the road?"

When I got back Trout was in the kitchen toasting English muffins and had the table set. We ate, talked about the house, and slowly woke up. We read the morning news, Doonesbury and Calvin and Hobbs. The two of us laughed at our ignorance as we stared down and tried to attack the crossword puzzle. Trout with all her brilliance got about five rows filled, and I did well with the three that had to do with movies that were made before 1958. We then put on jackets, headed out the back door, untied her bike and rolled it into the pump house.

The first thing I did was to show her the shower. When people would show up during the day it was always third on the list, right behind the lamp and stars, on my personal guided tour. It was a wonder of hot and cold falling water situated behind the shingled woodshed.

One would stand on smooth redwood boards, and while being exposed to every bird and deer within a hundred feet, or anyone staring out any of the windows at the back of the house, have the best damn shower ever.

In the winter it was an icy cold, heart attack test only for the foolishly brave, or the dead drunk. I never had enough courage to try it after October. Even though I had considered myself on occasions a drunk, I had never looked at myself as a stupid drunk. My German ex-girlfriend, Helga, used to walk out the back door stark naked on the coldest day in December, turn the water on to cold and stand under it for half an hour. I always thought that was the way she dropped her body temperature down to a level that was compatible with her heart.

Trout loved it, and couldn't wait for the warmth of the day to try it out. After she said it, I thought, please give me enough warning before you do, because I don't want to be anywhere near one of those windows when you stand there naked and wet with the sun turning your skin a glistening, pearlescent white.

We walked around the shed towards my studio, and on the way saw the first squirrel chattering its way into the new day. Trout and I entered the white, 700 square-foot, twelve-foot high, walled space.

By studio standards it was about a nine, and suited almost all of my needs. That is when I could get it together to walk the 150 feet from the house, which lately wasn't very often. It was full of all the tools of my trade; welders, grinders, drills and saws, and a cable ready TV to give me company on those long, boring, lack-of-creative-drive days.

A few years ago I would consider any studio that I had a sacred temple, where those late night conceptual visions would be, the next day, molded and formed into pieces of blessed work. But as we stood in the room and I looked around I saw things Trout didn't. There was the burned out frustration that hung from the walls. The coldness of the steel that hadn't felt a torch in weeks, and in the other room, the empty white pedestals that stood like unmarked head stones. I pushed us along quickly, wanting to get us out into the fresh air and away from a place that I felt looked and smelled like a crematorium.

We walked into the Zen garden and Trout immediately stopped. It was a signal that she was in the act of absorbing all that lay therein. It was indeed an angelic place and she gave out as much of it as she took in. I felt humbled, as I stood surrounded by the magnificence of 200-year-old trees, and of the natural nineteen-year-old beauty of her. I looked at her face in the morning light, framed by the camellia and fern. I thought if I could ever live to be as old as that redwood growing next to us, I would, for the next 200 years have that image of her standing there imprinted in my mind. It was an impression that would become ingrained in me. Much like that of the bark, as it through time, envelops itself onto the heart of that old tree.

We headed east past the old chicken coop and into the small wild blackberry-surrounded meadow which was full of knee-high grass and the fresh tracks of last night's deer.

The meadow narrowed down to a small path that wound through a grove of incense cedar, Douglas fir, and oak hung with wild grapes. To the right, towards the end of the path were the hives of thousands of bees that were used to pollinate the acres of apples that for a hundred years have grown on the land. There was an old hippie freak that was supposed to come out and collect the honey every few months and leave a jar or two for whoever lived in the house. I never saw him, and it's probably better I hadn't. I know for sure that if I would have ever seen him walking around in that knee-high grass in the morning fog with a long white coat wearing one of those screened masks, I would have probably assumed that he was a leftover intruder from one of my bad dreams, and with my scatter-gun, splattered him and that bucket of honey all over the field.

We continued along the path and reached the ramshackle old pig shed that marked the end, and northeast corner of the property. Trout and I turned right and decided to walk around the edge of the field. It was an imaginary line that circled the 13 acres.

As we turned the corner I pointed down to the right at the mass of six-foot-tall bushes that were erupting with flowers. They looked like giant breakfast eggs over easy. I mentioned to Trout that they were matilija poppies, whose snow-white petals encircled a yellow furry mass that was always dotted by some of the bees that lived next door. Whenever I walked by I always imagined a good-humored God playing his little joke on the natural plant restaurant that he placed on the world. It was His way of saying, "Hey waiter, I think there's something crawling in my eggs!"

As Trout stared at the sight, I sort of halfway chuckled, and she turned giving me her famous sideways look of, "What's so funny?"

I wanted to tell her what made me smile, but was afraid that she would find it dumb, and if it was anything I didn't need right now was for her, so early into her visit to find me a childish-humored dolt. That would come soon enough anyway, I thought, because in the weeks to come I'm sure that sometimes she would feel like she was living with a man who was the spitting image of a demented, Captain Kangaroo.

We walked on not saying much, just taking in the beauty of the land and enjoying the morning. We cut across the field and headed for the Monterey Pine that marked the far corner of the farm. It was the viridian green home of a red-tailed hawk that patrolled and controlled the skies over the field and vineyards next door.

As a boy in the valley town of Merced, I lived with a man who made the raising of birds his own Zen statement. He worked nine to five managing a fleet of trucks that delivered bread. When he came home he would retreat into his own little private world of birds. The man would spend countless feathered hours with his pigeons, dove, pheasant and quail. I grew up looking at him as some kind of small town bald Leonardo because somewhere in his heart was a pair of nonfunctional canvas wings which wanted desperately to get off the ground and fly.

I would watch him as he held a pigeon close, his palm holding its breast with his first finger between its legs and tail. His thumb, acting like a soft-fleshed weight pressed down on its back and held the bird steady and secure.

He would hold those prized racers tenderly to his chest and stroke their backs, all the while speaking to them in a low voice the small boy watching assumed was a secret tongue, and was one of the things he couldn't wait to learn when he grew up.

As I got older and started school, I began to emulate the man. I would come home, and just like him, sit in a chair outside the pens and for hours stare at the flightless scene behind the wire. I knew there was something special going on between him and his feathered friends, and I thought if I sat quietly without moving long enough, I would find out.

When he finally trusted me enough to unlock the cage and go inside when he was away, I would enter that inner sanctum with the same quiet respect as that of a devout Jew approaching the "Wailing Wall" for the first time. It became my seven-year-old private world, and if I hadn't yet learned the secrets that flew through the loft, then with enough patience, I knew I would by the time I was eight.

I spent so much time in that cage the birds started to believe I was a big mutated one of them. The first triumph of communication came one day when I laid on my back on the coop's sandy floor. Like Gulliver with arms and legs spread, I waited for the birds to come and bind me with quilled rope, and torture me with a soft-feathered secret knowledge that up until that time only my father knew. The boy, who thought of himself as an explorer of an up-until-now undiscovered, mysterious-winged world, lay prostrate in a pen inhabited by a majestic pigeon called White Kings. They were the bird of choice in all the "four star" restaurants in San Francisco. And my father raised breeders, the finest of the fine. The Kings looked down from their nests cocking their heads from side to side, trying to figure out why the big bird with no wings had suddenly fallen, and why was he laying like a soft-breathing, blue-jeaned mound between them and their food? After about an hour, they realized that they didn't have much of a choice. It was either walk around, or over me, or starve. After nervously talking about it in their cooed tongue for a while, I think they figured out that the dead-bird-kid lying there on the ground was harmless, and began their trek to dinner.

It was probably the high point of my young life, and better than any Christmas I'd ever had. In the short span of about ten minutes I had every bird in that pen either on my body, or close enough to touch. I must have lain there for hours. When I finally looked up I realized that my folks were home. It was clear to me that they had arrived, because my dad was standing outside the pen with the biggest pigeon-man grin that the limits of his face would allow.

After that day I knew that I had become a member of the most secret, two-man society of mystical-winged creatures in the world. In my young years that followed I would walk side by side, like a disciple of the religion of holy flight, with a man who did the best he could in his own way to teach me how to fly.

Trout and I looked up into the tree hoping to catch a glimpse of the master of an element which we call sky. The hawk was either gone, or somewhere looking back down on us because after searching the tree for a while we decided he wasn't to be found, and headed back towards the house.

CHAPTER 7

The fog began its slow burn, and as we walked over the moist furrowed field the sun-warmed, steamed-breath of the morning earth came alive, touching our legs.

We stepped over stones and a fallen tree, and approached the grove of oak and pine that sets to the left and in back of the house. It was a few acres that the local deer, and a no-man's land of poison oak, called home. The trees and brush were so thick that even on the brightest day you could only see about ten feet into a mass of moss gray and dark brown that I, not once, ever set foot in. The neighbors in back told me dark tales of crashing night sounds and poison vines that grew to a hundred feet choking the life out of trees and anything else that happened to venture in. Trout took a step back as I warned her of the menaced growth that lie ahead, and she assured me not to worry because it wasn't a place where she wanted to spend her summer vacation and, if the tales were true, the rest of her life.

We turned and walked past the huge pile of dead apple limbs. It was a monument to the wooden trees whose amputated arms would no longer jingle with the soft, sweet red jewelry called Gravensteins. We passed the rusty plow half buried in dirt, turned left and followed the picket fence that ended up at the front of the house. Trout turned with the porch to her back and watched as the morning sun took out its box of warm colors and began to paint the field.

She looked in the direction of the main road that was hidden by a row of tall pines. Even at a quarter of a mile away the subdued sounds of cars going by could be heard droning over the field. It didn't exactly sound like cars or trucks, but more like a rolling rumble which made her turn and say that it was a shame that no matter where you go, or how high up you climb, you can never escape "Them."

I told her I knew how she felt, and that I had also noticed it the first day I was here. But one evening while sitting on the mahogany bench swing that hung on the front porch, I decided that it sounded more like waves breaking on a distant shore, and if you listened closely and counted the sounds you might be lucky and hear a gigantic semi-truck seventh wave crashing against the asphalt beach just behind the trees.

Without saying a word, Trout smiled at my comment. Her eyes told me she understood what I was trying to say, and that was, if you sometimes can't handle the chaos that runs like a rampant elephant out there, you sure can come up with poetic solutions to deal with it.

We stood there for a while on our pretend sand dune beach listening to the morning commute and its white-capped storm moving towards town.

She told me that it was, indeed, a beautiful place, and was happy she came, and that if it was all right maybe tonight we could go for a walk.

"A walk?" I thought, hell, I felt so good around her that I would crawl around that rocky dirt field if she asked me too! Trout was putting out the strongest, "Nicest Female That I Had Ever Met In My Life," waves I had ever felt, and she's asking me if it's OK if we go for a walk? I thought about answering, "Sure, you walk, and I'll just fly alongside with the wings I sprouted the minute you stepped out of your car yesterday."

I didn't know what she was doing to me, but it was something that hadn't been done in a long while, (if ever). She had been there less than a day and I was already having feelings that scared the hell out of me. They were emotions that made me pull up the drawbridge. It was a defense against affections that seemed to be more than what I was supposed to be feeling. She was almost like family. That alone was a boundary I didn't want my emotions to cross. Her parents were friends of mine long before she was born, and I considered her mother one of my closest. Whatever I was feeling at the time was something I would have to bury, that is if there was any room left in the graveyard deep inside me where all my other secrets were buried fifty-one years deep.

Trout spent her first day reading and napping, and I spent most of mine watching her. I tried to act busy, cutting a trail back and forth to my studio. But every time I walked through the studio's double French door, my mind became as blank and empty as the 10-by-10 foot workbench that lay in front of me.

After awhile I gave up, thinking who in the hell am I trying to kid? If it's her, she doesn't care anyway. She probably already knew what I was up to. If it was me, then I wasn't as sharp as I thought I was. I could fool myself about a lot of things, but trying to find creative reasons to work wasn't one of them.

The place had become so quiet I didn't even know someone else was occupying it. I felt a presence in the house, but it wasn't movement or sounds that made me aware that someone else was there. Trout didn't move much anyway, and the only sounds I heard from her were the turning of pages as she lay on her back on the couch. It just felt like there was some kind of soft energy growing from the carpet and climbing the walls. It was a slow gracious movement that reminded me of one of those nature films where a field of daisies is shown in a 30-second time lapse sequence beginning from the planting of the seed to the final outward explosion of the petals. Realizing that the house was in the good "Mother Earth" hands of Trout. I decided to retire to my room and lie down and turn the worn pages of my mind and try and take a nap.

I awoke to the same silence that put me to sleep, and walked into the living room fully expecting it to be over-grown with wild flowers. There were no flowers, and no Trout. She was nowhere to be found.

I thought, she's either out taking a walk, or packed up and left. She probably heard me talking in my sleep, saying the same things that I was thinking just before I drifted off. If there had been any daisies growing on the floor, then the feelings I was having would have poisoned them with a guilt that would have made DDT look like watered-down Kool Aid.

I looked out of the kitchen window and saw her sitting on the bench next to the pond. She was deep in thought. It was nothing new for Trout; one just had to figure out what depth she was at before you dove in with any dialogue. I decided to leave her alone and let her climb out of wherever she was by herself. Whenever I was down there exploring those dark caverns and anybody shook my emotional shoulder, I would react like a man that had just eaten 25 tabs of high grade acid, believing that the touch was the tail of one of the giant lizards I was locked in the room with. If they were real lucky they'd get that blank 1,000-yard stare. The one you get just before some white-gowned nurse prepares to give you a mega-shot of Valium. One thing I learned about being on the edge of insanity myself was to never get sanctimonious about it with other people who were also caught in that web. It would be like one drunk telling another to straighten up and stop puking on his food. So I decided to let her be, wherever she was, maybe it was somewhere nice. At least she was in the Zen garden, a place that made any voyage of the mind seem like a pleasant cruise down some orchid-banked river. It was also a place where the garden spirits didn't want you coming in and fucking with the good karma they had been building over the last hundred years.

I walked into the garden one night with a good load on and sat down on the bench with a beer in one hand and five fingers of J.D. in a water glass in the other. I sat there peering into the pond trying to figure out if there was enough water in the bottom to drown myself. The spirits didn't like my presence. They thought if I kept talking loud I would wake up the baby owls just born in the tree above me. The garden spirits proceeded to do a number that would have made George Lucas's special effects studio look like some garage hobby shop.

Within a matter of minutes I found myself surrounded by a platoon of Halloween-masked, black-pajama-clad Viet Cong crawling through the ivy with rusty machetes in hand. I thought, man, I had played this game before, usually with scaled reptiles riding Black Horned Rhinos, or rabid bats trying to eat out my eyes, but this was about as real as it gets. I felt like I was sitting there with one of those cardboard masks of Richard Nixon welded on my face, and the first one to bring in my head got an extra month's allotment of rice.

There were times in Europe when I would hallucinate and see little ballerinas dancing on the windowsill, or negative space silhouetted people in the room, standing and talking and swaying with the shadows of the moon, but they weren't out to KILL ME!

These little black-pajama-wearing motherfuckers were serious, and I didn't know whether to surrender, run, or finally give in to my lunacy and jump head first into the foot of water at the bottom of the pond. By this time something had let the adrenaline-pissing blind butterfly out of its cage. It hit the side of my chest so hard it picked me up off the bench and sent me, spilling half my drink in the process, on a dead run to the back door. The rest of the night was spent with me sitting on the couch with my pistol in one hand and the TV remote in the other, watching reruns of "The Wonder Years," and anything else that would take my mind off my mind.

Trout finally came in looking peaceful and content, a sign that she was having a good day. We fixed dinner, sat around the table and talked, and after looking and failing to find a good late movie on the tube, said good night and went to bed.

The next days were spent just like the first. Trout read and napped, and in between, me watching her read and nap. I cut deep trails back and forth to the studio, always returning like the defeated hunter without any creative kills to lay on the table.

I was still broke, and was racking my brain about how to get something coming in. The five-day deadlines would soon be over, and along with them, the electricity, telephone, propane, and the cable TV. The television wasn't so important, but the cable radio was hooked up to it, and if I couldn't hear "KJAZ," the best FM jazz station in America, then I would go into some kind of withdrawal that would make trying to kick the crack cocaine habit a piece of cake.

I decided to hit up the developer who I had signed a contract with to do two gates at the beginning of summer. The gates were supposed to be have already been done, but construction delays and building permits were keeping the project two months behind schedule, and along with it my eating and drinking habits.

I went down and decided not to fuck with the truth by telling him something like, "my mother just died and I need the money for a casket," (bad karma), or, "I need an operation on my right hand, or I never will be able to weld again." No, I came right out and said, "I need a thousand dollars, and if you don't give it to me I will starve to death before the summer's out and you will never see those gates, or the two thousand dollar deposit you gave me when we signed the contract. He looked at me like he was thinking this was the last time he would ever deal with this artist-gate-maker, no matter how good he was supposed to be. He arrogantly peered over his glasses at me, and with his millionaire's, "I've got power over your life," chicken shit smile, cut me a check and went back to the paper work on his desk.

After I cashed the check I filled Vanna, (I had named my '68, white VW van, "Vanna White"), with gas. It had been so long since she had been filled up that I'm sure the colony of mutated insects living in the top half of the tank would panic, and like eight-legged salmon try to swim for their lives up the gas-hose-stream.

I drove home and spent the next hour at my desk writing checks that totaled $784.25. It was an amount that would keep the farm from crashing for the next few weeks.

It was decided that we would go to "Jasper's" and celebrate. It was a local pub and restaurant in downtown Sebastopol that had live music and the best hamburgers in the area. Trout and I had been there a few days before, and she had paid. It was a generous act that nevertheless made the hamburger and hand-cut-fries not as tasty as they could have been. I told her that this time it would be my treat, realizing at the time that it was just a small band-aid to cover the festering wounds of my manhood.

My father had instilled in me the moral ethic of, "Never let a woman pay your way." It was a silly rule of a lot of men of his generation, and one that nevertheless put me into bad trips of guilt whenever it happened. It also played hell with my wallet on a lot of those $150 first-date dinners.

Trout grabbed a towel and robe and headed out to the shower, while I grabbed a beer and headed for a point in the house as far away from it as I could get. I was already having enough night-dream visions of her which made me want to wrap my body in thorns, without having her see me accidentally walk past one of the windows that overlooked the stream of water that she was standing under.

The feelings I was having about her were building up daily, and I hoped the third eye she was born with wasn't looking through my chest, into my heart.

Trout was the kind of woman I had been looking for all my life, someone who would accept me with all my imperfections and respect me for admitting them. I was so worn out by women who had fallen in love with me wanting the creative adventurous life. They thought I would ride into their lives on a white charger and do something to them that had never been done before. After awhile they realized I wasn't the hero who would rescue them, and that I was, indeed, just another fragile human being with a crying little boy inside.

A man who had enough baggage to break the back of any charging white horse ever bred.

The process of molding and changing me into the "White Knight" they had hungered for all their lives began, for them, at about the age of twelve. It was during that time when they realized their father was too tired and too busy from punching a time card and paying the bills to fight off any dragons. The only Round Table he gave a shit about was the one down the street that sold beer and pizza.

I had met a lot of woman in my life and Trout was the only one I felt who could let me be myself. It was a quality that emanated from her being; an understanding that filled the air every time we were close.

Trout stepped out of the bathroom and said she was ready to go. I wasn't quite sure, though, if I was. I was sitting far across the room in a chair that, once you are in it, holds you down like a strong-handed, huge white glove. It had a grip on my body much like the sight of her; a grip that took hold and squeezed tight around my heart. I had never seen her look so beautiful. Her hair was still damp and hung down in long ringlets, which rested on her shoulders. She was wearing a light brown, sleeveless blouse with little buttons that fell like a row of pearl stars from between her breasts. The blouse hung about two inches over an ankle length, flowered cotton skirt, from which a pair of white feet and two Birkenstocks stuck out from the bottom.

She stood in the middle of the room totally unaware of the hundreds of albino hummingbirds flying around her body, and gave me a sweet smiled look, and said, "You ready to go?"

Sure, as soon as somebody pulls the switch on the fire works that went off and filled the room the minute you stepped into it.

I just sat there and stared, not so much out of rudeness or to make her feel uncomfortable, it's just that my eyes wouldn't blink anymore. The reason they couldn't blink was because white feathers were starting to fall from the ceiling and land on my face, filling my eyes with a down-like dust.

Trout got this embarrassed look on her face, turned a light shade of red, smiled, and asked, "What?"

Not only couldn't I blink or move, but also I was at that moment unable to speak. In my profession I was able to meet, hang around, and sleep with a lot of pretty women, but I had never been as fascinated with one the way I was at that moment with her. And the incredible thing was, she wasn't even aware of it.

When I lived in Germany I used to frequent a bistro across the street from one of the biggest modeling agencies in Europe. I saw women walk through the front door that could press the hormone, heart attack buttons of any straight man in the place. But Trout had it all over those women, and the wonderfulness of it all was that she didn't know it. If she did, she would be so far beyond that superficial bullshit that she wouldn't care. Trout had something besides her obvious beauty, and that was a poetic soul still held captive, deep in the marrow of her being.

"DAVIS!"

She was yelling my name with this big carp of a grin on her face, and said, "Get it together! What's the matter? Don't you want to go? Come on Davis, pick it up!"

I thought, sure I do. But first you've got to open a window and chase those hummingbirds out of the house. Then sweep up the three feet of white feathers that are covering the floor, and while you're at it, come over and pull these arrows out of my heart.

I slowly stood up, and said, "OK. But first let me go into the bathroom and throw some cold water on my face. And by the way, you look beautiful."

Well, I did it. I went and said something personal and crossed the line.

Trout was not one to handle compliments very well, and hearing from an older man that she was beautiful was a little more than she could handle. She looked away from my eyes and said, "Yeah, it is a nice dress isn't it?"

I thought, the hell with the dress, it's you I'm talking about.

"Yeah, it is a nice dress, but you look great, too."

Looking at an angle, towards the floor, she said with a voice I could hardly hear, "Thanks."

There was a treasure chest of femininity locked up inside that young woman standing before me. I wished at that moment that kismet had given me the key to it, because if it had, I would have gotten on the phone and ordered twenty dozen roses, then had them delivered by the ghost of Isadora Duncan, who would then swirl and float around the room throwing them one by one at her feet. I would ask the spirits to conjure up the phantom of Charlie Parker, and while Trout and I held each other close and danced around the room, he would stand in the corner and play a celestial version of "Body and Soul." The hummingbirds would pull at her hair, while a pair of snow falcons doing their ancient courtship ritual would dive and scream in the orange, smoked-filled air above our heads. I would feel her breathe deep, and watch as she exhaled all of the confused, woman-child, webbed-chains that had bound her to an identity she couldn't define.

We stood before each other separated by the thick walls that society and the unfairness of time and age had built between us. It was a wall that only the reckless or those hopelessly in love would dare to climb. As we walked down the steps and out to the car, I looked down at the pair of white falcons sitting on my right arm, and knew the truth. I realized that because of what I just felt in that room, I had become, indeed, a man hopelessly in love.

CHAPTER 8

We sat in the restaurant that night, ate our burgers and shared a beer. Trout might as well have been there alone by the way I acted, because I was definitely somewhere else, and she knew it.

After an eternal five minutes of silence, she asked, "What is it?"

I sure as hell couldn't tell her, because if I did, I felt she would pack up and leave, and I didn't think I could handle that. Not at that point anyway. So I said, "Oh, it's nothing, just some of that Davis mind warp that moves in and stays for awhile."

"Come on, we can talk about it if you want," she said, concerned.

"Nah, it'll pass. It's just one of those things. It's really not important."

Yeah right, I thought, just about as not important as a heart missing ten beats in a row. Trout was wise beyond her years, but even her "Eye of Athena" couldn't reach the depths of this one. This truth was buried in a place in my heart that no one had ever ventured. What Trout was feeling from me was an overwhelming sadness that I was doing my best to hide. It was the beginning of a period of bereavement over the loss of something that I knew I would never be able to have.

The next days were quiet around the farm. Trout spent most of her time reading, and if she knew what had moved in and occupied my mind, she didn't let on.

I started to teach her how to weld. She took to it well, despite her impatience and lack of confidence in herself. Trout constructed a lizard with a gaping mouth and dagger-like tongue. It was for certain a piece of art that the prophet in her had made, because when she showed it to me I was convinced it would be that exact face she would show to me if I ever told her how I felt.

There was something else that had been bothering me ever since she arrived, but feeling like it was none of my business, never brought it up. It was a question that, in the real world, didn't need to be answered. But ever since I discovered how I felt about her my world had ceased to be anything close to real, so I decided to bring it up that night during dinner.

Over the last couple of years I had heard rumors from my ex-wife and daughter that Trout was gay. Since I hadn't seen much of her during that time, it was something that I had never given much thought to. Looking back, I don't even know how I would have felt if I would have thought about it.

In the circles that I had moved in, (in connection with the world of art), I had met many people who were gay. I had liked or disliked them with the same approach that I gave to heterosexuals, and that was, if the person was an asshole, then the person was an asshole, if they weren't, then they weren't. If a gay friend tried to hit on me, I told him to go take a cold shower, and if that didn't work, to take a hike. I did the same thing to straight women. If I felt that their feelings for me were going to interfere with our friendship, then it might be better if we didn't see each other so often.

One thing that I have found out in this life is that when a friend wants your body, no matter what gender they are, and you don't want to give it to them, then whatever you both had in common with your minds always came in second. It was an unwanted attraction that could fuck up a friendship faster than anything I know.

The only difference with that and Trout was I had never been emotionally involved with a gay person. I'd heard it said that if you think a straight women can break your heart, try falling in love with a gay one. They'll take that red pulsating pump and bend it into shapes not even a cardiologist would recognize. The worst warning was, (and something that always put your dick into reverse and made it bury itself somewhere inside your lower intestines), that a man could never make love to a woman the way a woman can. Which was something that always seemed biologically obvious to me.

I guess what all those messengers of male inadequacies were trying to tell us was that it takes a woman to make another woman really feel good. The only problem I ever had with that concept was that until they come up with a rubber cock with a soul, then I think we still have a chance.

There were always the studs who were having so much trouble coming to terms with their own sexuality, who, when they saw a butch dyke biker walking down the street, would say something profound like, "All that chick needs is this 9 inches of blue steel hanging between my legs, that'd turn her around in a hurry." Yeah, right, I thought, what she would do is rip it off your infantile body and beat you to death with it.

I always thought the reason why a lot of women were gay was because there were so many guys walking around with that same attitude. I sometimes thought if I was a woman and that was the kind of quality I had to choose from, then maybe choosing to sleep with another woman wasn't such a bad choice after all.

The feelings I was having for Trout made me look at this life style with new eyes. They were eyes that, of course, only saw a relationship with her in a fantasy world.

From the minute she arrived and stepped out of the car I looked for things that might convince me that all of the rumors I'd heard were true. She did have a masculine edge to her, but it was something I had always seen in her, even as a child.

The way that she wore her hair pulled back tight; her taller than most men size, and the sloppy jeans with two funny Elmer Fudd shoes sticking out didn't help much. Even with all of that, and the influence of rumors I'd heard, I still saw a sensual female hiding behind that "Multi-Sex-Wear-What-You-Feel-Comfortable-In" disguise.

I sat at the table a few nights later watching her in the kitchen, knowing I was going to bring it up. Exactly how, I didn't know. I also knew if she said she was gay then it would destroy any chance I would have ever had, (that is, if chance could ever be misconstrued to mean that I wasn't old enough to almost be her grandfather, and I wasn't almost family, and why would she want to be together with somebody that loses his mind daily, anyway?)

I brought up the subject by using a story I had read in the paper that day. It was nothing in particular, other than it had the word "gay" in it somewhere. Me, being the astute person that I am, thought the word alone would be enough reason for her to look at me as a Catholic priest, and sit down at the confessional-booth-redwood-table and come out of the closet.

I might just as well have said nothing by the way she acted. She just kept going about her business making me feel like I had just said something like, "It sure is a nice day." The way I usually handle things like that, where I want a reaction and someone acts like they aren't listening, is to treat it like it was the most important subject since the assassination of J.F.K.

I started to talk about homosexuality in the same way that Jackson Pollack painted, with no beginning or end, confusing, and abstract as hell. I wanted a response, and if I didn't have enough nerve to come right out and ask her, then maybe she would say something just to shut me up. She walked back and forth in the kitchen with a pensive look on her face, which was the signal that I was evidently touching on something.

All of a sudden she walked over to the cutting board, and looking down at the garlic with the same concerned intensity one would have deciding whether or not to dice up the "Dead Sea Scrolls", said, "Davis, you know that I've been seeing women."

It was a quiet response. But one with enough defiance in it to let you know it was something she had given much thought to before she said it. She was also letting me know it was something she was prepared to deal with if you challenged her on it.

I recognized the tenderness of the issue. I knew that it was something I shouldn't make light of, or in any way, fuck with.

So I said in my best, "Oh really, who cares?" kind of a voice, "Yeah, I heard about it somewhere."

54

Which I thought at the moment it poured out of my mouth was the dumbest thing I had ever said in my life. Hell! It sounded like the mail man walked up to me, and while giving me the gas and electric bill, said, "Oh by the way, Trout is gay."

Still going about her business in the kitchen, Trout said, "Oh yeah, where'd you hear it?"

By the way I was acting, she was probably thinking I had seen it on the evening news.

"I think I heard my daughter and ex-wife talking about it. I think that was it. Yeah, I'm sure of it. I mean, who else would I have heard it from?" OK you made your point. I thought, now shut the fuck up!

Looking at me dead in the eyes, Trout asked, "What do you think about it?"

Reacting like she had just addressed that question to someone else in the room, I said, "Who me? I don't know. I really hadn't given it much thought." Like hell I hadn't, you lying son of a bitch, it's been running through your body all day with about the same intense speed as blood moving through your heart.

I stared down into my beer and tried to figure out how to deal with a situation that was a whole lot more important than I wanted to let on. And at the same time I knew she respected me, and at this point wanted a reaction that showed Trout and her choice the same respect. But I had a secret and that would keep me from dealing with this in an objective way. It had become a subject that I had brought up and now wanted to make go away. It also destroyed any fantasy that I had of us ever saying, "I do," having four kids, and living happily ever after in a small cabin in the woods.

I answered her with something about as safe and middle of the road as I could, with, "It's OK with me, after all it's your choice. If you're happy, that's all that matters." Not bad, I thought, good answer. So why did I have to go and fuck it up with, "But there sure are going to be a lot of broken hearted guys out there." Actually, I thought, there's only one that I gave a shit about, and that's the sad old dog sitting across the table from you.

It didn't take Trout long to react to that one. About a quick blink of the eye was my estimation.

She responded with all the conviction in the world, and with all the fire and rebelliousness of a person who was tired of hearing clichés like that.

"Yeah, but if I wasn't, there'd be a lot of disappointed women out there too."

OUCH! She might just as well have taken that garlic-coated steel knife and whiffed it across the table at me because the effect would have felt the same. Here I was with this monstrous secret trapped inside me, a secret that kept me from having any kind of sane intelligent conversation with her. On top of that, I was pushing buttons that were turning on music that I didn't want to hear.

She must have noticed something. Maybe it was my look. Maybe she felt the conversation was taking off and landing in a place we didn't want it too. It could have been she already knew how I felt about her, and not wanting to make my fall too hard, said, "But that doesn't mean that I've put the idea of men out of my mind, or out of my life."

I thought, WHAT? What the fuck does that mean? Is she trying to say that she's not gay? Or that it's just a trend? Is she just taking a break from the world I live in, the world of women and men? Maybe she has recognized my pain and thought I was having enough trouble dealing with the futility of falling in love with her as it was. She's probably thinking, the poor boy, he's in a no-win situation. Even if I weren't gay he wouldn't have a chance, and even if he had a chance to start with it wouldn't be worth a prayer in hell, because I'm gay.

I stood up and walked into the kitchen acting like nothing was wrong, which was hard to do because I was dragging my feet like I had on a pair of 30-pound shoes.

Trout saw me open the cabinet door and asked what I was looking for. "The aspirin," which I knew just happened to be in front of the pint of Jim Beam at the back of the shelf. I thought a shot would help me look at this with clearer eyes. Trout didn't know what I was drinking to. For all she knew, I was going to pour a toast and celebrate her coming out of the closet.

The eight-year-old had just walked in and taken over. The only thing I liked about him was that he didn't care what he drank. As a matter of fact when we would hit the bars, sad and broke, he'd settle for anything. He especially liked the stuff that caught fire when you dropped a match in it.

The eight year old was really feeling sorry for me, and in his best Bogart attitude, said, " *it's all right, nice guys always finish last."* "LAST?" Fuck! I'm such a loser she wouldn't even allow me in the race. Even if I was someone else and 20 years younger, and was lucky enough to get her into bed, she would probably laugh. She would be fulfilling all the fears that men have of hearing the stories from the prophets of heterosexual doom, that men can't satisfy a woman like a woman can. She would probably turn into some kind of bra-less reptilian goddess, and say something like, "You're so bad that the worst woman lover I've ever had made me feel better than you do!"

Well, the adult was getting a whiff of where the 8-year old was trying to take him. It was somewhere back in the fifties in the back seat of an emerald green, lowered 57 Chevy convertible on a first try to get it up attempt, which didn't materialize. The girl was thoughtful enough to tell her best girlfriend and anyone else who was sitting at the lunch table that cared to listen. Needless to say, the days that followed were ones of pure teen-age hell, and were almost enough reason to drop out of school and join the Navy. Every time I passed a girl in the hallway I knew they were going to point at my crotch and giggle, and if they didn't, I sure knew that they were thinking about it.

Those were the same feelings of inadequacy I was having, standing there staring out the kitchen window with a drink in my hand. I knew my thoughts were pretty distorted, and vaguely related to the conversation that Trout and I just had. But once that eight-year-old got his hands on my mind, (especially in a moment when I needed him the least), he could put a warp on it just like a hot torch does to thin steel.

I stood there and wondered if women really thought about what goes through a guy's head. I don't mean the ones that go around with their brains in their dicks, but the other ones. The kind of a guy I always considered myself to be. Had she ever gone to bed with a feeling man, one who could be tender to her and carefully take care of her needs and desires? Someone who would see her body as a soft dew-covered field of morning clover, and with his hands acting like a warm summer breeze, touch her gently with loving care. Had Trout ever slept with a man? And if she had, was it any good? Did she have anything to compare with as far as men and women were concerned?

I stared out the window deep in thought. My mind had become too much for the little boy, and he never liked it when I was locked into something serious and rational. So he would just pack up and leave. But he knew he had done some damage and would be back tomorrow to take a body count. I don't know why I have put up with him for as long as I have. I've thought many times I should have gotten rid of him years ago. But there were times when he came in handy and let me do things that were bad for me and hold my hand when I wanted to run away from things that would do me good.

I don't know how long I stood in front of that window. Trout was aware that my mind was somewhere else and called from the other room and asked if everything was all right. I said yes, and told her I was just looking through the night into the garden. I turned in her direction and saw by the look on her face that she felt whatever mood I was in was for sure, brought on by her. The last thing I wanted her to feel was any guilt by what she had said. If there was any guilt it was my department. She had told me the truth, and I had respected her for it. I was just having trouble at that moment respecting myself. If I were having these feelings for anyone else I wouldn't care. But Trout was special, and I always felt protective towards her. Now I had to fight the feeling of protecting her from myself.

I walked into the living room and looked through the TV Guide for a movie. We found something on AMC. It was an old John Garfield, Lana

Turner classic. We both watched, but didn't really pay any attention to what was going on. It was just a blur of black and white we were using to fill an uneasy quietness that I had created.

I would look her way as she sat on the floor and knew I cared for her deeply, possibly deeper than I had ever cared for anyone in my life. I wanted to tell her how I felt, thinking maybe it would make everything all right. Maybe then she would understand that my coldness and retreating to the kitchen window had nothing to do with what she had said or done. But I could tell by the look on her face that she thought it had.

I stood up, feeling like I should apologize, not so much for turning my back on her, but for falling in love. It was the first time in my life I had ever wanted to tell someone that I was sorry for caring so much.

It was a thought that confused the hell out of me, and made me think again that she would probably be better off if she left. But I knew if she did, she would take away a part of me that could never, again, be replaced.

I went to bed and lay on that fur-covered raft and floated down a river of thought that turned into sleep, and then into dream. In the dream I saw her on the beach wearing a wind-blown, silken dress. She was standing amongst a flock of swirling screaming gulls with her arms up and was singing to them in a tongue that only birds know. The gulls floated and landed on the ground and warmed her feet. They looked up flapping their wings and watched her cry. Her tears fell and splashed, and ebbed out with the tide. The gulls saw the sadness in her eyes and cried too. In my dream I became one of those birds, and tasted the sweet tears and cried with them. I tried to rip off my wings and stick them to her arms, but the wind kept blowing them away. Her eyes pleaded for me to help, but I was at a loss.

The gulls flew in slow motion and took me with them. We caught the wind, and as it took us higher and higher I looked down for the last time and realized I was powerless to do anything for her. She looked up at us hopelessly, and I saw in her eyes that she wanted so desperately to fly too.

I awoke from the dream wanting to go to her and hold her tight, to whisper that everything was all right. I wanted to tell her, yes, baby someday you will fly. And if I did have wings I'd rip them off and pin them to your arms and throw you into the air and let you sail away from all the pain I believe you've felt all these years.

CHAPTER 9

The next day I awoke trying like hell not to let my feelings show. I was at a point where I thought no matter what I did they would soon become as obvious as neon ink on a silk-screened shirt.

Trout was lost in her own thoughts, and I could only guess what they were. She acted concerned, which was really nothing new for her, except I was having the feeling it was something that had to do with me. I had blown women away before. It was always an inherent rage, much like an emotional Marciano right hand that struck when they least expected it, or a depression so deep that even with 3,000-foot eyes they were unable to see where it came from.

I had never chased a woman away by loving her too much. I sometimes made them want to leave because of jumping in that old Chevy truck and locking the doors. It was an iced, winter emotion that probably made them think that whatever warm feelings I had before falling asleep were passed in the morning along with all the other shit that I had accumulated during the dark hours of night.

If Trout were going to run it wouldn't be a rabid dog rage or a catatonic stupor that would scare her away. It would be the foul smell of a man whose heart was rotting because of the loss of hope.

The one-eyed raven had come in the night and had slept at the foot of the bed, a sure sign that it was going to be a bad day.

I awoke and went into the kitchen. Trout was still asleep, so being witness free I poured a bit of Kentucky in my coffee. I knew it wouldn't help me, but I thought the 100-proof rationale would at least help keep my pain at a manageable level.

There were days in my life when the need for the comforting warm breast of a woman was so strong the small boy in me would scream, and I would drink anything to keep him quiet. If Trout hadn't been there, that day would have been one of them. It was a side of me not many people knew, and I was going to do my best to include her in that group.

Booze has been the back-to-back buddy that has helped me to do the things in life I regretted the most. It has always been there egging me on when I got into my worst bar room brawls. If I got my ass kicked, it licked my wounds when I got home. Alcohol has put me into fits of rage where I would have enough adrenaline pumping through my veins where three good-sized men or a living room wall have trouble holding me back. I have been known to take a three-room apartment, and like a tossed grenade, turn it into a debris-riddled, one room flat. There were times when I was living in Europe that I gave into my depression and allowed it to rule me. Drunk and alone, I would go into a rage, and with my bare hands try to rip the welds and tear the seams out of a piece of my steel sculpture. I never totally succeeded, but I was able to change its form into a halfway decent piece of bloody, abstract art.

Most of the time I exploded when no one was around, but there were occasions when some poor soul was unfortunate enough to be a witness to this Vesuvius-like-explosion. It was an experience that must have driven a stake into their bowels, and put them as close to a war as they'd ever want to be.

My late German girl friend had a real knack of crossing my wires and overloading the circuits of a mind that was already carrying a load it couldn't handle.

When Trout arrived I was in the process of trying to put all those wires back in place, but I think I was still hooking up the red to the black because no matter how hard I tried the fuses would always melt and do a slow burn. Ever since the day she pulled in the drive I knew if anyone could calm this indefinable inner rage, it would be her. I knew, too, if she wasn't capable of doing it then nobody could, least of all me.

The day said hello with a burst of light setting the top of the pines laying to the east on fire. I looked out of the kitchen window at the stillness of the garden and waited for some movement of life. The quail were still asleep, and it appeared that my berry-eating friend, the wren, was going to have a late breakfast. There were fresh deer tracks imprinted on the dew-covered ground. The squirrels were quiet, and like the coons probably sound asleep. I imagined the red-tail perched high with feathers fluffed studying the field waiting for his late morning banquet beginning to stir in their holes.

Trout was also beginning to stir, and as I turned in the direction of the sound I saw her pass by wearing nothing but white panties and a wrinkled T-shirt. I thought, oh good, if I wasn't feeling bad enough already about looking at the thoughts walking through my mind I've got to catch her pass by half naked. There was only one remedy for the guilt, and that was a little more bourbon, but this time I thought, fuck the coffee, I'll just go ahead and suck it straight out of the bottle.

I already knew by the mood I was in that I was going to do something today to bare my soul. I didn't know what it would be, but I had been in these moods before, and no matter how hard I tried to divert the emotions nothing ever worked.

She came out of the bathroom looking at a back that was facing the window. Trout was wearing cut-off jeans and a T-shirt. With a voice sounding half asleep, she said, "Davis, good morning. What are you looking at?"

I turned around, and said, "I was just waiting for the quail to walk by. They always take their early morning constitutional in front of this window."

"I heard them outside the bathroom window," she said, with a bit of concern in her voice, "they'll be around in a minute."

I was thinking, great, maybe it's the diversion that I need to get my mind in another space. I couldn't wait for the parade of little top-notched, feather uniformed band members to strut by tooting their little quail horns. Maybe if I was lucky I could catch them at the half time show at the big-field arena where the squirrels and hawks play their daily game. The hawks usually won by a decisive margin. I often thought, if the squirrels would have had a better defensive front four they might have had at least a fighting chance. The rodents were quick, and had some pretty good moves, but the hawks had a couple of linebackers who were brutally swift, and had a knack at plugging up their holes. After the game you could see it had been a hard-fought contest because there was usually a lot of blood on the field. If you walked through the apple-leafed-confetti looking at the ground you might see the furry uniform of one of the losers without anyone inside.

There I was with the weight of the world on my shoulders and I was tripping on animal football. It was always a sure sign I was in deep trouble. I've been so fucked up at times I've sat in the field with a bottle of wine and imagined the crows as Stuka dive-bombers and the little swallows as British Spitfires. The house was, of course, a little flat in the London countryside. I was a downed "Limey" pilot sitting wounded in a field with a flask of good French brandy between my legs. My friends, the swallows, would dive and swoop in and out of the bad crows firing staccatos of feathered bullets. I always had my stereo turned on full blast, so loud in fact, that I often thought that it could be heard at that very moment in downtown Liverpool. I would put on a tape of the famous Gene Krupa/Buddy Rich drum battle. Beating out their fifty-caliber-double-paradiddles and machine-gun-rolls, with feet thumping against the bass drums they laid out an artillery back beat barrage that would make the ground shake.

This day wasn't going to be much different, I thought. If I wasn't careful I was going to find myself in the middle of a Zen garden resembling Central Park, talking to the wino snakes and gray dove bag ladies.

Trout saw me holding the sink down, and asked softly, "How you doing?"

It was a question she'd asked before. One she already knew the answer to.

I knew from the beginning she was a person I could never lie to. I was also certain I would never do anything I would have to lie about. The answers I gave were lies of a sort, but I'm sure she didn't see them as that. She knew what I would do was give her an answer that would keep me from laying my soul on the line. But today I was afraid I might pull away the layers of skin and bone that protected it and laid it out on the kitchen floor for her to see.

I answered her question with the same warped record reply she always got, "Oh, all right I guess. How you doing?"

Reading right through that dodge with her third eye, she said, "What's going on Davis? You've been so quiet this morning. Is it something I've done, or is it the conversation we had about my sexuality last night?"

"No, it isn't something you've done, I can assure you of that. As a matter of fact I feel good you're here. The place would be missing something important if you weren't. And about last night, I feel good about you telling me about yourself. I would have felt bad if you thought for some reason you couldn't."

She walked over to the stove and poured a cup of coffee, and moving to my left made sure she was in a position where I had to look her way.

"Well," she said, in a sweet, kind of demanding way, "if it's not me, and not about last night, then it must be about you. Maybe you should talk about it."

Yeah, she was right. Maybe I should. But I don't think the words would be able to crawl and work their way around this lump in my throat. I thought if she knew the truth, then she would know I have felt like crying ever since the moment I woke up. It was a smothered emotion, I had over the years, learned to keep inside. It didn't mean I wasn't crying, it only meant that whoever was around me at the time wasn't able to see it. They felt something all right, something that filled the air. It was a silent bagpipe dirge rolling off my face, wrapping around everything in the room.

I turned and refilled my coffee and leaned on the counter facing Trout. She was waiting, and sensed I had something to say. It wasn't something I wanted to say that was so important. It was something I wanted to feel. I wanted more than anything for her to hold me. And with my face buried in her hair to take her soft hands and brush my sadness away.

I opened my mouth and the words spilled out. It was an appeal that wasn't directed at her, but it was all about her. And if fate had been kinder, what she could give me.

Without looking her directly in the eyes, I said, "Trout, do you know what I've always needed most in life?"

"No, I don't," she said, with a gentleness to her voice.

"It's tenderness, a tenderness that's born in the soul; a tenderness that doesn't demand payback. It's something honest. An act that is as natural and pure as the deeply wanted birth of a long awaited first child."

I was getting serious. I knew it was the kind of mood that wouldn't go away until it broke every emotional bone in my body, and if I wasn't careful, Trout's too.

Trout didn't say a thing; she just leaned against the sink trying to peer through the heavy mist that had, all of a sudden, filled the room.

"So many times in life I've hungered for the perfect fingerless touch. It's an understanding that's much greater than words, one that will not betray. A touch that moves at you from another person and holds you with invisible arms, arms that reach out and lay a comforting cape over your shoulders. A cape that says, "Don't worry, I'm here. You can trust me. Everything's going to be OK."

I continued by saying, "We can call it mother or lover, or friend, it's all the same." I felt my eyes water just a bit. The soft mountain growing in my throat was doing its best to explode, becoming a sobbing volcano pouring warm lava tears down the front of my face.

"What I've always wanted was to be able to go out in that studio and use those tools, and with them, pour out all my creative guts, filling the work bench with the kind of art I've always wanted to make. Then after a hard day's work come into the house and be greeted by a loving tender being who doesn't say a thing. She just opens her arms, and with her eyes says, 'you did good, you made something for yourself. The hell with the money. The hell with the establishment. You just did something for your soul. I haven't seen it yet, but I already know it's good.' She would then hold me and tell me she loved me for who I am, not for who she wants me to be. She would take me to bed and caress my mind, becoming a soft cloud of understanding, floating unselfishly over my skin."

Well, I said it. I told her how I felt about her in a way I hoped she wouldn't recognize. She was moved and quiet. She stared into my eyes sending me a green-amber message of understanding.

I looked down at the floor in a way that probably made her think I was searching for the guts I had just spilled. Looking up at her with sad eyes and a touch of that eight-year-old's grin, I said, "Trout, how about a hug?"

She reacted by slowly pushing herself away from the counter, and with the softest nineteen-year-old smile that she had in her, said, "Sure."

We met in the middle of the room and I put my arms around her. The embrace became an eternity for me. It was a timeless act of trying to absorb every part of her I could. We pulled apart, and as her breast left the touch of mine I knew I had left a piece of me with her. I had opened the door to my soul and let her walk in and take a look at a special part of me. It was the part that occupied a deep inherent need that had never been fulfilled, and something that I trusted her enough with to hold. She had become the mother of all hearts capable of opening up the embryo that lay locked deep inside the core of my being. The only person I had ever met who I thought could give birth to the man I always wanted to be.

The rest of the day was pretty much spent by leaving me alone. Trout knew where I wanted to be, and that was a private place deep within myself.

CHAPTER 10

Trout's birthday was the next day. She invited her mother, my ex-wife and my daughter to come over and join in the celebration. I wanted to make her a nice gift.

I decided on a wire-winged clock that would be a Zen timepiece she could hang in her room. It would show her that the hours and minutes of the day could become a poem within themselves.

I went to the studio and proceeded to turn on the torch. The acetylene gauge blew up the moment I turned the valve on. It seemed the last time Trout had welded she had turned the pressure valve all the way to the right when she had finished. It was a wrong turn of the screw that meant when I opened the knob on the tank it would send a hurricane force blast through the little brass valves. It was a heavy acetylene storm that cracked the glass and permanently altered all the movable parts inside.

So much for the gift I thought. And being down to nothing but small change meant that all she would be getting from me would be a birthday hug.

I did my best to keep the episode of the broken gauge from her, knowing too well how she would react. Unfortunately the subject came up, and for the next couple of hours I felt like I was attending a wake for all the dead gauges that had lost their lives in storms like the one that had just taken place. Trout had enough guilt in her to make one think she not only had destroyed the gauge, but also had burned the studio down in the process.

I thought the only way to speed up the grieving process was to make a little cross with "Rest In Peace Sweet Gauge" carved on it. Then bury it, with her dressed in black standing by my side.

It was a dead pet ritual my dad always used on me. After my favorite pigeon's funeral was over, and after all the ice cream I could eat was gone, the ritual was one that usually worked. I would visit the bird's grave that lay in the corner of our back-yard- cemetery trusting in my father's words that the pigeon was happy and flying somewhere up in bird heaven. I didn't know if Trout believed in heaven, and I knew she was much too hip to believe in a heaven for dead welders, so I decided to drop the idea and let her mourn on her own terms.

The next day everyone arrived for Trout's birthday party. They were family. Three people who I hoped would never find out how I felt about her.

I believed if they did they would be the ones who would place the nails, and with hammers in hand hang my palms from the nearest wall.

I had to get my shit together and put on my best mask. One thing I didn't want was for them to walk through the back door and trip over all the guilt that covered the floor.

We decided to go out for dinner. I chose the Forestville Inn, a patio restaurant serving the best Mexican food in town. We sat outside, and over Dos Equis and enchiladas filled the falling day with birthday and family talk. It was a safe conversation. One that I felt would keep my emotions off the table.

I had a secret, and the little boy inside was dying to let it out. He said, *"If it would have been up to me I would have stood up and proposed a toast to love everlasting, wishing the old man and sweet young lady an eternal life of marital bliss."*

I sat there and fought with the little bastard throughout the meal. We finally compromised. I told him I would deal with this in my own way. I would lay it on the table in such a way that the secret would still be ours. The boy sat there sucking on his third beer and said, *"If you don't do something soon I'm going to get drunk and make you say something you will regret forever."*

So I brought up the subject of Walter and Hazel. Two dear friends who had experienced the kind of a life I wanted with Trout.

I had met Walter when I was living in Carmel going to art school. He was a writer, a Zen Buddhist, a severe alcoholic, a true Bohemian, and one of the best friends I've ever had.

When I met him he was on the skids, on his way down from a divorce. He was suffering from the loss and separation of his only child. I was twenty-two and he was forty-three, ages that are more appropriate for father and son than for best friends. Walter became my sage and mentor, someone who opened me up and helped me to set free a lot of the poetry that had been locked inside. We buddied around for a couple of years until I got the itch to travel. I said goodbye to Walter, telling him we would meet again. I strapped a few belongings to the back of my motorcycle and took to the road. On the way I got broadsided by a speeding '56 Chevy and almost lost my leg and my life.

I went back to my hometown of Fresno to recuperate. In the process I met the woman who, at that very moment, was sitting across from me eating salsa and chips. She was the woman who became my wife. In the course of our marriage we never lost contact with Walter. During that time he filled our life with volumes of wonderful short-storied letters.

My wife and I moved to Hawaii. I found a job working on the docks and she seemed content working in a restaurant waiting tables. At night, after work, I would paint for hours on an easel we had placed in the corner of the bedroom. We would go to bed and have the dreams that all young people who are in love have. The dreams took us to places that the cliché, "Nothing Is Forever" kept us from ever seeing.

My mother called one day and said my father was sick. We packed up, and in three days were back in the Central Valley of California. After two month's of hope and loving family care the Pigeon Man died, and with a pair of White King wings pinned to his shoulders flew off to bird heaven. It was a place only he knew. A place throughout his life he had tried so hard to show me was really there.

My wife and I left Fresno and moved north to Mendocino. It was a small coastal town that still had a wooden soul. In the meantime Walter had bottomed out and was living in a thirty-dollar a week hotel in the skid-row section of Oakland. I found out about it and got him a bus ticket north. I decided I had to do everything in my power to try and help him save his shattered life.

Walter came up and we found him a job as caretaker for a piece of property that sat in the midst of 20 acres of old growth redwoods. It was a five-cottage retreat called "Lost." It was named that because it sat in the middle of nowhere, and also fit the crazed and creative mentality of the Canadian couple that owned it. "Lost" lays in the middle of track that runs a train from the town of Fort Bragg to Willits. It's a famous tourist ride called the "Skunk Train." Every couple of weeks we filled a box with the staples of his life. We stuffed them with canned food, coffee and milk, and a few half gallons of halfway decent wine.

Walter's life improved and he was finding some substance again. He wasn't writing, but at least he was beginning to think clearly, and he always knew that down the tracks fifteen miles away he had a couple of friends who loved him a lot.

Whenever we saw him I could see that he was slowly getting better. His teeth were still bad, but he was gaining weight and his eyes were clear, and like his heart, the skin on his face got healthier and had ceased to die and flake off.

Walter was the one who told me that when you lose hope the soul dies. He said when that happens it's just a matter of time before bad wine, or a speeding truck, or a loaded .38 takes your life away. He was still struggling with hope, but at least he was still alive, and we were doing our best to keep him that way.

One night my wife and I were in town at a bar and restaurant called the "Sea Gull." We were sitting next to a table of young college girls that were down from Fort Bragg. They joined us and talked of their summer plans,

plans they hoped would take them away from a small lumber town that was dying a death as quick as the giant trees that surrounded it. They told us that the following week they were going to take a ride on the "Skunk," and go to the town of Willits to shop.

I told them they would have to stop and visit Walter who was kind of lonely and would love to have visitors. I said he possessed a great mind and was a well-known writer down on his luck. I also told them not to let his looks scare them away. I assured them that his long thinning hair and gray beard were part of a costume he had put on after the war and hadn't taken off since. Also, if his teeth bothered them to just look into his eyes when they spoke. And the dust of a skin that covered his face wasn't contagious. It would go away as soon as his soul healed.

Hazel, one of the girls at the table, seemed to be real interested. She was an English Lit major. Maybe she was thinking, here's a chance for her to meet someone who had written a best seller and had rubbed elbows with people like Mailer and Hemingway.

Hazel was a pretty girl, a touch overweight, but with the kind of mind that would tune into Walter's in a minute. They said they would, and should they take a gift. I said he was fond of wine. If they took him a bottle maybe he would recite them a poem in gratitude. They asked what kind of wine he liked, and I said that as long as it was the color of blood he didn't care. They looked at each other giggling and acted like they couldn't wait for a meeting with the creative creature living up in the woods.

In telling the story that night I probably stressed at least fifteen times the twenty five-year difference in their ages. Maybe I was trying to let them know that if they ever did find out how I felt about Trout, it was all right, because Walter had done it. He was a good guy. He was kind and intelligent. He wasn't a lecher. And he had even written a best seller!

I continued with the story, telling of how Walter and Hazel fell in love, got married, and moved to Berkeley. Hazel got her degree and became a librarian. I stressed the point again that, despite their ages, they lived a life of shared interest and bliss, conquering all of the social stigmas that threatened their welded together hearts.

I went on telling them how Walter continued to drink and fight the demons of his past, and of the time he cried and told me of the decision to give his daughter up. And of how he hadn't seen her in 13 years.

One morning Walter awoke and coughed up about a pint of blood all over the bathroom floor. At the hospital the good doctors had told him he had been visited in the middle of the night by his liver's worst nightmare, and cirrhosis had finally come to collect some dues.

Walter straightened up, quit drinking and started down the path of healing body and mind.

Hazel got a job at the university library in Belfast, Ireland, and she and Walter made a move that fulfilled a dream for them both. Walter felt good and began to write again. In his many letters he told me he was writing the "Great American Mystery Novel." His letters had finally begun to be filled with hope, which meant to me that his soul was getting its second wind and might run for another twenty years.

I was living in Germany at the time and had hoped that I could go to Ireland that summer for a much-needed reunion, to touch again a man I dearly loved.

A month went by with no word. I thought it strange, because he never failed to write. One morning I went out for the mail and in the box was a letter from Hazel. The minute I saw her name on the return address I knew what was inside. I became racked with a sad fear, a fear that kept me from opening a letter that had gained fifty pounds in the time it took me to read her name.

I put it in my pocket and went to the corner pub and started drinking. I knew that whatever was inside was going to cause me pain, and it was a hurt I knew I couldn't face with all my senses intact. I opened the letter and read that Walter had, indeed, died. He had gone into a coma and bleed to death from a ruptured artery in the throat. It was a part of the disease. The part that hangs around, then when you least expect it sneaks up like a thief in the night and cuts your throat. Hazel was heart broken, and I could read it in every word. She told me how much she had loved him, bad teeth and all. She didn't know how she could go on.

I spent that night in memory, toasting him with the same poison that took his pained life. I saw him choking on blood flowing from wounds that all his new hope had failed to heal.

The story had gone from apologetic purpose to a homage of an old friend. And as I looked in Trout's direction I saw she wasn't so much impressed by the difference in their age, or the love they shared, but more by what I was feeling, and of how much he had meant to me.

After dinner we all went to my place for some cake and coffee. Trout's mother and I found ourselves alone in the kitchen involved in a conversation about her daughter. I was nervous and trying hard not to show it. I told Trout's mom how much I enjoyed having her daughter there, and how wonderful it was to have a woman around that had so many of the same interests I did. I discussed her love for jazz, and how she was the first woman who recognized all of the great names I would throw out. And of how we would talk about poetry hours on end, sitting around the heart of the table in the next room.

I mentioned how we could find peace together, and knew when each other needed space. And of how we made sure that one another found it. Before I knew it I had painted a picture of two people who were made for each other. A perfect match made in heaven.

The eight-year-old screamed in my ear, *"You had better slow down or it's going to sound like you are on the verge of asking for her daughter's hand. If you cross the line I'm going to desert you and leave you alone, making you handle this one on your own, as an adult."*

Her mother seemed to like the fact that we felt such a bond. She even told me that earlier in the day when the both of them had gone to the store, Trout had told her she loved me. She said if she ever got married, it would be to a man just like me.

I thought, don't say things like that to me, not now, not in the kind of shape my miserable mind is in. Fuck! Mom, don't give me hope. You don't know what it does to me when she just smiles and looks in my direction. Now you're telling me she loves me!

Well, I didn't care how many witnesses were in the house. I just walked straight over to the aspirin cabinet, pushed that bottle of Bayer aside and reached for the real painkiller. I did have the sense to pour it in a glass with ice. And I did have the courtesy to ask anyone else if they wanted one. But after seeing that I had used the biggest glass in the house, using up most of the whiskey, they decided to stick with beer and let me go into an alcohol coma alone.

My actions woke up the little boy who decided he needed a drink too, and after the first gulp kicked me in the heart and got it pumping again. He grabbed my hand and took me over to the emotional corner. He said in no uncertain terms that I was getting myself all worked up over nothing. *"Of course she loves you, you dumb skinhead. She's always loved you. MY GOD MAN, YOU'RE ALMOST LIKE FAMILY! Why shouldn't she love you! And the marriage thing, she was just saying that to make her mother not worry, and to assure her she was in the hands of a man with good character."*

"GOOD CHARACTER?" I answered, "You call a man in love with the teenage daughter of good friends, GOOD CHARACTER? Hell! You might as well just go ahead and change my name to Jerry Lee Lewis and move me up to the perverted, incestuous hills of Tennessee. What the fuck is wrong with you, kid? You been smoking something I don't know about?"

Well, the boy didn't let up. He added to my confusion by saying, *"Listen, just last week she said she was gay. Do you really believe that a gay chick would want to marry you? That's like saying that the daughter of The Grand Dragon of the Ku Klux Klan has a thing for Jessie Jackson. Man! Davis, GET REAL!"*

The kid did have a point, but I persisted and said, "OK. If that's true, then why did she also say it didn't mean that she had discounted men entirely?"

The kid, in a voice that couldn't believe I was still hanging on to the subject decided to end it all right there, and cutting me where it hurt, said, *"Listen fuck-head you are 32 years older than her, which doesn't just make you a man, it makes you an old man, and a dirty one at that."*

Well, the kid had me, no two ways about it. He hit me where it hurt. He put my fantasies where they belonged, right at the bottom of that empty glass I was holding in my hand. You talk about a beat dog with no hope of ever freeing himself from a leashed pole. The kid had just taken a two-by-four to me and brought me right back to hard reality.

The party ended and everybody went home feeling good, and assured Trout was in good hands. I could tell she was happy they were gone. She didn't like crowds much, and I'm sure she would have just as well spent the big day alone.

It was late, so I said it was time for me to go to bed and walked up to her to give her a birthday hug. It was going to be as reserved a hug as there ever was. But when we met and embraced I couldn't help to absorb again, all that I could.

There was something different this time. Something was moving between us that I hadn't felt before. It had more tenderness to it, and for a couple of seconds I could have sworn it almost started to grow wings. When we pulled apart she didn't just softly drop her arms and step back like she usually did. This time she floated, turned to the side and smiled out of the corner of her eyes. She then let her hand slide down my arm and out the tips of my fingers.

We said good night and went to bed. I lay in the fur-covered pool trying to put meaning to the embrace. I fell off to sleep with the kid reminding me one more time not to read too much into it. *"She does love you, and it's no secret. But the love she has for you is just a drop of dew compared to the river of feeling that's running through your heart."*

CHAPTER 11

The next few days passed with both of us looking for more time alone. We still went through our daily ritual of sitting around the table trying the crossword puzzle, and talking of poetry and anything else that came to mind. We touched more. A shoulder squeeze of support now and then, or tender high fives, but it didn't matter what they were, because they were still harmless acts of affection. The hugs were becoming more and more meaningful. These were explained to me by the little boy running inside my brain of just being a normal progression of feelings between two people who had spent three weeks of 24-hour days together.

I hadn't worked since she had arrived. It seemed I was too busy working on myself, unable to concentrate on anything else. I knew that it was just a matter of days before I would tell her of my feelings, and then ask her to leave. It would be a storm-ridden day on the farm when that happened, because I knew I was in a no-win situation.

I knew Trout well enough to know that whatever happened, she would have a tough time handling it. Just the day before I had asked her if she still felt good about being here and she told me, without hesitation, that there was nowhere else she would rather be. It was a declaration of how good she felt being where she was, and I was kicking myself in the ass for having to be the one to take it away from her.

I knew that when I told her of my feelings she would first be in disbelief, thinking, how could he love me? Then, in her soft understanding way she would nod her head and tell me she believed, too, that she should pack her things and go away.

Visualizing her driving down the road because of the barrier I had built would take my fragile mind and drive it deeper than it's ever been before. And as Walter always said, "When hope dies, so does the soul." Which meant that after waving goodbye to her I'd step out into the road and kiss the front end of the first big truck that came by.

The weekend was approaching and we had planned to go to an outdoor art and music festival that was happening in the little ocean front village of Jenner. It's a beautiful little place on the cliffs overlooking the beach where the Russian River empties into the sea.

The show was typically bad, with the same artsy crafty shit you see at them all. A band called "The Swamp Dogs" took the Louisiana funk sound and blew it across the beach like alligators going for a jive driven swim. They were worth the trip, and as we stood there taking it all in we reached down and held each other's hand. It was a move that seemed as natural and comfortable as the tambourine-grasping grip of the man on stage singing the blues.

There was definitely something floating between us, but the eight-year-old who was tagging along kept reminding me that it was all in my head. *"So what if she's holding your hand?"* He said, *"She probably does it with everybody at art shows."*

We drove down to a rocky beach and with Trout's camera in hand walked over the tide pools. I laid back on a big warm rock and watched her out of the corner of my eye. She was busy looking for little treasures with her fish-eyed lens, pausing now and then to take shots of weathered driftwood pieces and storm-mutated stones.

I left her alone and laid back and tried to enjoy the day. The gulls followed her around, probably thinking that the camera in her hand was a box lunch, which she would at any minute open, emptying leftover tuna fish sandwiches and potato chips onto their sand-covered table.

Leaning back on the hard stone I watched her kneel down and stare at the tide pools. The rock was an appropriate place for me to come to terms with what I felt I had to say. It was jagged and nailed like a Fakir's bed. It pushed hard against my back trying to force the truth out of me and into the open air. The butterfly moving in me became an albatross of bad omen, and the little boy was riding on its back. He was a flying rodeo rider bucking around deep in my guts yelling at me to keep my mouth shut. If you do he told me, you could at least have her around for another day. I took the advice and decided it was too nice of a day for me to have to ruin because of what I felt I had to say.

We walked to the parking lot and left in a car that was like a buried time capsule. It was void of air and sound and filled with secret emotions that someone in the future would dig up, read what was inside, and say, "Man, I glad it was him going through that shit, and not me."

The mood in the house was definitely different. There was a pall that covered everything within reach. Trout was deep into herself. It was an intense activity of her mind that her furrowed brow and solitude seeking eyes easily gave away. I figured she knew what was going on inside my heart and was making the decision to leave. I felt like a rotting piece of garbage, knowing I was about to chase away something I had gotten to love so much.

The next day we had planned to go up and spot-paint a gate I had installed a few months earlier. It was in the mountains behind Santa Rosa; a beautiful spot full of dry oak, moss covered stone and manzanita.

We made the drive and, after arriving, unpacked the paints and brushes. Trout wearing her little brown beret proceeded to cover up all the mistakes

I had earlier made. She berated me like a critical blue jay for doing one of the worst paint jobs she had ever seen. I explained that I did it in the week following the departure of the female commandant of the Nazi SS. I said if she saw any little skull and crossbones drawn in the steel to go ahead and paint over them, because she probably put them there as part of the perpetual hex she had placed on my life.

It was the "Voodoo gate," as I had named it, and I was working on it when Helga left. I had welded together and humped those two nine-foot, 350-pound sections all by myself. One day I dragged them both from my studio door over fifty-feet of soft ground and tied them down upright in the yard. I was going to paint them, so I had them braced with steel rod, and like a picketed tent tied them down with rope and staked them to the ground.

While "Sheena" was out in the front of the house collecting dead bugs and rotten squirrel tails for a cool drink she was concocting for me I walked by the gate with spray gun in hand. My mind wasn't on the gate or the maze of rope that lay in my path; it was on the war that had transpired in the house the night before. It was a war with only one prisoner taken, and that was the man who was about to put the finishing touches on an iron barred symbol of the prison he had put himself in.

I walked by the gate and the tentacles of rope that she had just given life to reached out and grabbed my leg. Tripping, I fell to one knee and became entangled in the nylon snake she had put in my path. The gate started to tip, then slowly fall, and with the cast iron arrow tips that I had stuck to the top, landed on my back. I couldn't free myself and the weight pushed me farther into the ground. I knew she was flying up there with the crows looking down and watching as one of the poisoned points dug deeper into my back. By this time I was down to both knees, a place where she exactly wanted me to be. The gray squirrels screamed and the covey of quail exploded into flight, while buzzards began to gather waiting for a sign of my last breath. I was covered with wet paint as slick and fresh as blood and my knees were shoveling into the moist earth digging my grave. The wind had been knocked out of me and I wasn't able to yell for help.

I figured it was all over and this cursed steel motherfucker was going to take my life, and the incredible thing was, I didn't care. I knew that sooner or later the arrow would drive itself through my back and into my heart, and it would be an end to a man who had lost all his strength and given up.

The sorceress crow had seen me brought to my knees and felt that my punishment had been long and painful enough. She transformed herself back into beautiful beast, walked around the corner of the house and screamed. She ran up and soothed the snakes then untangled the octopus around my leg. With her help I grunted that monster off my back. I was arching my

74

back reaching back with my hand searching for blood when I heard her say something sympathetic, "Next time you should be more careful." I groaned out a scream and told her to get the fuck out of my sight and to go back in the house and finish her brew because I was going back into the studio into my secret stash and prepare one of my own.

As I watched Trout up on the ladder painting the gate with the same tender care that was used on the ceiling of the Sistine Chapel, I thought, my God, there is a woman out there who can feel and who is soft, someone that cares. I knew if this gate was to fall on me again out here in the wilderness she would lift it off my back with all her poetic Wonder Woman strength, lay me on the ground, and with her Rembrandt-colored hands soothe away all my pain.

We loaded up Vanna and headed back. I was becoming overwhelmed by her presence and of how much I cared her. I felt that the flammable love I had for her was about to ignite and catch the car on fire.

We pulled up to a red light; an appropriate place, I thought, to confess my feelings. Looking straight ahead for the signal of green, I suddenly said, "Trout, there's something I have to say. I just want you to listen and hear me out. It's not easy for me to do, but it's something that's been on my mind for days. I don't want you to think badly of me for saying it. I just hope you will understand."

She looked straight ahead, and I'm sure had no idea of what was to follow. I thought I'd better hurry up and get it over with because she was getting that look she gets when she thinks that she has done something wrong.

"Trout," I said, "I've begun to have some feelings for you that go far beyond what we have felt for each other over the last twenty years. I have begun to view you as a woman; a woman that has moved into my heart and created a wave of affection that I have never felt before. I have become tremendously attracted to you and I am honestly at a loss of what to do with my feelings. I wanted to get it out and lay it on the table before you felt them and interpreted them as something that would offend you. I didn't want these feelings to rub off on you in a negative way and ruin any of the nice experiences we have collected over the years. I know that I will never be able to see you with the same eyes that I did before, so I think maybe it would be better if you left before I do anything which would make you lose respect for me."

Trout continued to look straight ahead, and the car suddenly became as silent as a tomb for dead roses. I had gotten so serious, the minute I opened my mouth the eight-year-old opened the door and bailed. He knew he didn't want any part of this. This isn't work for a kid, he thought, it is something that a man would have to take care of.

Well, there it was, you said it Davis, you got that load off your mind. I thought that if she could have heard this butterfly beating against my ribs she would have panicked and bailed too. I was waiting for a reaction, anything to break the silence. Trout was still staring through the windshield. I thought by the look of her concentration, maybe she was watching our friendship sprout black wings and fly away down the road.

Without looking to the side, she said, "I've got something to say too. I've also been having the same feelings, and they've been with me for a few days. I also don't know what to do with them, but I just want to say that I'm not going to leave right now. I would like to have some time to think about it."

When Trout said she wanted to think about something, you knew that it was as serious as an eighty-year-old's third heart attack.

My feelings were in such a state of confusion after her response that I didn't know what to think. If anything, her reply had just made an impossible situation even more unimaginable. Now what was I going to do? I was overwhelmed by the fact that her feelings for me ran deeper than I thought, but it was just going to make the inevitable that much more difficult.

What in the hell did she see in me? I was nothing more than an old dog of a used Chevy that hadn't had a tune-up in years, and that young flower of womanhood sitting next to me was falling for me, and might even like me enough to jump in and go for a ride.

Come on Walter, I said to myself, you never told me about this, what happens when hope knocks at your door and you're afraid to answer? What happens if I grab on to that passing golden arrow of life and then she leaves?

I was afraid to say anything more. Everything I wanted to say had been laid out on the front seat of the car. I didn't want to demand that she leave because Trout doesn't like demands of any kind, especially those involving decisions that others are trying to make for her. If there was anything she wouldn't respect, it was for me to try and force her to do something that she was totally capable of doing herself.

The only thing I knew for sure was that the car had taken on another passenger. It sat between us all the way home with its arms spread, all the while touching each of us on the heart with its hands.

The mood around the house had changed. It was now inhabited by two people who had jumped the fence of family into a field containing other walls, walls that were just as difficult to climb. The next couple of days would be ones of different eye contact, softer and with more meaning. Efforts were made by us both not to get too close. We both knew that if anything could ruin the friendship, it would be that of irresponsible thought sending us both crashing into a guilt-ridden abyss.

After three or four days the need to touch overpowered everything else, so our hours of talking about what was happening between us were often done holding each other's hand. It was a simple act of caring, and of giving each other some support when we got to the point of laying our feelings out on the table. We talked endlessly about responsibility and the dangers of what we felt. I gave Trout plenty of space to sift through the feelings that were pouring through her mind, and she in turn gave me space of my own.

Five days had gone by and we were both getting to the point of knowing that something had to happen. I felt whatever it was would have to be better than what we were both going through. I felt for Trout, and tried to guess what filled her preoccupied head. But there wasn't much of a clue, other than knowing that day-by-day her feelings for me were starting to show. It wasn't anything tactile, or a word, it was just the way she filled the room when I was in it. She didn't walk anymore, she glided through the house, and she didn't stand, she hovered. She had become a sparrow hawk who has the gift of catching the vacuumed air, suspending itself effortlessly over a field. Trout would float over the room looking down with thousand-year-old eyes at the new feelings that had moved into her twenty-year-old skin. I watched her struggle and search, but knew that she didn't want me to interfere. So I waited for her to make a decision, and I hoped it would be something that wouldn't add to her already troubled life.

One day I missed her in the house, and knew where she would be. I peered out the kitchen window and saw her lying on her back on the Zen garden's stone bench. She was staring up at the trees, and knowing her state of mind I was sure she wasn't watching for birds. I felt that if there was a bird that could have answered her questions, I would have by now gotten to know it myself, and with it carefully in hand walked over and laid it in her lap.

I decided to go out and see if she wanted to talk; a presumptuous move considering where she was but, nevertheless, one I felt I needed to do. I approached her like a hunter with an arrowless bow, one who doesn't want to shoot, but only to touch a sleeping deer.

I asked softly, "Trout, is everything OK?"

She answered with a quiet voice, saying, "Yes, I'm just trying to figure some things out."

"Well, if you want to talk about it, it's OK with me. There's something I want to repeat anyway."

We had already talked about her looking for a father figure in me, and I wanted her to give that more thought than anything else. I knew no one could ever replace him in her mind, but he had only been gone less than two years, and she missed him desperately. I didn't want her to confuse her attraction for me with the loss of him. He had been a friend of mine and I wasn't going to dishonor that by taking advantage of one of her most sacred needs.

I said, "You know we have talked about you looking for a father in me, and I just want to again say how important it is for you to look into that and try and come up with an answer. If that is indeed the truth, then you and I both know what we feel for each other will never travel any farther than today."

Still looking up at the trees, she said, "I have thought about it a lot and have come to the conclusion that the reasons for my feelings aren't a part of that. I'm sure it's there somewhere, but if it is, it's so small I can hardly see it, and if I can't see it then I'm not going to give it much importance. I have decided that what I feel for you is strictly between a man and a woman, and nothing else. It's funny, but I was just thinking that, oh my God! This is Davis I'm falling for, the man who used to baby-sit me as a kid! I mean, isn't that the craziest thing you've ever heard?"

"Yeah, it sure is," I said, laughing.

We both smiled at the truth and seemed relieved we were coming to terms with the anguish that had been filling us for days.

I left her alone and returned to the house and decided that this wasn't in our hands anymore and I would have to let destiny take over and run its course.

That day, Trout and I knew we had climbed the big tree, the one with the great view from the top, but once you got there and looked down the thought of falling scared the shit out of you.

We ate dinner that night sitting at the table and acting like we had met each other for the first time. It was a meeting of innocence; one of two people acting like they had never fallen to the depths of another's heart before, and of not knowing how to act when they got there. We were children gazing down at precious stones wanting to hold their beauty, but afraid to touch them for fear that they would break. Trout and I knew the next step, but it too seemed as impossible to take as the one we had been struggling with for the last week. The thought of touching her in secret places let loose the cocooned Monarch that flew down my chest and into my loins. It fluttered between my legs begging me to let it loose. It didn't matter how much I loved her, or thought of her as a mature twenty-year-old, there was still a little girl running loose in that woman sitting across from me and that was the person that I was afraid to touch. I felt, too, that she wasn't some innocent waif who was going to have the doors of erotica opened for her by me. Trout was the kind of person who had a wind of passion blowing through her. I also believed that she was the type who could use the sensual pleasures as a way to turn her back on the cold throes of hurt and sadness.

Trout had a sensuality that ran from her pores. It was something that walked with her into every room she entered. She wasn't really aware of it yet, but it was there. I saw her wearing it like a crystal veil the minute she arrived. It was something that had attracted me to her immediately, and something that also scared the hell out of me. I knew how that magic magnet had pulled me in before. It had taken me on some travels of the heart that had left me by the side of the road, run over and bloodied lame. I knew poetically that whatever was going to happen between our bodies already had, it was just going to take the embrace of the skin to complete the act.

That night we walked arm in arm into the field. We were stargazers daring the heavens to show us something bigger and brighter than what was glowing between us.

We tried hard to find Jupiter and the Milky Way, and debated whether that was the Big Dipper up there or his little brother. The bats, flying at the speed of night sounds, feasted on the wing to the tune of lightning bug songs. I yelled at Trout to look, and didn't she see the fluorescent bird that had just landed in the tree. Look how the owls are exploding in flight, raining down feathers of ember shrapnel at our feet. The squirrels were celebrating with candled lanterns in hand, and the night birds did us a favor by lighting their tails on fire, doing loop-the-loops before our eyes.

The red-tail swallowed fire and sparked the trees as he flew over us and screamed. A hundred deer ran from the grove, and with red ash horns raced through the night. The quail awoke and tied sparklers to their heads and erupted through the orchard in a blurred, comet flight. The coons entered the ballet and offered us glittering rubies with their little hands. The blue jay did me a favor and ignited his head, which let off a violet smoke that encompassed the pine. The oak danced in the orange, brilliant storm, and dropped glowing carbonated leaves on the ground, while the eucalyptus turned neon blue.

The cars passing by on the road were meteors on their way to town, and the house down the drive exploded in napalmed flame to light their way. Gravity took a rest and allowed the stars to fall, which landed and bounced off the field like celestial hail.

The night and everything in it had become ours. It was an ebony-filled musical wind with Brahms and Bird playing heart tune duets. The white pelican choir sang soft hymns while the silver crow blew yellow smoke through a flute. Molten moss began to grow from a tree, and while blazing down the trunk filled the furrows with flowing lava stones. The breeze became moving glass, melting white hot on the pond, which reflected a Tibetan moon filled with ivory colored African cranes.

We didn't move. We just breathed in and engulfed the night. Trout's face had become a soft-oiled pallet of warm Cezanne hues, and her hair moved like Gauguin's brushed Tahitian grass.

We were caught in the moment of an inherent storm; a predetermined fire that was going to blaze and burn down all the walls that had kept us apart.

We held hands and walked back to the house covered with a clinging, sweet tasting, golden ash.

Trout lay on the big couch and I sat across the room on the small one. We had tried to watch a film, but became disinterested, realizing there wasn't anything on that was as important as us. It was getting late and the room was starting to fill with tense, delayed goodnight words. I was becoming overwhelmed by feelings that grabbed hold of my guts and weren't about to let go. I stood up and looked her way and said, "Well, Trout, guess it's time for me to go to bed."

She didn't move or speak; she just lay there like a bouquet of white flowers waiting for someone to hold. I walked over to her, grabbed her hand and knelt at her side. The words fell from my mouth much too quickly for me to grab hold of and pull back. I said, "Trout, would you like to go to bed with me?"

She didn't answer right away. She just looked into my eyes asking herself the same question. I was nervous, and afraid that I had assumed too much and had stepped over the line. The boy popped up and said, *"Don't act like a fool, and not ruin a good thing, enjoy what you have and forget about the rest."*

I could tell she was pondering the idea. It was a look that flowed from her eyes and covered the couch.

She answered, "No, it sounds appealing, but not tonight."

"OK" I said apologetically, "No problem. Hope you're not offended, but it was just something I had to ask. It's all right. I understand."

"It really does sound appealing," she said, "I'm just not sure how I would feel in the morning."

Still holding her hand, I said, "Trout, really it's all right. I understand. I don't want you to do something that you don't feel good about."

"It's not you," she said, "it's just me, and well, I just don't know."

I didn't want her to feel pressured. It was the last thing I wanted to bring into this, so I dropped it. I stood up and said good night, and how about at least a hug. She rose like a tall lily growing from the couch and met me in the middle of the room. We hugged tenderly with cotton hands and slowly pulled apart. Trout and I faced each other just a pulse beat away, not wanting to leave. And as slow as an awakening breath, we drew together and kissed.

The kiss was an act that had earlier in the day begun when the heart spirits had connected our mouths with an invisible Corinthian thread. Now, they had just entered the room and simply pulled our lips together. It was short and soft and open. It wasn't passionate or wet. It was dew-covered and warm, and moved through me like blowing fern. Trout opened her eyes and stared into mine, then we moved apart. I said good night, and she nodded her head. After taking about three steps I turned around and said, "Trout if you change your mind, you'll know where to find me." She smiled with a shy understanding, turned, and walked to her room.

I lay in bed watching the rose bend over the picket fence, while the ivy reached up and touched its stem. The caress by the dark green leaf on the neck of the soft rose covered my mind, as a night bird flew into the room and with its feathered tips, closed my eyes into sleep.

CHAPTER 12

The next day was a monument to hidden emotions. We both knew what had happened the night before was too important to talk about, and we didn't want to discolor it with words. Tender looks were with us in the house and they moved like warm air between us whenever we passed.

I tried to spend some time outside, thinking if I kept busy whatever was happening between us wouldn't jump up and land like a thousand-sharp talons digging into my chest.

It was afternoon, and I walked into the house to find Trout lying on the floor in front of the TV. It was as if she had called me to come and sit by her side. It was that silent voice that I followed into the room, a voice that told me to sit down and touch her hand.

What happened next was as natural as rain falling on grass. She looked up at me and hooked my eyes with her own, and with gray green alpaca twine pulled me down. I touched her hair and her face and my callused hand traced a line down the side of her neck. The silken thread was being pulled tight, and again drew our mouths together. Trout and I floated and absorbed each other's face, and the smell of her skin and warm breath brought out feelings of pent-up passion I'd forgotten I had. Trout had grabbed me with soft-finned hands and was dragging me down to depths that I'd never felt. I thought if this is what drowning was supposed to feel like, then I hoped I would never see dry ground again.

I unbuttoned her blouse and laid my face on her breasts. She pulled off my shirt, and with forceful hands pressed against my back gluing my chest to the soft whiteness of her porcelain breasts. I was like a blind voyager using my hands to guide me over a landscape whose paths I'd never seen. With both hands she grabbed my face, and said, "God, this is good."

It was a compliment of passion that erased the fears I had of being the worst lover she had ever had, and something that made me stop and say, "That's nice of you to think that. I believe there's a big chance that it can get better, maybe we should move to the other room."

She didn't say a thing; she just looked at me with her mouth partly open and nodded her head once.

We walked together to my room and laid on the bed, and within the time that it takes to take off two pairs of pants and socks, we began with all the trust and care in the world to make love.

Trout was tender and soft, and never left me alone. She moved like a rainbow scaled fish with her mouth swimming over my skin. I was careful with her, and didn't want to break any of her fragile first-time-in-bed experiences with me.

I entered her and heard her sigh and moan soft woman songs, which traveled with her grasping fingers over my back. It was as if what we were doing was an act and prophecy of love that had been there forever; something that long ago had been written on our certificates of birth. It was as natural and predestined as an embryo's first beat of the heart, and I had never remembered loving so deep.

I was worried about filling her with the essence of my life and giving her a little, bald mustached one of her own, so I pulled out in enough agonizing time and erupted on her soft-bellied flesh. Trout was flying and I didn't want her to come down. I was one who believed not to ever let a woman have to end her pleasures with the explosion of mine. A symphony was playing in her head and I wasn't about to let it end.

With all the delicate knowledge of my hard-ridden 51 years I traveled with my face down her breasts, over her ribs, and her plateau of life. I smelled her womanhood and paused at the entrance to her sacred garden. She pulled herself up to her elbows, and with her eyes closed and mouth open, looked up at the turquoise cloud that had just formed over the bed. With my lipped breath I touched her deep and moved her magical chime, then watched it send arched waves of gratification rolling up her back. Trout shook and grabbed the side of the bed and shrieked, "OH GOD," which was a compliment, because she was acting at the moment like He was the one that had just given her that sweet, screaming orgasm. It bounced like a velvet ball off the walls and echoed through the halls of the house, and sent the birds on the porch into a frightened flutter.

If I would have had hair she would have grabbed it and pulled me up towards her, but she had to compromise, and instead grasped my head tenderly with her palms and met me halfway, kissing my eyes. I lay on her stomach and heard her breathe, then listened as her heart calmed to a slow, satisfied beat.

I inched up to her side and said, "Trout, for our first time that wasn't so bad. The great thing is, it gets better."

She sighed, and said, "It was more than that. It was wonderful. You were wonderful."

I thought, does that mean that I'm not worse than the worst woman that she's ever made love with. Maybe the prophets of male doom were wrong. Maybe I do have a chance. And if it does get better than this, then I had better start taking more vitamins, because Trout had a good chance of wearing this old dog out.

I asked, "Trout do you think that maybe you might be sleeping here tonight?"

"Are you kidding?" she answered, "I'm never going back to my room again!"

We spent most of the day in bed, napping, touching a lot, and laughing about where we had found ourselves.

Trout said, "You know the night we kissed and then we went our separate ways?"

"Yes," I answered, lying at her side about an inch and a half from her face.

"Well, I went to my room and laid there for hours. I couldn't get the thought out of my mind that I had kissed you, MY GOD!"

"Yeah," I said smiling, "I was thinking the same thing about you. It was amazing, but I didn't even feel bad about it, as a matter of fact I laid there all night hoping you would come in and slide into my bed."

"I thought about it, believe me," she said, "but I was still worried about how I would feel the next morning."

"Well, how do you feel?"

"Good, real good," she said, reaching over and kissing my forehead.

It was a wonderful day. I had forgotten what it had felt like to feel good and to lay next to someone as warm and caring as her. As we lay there watching the roses try to grow through the walls, I thought, here we were, Trout and me. We had finally found that karmic bond and it was taking us on a fur-covered swim, with us holding our breath and diving as deep as we could.

We lay there with and rolled in a warm earthen bed and howled at a moonless day. We were a pair of white forest wolves who had run through the pack and chosen partners. Trout and I had become spawning salmon laying in a warm summer pool taking the plunge into a tabooed world; a world we knew would have to be our own closely guarded secret.

The day's that followed were spent with Trout and me never leaving each other's side. If we weren't touching, then we were laughing at the sun. If we weren't sitting at the table talking about the pleasures and the dangers that lie ahead, then we were laying in bed acting like Mr. and Mrs. Cortez discovering New Worlds at the ends of our wind-driven, white-sailed hands.

Trout was fascinated with my body, which for my age was holding together pretty well. She explored it and studied every part, and over the next few days became a dermatologist of the heart. Trout told me she hadn't seen that many naked men, especially none at the microscopic closeness that she was studying mine. We talked a little about her past and the couple of unsatisfied sexual relations she had with younger men. Trout was much too sensitive to have to bear through a night laying next to a man who only thought about himself, so I made a mark in my mind to never let her have to go through that with me.

I didn't know where her fondness for women came from, and in those moments, I really didn't care. I only wanted to show her that there was a man out there who would treat her tenderly, take care of her desires and love her deeply at the same time. It was something I knew that I had always longed for, and in the weeks that followed, a loving touch I myself had finally found. Trout had the heart of a poet and took it with her when we went to bed. With it she wrote soft-penned sonnets on the pages of my skin.

Trout never did go back to her room. It became a giant closet that she would sometimes walk into to pick up some things.

We lay there one evening and decided that, from that moment on, my bedroom was to be called The Pond. A perfect name, I thought, for a place where we could swim in those lily-filled, warm summer nights.

There was a night, a week or so later, when I took some alcohol-backed 50-year-old aggression to bed with us. I didn't know where it had come from. It was just some old rust that had flaked off and filled my veins and turned my touch into a hard steel brush. I made love to her like she wasn't there and gave her a glimpse at the kind of men she didn't like. I was dominant and insensitive, and she pushed me away and let me know that wasn't what she wanted. I had always been careful with her, and she knew it. One night I told her I would never do anything that would assault her right to choose. She assured me that if I ever stepped over those boundaries she would let me know.

That night she did, and pushed me away. I left the room and sat on the couch knowing that I had disappointed the hell out of her. For the first time since we had opened our hearts I felt like a piece of rotting flesh. My anger-filled past had crept up in the night disguised as passion and had left green moldy scales scattered over the bed. Trout was someone who I had begun to love more then any other woman I had ever met, and I felt I had just treated her like a whore.

I sat on the couch and popped a beer, and if I could have stepped out of my body I would have unmercifully kicked the shit out of myself. I would have used all that aggression, and like a good street fighter friend once taught me, kicked my balls up through my throat. I sucked my brain for the reason, and found that I was still angry with the woman who had lived here before. Taking it out on Trout was an act that I compared to pissing on the Pigeon Man's grave.

The German Frau had taken away all my pride and had put my ego on the rack. She had taken my heart and painted it black, and had fucked with my mind so badly I still hadn't gotten rid of the rage, and at that moment the sweet young lady in bed was paying for it.

I sat there and recalled the night, after a good day's work in the studio, where I brought in a new piece and hung it from the ceiling. Helga was perfect at playing good-cop-bad-cop, and was the walking definition of sadistic afterthought. She liked the piece, "but why isn't it something with worth, and why don't you change your style, and why in the hell aren't you making things that sell?" Well, that got her venom-powered motor started. The theme wasn't about my art any more, it was about me and my lazy American character and my worthless artist's soul. She ended her assault by saying, "why haven't you ever done anything with your life?"

I figured I was only born with a hundred fuses and that night she had just burned out the 99th. Acting like I had just swallowed a pound of "Meth," I shouted, "WELL FUCK IT! If it's not worth anything then let's just rip it off the wall and bend it into something you might like!" I then proceeded to tear that steel-wired-work apart. It lacerated my hands and I bled all over the floor. She still wouldn't shut up, so I just picked her off the floor, walked into the bedroom, and like a little Bavarian doll threw her on the bed slamming the door behind me.

I got in my van and drove to the nearest bar, hoping that somebody would try and fuck with me. But walking in the bar room door with my crazed look and bloody hands, made even the drunken construction workers turn their backs.

I sat at the bar and ordered a double Wild Turkey with a Bud back, but was shaking so badly I couldn't even drink. The woman bartender asked me if I was OK, (which made me think she was either blind, or dead drunk), and did I want a towel? By this time everyone had moved about 10 stools down. None of them dared look at the seething, sobbing man on their left who was no doubt the most dangerous, insane looking thing they had seen since Crazy Harold the town drunk ate some PCP and tried to chew the head off his neighbor's dog.

I saw the bartender on the phone talking in hushed tones, and thinking that any minute the local "SWAT" team would be kicking in the front door, left and headed straight for "Crises Intervention Clinic" at the county hospital.

I walked in and was met by a uniformed security guard who noticeably twitched when he saw me. He looked at me and saw that I was in such bad lethal shape; he reached down at his side for an imaginary gun. Finding none, he cautiously stepped aside and pointed down the hall to a room that said "Crisis." As I was walking down the hall, I thought that the room better be big, because I've got enough "Crisis" in me to balloon out the walls.

The therapist told me I was suffering from "Battered Wife Syndrome" in reverse. It was a definition of my condition that immediately made me think that the bitch not only torqued out my mind, but also had turned me into a weak-kneed, transsexual.

I went home that night and slept in the spare room, and the next day told her she had to leave. But that night in bed with Trout I had invited her back in. It was clear to me as I sat on the couch that I had to kick her out again and get that anger out of my life forever.

Trout came out and sat next to me. We talked, and I told her of my hurt, and promised it would never happen again. I told her of how deeply I cared for her, and if I was younger and she was a little older I'd ask her to marry me. Trout looked at me with soothing eyes, and said if that were the case she wouldn't hesitate, and would say yes. We went to bed and she held me, giving me all I needed. Before I fell asleep, I saw the truth. I knew that I wasn't younger and she wasn't a little older, and this sweet love wasn't destined to be long-lived.

I had often told Trout I loved her. It began the first time we were in bed. She accepted it with tenderness, but was reluctant to mouth the words herself. It was a commitment that scared her. Being the way she was, she would have to give it much thought before she laid it out for me to see. After a few days she gave in to the emotion. We were lying in bed one night after taking a ride on that amorous cloud that floated over us every time we walked in the bedroom. She told me that yes, she did love me, but wanted to wait to make sure that was what she felt before she reached over and put it in my hands.

It seemed like the bond had finally tied itself. We felt wonderful together, and Trout was slowly removing the rust that had permeated me. Our adventures in bed were always exciting, fulfilling the both of us. I couldn't remember ever making love with someone so tender and concerned with my needs.

I always wanted to sleep with a woman and be so wonderfully in love with her that I could honestly say, "this is it, this is the last woman I ever want to make love to." It is the ultimate definition of fulfillment, and of the word "Forever." I knew with Trout I had finally come to that point. It was an act of commitment. It was a deed that, after we made love, moved me like a high tide wave and laid me gently on the warm fur-covered beach.

I was so deep into her and what she meant to me, that I would have done anything to make it last. If it were marriage, then I would have driven us to the altar that day. If it were a child she wanted, it would have been born exactly nine months after the word of her wish left her mouth. When times got hard I knew I would go out and chop cotton, or dig ditches in a field, or anything else that raised blisters on my hands to keep her stomach full. But

I couldn't kid that wise child in me. I was telling myself that she was the last woman I ever wanted to make love to, and here she was still working on her first man.

Trout was often in turmoil with her feelings. She knew what we had was special and told me more than once she had never been happier and knew that no one would ever love her as much as I did. But I knew she also saw in our love a prison that had the capability to steal her precious youth. It was a point well taken, and something that, as the weeks went by, was beginning to make me feel more and more like a thief. It didn't really matter at that point what was going to happen in the end. I would just bury the prediction and continue to love her as much as I could.

We were in bed one night, and Trout's lovemaking had taken me to a place where I had never been before. I was inside her taking a ride on the white unicorn. It was a slow and soft beat, like an African's hand on a leather drum. I was at her ear and the words just rolled out and covered her hair. I said, with all the tenderness in me, "Trout, I do." She knew what I was saying, and how much it meant, and that I had just taken The Pond and turned it into a soft-watered, chapel aisle. The words started at my feet, moved up my loins and through my gut. They paused at my heart becoming a warm summer tide ebbing into her ear. She didn't react, she just held me caressing my head into the sleep of night.

It was another step, and I had taken it first. It was a mark of the eternal love that had moved in and set up house in me. I repeated it often in the days that followed, always when we were in the heights of passionate flight. They were two words that flew from a falconer's glove sending the sacred, taloned bird of entrustment screaming through the room.

Trout worked the words, and their meaning back and forth in her head before she would dare whisper them out loud. They weren't words I would demand. They were also two words that I never expected to hear.

Some weeks later, and deep in the layers of the fur-covered bed after absorbing each other, Trout touched my face, and looking through my eyes, said, "I do."

I thought, my God, what else is there. This is all I want. This is all I ever wanted. If I died right now I would feel blessed because I had reached the plateau, the one I've been trying to climb for years. I have reached it with a woman who I believed I have loved all my life and a thousand life times before.

Two day's later I awoke and heard that Trout was already up. On the pillow next to me was a folded note, which I opened and read. It was a poem that, unbeknownst to me, Trout had written the night before. It read,

"Two Words"

Nothing seems quite the same
Since the day you spoke of marriage.
You wanted my eyes to vow affirmation,
Knowing that my voice never would or
Never could, but they just stared back
At you, not knowing what to do.
Your face divided into three pieces,
Like a mathematical pie, one eye looking
Serious, the other seeing loss, your
Mouth grinning and releasing chuckles.
The last piece of the equation confused
Me most (I never was good at math),
But I imagine that was your intention
To confuse me, to deviate my attention
With a laugh that quietly pleaded
For me to play along, yet opened
A door to escape, in case I didn't.
That night in bed, when our bodies were
Warm and excited against each other,
You looked at me. Your face was whole
And consistent with longing, and your
Mouth steadily whispered I DO!
Those words, those TWO WORDS,
Took me to a place with which you
Have long been familiar-a place
Where hope and tenderness disregard
Reality just to get through it.
I opened myself up in that place, gave in
To myself, and repeated the TWO WORDS
As you slipped into me as easily and
Comfortably as a familiar finger
Slips into the warmth of a wedding band.

CHAPTER 13

Trout and I were keeping our secret well hidden from the people who we didn't want to find out. There were a couple of friends of mine who had dropped by and, on the phone later, told me they felt there was something going on between Trout and I the moment they had walked into the house. We talked daily of letting it out in the open, but somehow always drew back when it came to the moment of truth.

Trout and I hung out at Jaspers a lot, where we would have a couple of beers and eat our favorite burgers. The music was always good, and some of the best groups in the area would play there on weekends. When we were inside, sitting across from each other at a table, our emotions always took over and we couldn't have cared less what strangers thought. Often, when we went to town to shop, we raised the eyebrows of some straight-laced women and of men who enviously wished it were happening to them. It was mostly women who judged us, especially after they first saw us as a nice father and daughter team. Then their faces would drop like a bad kidney stone after they had witnessed Trout wrap her arms around me in the super market parking lot, and like a grocery cart-pushing vampire, tenderly suck my neck.

We would always give them a little extra after we loaded the bags and stepped into Vanna by acting like a couple of teenagers parked at Lovers Point. The women would huff away with their noses in the air acting like they were trying to smell that old pervert in the car. It seemed like they were praying to God to have him save the poor child who, (they knew for certain), had recently been hooked on drugs by the molester with the shaved head. Their husbands, who were unhappily tagging along, would think, (I'm sure), "The lucky son of a bitch! How did he get a hold of THAT! He sure isn't rich by the looks of that old beat up van, and he certainly is no Brad Pitt!" Trout and I would crack up all the way home and look at each other with smiling eyes knowing that it was none of the above, but something a whole lot more important.

One night in Jaspers, a night where Trout and I were especially enamored with each other, we ran into a friend of mine who also happened to be a friend of my daughter's. It didn't take long for her to mention to my daughter that her father sure had a pretty young girl friend. My daughter told the friend that it couldn't be. It was probably Trout she had seen, and Trout certainly isn't my dad's girl friend. Our friend said that somebody should have reminded him of that fact as he was kissing her on the ear in the middle of the dance floor in front of 75 people.

The sky had suddenly fallen and landed with Volkswagen-sized meteors right on top of Trout and myself.

The phone rang the next morning. It was my daughter on the line and she didn't fuck around with, "Hi, how's it going?" No, it was, "Dad, do you and Trout have a thing going?" She had seen me involved with a lot of women in her 25 years, so normally she wouldn't have given a damn. But this was different, this was Trout, and she's only 20, and besides that, she's GAY! I can still hear the words, "I think you are disgusting" blasting through the line. Those were the ones that stand out the most, words that are still tattooed on my ear. I tried to explain about love and of how when something good and honest comes passing through your life you should grab onto it, because it may never pass by again. I told her that maybe I didn't have many years left, and I was really happy. I had talked for about five minutes before I realized that she had hung up right after she had told me I was disgusting.

To say the least, my daughter's jibe cut me off right about hip level and drove me alone, teary-eyed into the Zen garden.

I knew my daughter would have found out eventually, but I wanted to be the one to tell her. If my ex-wife didn't know by now, she would in the length of time it takes for a voice to travel over ten miles of telephone wire.

After a few minutes of reflection in the garden I returned to the house and called my ex-wife. Listening to the phone ringing made me think of a man strapped to the electric chair waiting for a call from the warden saying that his pardon had come through.

She picked it up, and I said, "Hi, it's me, how's it going?"

Anybody else would have answered, "Probably not as good as you, you lecherous bastard!" But my ex-wife was cool, and in cases like this, usually non-judgmental. If the tables were turned she might have jumped on this magic horse herself.

I said, "There's something I've got to tell you."

"I already know," she answered matter-of-factly.

"Oh, I guess the kid must have told you."

"Yeah, about five seconds after she heard it."

"Well, I know it sounds crazy, but it was just one of those things that happens. And you know how much Trout and I are alike, and we have so much in common, and, and, and, and."

"Davis, it's OK. I understand. If you guys are happy and no one is getting hurt that's fine with me. I just hope you both know what you are getting into."

"OK, but I still want to get together and talk about it," and hung up.

Trout and I looked at each other, and at the same time said, "Two down, one to go," meaning that the "one" was The Big Kahuna, MOM!

We spent the whole night discussing what had happened, and of how it was going to affect what we were feeling for each other. We both agreed they were all going to have to accept it, because we weren't going to break it apart no matter what anybody thought. We tried to convince each other that once they realized how wonderful we felt with each other maybe they would understand.

The next day Trout drove down to San Francisco and told her mother. It was easier than we both thought. Her mom respected me and knew I would handle her daughter with gentle and responsible hands. Her main concerns were the grandmothers, and the "Hit" men they would hire if they ever found out.

The next day I called her mother and talked it out. She said if Trout was going to choose to be with a man, then she was happy it was someone like me, and our difference in age didn't matter. She just didn't want it to interfere with Trout's education, and hoped I would respect that. I told her I did, and not to worry, everything would work out just fine.

Fine? I asked myself? How in the hell did I know that? Here was Trout starting to tell me everyday how cute the babies in the TV commercials were, and wouldn't it be nice to have a kid.

What I had failed to tell mom was that over the last month her daughter's womanhood had blossomed, and with it all of her female-nurturing fantasies.

When we first got involved we talked about all the responsibilities that went along with what we were doing, especially the things that we were doing in bed. For over a month we had used condoms, those little things that, before you put them on make you think they will strangle your dick and choke the life out of it. We tried everything; rubbers, withdrawal, rhythm, foam, and praying to all the Gods who ever had their names carved in stone.

Trout and I finally decided she had to go on "the pill." So she went to family planning and got a three-month's supply. She was told to start them after her next period, one week away. In the meantime I was confronted with Trout's nurturing seed and its daily growth.

At the beginning of our love affair she said adamantly that if she got pregnant she would get an abortion, no two ways about it. The word sent chills up my spine every time I saw the woman I loved dearly strapped to a table getting rid of something that we had created, and of what it might do to her emotionally. So we were extra careful. I felt I knew more about birth control than she did, and knew the responsibility was mostly mine.

About a week later while sitting on the couch she said if she were to get pregnant, she would have the child.

"Sweetheart, what did you say?"

"I said if I got pregnant, I would have the child."

Already knowing Trout always thinks things out before opening her mouth, I still said, "Do you know what you are saying?"

"Yes, I do," she said defiantly.

And by the way she looked me in the eye when she said it I was convinced she would never let anyone cut out of her the life we would both be sharing.

I knew what a child would do to her young life, and what an anchor it would become. I tried every argument I could think of to get that thought out of her head. I even pulled out my drivers license, and while pointing my finger at the date of birth, said, "Look, born 1942, that means when the kid is 18 I'll be 70. Did you hear me? 70! That means I will be watching his High School graduation from a TV monitor in Intensive Care!"

"Davis, I don't care, it doesn't mean I'm going to try and have one, it just means that if I did got pregnant that's the decision I would make." Which when translated correctly meant that until she got on the pill I would become as impotent as a run-over snake.

It was on her mind all right, and something we would sometimes use as an affectionate bond, and a topic to express our love. I couldn't deny that it was part of my fantasy about us, and something I would use to kick the ass of fate whenever I could. Having a sweet child with Trout would be for me a dream come true. I had already helped raise one, and knowing that I had learned a lot in the chaotic process felt that maybe this time I would have more to offer. It was just a fantasy I told myself, because in my heart I knew that someday Trout and I would have to end what we now had.

One day watching Trout chop kindling, I said, "Hey baby, chop that kinlin!"

She answered in her best southern drawl, and said, "That's right honey, I'm cuttin' that kinlin!"

It just came out of the blue, and I said, "Trout, I've got a name for that kid you're always dreaming about."

"Yeah, what is it?" she yelled back, not missing a stroke.

"It's Kinlin. What do you think?"

She put the axe down, looked up at me and said, "Yeah, I like it, Kinlin, Yeah, that's it!

From that day on whenever we spoke of a kid, one that I sadly hoped we would never have, we called him Kinlin!

Trout and I would lay in bed at night and talk about Kinlin, and she would ask questions like, "Do you think he would be smart?"

"Smart?" I would incredulously say, "Hell, that kid would be so smart that he would be reading Rilke in the original as the birth doctor swatted him on the butt."

"And what color would his eyes be?" she would ask tenderly, while looking into my mine

"Just like yours Trout, gray green, with a few amber flecks."

"And what about his hair, what color would it be?"

The longer the conversation got, the closer we got, until by the time we were through our eyelashes were touching.

I said, "A mixture between yours and mine, that is when I had hair, then it was dark brown."

"He will be creative, won't he?"

"Oh, yes, sweetheart, as a matter of fact when all the other kids in kindergarten are picking their noses and finger painting, he'll take out some oils and do things that would put Matisse's French period to shame.

We would end with my fingers brushing her hair as she fell, with all her motherhood dreams, into a contented sleep.

A week passed and Trout and I anxiously waited for her period to begin. She checked her calendar and saw that she was late.

"How late?" I asked.

"3 or 4 days," she said, "but don't worry, I'm sometimes late anyway."

OK, I thought, I won't worry, like hell I won't! Everything that went through that young woman's mind was of concern to me. Everything that caused her pain caused me pain, and I knew that this must have been on her mind constantly. It was also something that, if she ever did get pregnant, would bring this relationship out into the open and lay it in front of some eyes that we had hoped would never see it.

The mother of her father was one. She loved her grandmother very much and was sure she would take it hard. Her grandmother and aunts lived in the same area as my uncle, and if they found out, then so would he. The man was ninety years old. In my eyes he was a replacement for my father. I knew the man loved me like a son, but this would be something he would have trouble understanding. He would try his best. He might even lie about his emotions. But I knew that somewhere in that old cattleman's heart he would think it wrong, and I'm sure he would respect me a lot less.

Another week went by, and still no good news. The pills were lying unopened on the shelf in Trout's closet. Every time I looked in I could swear they were collecting dust. Trout was worried, and it was playing hell with her mood. The relationship that had been putting her through sweet bliss was now grabbing a hold and giving her a reality check.

It had been ten days, and Trout couldn't stand it any longer. She told me she had to go to town, and instinctively I knew which part. It was the Kaiser Medical Center. I didn't say anything, or ask her where she was headed. I'm sure she felt I already knew. Trout walked out the door appearing to have the weight of the world on her back. She reminded me of one of those women who had just returned from an African well with a hundred pounds of water-filled jugs across their shoulders. A burden they had picked up ten miles away.

It turned into a long day. A day where I could have sworn I had seen the seasons change. As I stood staring out the kitchen window I saw her car coming up the drive, and walked down the back steps to meet her.

She didn't say a thing. She didn't have too. I saw it in her eyes. We faced each other, and without a word, she wrapped her arms around me and I felt her start to shake and slowly begin to cry.

I said, "Tell me about it, what did they say?"

"I'm pregnant."

Those two words, just as important and powerful as the other two words we had been mouthing over the last month came out of her warm, tear-filled breath and rolled down my neck.

"Are they sure?" I asked.

"Of course they're sure. If they aren't, I am. I can feel it. I have for the last few day's. It is just something I know. I can't tell you why. I just know; that's all."

I didn't really know what to say. I just held her, looking over her shoulder at the tall pine moving in the late afternoon breeze. I thought that the karmic bond I have always felt, the one born with Trout and me had taken another step. I knew too, it probably wouldn't be its last.

Over the next days Trout and I spent most of the time in bed. We were like two twin embryos glued together. I knew The Pond wasn't just ours anymore. There was a little tadpole swimming with us amongst the lilies. Trout would go from bouts of deep depression to high-flying euphoria, wanting to make love whenever possible.

She would use it as a confirmation of our love, and also as an escape from her fears. In those moments I would lay in front of her all the tenderness I had. I would sometimes find her alone out in the Zen garden deep in thought. Looking at her there, I imagined her twenty-year-old tears slowly filling the pond. She would grab a hold of me at the most unexpected times and sink as far into me as she could. There were other times she would take off alone and go for walks that seemed to last for days. I knew it was time for a talk. We had a decision to make.

That night in bed I brought it up, and in doing so, felt like a black hooded executioner. "Trout, we've got to talk about it. There are some issues here that are not going to go away. I know how you feel about an abortion, but I think it's something you should seriously consider."

"I have been," she said, "and it's a choice I have decided that I don't want. I've decided I will have the child."

"Trout," I said seriously, "don't you realize how this is going to effect your life and everything you do from now on?"

"Yes, but I feel it's something that was destined to be. Just like what has happened between us. It is something I just can't bring myself to kill. I feel that destroying it would be the same as to destroy everything we have had."

Trout was saying things I could just as well have been saying myself. My argument was turning out to be one of rational ideas, but one without any soul.

I said, "OK, if that is your choice then I'll never let you be alone with it. I'll hold your hand and your heart all the way."

"I know you will," she said, "but don't forget, you're going to need someone to hold your hand too."

She was right. I was trying to be strong and give her all the support I could, but this thing had taken its toll on both of us, and it was beginning to have its effect on me.

I saw myself as a father at 52, one that was having enough trouble supporting himself, let alone two others. It could also strain and possibly break my friendship with her mother. She was a person who had entrusted her daughter to me, and my so-called responsible hands. It would also create waves of jealousy in my daughter who still was angry with me for me abandoning her as a child, and could tear apart a relationship that I had so desperately tried to rebuild. She was coming around to the point of accepting Trout's and my relationship. She hadn't given us her blessing yet, but was doing her best trying to understand what we meant to each other.

I had totally blocked my mother's reaction out of my mind. I had already decided that I would lie like a dog from hell if she ever asked about Trout and I. Keeping a new grandchild a secret around that intuitive 82-year-old mind would be tough, and being the kind of mother she was, could always tell when I was lying. The rest of the world I could give a shit about. It seemed it was too busy trying to destroy itself without having to be concerned about us.

CHAPTER 14

The next two weeks were fragile ones around the farm, so I decided to start to work on my exhibition for September. I had to get twelve new pieces together, and since I already had the concept and ideas, it was just a matter of going out and braving the heat of the Crematorium.

One day Trout came in with the mail. It had become one of her rituals, and a chance to get away for a walk alone. She came in and handed me the usual bills and other nonsense mail, which would lay unopened on my desk for days. This time she had a card from an old friend of mine. While staring at the 3-D picture of Christ on the front Trout gets this weird look on her face and says, "What the hell is this?"

I turned the card over and read the name at the bottom, "It's a card from Jose. I told you about him, didn't I?"

"Yeah, I think you did. Isn't he the guy you used to buddy around with in Europe, the one that could open a bottle of beer with his teeth?"

"Yeah, that's Jose, craziest son-of-a-bitch I ever saw."

Trout was as curious as me about what was written, and said, "What's it say?"

"Here, I'll read it to you. It say's,"

AMIGO...

I'M SITTING IN A BAR IN MAZATLAN ACROSS FROM A WOMAN WHO REMINDS ME OF A PIECE OF LUGGAGE. SHE HAS SKIN LIKE AN ALLIGATOR, AND LOOKS LIKE SHE HAS BEEN HANDLED A LOT. I THINK I WILL GO AND MAKE HER A DRESS OF TRAVEL POSTERS, AND THEN TAKE HER TO BED.

JOSE

P.S. I AM HEADING FOR BAJA TO VISIT MY UNCLE, AND THEN UP TO SEE YOU.

"Is that it?" asked Trout, looking like she had just swallowed the daily cross word puzzle.

"Yeah, Jose always did write strange cards. When he's drunk he believes he's Mexico's answer to Richard Brautigan. About five years ago I gave him a copy of Brautigan's 'Revenge of The Lawn' and he hasn't been the same since."

"What was his name again, Martinez?"

"No, Mendoza, Jose Mendoza."

Trout seemed like she was interested. I thought that anything that would keep her mind off of what was going on inside her was something to pursue.

She said, "I forget where you told me you met him. Wasn't it in Spain?"

"No, it was in Greece in '77. I was in a little village off the coast; down at the southern tip in the area known as 'The Three Fingers.' If you look on a map you'll see that at the bottom of Greece the land spreads out like three fingers of a hand. I was in a little fishing village named 'Monemvasia'."

Trout's interest was sparking a bit. I think she wanted to talk about something other than the Aries baby that was just starting to form inside her beautiful stomach. The doctor figured it would arrive sometime at the end of March, around the week of the 24th, two days before my birthday.

Trout had taken to ground lately spending a lot of time under the covers. I thought, maybe she was trying to hide from a karma that she had no choice but to face. She was still bent on going ahead with the birth, and I hadn't discussed the other option since that last time in bed.

I couldn't even stand to think about the word abortion, not when it came up in the same thought that Trout occupied. I had even taken Brautigan's book of the same title off the shelf, realizing that there wasn't any poetry in the word as far as I was concerned.

We were sitting at the table, both of us on the same bench. It was a position that we often used, one with me straddling a bench and Trout laying on her back with her head and shoulders on my chest. I wrapped my arms around her, resting them on her breasts, with my face becoming entangled in her neck. It was a good place to tell her about Jose, as long as I didn't become lost in her hair, an act that almost always made me forget my name. Trout said in a dreamy kind of a voice, "Tell me how you met him again, I forgot."

"Yeah," I said, visualizing the moment perfectly in my head. "Well, like I said, I was in Greece in this little village. It was a fantastic place with a population of about 300. It had one hotel, a couple of bars and restaurants, and right across the harbor was an old fort called 'The Castro'." It sat on a small island connected to the mainland by a centuries-old stone bridge. During the days of the Greek empire it was one of the fortified, stone walled sentinels protecting the southern sea entrance to Athens.

The village sat in a rock-walled harbor that was filled with crystal clear blue water, dotted with those little Greek wooden fishing boats, and directly on the water was the hotel and patio restaurant. It was late September, and off-season, so there were just a few tourists there.

I had met a Swiss guy by the name of Peter Schneider. Peter was about my age, a journalist who was there seeking some solitude and inspiration for 'The Great Swiss Novel'." He existed by freelancing for Swiss newspapers and magazines, and like me, had bad relationships with money. We had met in one of the two bars and became good buddies, spending our days and nights drinking six star Metaxa and the local rotgut beer. Peter had a great mind that had the tendency to become touched with, and invaded by, occasional bouts of insanity. He was a perfect pal for me, because we often felt like we were wearing the same head. He rented a place up the road, a small walled-in villa with an outdoor toilet and no hot water. Peter was a Spartan type anyway, and hated living in the spotlessness of Zurich. So every time he sold a couple of stories he would hop on a plane and fly down.

He had been doing that for years, and in his 'Soul Voyages,' as he called them, had picked up a decent knowledge of the Greek language. And since no one spoke English in town, having him for a companion came in real handy. Peter's English was excellent like most educated Europeans, but he had this heavy Swiss accent, which always made him sound like he was singing out of tune whenever he spoke. Anyway, Peter and I were sitting at the outdoor cafe one afternoon eating lunch and drinking beer. We were two of the six or seven customers in the place. The rest were a couple of Germans who had sailed in on their 60-foot ketch that had 'Hanover' painted on the side, two French honeymooners, some locals, and Jose.

Jose was sitting by himself with nothing on but a pair of cut-off jeans and a pretty good buzz. He was having this mumbling conversation with no one in particular, just sitting there talking to a loaf of Greek bread and a beer glass full of Retsina. Retsina is that Greek white wine that I sometimes thought also powered their cars. Jose was about thirty, but that day looked a lot older. Closer to a good looking fifty would be more like it. He had a handsome face, definitely Latin, with the hard natural strong body that comes from being related to people, who have for hundreds of years lifted the loads of the rich.

He had a strong-jawed face with a black mustache and long black wavy hair that hung to his shoulders. He would have had an intense wild look about him if it hadn't of been for those two obsidian, sensitive eyes that were set deep in his head. They were, at that moment, filling his face with the kind of expression that goes along with someone speaking to a loaf of compassionate, and understanding bread.

I couldn't help but stare at him, but had to be careful about it, because he was the type that would stare back until you got real uneasy and looked away. I could see right away that Jose was no guy to fuck with. It was just a way he had about him, an attitude I had learned to recognize in people over the years. I could tell that he was a man that could definitely take care of himself, and a man that you would want covering your back when things got rough.

He had a tattoo on his right upper arm, but it was too far away for me to see what it was. It was kind of lost in brown skin that had become deep Mahogany from too many years of shirtless days in the sun. There was something about him, though, that was different, and made him stand out. You know the type, they can walk into a room with a hundred people milling around, and all of a sudden it seems like they're the only one in it."

"Yeah," Trout said, totally engrossed with the story.

"So, anyway, Peter and I decided to ask him over for a drink, that is if the loaf of bread didn't mind, so Peter said, 'My friend, how would you like to join us for a drink'?

Jose looked up, and around, not quite sure that it was him that Peter was talking to. Peter said again, 'Yes, you, would you care to have a drink with us'?

Jose shrugged his shoulders, and with his thumb pointed at his chest and asked with his eyes, 'Who, me'?

I was thinking, no man, that loaf of bread you are involved with. I said, 'Come on over and bring your friend', which he did. He picked up the bread and his glass, which was almost empty, and walked over and sat down."

Trout was listening intently, and asked, "Did he really bring the bread?"

"Yeah, he did," I said.

"What was he doing with it beside carrying on a conversation? Was he eating it, or what?"

"Hell no, you don't eat a friend, especially one that listens so good."

Trout bit me on the arm, which meant she thought that I was fucking with her mind, and said, "Come on Davis, this is supposed to be a true story."

"It is true. Have I ever lied to you?"

"Well, that first night in bed when you told me you were a virgin was stretching it a bit," she answered, chewing on my arm.

Her actions were a signal for me to bite her neck, and nibble her ear, which was the same as saying, "I'm tired of stories, let's go take a nap."

Trout was an expert at interpreting my actions, "We can do that later," She said, "I want to hear the story first."

"OK. Anyway, Jose sits down and we introduce ourselves. He gives us his name like it has royalty to it, that the name Jose Mendoza is the only real Mendoza in the world, and anybody else with the same name must have copied his. He's proud of his heritage, and the fact that he is one-quarter Yaqui Indian. He told us they were the first Apaches, and that his great grandfather was a medicine man. Whenever he said the word 'MEXICAN,' it was as if you could read the words coming out of his mouth in capitals and bold 24-point-type. Jose is a man that it's best to never use the word 'Greaser' around unless, of course, you are looking for a reason to try and find a hard definition for the words, 'Mortally Wounded.'

We tell Jose what we do, that I'm an artist and Peter is a writer. I ask him what he does, which he answer's. 'I am the soul of Don Quixote. I am Emilio Zapata incarnate. I have drunk tequila with Pancho Villa and stolen women from Don Juan. I am the King of Vera Cruz, and once in a while I drive hot Porsche turbo's from San Diego to Mexico City. Right now I am hiding from a very rich man who hired me to bring his 55-foot ketch from Acapulco to Crete. A five-hundred-thousand-dollar piece of hand-made teak, which I left somewhere on the coast of Italy, stuck in some sand.'

Well, Peter and I would have a hard time topping that, and that was just for starters. During the next week of sleepless nights and passed-out-on-the-sand days we heard enough unbelievable, but no doubt true, tales of love and war to raise the ghost of Cecil B. DeMille and put him back to work on a hundred non-stop epics; all starring, of course, Errol Flynn Mendoza.

The guy was unbelievable, and had Peter drunkenly talking about writing the Great Swiss Novel, featuring a Mexican Apache driving stolen Porches, smuggling dope through the hills of Zurich."

Trout was getting excited and got up and opened me a beer. She had sworn off any alcohol and cigarettes until the little mustached baby was born, but was rewarding me for getting her mind off things that were too serious to think about that day.

Trout asked, "Did Jose really smuggle dope?"

"Evidently. It seems that Jose used to be one of those hemp backpackers, crawling on his hands and knees, hauling five or ten kilos at a time into Texas."

"Did he ever go to jail?"

"Yes, but not for hauling dope. It seems he spent a year in a Mexican state prison for beating a man half to death."

"Beating a man half to death? That's not very nice. Please tell me he had a good reason?" Trout asked the last question just like a little girl begging her parents to reaffirm her belief in Santa Claus.

"Well," I said, "it seems that Jose had this mongrel of a dog which he kind of adopted and kept at his uncle's house in Baja. Whenever Jose would get back from one of his adventures he would go there to relax and take his dog fishing.

One day when Jose returned from a trip, his uncle said that some fishermen from down the beach had shot it and used it for shark bait. From what Jose told us, he doesn't remember much of what happened. He and his uncle killed off a bottle of mescal and went looking for the worm-sucking snakes that killed his dog and found them on their boat at the pier.

Jose, if he remembered right, set the boat on fire as they slept. It was an act that sent them in a panicked flight towards the dock. Jose's uncle pointed out the one who killed the dog, so Jose used the reel end of a bamboo deep-sea-pole, and beat the man into unconsciousness.

Jose could have gotten away, but insisted that his uncle take a photo of him and the killer. Jose hoisted the guy up, tied with a rope under his arms, to a crossbeam on the dock. He then stood with the bloody pole in his hands, smiling proudly with his catch. The police arrived just as the camera clicked, and then used the picture as evidence when Jose went to court. The story became legend around Baja, and is always a guarantee of free drinks whenever his uncle retells it in the local bars."

"Is that really true?" Trout asked, exactly the way she would after her folks told her that there was no Santa clause.

"Well, Trout, I don't think Jose's the kind to lie, at least he's never lied to me, not that I know of anyway. One thing I know about Jose is that he's got honor, and if he is your friend, then he's a friend for life. Jose would never lie to a friend or try to steal his wife. He would steal someone else's wife, but not a friend's."

"This man is coming here?" Trout turned around and strained her neck, looking like she was expecting Attila The Hun to be the one we were going to have visit us.

"Don't worry, Jose is the sweetest guy in the world, just don't ever fuck with his dog," I said smiling.

Trout bit my arm again, which made me kiss her neck and blow in her ear, which made us both think that maybe a nap was in order.

We went and laid in bed, and just as I was running my finger down the inside of her arm on the way to her left breast, she say's, "Wait a minute, what about the tattoo? What did the tattoo say?"

I was thinking, the hell with his tattoo, I'm just getting ready to do a little tattooing of my own on this soft range of mountains on your chest.

"Davis, the tattoo!"

"Oh, yeah, the fucking tattoo."

"OK. After we had invited him over for the drink on that first day, I kept looking at it, but thought that it would be rude if I came right out and asked him what it meant. You see it was in Spanish and I hadn't the slightest idea what it meant."

"Well, what did it look like?" Trout asked that with a touch of impatience in her voice, which told me to get to the point.

"It was a heart that was cracked in the middle, and underneath the heart was written, 'EL LADRONE'."

"Well, WHAT DOES EL LADRONE MEAN?" She was getting serious, and wanted the puzzle solved, now!

"OK, I'm getting to that, just hold your little sea horses. So anyway, we'd been sitting in the bar about four hours, and were pretty fucked up. Jose had ordered some goat cheese to eat with his friend, the bread, and kept trying to get Peter to ask the waiter if they had any Tequila. We both kept telling him that it was impossible, but he insisted anyway. Peter got tired of trying to figure out how to say Tequila in Greek, so he finally gave in and settled for a fifth of German Schnapps that some tourist had left behind as a present to the owner. The owner didn't have the slightest fucking idea what we wanted; he just knew that from what Peter described, it was clear as water, sometimes had a worm in the bottom, and got you really drunk.

Well, the poor old owner of the bar felt like he had failed at his job by not having any Mexican booze in the house. Peter told him in Greek that it was OK, and just go outside and secretly dig up a worm and drop it in the bottle. He told the old man that Jose was so drunk he wouldn't know the difference.

So the owner goes outside and comes back in with a bottle of clear booze with a worm in the bottom, but on the way he stopped by the kitchen and told all the help what was going on. Well, the cook, and dishwasher, and their families peered around the corner waiting to see this strange man, who was by now reciting passages from, 'THE TEACHINGS OF DON JUAN: A YAQUI WAY OF KNOWLEDGE.'

The owner brought the bottle, and acting like he was serving Aristotle himself, set it on the table, and said, 'TAKIA'!

Jose looked at the bottle, which was missing a label. The old man thought that Mexican liquor shouldn't come in a German worded bottle. He tried, but couldn't get all the paper off, so some just hung in shreds from the glass.

By this time everybody in the place was waiting for the 'Crazy Fucking Indian,' who had tied a bandana around his head, to tip the bottle, drink some, and die slowly of some unknown, earthworm parasitic disease.

Jose got up real close to the bottle, about an inch away would be my estimate, and stared at the worm. We thought that Jose was so drunk, he wouldn't be able to tell the difference, but he didn't need to taste it to know that he had been screwed.

Jose stood up and kicked his chair backwards, halfway across the room, looked at the bottle and screamed, 'THIS IS NOT TEQUILA'!

'How do you know?' I asked.

Jose looks at me, then at Peter, and then at the owner, and then looks at all the people staring at him from around the corner like we were the dumbest motherfuckers in the world. I looked at Peter, and we both just shrugged our shoulders, with this 'What the fuck' look on our faces.

Jose is staring at the bottle, with his finger pointing like one of the accusers at the Nuremburg trials, and says again, 'THIS IS NOT TEQUILA'!

'WHY NOT'? We all say in unison, in Greek, English and Swiss.

'BECAUSE, THAT IS NO MEXICAN WORM'! Jose said, with wild eyes.

The place was dead silent. Peter and I are the only ones that knew what he said, but everybody else seems to know what he just said. The poor owner is standing between Peter and me with his shoulders slumped, his arms spread with the palms up, and a look on his face that is painfully saying, 'You guy's said worm, so I got a worm.'

I bite the bullet and ask Jose, 'Jose, how do you know that it is not a Mexican worm'?

'BECAUSE AMIGO, THIS WORM IS BROWN, AND A MEXICAN WORM IS GRAY. I THINK THIS WORM IS STILL ALIVE, AND IF THAT WORM IS STILL LIVING AFTER FLOATING AROUND IN THAT BOTTLE, THEN IT IS NOT FIT FOR A MEXICAN TO DRINK'!

Jose did have a point about the alcohol content not being enough to kill a worm, and if it couldn't kill a worm, then it sure as hell wouldn't get a Yaqui Indian drunk. It did look like it was sort of alive and snorkeling around in the bottle.

We finally admitted that, yes, we did try to pull the worm over his eyes. But what the hell, Jose, loosen up, it's still booze. After asking for four shot glasses we proceeded to drink the crap, plus all the Metaxa in the place until we all got snot-slinging drunk and went out and fell asleep on the beach."

Trout was, by this time, lying on my stomach with her face about an inch away from mine blinking her eyes in disbelief, when she finally realized I didn't tell her about the tattoo. She bit me on the chin and said she wouldn't let go until I told her about the heart on his arm.

"OK, OK, I'll tell you," I said, screaming in pain, "the tattoo said, 'EL LADRONE.' In Spanish it means 'THE THIEF'."

"The Thief?" Trout said puzzled, "What thief?"

"Well, I asked Jose that myself, saying, 'Jose, why 'THE THIEF'?"

"Amigo," he said, "it says 'THE THIEF' because of all the hearts that I have stolen in my home state of Sonora. You see amigo, I am more famous than Casanova, and more notorious than Geronimo, and I am the bastard son of Don Quixote."

Trout looked at me out of the corner of her eye, and said, "Is this all true?"

"Trout," I said, "Have I ever lied to you? And by the way, where were we just before this story got under way?"

"Just about ready to go for a swim, remember?"

As we slipped under the covers, I thought, if there was ever a "Thief of Hearts" it was her, because she had mine and I knew I was never going to get it back. If I ever did, it would be so broke and bent it would never work right again.

As the days went by, I told Trout more stories about the adventures of Jose and I. She was often lost in thought, and again swinging through moods that would have her dancing around the room with me, or hiding under the algae at the bottom of The Pond.

CHAPTER 15

It had been about three weeks since we had heard of her pregnancy, enough time for her to realize that there was a life growing inside of her. The boyfriend of her sister said, after he heard of our relationship, that it would be good for her, and it would bring out her womanhood. Well, he was right on the money with that one. I had brought out all the womanhood she will probably ever have, and along with it a little hand holding, diapered kid. She had already decided that it was going to be a boy, and since we already had a name, then at least that problem was solved.

She had all but ceased to talk of going back to school. It would become a truancy that would send the new grandmother scraping her nails down the first available blackboard. She had been investing about twenty thousand a year for Trout's education and wasn't going to take the pregnancy, or the loss of the PhD-programmed kid's failure to return, lying down.

Trout had been going back and forth trying to decide when to tell her about her being pregnant. She wanted to drive up one weekend just to get it off her chest, but I had used all my persuasive powers and talked her out of it. But I knew that it was just a matter of time before it had to be done. Then it would just be a matter of months before everybody knew, grandmothers, hit-men, uncles, and of course, my mother.

I did my best to put all that out of my mind and tried to work towards my show. I could pull out maybe four or five hours a day and that was it. One of the main forces driving me was the need for money. It was a constant preoccupation that lay on my chest like a 500-pound safe every morning when I woke up.

There was a mountain of irony in all this. When Trout and I first realized what was going on between us, we both agreed it was something that probably wouldn't last. We talked about it like a couple of real responsible adults, and agreed when that happened we would just move on and always remain good friends. It looked great on paper, but the only problem was that this little boy in me had a hard time reading fine print.

We both knew in our hearts that it couldn't last forever, and I didn't want to have any illusions about it, but the childish boy in me had other ideas. He was raised with the Mickey Mouse Club and Batman, and saw us beat the shit out of the Nazis. To him anything was possible, and if so, then this would be a piece of cake. He said, *"If she had the kid, then how could she ever leave you? That would be breaking up the team. What would Batman be without*

Robin, and Lois Lane without Clark Kent? Hell, can you imagine Tracy without Hepburn?" No matter how hard he tried, he always fell short on realities, and this relationship was about as real as you get. I'd already gone through a divorce and the trauma of loss of family, and here it was staring me in the face again. No matter how tender we were with each other, and no matter how much love existed, the young woman was only twenty and had a life ahead of her. What would happen if she said, "Fuck it, I don't want this. I want to have fun, and travel. There are things I have to do!"

What then? I would be a single parent who would get phone calls and visits from a woman I would love forever. The kid wouldn't be a dummy, he would see me slowly rot and miss her like an amputated arm. She would go on with her life, meet someone else, and maybe take the kid. I would just slowly roll over and die. I would go to Bohemian heaven and meet Walter and seek advice. He would say, "Kid, it was a no-win situation from the beginning. It was an opium-cloud-love, full of good whiskey dreams. Look at Hazel and me. I finally make it, and BOOM! I get my throat cut! It's karma kid, and it has eaten out my liver and broken your heart. But if I have ever taught you anything, it's that nothing is forever, so quit getting your hopes up. It's over, and you'll never get her back. It is the death of hope that killed us, and nothing more."

I knew that if she ever took the child and left me, then it would just be a matter of time before I took this kid in me in hand and drink myself to death. And I'm sure I would fulfill my dream of having her be the last woman I would ever sleep with.

Trout's worst fear was to fail me, and that covered a whole range of things. I could see her fight the feeling of wanting to leave and never in her life coming to terms with it. It would be a hard ride for her, and she would never find peace with it.

If she left, the pond would turn into a swamp and the Zen garden into dust. The red-tail would die and rot in the sun, while the squirrels would cut off its head and stake it out in the field. The albatross would gather and fill the house, while the bones of white pigeons would erupt and grow like dead grass amongst the furrows and stone. The ghost of Mozart would play a black harp, and the hope spirits would throw gasoline on the redwood table and watch it burn into an ashen mound. There would be no turquoise wind and no white ravens or feathered landscaped trees. The Pigeon Man would moan lamentations and hold my hand as hope slowly died. He would watch as my soul grew charcoal wings and drift into a moon-less night.

Trout would bend down and see it all reflected in the murky pond and would never walk straight again. And I would never have the chance to give her the wings I hoped she would use to help her get off the ground and fly.

Whenever she got depressed we would lie in bed, and I would tell her stories. They were mostly about Jose and I. It was the one thing that seemed to relax her mind.

She talked a lot of Kinlin; the child she believed was destined to be. Her usual contact with her friends from school had dropped to almost nothing, and she hadn't told any of them about her being pregnant. It was as if the treasure that she had inside was too precious to share, and she was sure that most of her friends would have tried to talk her out of it anyway. I think sharing the news was something she just wasn't ready to deal with, and I sometimes wondered if she ever would.

My stories of Jose kept her fascinated, and the hardest thing for her to believe was that they were all true. Jose was an incredible man, and a friend for life. Contrary to all of his womanizing, Jose was a man of honor when it came to respecting a friend's lady. Once he had met Trout, and saw what we were sharing, he would treat her like a sister. He was the only friend I had that I could trust enough to not make a move on her. I could be called away for a year, and all I would have to say was take care of her for me, and I know he would. He and I had been through so much together, that if there hadn't of been trust between us, we both might not be alive.

In Berlin, he had been hassled by a group of skinheads who mistook him for a Turk, and while I was in the bathroom of the bar, they proceeded to kick the living shit out of him.

I heard the ruckus and ran outside to find him on the ground with five Neo Nazis putting the boot to him. I jumped in, and they turned on me, and brutally kicked the shit out of us both. Jose never forgot it, and still to this day says that if I hadn't jumped in they would have killed him. I always tell him that they decided to kill me instead, and the next day it felt like they had. He still says I saved his life, and being the true Yaqui he is, insists that he owe's me a life in return. Since that happened back in '83, we've gotten in enough bad situations where I've said he's paid me back, but he won't except it, and says I'll know when it happens.

In bed one night I told Trout about the time he and Peter, myself, and an Iranian poet friend of ours got into it with some members of the University of Southern California rugby team.

"The three of us had become good buddies in that little village in Greece, and along the way picked up Yesaf the poet." I said to Trout, excited that I was getting to relive that time in Greece. "He was an expatriate and a pure pacifist on his way to Paris to escape the war between Iraq and Iran. He was one of Iran's most well known poets, and a genuinely sweet guy. When I first met him, his softness and tender manner made me think he was gay. It was a misconception on my part, and in reality, he was asexual.

I was the first American he had ever known. He told me that he was always taught to stay away from us because we were hedonists and the personification of the Devil. From the time that he began school, it was pounded into him, and something that he actually believed. Over the weeks, Yesaf and I became close friends, and he would sit outside with me at the patio bar and read me his poetry. It was written in the ancient way of Persian verse, where it is more sung than spoken. Even though I couldn't understand the words, they were still the most beautiful sounding poems I had ever heard.

Jose would get drunk with Peter and recite Mexican and Swiss sonnets, while Yesaf would be singing in Persian in the background. The old Greek bar owner would have a few pops and quote Socrates, while I would play congas on the table and do my best imitation of B.B. King. We were the 'International Happy Hour,' 24 hours a day.

The four of us took a boat to Piraeus. It was the waterfront area of Athens surrounded by bars and restaurants. It had a huge harbor full of some of the nicest boats in the world. In the evenings the very rich would sit around the decks of their yachts and drink cocktails and read the financial times.

We ended up in a tavern down by the water, which had a few locals in it, some deck hands from the yachts, and some college guys who were pretty loud and very drunk.

We sat at the bar drinking whisky and cold beer. Peter had ordered a tray of assorted Greek food, which consisted of rolled grape leaves, Zatziki and bread, olives, and deep-fried sardines. Yesaf didn't drink. He didn't have to. He was high on something else. It was the 150-proof written word, which he was constantly scribbling down on a little note pad that he carried in an old leather shoulder bag.

Peter and Jose were fucked up, and had been ever since we left on the boat at eight-thirty that morning. Peter had scored some hash from a deck hand in the basin, and had been stuffing the ends of his cigarettes with it all day. Jose had found a few "Bennies" in the watch pocket of his jeans, which we split three ways. It was an act of ingestion, which made Peter kind of flinch, and put him into a mood where he spoke nothing but French the rest of the night.

Yesaf was scribbling and drinking orange juice, singing in some ancient Persian tongue. They were melodies that made the bartender go and turn the music up to a point that made Jose tell him, in Mexican, to turn the fucking thing down. The bartender was confused as hell, and had to ask Peter in Greek if we were a United Nations delegation. Peter said no, as a matter of fact we weren't, but we were a band of mercenaries on our way to Africa to assassinate a Congolese king, and if he wanted to go, it was all right with us. Peter said that he was the captain, I was the sergeant, Jose was the private, and

Yesaf was the medic, and it would be great to have a bartender along to mix the drinks after we had shot the king. Needless to say, the bartender didn't hang around our end of the bar very much. So Peter asked him to put the bottle of Jack Daniels, some ice, and about ten beers in front of us, and then take a break.

Everyone was having a good time except Jose. For some reason the bennie didn't mix very well with what was going on in his mind, and he had become as somber as a judge.

The five husky college guys wearing the U.S.C. rugby sweatshirts at the other end of the bar became real loud. We didn't pay much attention to them because we were having our own kind of fun, involved in "The International Happy Hour," and trying to carry on a conversation in four languages, (actually five if we counted Peter's broken French). Jose was busy trying to write poetry with a ballpoint on the underside of his arm, which made him look like a blue ink smeared, poem-tracked junkie.

We had become the "Four Amigos" sitting there. In fact, four of the most insane amigos the bartender had seen in a long while. A fact made much more believable after Jose reached over and bit off the caps of three bottles of beer, and spit them in his direction.

One of the college boys walked over to us and tapped me on the shoulder and said in a rather arrogant and demanding tone of voice to ask the guy next to me how to say, 'Do you want to fuck?' in Greek, mistakenly thinking that Jose was Greek. I said he wouldn't know because he's Mexican. A statement which made the college boy get this disgusting look on his face, and say something to the effect, 'You leave California to get away from the little 'Cholo' motherfuckers, and no matter where you go there they are eating their greasy tacos.'

He then turned around and started to walk back to his friends, when all of a sudden a sentence in Spanish swept across the bar and hit him like a flame-thrower in the back of the head. Well, the "All American" didn't understand what it meant, but he certainly got the drift of the tone. It was a verbal knife in the back, which made him walk back to me, and again asked me to tell him what Jose had said. I answered that I didn't speak Spanish, so maybe he should ask the man who said it.

He got all puffed up, looked at Jose, and asked him what he had meant with those words. Jose reached over and grabbed a bottle of beer, bit off the cap, and spit it at the 220-pounder, hitting him in the chest. Then Jose told him that he had just said, 'Your mother is a whore working in a colony of leprosy-infected Ugandans.'

By the way the college boy flinched, one would have thought he had just been spit in the face by a mouth full of dog piss.

It took about five seconds for the kid to react, and about four for Jose. Jose had taken the bottle of beer that he had just bitten the cap off of and threw it, hitting the Neanderthal in the middle of the forehead. A pretty good shot, I thought, for someone so drunk. It didn't knock him out; only back about three steps. The worst thing was that it had opened up a twenty-stitch gash between his eyes that bled like hell, and momentarily blinded him. Afterwards Jose told me he would never hit a blind man, but this was different, because the kid was only temporarily blind.

Jose was pound-for-pound one of the toughest men I have ever seen, and almost unbeatable when his nationality was insulted. I saw him hit a guy so hard in a bar one night for calling him a 'Wetback,' that the guy hit the floor and started to twitch and involuntary shake his legs. Afterwards, I said to him that he shouldn't have hit him so hard, and I thought he had killed the guy. Jose just looked at me and smiled and said that he was just teaching him to do the 'TUNA'; the harpooned, on the deck, twitching dance of the loser.

That night in the Greek bar, we got into one of the bloodiest fights of my life, and Peter, Jose and I, with Yesaf playing medic, barely got out alive. We could have probably whipped them if we hadn't been so drunk, and if Yesaf hadn't kept interfering by trying to give first aid to the guy that Jose had first hit. I got socked more times by just trying to get him out of the line of fire. After Peter took a stool over the head, it was just me and Jose, a couple of tired, drunk hombres taking on four, (in much better shape than we were), rugby players. The cops came, and seeing that the four of us had been punished enough, took our names and let us go. The bartender was impressed by our futile courage, and said that the college guys had started it. On the way out the door the bartender gave Peter his address, and told us to have a nice trip, and to be sure and send him a card from Africa."

Trout looked over at me, yawned and said, "Come on, he didn't say that, did he?"

"Of course," I said. "After he saw Peter yelling, and giving orders in French, like a true Legionnaire captain, and me trying to rescue our medic from the trenches like a good sergeant, and Jose going for the 'Medal Of Honor' like a dedicated private, he couldn't help but believe we were four of the toughest mercenaries he had ever seen. I swear Trout, it's the truth!"

She gave me that Trout look of, "Come on, you're pulling my fin again," and said, "How long do you think Jose will stay?"

"I don't know, why?"

"Because it sounds like you and he will get into nothing but trouble if he comes, and I don't like the idea of you getting hurt. You're not a kid anymore you know."

Way to go, I thought, hit me below the belt. "Of course I'm not a kid. Would you like me more if I was?"

"No baby," she said, smiling, "I like you just the way you are. Old, bald, gray, skin like suede, and great in bed."

"Greater than the worst woman that you've ever slept with?" I asked, half joking. "You wouldn't kid a tired old man now, would you?"

"You're the best lover I've ever had, and that is the truth. Now why don't you come over here and prove it to me one more time."

CHAPTER 16

The next day I was trying to get a piece finished for the exhibition, and was struggling like hell with it. My mind wasn't in the right space, and was preoccupied with Trout and what she was carrying inside. I had begun to act like her, roller coastering with moments of proud father euphoria, then sinking to the depths of imagined, despaired future responsibilities.

She often spoke of Kinlin as if he were already there, and talked of the adventures the three of us were going to have. It was again the "Forever" syndrome I so much wanted to believe existed, but deep in my heart knew didn't. It would put me into the throes of hopelessness, and they were moods I had trouble hiding from her. Trout had enough problems filling her mind without the addition of mine, so I did my best to keep them to myself.

I hadn't talked to anyone about this, just Trout, and there were things I couldn't even tell her. They were too heavy for her to hear, and would just be an extra burden, so I kept them to myself and wished that Jose was around. He was the one man I could talk to and he always found time to give you his ear. He was crazy and a fuck up, but he had a sensitive heart and would always open it to a friend.

I turned off the welder and headed for the house and sought out Trout for a supportive touch. I found her on the bed with her arms covering her eyes. She was quietly crying. I sat by her side and touching her hair asked, "Trout, what is it, what's wrong?"

Sometimes in these situations she would turn away, which was a sign that she wanted to be alone, and I usually left it at that. This day was different. She turned away, but at the same time grabbed my arm telling me that she didn't want me to leave.

I knew it was serious, but didn't want to press her. I knew she would tell me when she was ready. I touched her hand, and with my other hand gently brushed her hair. I could always calm her by using my fingers like a comb. I said again, "Are you OK? Is there something that you want to tell me?"

She squeezed my hand, and half sobbing said, "I lost him."

"What do you mean you lost him, who?"

"Kinlin, I lost Kinlin, he's gone and we'll never have him back."

Gone? I thought, shit, what is she talking about?

"What happened Trout? Tell me, please?"

She looked up and threw her arms around my shoulders and sobbed. I felt her breath on my neck; it was warm and smelled like pain. Her tears glued her face to mine and she was now openly crying.

I said again as soft and undemanding as I could, "Trout it's OK, please tell me what's going on."

"I felt like I was starting my period, but it was different. I had a sharp cramp and then just started to bleed."

"Trout, what do you mean, you started to bleed? Did you have a miscarriage?"

"Yes."

"Are you sure, how do you know for sure?"

"I rushed into the bathroom and grabbed a towel. I was bleeding much worse than a normal period, and it was strange, much thicker than normal. I knew exactly what had happened. I knew I had lost him."

"Well, are you all right? Trout, ARE YOU OK?"

"I don't know. I'm pretty dizzy."

"Are you still bleeding?"

"No, just a few light spots, kind of like a period."

"Well, I'm going to call the hospital."

Squeezing my neck hard, she said, "No, I'm OK. Don't! Just lay here with me for a while. I'll be all right."

She wouldn't be OK. Something had just been wrenched out of her that she had begun to love. It was a loss of the growth of hope, because Kinlin was hope for us both. He would have always been there to remind me of her and of what we have shared. He would have been the knot that would have tied the karmic bond that would keep us in touch forever, no matter how far apart we were.

I was as sad as Trout, and with her warm, tear-filled breath on my neck I began to silently cry too. Trout had lost a part of her flesh, a warm, blood red, living attachment that had been tied to her like growing roots to a live, breathing tree, and because of it she was deep in the throes of loss. Trout's pain was always mine to share. I wished at that moment I could have taken it all, pulled it inside my guts and freed her of whatever ate at her heart. I had this overwhelming fear that we had not only lost Kinlin, but we would lose each other. I knew Trout, and it would take her many painful, alone-by-herself months to get over this. I knew, too, that her moods wouldn't have room in them for me.

I lay by her side with her head on my chest listening to the sound of her tears as they rolled off my arm and splashed, creating endless wailing child ripples, over the surface of the fur covered bed.

Trout stayed in bed and slept for two days. She lay there with her back to the door facing the window and the wild white rose. I felt it was just a matter of time before she would tell me that she had to leave and get away from the memories of the house. It was something I was preparing myself for but had not mentioned. I slept with her and was careful not to disturb her mourning. I knew that's what she was doing. She was mourning the loss of a boy who she already had known by the color of his eyes and the darkness of his hair, and the creative spirit I had promised he would have.

I feared if Trout believed that this was the kind of pain born from a relationship with a man, maybe she would again seek refuge in the safety and comfort of a woman. It was a cancerous fear that always ate at me somewhere deep and private. It was now starting to surface becoming a razor sharp claw, crawling up my throat. I was afraid to ask her anything, afraid of what the answer might be, and scared to death I wouldn't be strong enough to accept another loss.

Two weeks had passed and I felt like a stranger had moved in and replaced Trout. She hadn't laughed, hadn't gone outside, and had lost about ten pounds. I was worried about her but every attempt I made to cheer her up failed miserably. There wasn't a Jose story incredible enough to make her crack a smile or a touch tender enough to make her want to make love; something we hadn't done since before the Kinlin tragedy. If my worst fears were true and Trout was thinking that being with a man wasn't what she wanted, then she was on the right track, because she had suddenly taken our bedroom and turned it into ice.

I finally broke down and suggested that maybe it might be a good idea if she went and visited her sister in Santa Cruz. It wasn't what I wanted, but I thought, maybe it could be something that would be good for her soul. She reacted like I was trying to get rid of her, and said in effect that she had just lost one person she loved and wasn't in the mood to deal with the absence of another. So I dropped the idea and decided to tough it out.

I had all but stopped working, and saw the commitment to the show slip away. I was so empty inside that nothing I could have made would have been worth a shit anyway, and I was at the point again of going out and torching the studio.

I spent a lot of time in the Zen garden pulling weeds and trying to patch the cracks in the pond. I spent hours watching the hawks and the squirrels play their daily game. My drinking increased, but was having no medicinal effect on my mood. Trout didn't like me to drink, but at this point she didn't notice or care. It was just taking me deeper into places I'd already been, and I was becoming a drugged tourist, booking myself into the five dollar a night hotels of my past.

I watched the hawk and imagined it watching me. I remembered when I was eleven and my father had brought home a mature red-tail about one short day away from death. The Pigeon Man knew how much I wanted one and had passed the word around to his bird buddies to keep their eyes open. I had read every book pertaining to hawks and falconry that the local library had, and because of that had become the youngest authority on falconry this side of Yemen.

One evening, my dad brought me a cardboard box containing a sick and wounded hawk. I looked inside and saw him lying down and unable to move. The Pigeon Man said that a fireman had found him in a field shot through the wing. He told me that if I didn't get some food into him immediately the great bird would probably die before morning.

The Pigeon Man and I ground up liver and beef. I sat with the bird on my lap, and like the mother of all hawks, crammed the food down its throat until its crop was full. After a week of this dedicated care the bird finally stood and looked at me like I was Jesus of Nazareth, who had just given fresh water to a dying man.

The old hawk became my best friend and would sit on my arm and tell me the secrets of living in the sky. We would talk for hours about squirrels and ancient Indian rites and of the days when he would be able to fly again and we would go and hunt rabbits.

Two years later, standing alone in the back yard after school, I sadly let him go. I tried to throw him off my arm, but he didn't want to leave; he had more stories to tell, and he knew I had much more to learn. I knew it was for the best, and he should be out there free, hunting with his friends. With all my 12-year-old strength I tossed him in the wind and watched him clumsily lumber away. He flew to an old palm tree, landed, and looked back. We stared at each other for a while, then I said goodbye and watched him as he slowly caught some wind and flew away.

During those days when Trout was locked up within herself I would sit on the stack of cut apple wood in the field and watch as the hawk flew overhead, wondering if it knew who I was. Maybe the word had been passed down in the lore's of "Dead Falcon Scrolls" and the screams I heard daily were really the sounds of winged appreciation for saving an old grandfather's life.

Trout needed her life saved. I felt she was going to shrivel up and die if she stayed here much longer. I would have hand fed her if I could have, but she wouldn't even accept my touch. It had been three weeks and Trout was withering away emotionally and I was at a loss about what to do for her. I'd thought about calling her mother, but knew that Trout wouldn't want that. What I didn't need right now was for her to think that I had betrayed her trust. I had given her something she had begun to love, and then suddenly it had been ripped from her body. I wondered if she was holding me to blame for some of the pain she was feeling. We hadn't even talked about the day of Kinlin's bloody death, and I was afraid to bring it up for fear it would set her back further, if that was possible. She had always complained that I didn't open up enough to her, having at times become an issue in the relationship. But I was willing to open up the doors of communication now. I knew it was the thing that might save this relationship, if it still was capable of being saved, but Trout wasn't talking and wasn't listening, and I could only guess what was going through her head.

CHAPTER 17

I was standing at the kitchen sink staring out into the garden. It was 11 o'clock in the morning and I had just opened my first beer, the first of six I would probably drink before dinner.

I saw the squirrel that was sniffing around the base of the bay tree take off in a startled chattering run and climb to the top. He looked down and began to loudly scold the car that was coming down the drive. I peered around the corner of the window waiting to see what was accompanying the sound of gravel being kicked to the side.

A beat up old Ford pickup pulled in, and out stepped a black-bandana-wearing bandit by the name of Jose Mendoza. I went to the back door and stepped onto the porch and screamed, "Amigo, you made it!"

"Compadre," he yelled back, "I am hot and must have a cold beer. If I don't have one in my hand soon, I will fall down and die right here on this beautiful ground."

It was great to see his face, and the big Mexican smile covering it.

"Amigo," he yelled again, "I have brought a friend, a little fish all the way from Baja, California. He is like an old Indian who, when I got lost, showed me the way."

What the fuck was he talking about? Has he brought some fish for dinner and an old Indian to share it with?

"Jose, what are you talking about?"

He walked to the other side of the truck and opened the door and lifted out a kid that looked about four years old, and said with a big flair of his left arm, "Amigo, I want you to meet my friend, 'Little Fish'. 'Little Fish', I want you to meet my best amigo."

I didn't know what to think. Was this little boy who was wearing a faded pair of jeans and a Dos Equis T-shirt, and a pair of leather sandals a product of one of Jose's liaisons, one that some broken hearted woman had thrown in his lap telling him it was now his responsibility?

Jose said, "Amigo, isn't this the most beautiful boy you have ever seen, he is a prince, and a prophet, too!"

I thought, man, Jose must have got a hold of some good weed on the way down, and had just smoked most of it turning into the drive.

Jose let the boy down and grabbed his hand and walked towards the house. About halfway there the shadow of the red-tail appeared and crossed the boy's face. He looked up just in time to hear it scream, and with his free hand pointed to the sky, then looked at me and smiled. The boy was beautiful, but didn't look Mexican. I was curious as hell to find out where Jose had gotten him.

Jose approached me and we embraced. It was a strong hug, one of two friends that hadn't seen each other in awhile.

Jose looked down and said, "Little fish, this is my friend, the one I have told you about."

The boy looked up into my eyes and seemed to know I was exactly that. I said, "Jose, who is he? Come on tell me. Is he yours?"

"No amigo, I found him."

"You found him, where?"

"In Baja. Well, I didn't exactly find him, my uncle did. Amigo, it is a long story, come, let's go into the house and I will tell you."

The noise had stirred Trout, who walked out of the bedroom and into the kitchen. There was Jose and the kid, a sight that made Trout even more speechless than she already was.

I said, "Trout, this is Jose and a little friend of his, everyone, this is Trout."

Jose said, "Trout, if you are the woman of this man then you are much too beautiful and too smart to waste your time with an old crazy fool like him. If you really do love him, then you must have a very patient and forgiving heart."

Trout actually almost smiled, and replied, "So you are the infamous Jose Mendoza. I have heard many stories about you from this old man here. Nice to meet you."

Trout looked down into the eyes of the boy, who couldn't take his off of her. She turned to the side and looked at me, then back down again at the kid.

She said, "What's your name?"

Jose answered for him, "He doesn't talk. He seems to have a way of communicating without needing to. My uncle found him on the beach and named him Little Fish."

"Found him on the beach?" Trout said, with her eyes wide open. "Where?"

"In Baja," Jose answered.

"Baja?" Trout said.

"Yeah, in Baja all by himself walking on the beach stark naked with hundreds of sea gulls flying around him."

At about that time the boy reached over and grabbed Trout's hand and pointed to her room, and with her in hand led her into it.

He walked in the door, looked at her, and pointed to the stars on the ceiling. Trout called my name and I walked in. By that time the boy had reached up with his little arms beckoning for her to hold him. I walked in and saw Trout holding the boy up high enough so he could touch the stars with his fingers.

Trout looked at me with this amazed look in her eyes, and said, "Davis look, he led me to the stars. What does he want? How did he know they were here?"

"I don't know. It's weird."

Jose had just walked in and said, "No amigo, it's not weird. The boy knows things that no one else does. I told you, he's a prophet."

The kid brought his gaze down from the ceiling and looked at Trout. He felt safe with her and acted like he had known her for a thousand years. He rested his head on her shoulder and began to cry soft tears, tears that ran down her back and made her grab him tight with her hand tenderly touching the back of his head.

Trout rocked him softly and spoke soothing words. Trout's eyes began to fill too. Jose and I looked at each other and shook our heads.

Trout said, "I think he's tired. I'll take him into the bedroom and lie down with him."

Trout went with the boy still holding onto her tight. They walked into the bedroom and Trout laid with him on the bed. I watched her give the child all of the tenderness that she had been holding back from me. She lay there next to him and watched him as he closed his eyes. She whispered for me to close the door. I shut it silently and walked back into the kitchen and opened beers for Jose and me.

We held our beers up and clinked glass, and both knew that it had been too long since we had seen each other.

Jose said, "Amigo, this is a beautiful place. Remember that time in the south of France when we met those two Swedish school teachers and we spent some time at the villa they had rented for the summer? This place reminds me of it, only nicer. Man! IT IS GOOD TO SEE YOU!"

We hugged again, and I went to the aspirin cabinet and brought out what I had left of the quart of Jim Beam.

Jose said, "NO! I have some Yaqui fire water in the truck. My uncle saved it for me and told me to give it to you with his best wishes. Wait a minute, I'll get it."

Jose leaped down the steps like a little kid going to get the new bike he got for Christmas. Jose got excited by the littlest of things, and would use the simplest of occasions to show you that he was really a ten-year-old-boy inside.

He ran back taking two steps at a time, and set a canvas bag on the counter.

"Look," he said with a huge grin on his face, "Indian holy water, now we're going to have a real drink!"

I got out two glasses and let him pour, because if you didn't he would grab your glass and fill it to almost overflowing, saying something like, "Amigo, that is not a drink. That is a taste. This is a drink!"

Jose and I sat at the table eating cheese and bread, and drinking with the beer, the strongest Tequila I have ever tasted. Thank God that he had brought the lime, because Jose thought it a sacrilege to drink anything brewed in Mexico without it.

We toasted to all the dead Yaqui's that had lost their lives to the coming of civilization, and to a soccer player, (that I had never heard of), who had just been killed in a motorcycle accident. "The future of Mexican Soccer has died," were his exact words as he held his glass high.

I asked Jose about the kid, and exactly how did he come across him?

"Amigo," he said, "as I told you, I went to my uncle's to visit and to have him fix my clutch. The old Ford has not been feeling well lately. Anyway, I drive up to the house and knock on the door and my aunt opens it and I walk in. Sitting at the table eating a cantaloupe is the boy, so I ask who he is. My uncle comes in and tells me the story in a way that made me think by the way he was acting that he had found another baby Moses. He said he was on the beach doing some surf fishing at about six in the morning, when he sees a flock of sea gulls milling around something about a hundred yards up the beach. He strains his eyes and sees that it is a little child standing in the middle of them, all the while the gulls are screaming and flapping around him. He takes off in their direction worried they will hurt him, but halfway there sees that the boy is not afraid and appears to be talking to them.

I look at Jose and roll my eyes toward the ceiling.

He notices, and says, "I know it sounds crazy, and my uncle might drink a little too much, but he has never eaten mushrooms, so I know he wasn't having an hallucination."

"OK. So then what happened?"

"My uncle goes up to the boy and asks him in Spanish who he is, and the kid just looks at him. Then he asks the same question in English, and the kid still looks back with nothing to say. So my uncle takes him home and gives him something to eat, and then they drive to the village to look for his folks. No one has ever seen the kid, and the police don't have any missing person's report, so my uncle takes him back to the house. For the next couple of days they ask everybody around if they've heard anything about a missing kid and no one had. After a while the little boy seems to understand the question of home, and where is it? Every time my aunt or uncle mentions the word home, the kid looks them dead in the eye and points his finger in the direction of north. My uncle spent three days traveling in a circle that covered all the land in a fifty-mile radius north of his place, and still no one had ever seen the kid. They figured out that north is up in the States and maybe in California. When I arrived they suggested that I take him along with me, and that maybe you could help me find his parents."

"You mean the cops didn't try to look?" I ask.

"Nah," he said, "those lazy Mexicans acted like they didn't even care, saying, 'It ain't our problem, man.' So here I am, and here he is. Now what do we do?"

"I guess go to the police, I don't know how else to approach it."

"But amigo, what if they put him in a home? The kid has got too much soul for a home. I tell you, he is special, and he's a fucking prophet!"

"What do you mean a prophet? What did he do? Read that nasty palm of yours? Fuck, the kid can't even talk!"

"Amigo, I told you he doesn't have to, he already knows everything!"

"Jose, what do you mean, he knows everything?"

"Well, I'm going to give you an example," first pausing to toast the boy for the forth time. "Listen, I only had your old address in Petaluma, right?"

"Yeah, I know, my ex-wife forwarded me your last card."

"OK." Jose said, acting like he was getting ready to tell me about a squadron of UFOs he saw on the way up here, "I found your ex-wife's house. But the minute we pull into the place the kid just shakes his head back and forth, so I ask him what's wrong and he just keeps pointing his finger north. I get out and talk to your ex-wife and she tells me how to get here. So the Little Fish and I head over here and get lost somewhere in a town called Graton. The place was full of Mexican farm laborers and none of them knew how to get here. The kid pokes my arm and points up the road, so what the fuck, I was lost anyway, so I just followed his finger. We get on the main road out in front and are coming down the hill when the kid jerks my sleeve and points at the three mailboxes. I slow down and he points towards the grove of trees that are at this time, GROWING OUT THIS FUCKING WINDOW! So, here we are!"

"Now wait a minute," I said, with a look of disbelief, "you mean the little boy in the next room pointed you all the way here?"

"Amigo, I know it sounds like I have been drinking some bad Mescal, but on the grave of my dead mother, I swear it is true!"

I knew that Jose would never swear on the grave of his dead mother unless he thought it was the truth, but a kid who has never been here before showing him the way was pretty hard to believe.

"And amigo, look how he acted when he got here. It was like he had already been here before. What about the thing with the stars? And look how he took to Trout. I tell you the kid is special."

Pointing to the stars was strange, and he did grab onto Trout like he never wanted to let go. They did seem to have some kind of a bond. Maybe it was just lonely woman meeting a lonely child, both of them recognizing there were some needs that had to be filled. Whatever the reasons were that had given her some momentary peace, they were all right with me. If it was that kid in there asleep next to her that was helping, then it was OK with me if he spent the night.

Jose and I continued to drink and tell our stories. It seems that he had been involved in working on charter cruises in the Caribbean for the last year. Jose was a hell of a sailor, and could usually hire on whenever he wanted. The only problem was that sometimes he would help get the boat there, but wasn't to be found when they wanted to sail it back.

We were getting hungry, so I called out for a pizza that we would have to pick up in half an hour. We were also out of beer, which tonight would be of much greater importance than food, but Trout and the boy would be awakening soon and would no doubt be hungry.

Jose and I headed for Forestville to the pizza joint. It was a short drive that took about five minutes. On the way we talked about Trout and me. I told him what she meant to me, and he said, "She is a beautiful woman, but I see she is troubled amigo, and you know that it is dangerous to love her so much."

"I know," I said, "but it has gone beyond the point of no return, I have ripped open my chest and allowed her to move in, and no matter how hard I try to talk myself out of it, I still find myself hopelessly in love."

Jose was about half drunk, but it never interfered with his intuition and ability to read people. He said, "You have been in love before, but you always held something back, do you mean this time you have really pulled out your heart and laid it on the table?"

"Yeah Jose, I have, and it is much too late to try and get it back."

"Did you also go out into your studio and get a big hammer and lay it along side of it?" he said, smiling.

"Jose, don't fuck with me now."

"Man, I am not fucking with you. You know how I have always been honest with you, right?"

"Right!"

"You are my friend and I don't want to hurt you, but I think that this woman is going to break your heart, and it will take a long time to stick it back together."

"I know," I said, "I have the same feeling, but I can't change the course that this love is taking me on, and I wouldn't change the experience for anything. If it kills me, then maybe it will be the sweet death I have always looked for."

Jose looked over at me and grabbed my shoulder and squeezed hard and got a big Yaqui smile on his face, and shouted, "AMIGO, I LOVE YOU MAN! You still have the heart of a poet, you will never change, and if you die of a broken heart I will jump in the middle of the burning pyre and rip it from your body and take it and lay it in her hands."

"Jose, you are a crazy motherfucker, and the scariest thing is, I'm afraid that you would do it!"

"DO IT? You bet your fucking ass I would, quicker than the last beat of a dying man's broken heart!"

We got the pizza and some beer, and drove back. Jose was ranting and raving about the power that women had over us, and decided that we were nothing but a bunch of weak son's a bitch's, but how horrible life would be without them.

We walked into the house and saw that Trout and the boy were up. She was sitting on the couch with him on her lap, talking to him. The kid was staring into her eyes with this incredible intense look on his face, fixed on her every word.

She turned to us and said, "Hey, the boy can speak!" She then took her finger and pointed it at herself, and said, "What's my name?"

The boy looked at her and smiled, and said, "Trout."

"See! He can talk," she said, with the first real smile I'd seen on her face in three weeks.

I looked at Jose, and Jose looked back and said, "I told you the kid is a genius, a genius who is also a prophet."

I was confused as hell. Jose said that the kid hadn't said a word since he was found, and now he's talking to Trout. Well, maybe he can say pizza, because I bet he's hungry.

"Hey you guy's, we've got food," I yelled, "half vegetarian, and half sausage! Get a plate and take your pick."

Trout starts to get up and the boy reaches up with his arms and gestures for her to hold him. She reaches down and picks him up and walks over to the table. The two sit down opposite Jose and I. The kid had a thing for her, and showed it by crawling up on her lap, looking up at her for the sign that it was OK to eat.

The twilight was coming through the window covering Trout and the boy with an opaque warm glow. I looked at him and noticed his eyes. They were a gray green, with slight amber flecks, and they were so much like hers that it looked like Trout had just taken hers out and placed them in his head. His hair was dark, and his manner was soft and tender. He was indeed a beautiful boy, and if there had ever been a Kinlin I'm sure he would have looked just like him.

I said, "Trout, did you look at his eyes?"

"Yes, aren't they beautiful?" She said, staring into them.

"Yeah, they sure are, almost as gorgeous as yours," I said.

Trout asked, "How old do you think he is?"

Jose blurts out, "I think he's about 150!"

Trout smiles and say's, "No, really."

Jose say's again, "I tell you, that kid is the oldest person that I have ever seen! He's at least 150, maybe older."

I jump in and say, "I think he's about three and a half, maybe four."

Trout say's, "I wish he could tell us."

"Why," Jose said, "even if he could talk, he probably wouldn't be able to count to a hundred and fifty! I tell you, that kid is ancient!"

Trout and the boy were sharing a piece of pizza, and for the first time in weeks she was happy. I always tried to imagine her as a mother and how she would act with a child on her lap, and now I was seeing it. She was as tender and caring as I imagined her to be. The fear hit me of her becoming attached to him and then having to let him go. It might be as hard on her as the loss of Kinlin.

Trout and the boy finish, and she say's they are going to go for a walk. She wants to show him the farm, and the bees, and all the wonders of the Zen garden before it gets dark.

Trout picks him up and they walk outside where she puts him down and grabs hold of his hand. I see them through the front window walking hand in hand across the field, all the while Trout looking down and telling him about the treasures of nature that lay before their eyes.

Jose looks at me with his sensitive, knowing eyes and says, "Amigo, Trout is not only in love with you, but I think she has fallen in love with that boy too. Most important of all, I think the boy has fallen in love with her."

"I know," I said, "I've seen it too. What the fuck am I going to do?"

"Nothing man, it is destiny." he said, "If you wanted to change it, you wouldn't be able to. You told me in the truck that she lost that little boy she had gotten to love. Remember?"

"Yeah," I said.

"Well, she has gotten him back, and it is now out of our hands."

"But what about going to the authorities, and trying to find his home?"

"He is home, amigo."

"What? What the fuck are you talking about?"

"I tell you, the boy knew where he was going the whole time we were looking for this place. Amigo, the boy is home. He is yours forever."

"Jose, are you trying to tell me that when he was in Baja, this is the place north that he kept pointing to?"

"I know it sounds strange and hard for you to believe. My aunt is one who knows, and she told me that the boy is not of this world, he is blessed, and I think that Trout is not only his mother, but you are his father."

That last line stood me up and headed me straight for the kitchen and the Jim Beam, which I grabbed, and reaching for the first glass, filled to the brim.

I came back and killed half of it and looked Jose in the eye and said, "How do you know this?"

Looking at me with all the seriousness that he had in him, Jose said, "There is an old Yaqui belief that a death is also a birth, and that when something or someone dies then it is born again somewhere else. Sometimes as an animal or fish, or another person, but it is their explanation for the cycle of life."

"Are we talking about reincarnation here?" I said.

"Yes. That little boy outside is hope, and even though you have lost faith in it, the spirits haven't. Hope didn't die in that toilet, it was born the minute he walked through that door, and I tell you man, you can look forever for the parents of that kid and you will never find them. The kid has found them."

The whole conversation was so far out I didn't know what to think. Maybe the booze was getting to us. Maybe his uncle did grind up some mushrooms and lace the Mescal.

I had read about reincarnation and the Dali Lama, and the Tibetan monks. I had found it plausible, but I was pretty much of an agnostic about it and all other theories of creation that I'd heard about. This was something I would have to look at with very sober eyes, and it didn't look like tonight was going to be the night for it.

We saw Trout and the boy approaching, and Jose said, "Amigo, don't mention our conversation to her, not yet. Just watch and maybe you will see it unfold and become as natural as the growing of grass out in that field. Just be tender to her, the same way you would be if she had actually given birth to that little boy today."

Trout and the boy came through the door with a handful of wild flowers and went into the kitchen to look for a vase. I watched her and saw how she sat him on the counter and tenderly cut the stems and placed them in the glass vase. The boy watched her like a student of Zen, and after every cut would look up at her to see if she was satisfied with the length, and the spot she had chosen to put it. She handed him a flower, and watched with adoring eyes as he chose a spot in the middle, and like Cezanne putting the finishing touches on a still life, moved his head from side to approving side.

Trout had finished with the flowers, and picking up the boy said, "I think this guy needs a bath. Jose does he have any other clothes?"

"Yeah there are a few things in the car in a bag, but there's not much. My aunt went to the neighbor's and asked for a few hand-me-downs of their son's. Wait a second and I will go get them."

Jose went outside and came back with the bag and handed it to Trout.

Trout looked kind of puzzled and asked Jose, "Jose do you know if this kid is toilet trained?"

"Yes, my aunt told me that every time he had to go, he would walk outside. So the next time my uncle had to take a piss, she had the boy go with him to the toilet and watch, and he picked it up the first time. Taking a crap in the toilet was a little more difficult. It took him two days to figure that one out. She said he acted like he had never seen toilet paper before."

Trout looked at us and shook her head and said, "Is this kid from outer space, or what?"

Jose answered, "Close to it."

Trout looked at him, trying to figure out what he meant, then said, "Nobody disturb us now, this little boy needs some privacy."

"OK" I said, "and by the way, have you figured out where he's going to sleep tonight?"

Pausing at the bathroom door, she said, "Yes I have, right between us!" and before closing it, looked back at me with that little carp smile of hers.

Jose held up his glass toward me and said, "Amigo, your Trout has just swam up from the dark bottom and is now basking in the warm sunlight near the top. She is happy. The boy has given her back hope. Maybe now he will do the same for you."

Trout's mood had definitely changed, and it was written all over her face. I wouldn't know about mine until tomorrow after I sobered up.

I stood up and sneaked over to the bathroom and slowly opened the door and peeked inside. Trout was neck deep in water and so was the boy. She looked up and screamed, "Hey, how about a little privacy, huh?"

"Oh sorry," I said, "it's just that I've never seen a big fish and a little fish in the tub at the same time. Is everything OK?"

"Yes it is," she said, "now if you would just close the door, I can start to get this kid clean."

Before leaving I whispered, "Hey, remember the second day after we first made love and I came into the house and knocked on the bathroom door. You said with this deep sexy voice to come in, and you were lying in the tub with little rings of soap around your breasts? Then I proceeded to give you the best bath you said you'd ever had?"

She gave me this look of disbelief and nodding her head towards the kid said, "Sssssshhhhh!"

"Well I just wanted to remind you, that maybe we can do it again some time soon, OK?"

"If I say yes, do you promise to leave?"

"Yeah," and looking like the eight-year-old in me had just lost his puppy, said, "are you sure about the sleeping arrangements?"

Looking back at me like someone who knew they were going to get their own way, answered, "Just tonight, please?"

"OK Trout," I said, "anything to make you happy."

No truer words were ever spoken. I would have done anything to make her happy. Hell! I would have offered to sleep on the floor next to her and the kid if that would keep that smile on her face. Maybe Jose was right, and the kid was supposed to be here. Maybe the kid is hope incarnate and was sent here to save her fragile life, and while he was at it, maybe he could work on mine too.

When Trout and the boy came out of the bathroom Jose and I were deep into a discussion about as abstract and without end as Art Pepper high on heroin lost in a ten-minute solo.

Trout said, "OK guy's, we're going to bed and read, so if you could just keep it down a bit, maybe the boy will fall asleep."

"You know," I said, "it's a shame to keep calling him kid, it's too bad we don't know his name."

Jose popped in with, "It's Little Fish, I told you already!"

"Nah, it's cute, but not quite right for him," Trout said.

She then gets this warmhearted expression on her face and turns my way with a soft, pleading look and says, "Do you think maybe we could call him Kinlin? That is until we find out his real name?"

I look back and smile and say, "Yeah Trout, if I've ever seen a Kinlin that's one. Yeah, Kinlin sounds good to me. What do you say Jose?"

"Hey man, it sounds like a good name to me, except it reminds me of firewood."

Trout looks at me with the most peaceful grin I've seen in weeks and says. "OK, Kinlin it is. I mean, he even looks like Kinlin doesn't he?"

"Just like him, sweetheart, just like him," I said.

She walks over with the boy in her arms and gives me a kiss, and as I say good night the boy reaches out and hugs my neck. I reach out and touch his velvet face. "Good night Kinlin, sleep tight and keep the dragons away from Trout tonight."

They walk away to the bedroom with Trout wearing a long white robe and Kinlin an extra large T-shirt that hangs below his feet. Trout gets to the door, turns and says, "Good night Jose and thanks for bringing him, and don't get the old man too drunk tonight, he's not as tough as he used to be."

Jose looks at me like someone just said that the Pope wasn't Catholic, and said, "You aren't?"

"No Jose, I don't think so." I answered.

Jose is pretty fucked up by now, and is staring at me from across the table looking like he has just heard for the first time that I am a cross dresser.

"What the fuck did she say? Man, you were one of the toughest son's a bitch's I've ever seen, and I bet you still are. Remember the time you kicked the shit out of those five Nazis that were trying to kill me?"

"Jose, you got it wrong. Those skinheads almost killed us both. Don't you remember?"

"Oh, yeah, but they were lucky we were drunk and in a good mood or there would have been hell to pay!"

"Right!" I said, "Jose, I'm going to bed, come on I'll show you where to sleep."

I showed him to the room with the stars and said good night. He looked at me and said, "Good night my friend, I am happy to be here. You are my brother and to see you again makes my heart feel good. Tomorrow we will celebrate the smiling face of the woman that you love and the birth of your new son."

He laid down on his back and I turned off the lights, and he said, "LOOK! Amigo, I am in heaven, there are stars everywhere!"

"Good night Jose," I said, "have a nice voyage."

I went to our room and looked inside. The boy was wrapped around Trout deep in sleep and holding on for dear life. Trout looked up and put her finger to her lips, and with her eyes asked me to lie down. I lay there with the boy between us, and with the light of the winged lamp filtering through the room, stared into her eyes. She was radiant, and glowed like the feathered wing next to the bed. We moved as close as we could to each other without disturbing the boy and kissed as tenderly as we had the first time.

I asked, "Are you happy?"

"Yes, very happy," she said, holding me with her eyes.

"Good Trout, I'm happy too." I said.

I was reaching over to brush my fingers over her eyes and close them into sleep when she looked into mine and said, "There's something I've been meaning to tell you, something you haven't heard in a while."

"What's that?" I said.

She moved her face to mine and as she placed her lips on my eyes, whispered, "I do. I really do."

I touched her face and answered, "Me too, Trout, me too."

The three of us fell into a sleep that was free of demons and scaled reptiles, and there were no furred bats, or rabid rhinos.

The boy had brought Excalibur to bed with him and it glowed in the dark as a warning to all the black beasts that would dare trespass and disturb the harmony of our first night together. It would also be the first good night's sleep that I had had in a month.

CHAPTER 18

The next day the four of us played soccer in the field, with Kinlin falling down in big clouds of dust after every third step. Jose took him squirrel hunting with the stick guns he had made and Trout and I renewed a love that was reborn the night before, as we had fallen into harmonious sleep. I thought this was the way it was supposed to be. This was how the sun was supposed to shine and warm the dust kicking at our feet. Jose was all heart, and had begun to tell Kinlin that from now on he was, uncle Jose. He kept telling Trout that he and the kid were, from that point on, to be known as Don and Sancho.

We picnicked in the orchard with Jose playing his guitar and singing Mexican love songs. Kinlin was always at Trout's side looking up at her with adoring eyes. I thought that if that was the way a boy was supposed to look at a mother that he dearly loved, Kinlin had it down pat.

Jose went to the store and bought a case of Tecate and a huge bag of limes, and couldn't resist bringing back a kite with a fire-breathing dragon on the front.

We spent the afternoon drinking beer, flying the dragon kite, and listening to Jose tell unbelievable tales while holding the ever-present bottle of cerveza in his hand.

Every ten minutes Trout would interrupt him and say, "Nah," or, "Oh my God!" or, "I don't believe it!"

Jose had found an audience. Every time he would get into a tale that included me, one that I didn't want her to hear, I would throw a rock, which thudded and bounced of his chest, which would make Kinlin giggle and throw rocks at him too. Trout would step in acting like any good mother by admonishing the two of us for teaching the boy bad habits. Jose always brought up the fact that teaching a little boy to throw a rock straight was just like teaching him the facts of life.

The red-tail flew overhead and screamed down to us, which made Kinlin turn his head to the sound. Then with his finger pointing towards me, looked at Trout and smiled. It was an eerie feeling, because he acted like he knew that the bird and I had a sacred union.

He was picking up words left and right, and had learned, "Jose," "Trout," of course, and Trout had secretly taught him to call me "Bird Man." He liked me, but the bond he felt for her was stronger, like it was inborn.

He was sometimes affectionate and would find me wherever I was, crawling on my lap listening intensely as I told him stories of my battles with winged dragons and fanged serpents. I wasn't sure if he understood what I was saying, but it didn't matter. It was a chance for me to be close to him and to imagine he was the son I always wanted.

I would tell him of the days in my 1,000-year-old past when I had fought single handedly against hordes of reptilian warriors riding snakes with a hundred legs. His little eyes would get wide, and his mouth would drop open when I described my great charging horse with its white-scaled body running through the night with its tail on fire, as I slew the enemies of all good men. Trout would always stop me when I got to the good parts, afraid the kid's mind might turn into something as bizarre as mine. I told her he probably couldn't understand me anyway. If he did, then it was important that he knew, because who else was going to carry on the legacy of all the poet warriors that have fought and died against the eternal, evil tribe that calls itself, "The Dream Killers."

Kinlin loved my stories. Jose carved him a wooden sword which he painted silver. Kinlin and I would walk through the Zen garden, with him brandishing his blessed cutlass, fighting vampires and packs of yellow jackals, which would try and surround our undying spirit. I would charge through the bush shouting our own private war cry of, "Above anything else, don't let them eat your poems!"

One night a couple of days later, the four of us had tuned into an old western on the television. It was a movie where the cavalry is charging down on a band of defenseless Indians; and while the women are picking up their children and running for their lives, Kinlin blurts out of nowhere, "DON'T LET THEM EAT YOUR POEMS!"

Everybody just stops what they are doing and turns towards him with their mouths open. Trout say's, "MY GOD, he just spoke a sentence! Where did he learn that?"

Kinlin somehow recognizing the gist of the question turns towards me with a sheepish grin on his face, and also one touched with guilt. At that moment I think he felt he had just given our secret battle cry to the world.

Trout said, "Davis, did you teach him that?"

"Yeah, I guess I did. Hell, I didn't know he could repeat it."

"What does it mean?"

"It's our sacred battle cry, the one our secret society of poet warriors screams every time we go into battle. Do you want to see our tattoos?"

"TATTOOS?" she screams, as any concerned new mother would, imagining Kinlin and I down at "The Parlor" sitting there while some drug crazed, heavy metal type punctures our bodies with AIDS-infected needles.

"What do you mean, TATTOOS?"

About that time, Kinlin lifts up his "Save The Whales" T-shirt and proudly shows off the flying eagle clutching a flaming sword in its blood red talons that I had so painstakingly drawn with colored felt markers.

Trout looks at me and says, "Now, how am I supposed to get that off?"

"You're not supposed to," I said, "tattoos are there forever, besides, you have to have one to belong to the club. Jose show her yours."

Jose lifts up his shirt and gets this big Yaqui grin on his face acting like a boy showing off his first erection to his folks. He had drawn it himself while looking in the mirror.

Trout asks, "What is it?"

Jose explains, with a look on his face that shows the piece of art needs no explaining, but says anyway, "As you can plainly see, it is a flying fish with a book tied to its back!"

"A book?" say's Trout, "What kind of a book?"

"It is, 'Rommel Drives On Deep Into Egypt' by Richard Brautigan. I was reading it last night in bed and thought it would make a great tattoo."

"And you, Bird Man?" she says, with a curious look.

"Oh, yeah, well Kinlin drew mine, here I'll show it to you."

I unbutton my shirt and showed her his drawing.

Trout turns her head to the side and say's, "What is it?"

"Can't you tell?" I ask with this unbelieving look on my face.

"Well it kind of looks like a rock with some weeds growing out of it," she said with a puzzled look on her face.

Kinlin looks over at her like she had just said a swear word.

"THOSE AREN'T WEEDS,"I said. "Those are FEATHERS!"

"Feathers?"

"Yeah, FEATHERS!"

She looks at Kinlin acting like he could answer her next question. "What is it supposed to mean?"

"Well, we were doing our tattoos," I said, "so I let him do mine. I didn't watch him do it, but I did look at his face as he drew it, and in it saw all the concentration of da Vince painting the Last Supper."

Trout, dying for an answer, asked, "Well, what does it mean?"

"OK. When he's finished I take a look, and then shrug my shoulders. It was kind of like 20 questions until he finally got the point and with a smile on his face pointed to it and then to my face. Well, I mimicked him doing the same thing, and he smiles and nods his head up and down.

Trout says, "Do you mean that he has done a portrait of you?"

"Yeah, I think that's what it is," I said.

Trout gets a sly smile and a knowing look on her face, and say's, "Well Davis, he got you pretty good, didn't he?"

Yeah, he did, I thought. The kid has only been here a couple of days and already he reads me like a book. He sees the same rock walls Trout has been seeing ever since she arrived. When he walked into the house for the first time he was probably wondering what that old truck was doing parked in the living room. The kid is probably so intuitive that he knew the answer to that after just being around me for a minute and a half. Now he has inscribed this fucking rock and feathers on the skin that covers my heart, and like a bad rash I have the Pigeon Man's legacy tattooed all over my chest.

It was amazing, but the eight-year-old inside me had been staying away. Oh, he had dropped in a few times to sit down with me and have a drink, and to tell me it was OK to have another. But basically the little son of a bitch had left me alone. He came around one night when Trout was pregnant to remind me what a shitty father I had been with my own kid. And how I couldn't even handle a harmless eight-year-old like him. So how could I expect to be a responsible dad to the new life growing in her stomach? Now the little monster has sent a friend of his to remind me of my failures, and he didn't just send some whiny little kid. He delivered on my doorstep a 1,000-year-old prophet.

Kinlin was no ordinary child. I had noticed that after the first day. I always had the feeling when he looked at me he was looking through all the walls I had built over the last fifty years. I also felt he had the spiritual power to open all the caskets that my dead hopes and dreams were buried in.

Trout brought a mirror with her that she made me look into every day. Now she had given it to the kid who has tied it to a sacred leather thong, and like a shaman displaying a new found token of the God's, has been religiously wearing it around his neck.

I was beginning more and more to see Jose's interpretation of the kid turning up in our lives as no accident, and as some part of a predestined plan.

His actions around Trout could only be explained as those of a little boy finally finding his mother. I still didn't know how he felt about me, or whether he saw me as father or friend, but if the karmic bond I had always felt with Trout was true, then maybe he was put into our lives to help tie the knot. The entire idea of it boggled my mind and forced me to think in spiritual terms that I had never thought of before.

He was the spit and image of the child Trout and I had expected to have. The day he arrived and walked in the back door you got the feeling he had finally found his home. Kinlin had brought Trout out of her shell and made her blossom into the woman that she had so desperately been trying to hide.

He had become a thirty-pound bag of spiritual confetti that had burst open and rained multi-colored flakes of womanhood over her troubled soul which fell from her hair like comets with every step she took.

I thought, how could she ever leave now that he has come into our lives? If she did tire of our love and the responsibilities that go with it would she take him with her? Was I setting myself up for the ultimate hard fall by investing every ounce of hope I had left in me by creating the illusion of foreverness? Nothing was forever. There really aren't any white-picket-fence dreams in the book that has been written about my life. I am just kidding myself to believe there were. Those dreams all died in the forties, somewhere on those elm-lined streets I ran through as a child in that little valley town of Merced.

The American Dream was born in little towns like that. Nobody got divorced, and if they did, the kids at school treated the torn-apart kids of the split marriage like the whole family had come down with the plague.

The only homosexual that I had ever heard about was the high school art teacher, who, like a bad "B" movie, left town and was never seen again.

My buddies and I grew up in the forties and fifties believing there wasn't a dragon big enough that we couldn't slay. Me being a football star for U.S.C. was already a known fact around my household by the time I was ten. There weren't failures, they were just called punts that were dropped, which had to be picked up again and run in for a score.

Those were the times of the "Big Bedroom Door," where all the whispered secrets of the society inside were locked up and kept from our innocent little eyes. There came a time in the early fifties where I dared to peek through the key hole, and saw a room inhabited by cannibalistic demons who fed on the hearts and spirits of everything I believed was good.

I saw my heroes as vulnerable beings, whose armor overnight became as thin and full of holes as the hope that was born in me on those warm, summer green playground fields. My favorite singer, Johnny Ace, shot himself in the head, and Superman was really a drunk. The Marines had retreated in Korea, and some of my tough-guy idols in Hollywood seemed to like men more than women.

My baby sitter, I was told, screwed half the football team, and then went back for seconds. The men who drove trucks for my father let me know, in hushed tones, that the women they were married to weren't the only ones they loved, and that the heart had enough room for a lot of beds. I was taught that the black kids I played baseball with had two names, one was, "Way to hit, Charles!" and the other was, "That little nigger, Charley, just dropped the ball." My big brother, who tuned me onto jazz and duck tailed hair, and who used to beat me up harmlessly as a kid, turned himself into a mean drunk who, later on in life, tried to seriously left hook me every chance he got.

The Pigeon Man was the only truth I had left, and he died before he could put it into words. He had wings and talons and a crop full of life, but he always held back and flew north whenever it came time to tell me how he felt.

Now my life was inhabited by a mini prophet, a drunken Yaqui warrior, and a woman who had the mirror of my life strapped to her chest, and I was finding out that these three people knew me better than I knew myself. I trusted them more than I had ever trusted anybody in my life, and if anyone of them would ever betray me, I knew that I would end up somewhere with the Pigeon Man, lying down and feeling the soft feet of celestial birds perched on my chest.

Kinlin had been with us for three days and was still sleeping in our bed. I told Trout it was time to cut the cord, and put him in his own room and to retie our own. She reluctantly agreed. We both decided that Jose would move into my studio and Kinlin could sleep in her old room.

We hadn't discussed him leaving, or looking any further for his roots. Trout wasn't about to bring it up, and I didn't have the heart to, so I thought for the time being I would just let it rest. I was also getting the gnawing feeling that Jose wasn't far from wrong, and that the kid was already home. I decided that in a few days I would go to the authorities and get a list of all the three-to four-year olds that were missing, under the guise that I was doing some research material for a book I was writing.

Jose and I spent a couple of hours putting the extra room in my studio in order. It was a nice, white airy space, with a sink and running water, a bathroom and a fridge. We brought in a bed and a soft chair, and a floor lamp to set next to it. He was pleased, and knew it was for the best, and that the boy needed his own room.

In the meantime, Trout and Kinlin were busy getting the other room in shape. Trout had finally moved her things into my closet, a move she had up until now been putting put off. I felt she had been reluctant to do it, because it would have just been another big leap into the lake of commitment, an extra chain she would have to pull off if she ever decided to leave.

Kinlin seemed excited as hell about moving into the room, that is, after she let him decorate it himself. The first thing Trout did was to get this huge roll of posters out of the closet and spread them out on the floor. She then let Kinlin know that it was up to him which ones he wanted to hang on the wall. He walked back and forth over them in deep concentrated thought, and finally picked a couple of my old exhibition posters. He also chose one of a Braque still life advertising a Paris retrospective, and one of Picasso's bronze goat from a Museum of Modern Art show.

I let him rummage through my extensive feather collection and told him to pick out what he wanted. When I opened the big plywood box and

136

exposed about fifty plastic bags of assorted feathers of all imaginable colors, he threw his arms up into the air acting like we had just unearthed a chest of ancient jewels. I could see his little incredible mind working, thinking that what we had just done was violating a tomb for all the beautiful birds that had ever flown. Trout got the staple gun, and with Kinlins' hands full of his favorite plumage, proceeded to tack them wherever his finger pointed.

He looked through an old *National Geographic,* and chose a photo of a polar bear family frolicking in the snow, and one of a Cheyenne medicine man in sepia tones.

I built a small desk with a wooden box for a stool, and put the set of felt tips I had given him, plus a stack of blank paper, in the middle.

The day before, Trout had taken him to a second-hand store to get him some clothes, and noticing he had wandered off, found him in the used book and magazine section. The children's books didn't interest him, but he did find the art books and *Field and Stream* magazines more to his taste, so Trout picked up a few and brought them home. Kinlin placed them neatly on his new desk, all ready and waiting for him to do some serious reading.

He insisted on having a winged lamp like the one we had in our room, so I got my perfectly preserved, and much treasured, red-tail wing, attached it to a base, and gave it to him for a present. He seemed to understand the gesture and smiled, then reached out and tenderly touched my leg. It was Kinlin's way of saying thank you, and a touch I would learn never needed words to be understood.

Trout let him go through some photos of us, and he picked out one of her and I sitting together in a chair. He pointed to a place above the head of the bed, beckoning Trout to tack it on.

Finally he took a portrait that he had done of Jose, one that had him looking like a cross between a Mexican bandit, and a beardless Jesus. With some scotch tape he attached it to the back of the Picasso goat. Jose walked in, and seeing him doing it, started to bitch about the fact that Don Quixote rode a donkey, and not some bearded, smelly, garbage eating beast. Kinlin acted hurt, and Jose noticed it. Jose cheered him up by saying that he had thought it over, and was proud to ride on the back of a golden goat, especially one that was made by a great master, a man that had Spanish blood flowing through his veins.

We all stood back and admired the room. Kinlin took us on a tour, using his little magical finger to point out his favorite pieces. He was proud of his own space, and would, as the weeks went on, turn it into a poetic playground. The room was a giant fetish, and Kinlin had placed his own private spiritual meaning on every feather and picture he had so thoughtfully hung.

CHAPTER 19

Kinlin had his space, Jose had his, and Trout and I finally had back ours. If there was ever enough reason to celebrate, then being able to go for a swim again with her was it.

That night Jose decided he was going to cook dinner, an Aztecan feast as he called it, prepared in a way fit only for kings, virginal princesses, and assorted priests. He headed out the door to go shopping, with Kinlin tagging along. I watched them get in the truck, and saw Jose tie bandanas around both of their heads. The squirrel chattered and hopped around the bay tree, as Don and Sancho rode that old burro of a pickup in a cloud of dust down the road.

Kinlin wouldn't let Trout wash off his tattoo, and walked around without his shirt as much as possible. The second they had slammed the truck doors he had it off and, like an unwanted layer of skin, threw it on the dashboard. Jose was teaching him Spanish, and as I watched them top the last hill with their arms moving with wild gestures, I could only imagine what the two bandits were talking about.

With them gone, Trout and I finally found us alone. It was the first time since Jose and Kinlin had arrived.

The house had suddenly taken on a Mojave duned stillness, and the tumbleweeds found themselves blowing over slowly, in the direction of the cactus flower setting at the beating heart table. I scooted next to her and she leaned against my chest.

She had just showered, and smelled like a breathing bar of lavender soap. Her hair was still damp and pressed cool against my face, and as I became lost in the moist, dark brown forest grass, I realized how much I had been missing her. I had longed for her smell, and the sweet warmth of her breath, mixed with the tenderness of the words that filled it. It had been weeks since we had made love, weeks that had turned into an eternity of empty calendar touches.

She opened her robe and placed my hands on her breasts, and said, "It's been awhile hasn't it?"

"Yes," I answered, "It has."

She laid her cheek on my arm and said, "I missed it."

"Me too, Trout, me too.

"Do you want to dance?"

"Yeah, that would be nice."

We walked over and put on the R and B station, and like two flamingos with wings unfolded, touched with feathered arms.

We drifted and moved to a tenor saxophone breeze, while the oak stared through the window and accompanied us with a late afternoon rustling of its leaves. Trout stepped back, and like an orchid breathing in its first light, opened her white petaled robe. She pulled me to her and placed my hands on her hips, and with her eyes telling me what we both needed, danced me into the bedroom.

We both knew that Jose had taken Kinlin so we could have some time alone, and he would stay away long enough for us to make sure we had it.

Trout let her robe drop to the floor, which landed on the rug like a cotton shadow. She stood in front of the late afternoon light coming through the windowed glass, and I watched the warm flush of the closing day reflect off her milked skin. Trout was showing me with her eyes that she had stepped out of the gray shade that had been covering her for over a month.

She undressed me tenderly, like I was a full mooned night, and my clothes were sewn together stars. Trout laid me on the bed and covered me like a soft summer eclipse, sending me into a sweet celestial darkness with the warmth of her breath on my eyes. She rubbed her skin with almond scented oil, and began to float over me as if she were a lotioned cloud.

Trout had filled The Pond with lilies, whose wet leaves moved and brushed against my body. They were gathering in my loins, blown there by the current of her touch. Her mouth was warm spring water sliding down my chest and running over my ribs. It paused at my stomach, and overflowed onto my thighs, and like a swirling, cascading wave, engulfed my hardening flesh.

She took me deep into blue violet waters where I saw the castles of Atlantis covered with silken grass. The pearlescent scales of Neptune reflected in her eyes, as her mouth whirled around me, and began to tap the geyser between my legs. I bent down and touched her face with my palms, and turned her gently onto her back. Trout was a warm moist lagoon, and like a boat full of beating hearts, I drifted into her. The air above us filled with powder blue cranes. I watched her eyes open wide and behold the wonder of their wings, flapping against the off-white walls.

Every movement of my groin released a hundred butterflies that were being born between our legs. They opened their wings and tickled our skin, and with every delicate thrust, a hundred more were born. Pelicans flew through the walls, and with wings beating, cooled my back. The hummingbirds returned and circled her hair, grabbing at strands, laying them Medusa-like on the pillow behind her head.

Trout moaned like a pine in the wind, and her sighs seethed from the pores of her skin. I reached down with oiled fingers and gently stroked her garden of silk, and watched as she sat up and clawed at the sheet. Her backbone bowed like a willowy branch, and I felt the primrose scream begin at her legs and flow from her throat. I had waited for her, and with all the month long essence that had welled in me, erupted inside of her.

The startled birds took flight, and as the pelicans dropped petals of rose on the bed, the cranes moved their wings and fanned the heavy, mist filled air in the room.

I lay on her stomach and listened to her heart ripple against her chest. She was lost, flying up somewhere with the birds, and I was in The Pond, basking with the golden fish. Her body glistened with oil mixed with sweat, and I saw images of rainbows reflecting off her breasts. Trout's skin was absorbing me, and as I floated an inch from her heart, I thought, how could I ever live without her. She was the sum total of every poem I had ever written, and every sculpture I had ever made. She was the nectar of all the flowers I had ever seen, and her scent was filling my lungs with perfumed smoke. I felt at that moment that I had loved her in life times before and, I knew too, that I would love her till this one ended.

I pulled myself up even with her eyes, and said, "Trout, it was never better than this."

With a flushed face she stared back and said, "Yes, it was so soft. For a minute or two I felt like I was up somewhere soaring with the birds."

"Yeah, I know," I said, "I watched your eyes grow wings. Whether you realize it or not, sometimes when we're making love, you splash out of The Pond like a snow goose catching the first cloud heading south."

"Oh, I was up there," she said, "was I loud?"

"Not too bad," I said, "kind of like a runaway freight carrying a load of cymbals, or maybe even a factory for smoke alarms that just caught fire."

She chuckled, then got real serious and said, "My God! Do you think Kinlin will be able to hear us?"

"Nah, and even if he does he'll just think he's hearing a cat giving birth to a truck."

"Come on Davis, I'm serious."

"OK. Why don't I just go into his room and close the door, then you scream, and I'll see whether I can hear it or not."

"You're joking," she said, looking out of the corners of her smiling eyes.

"Joking?" I said, standing up and heading for the door, "Hell, I don't want the kid to be traumatized thinking that the sounds that he might be hearing were of me taking out your appendix."

I walked into his room, shut the door, and yelled, "OK Scream!"

Hearing nothing, I yelled louder, "Come on Trout, scream!"

She yelled back, "I can't!"

"Why not?" I answered with a skin-cracking grin on my face.

"Because I don't know what I sound like when I'm having an orgasm, that's why."

"Well," I said, "just try a little method acting, and imagine yourself as an African elephant giving birth to 1,000-pound Siamese twins, after a six-week labor."

"Davis, this isn't funny, get back in here!"

I walked back in and saw her with the sheet pulled up under her nose, mumbling, "I don't like this game."

"Listen Trout," I said, "to tell you the truth, Kinlin is so endowed with supernatural powers that he doesn't have to hear us making love, he can probably tune in and feel it."

"Do you think so?" She said, pulling the sheet down.

"Yes," I said seriously, "the boy has something very special going on inside of him, and for him to figure out when we are sharing something intimate behind closed doors, would be a piece of cake."

Speaking the words tenderly, she said, "He is special, isn't he?"

"Yeah, he is, Trout."

"Baby, isn't it amazing how much he looks like the Kinlin that we talked about having, and of how much he looks like us?"

"Yes," I said, realizing that this was the first time she had brought it up.

"And isn't it amazing that Jose's uncle found him at about the exact same time I had the miscarriage?"

"Yes," I said, again, realizing where this was headed.

"You know, I've been thinking, and maybe you might think this is crazy, but isn't it possible that he could be a reincarnation of what I lost?"

She said this with questioning eyes, but with a look that also suggested that she wanted some affirmation that maybe it was the truth.

I entered this carefully. "Yeah, I have thought about it, but I'm a real skeptic when it comes to those things. But to be perfectly honest, it has entered my mind lately."

"You too?" she exclaimed, grabbing my arm.

"Yes," I answered, "there is something about all of this that is uncanny. I can't define it, but I feel there is a natural union between the three of us, and especially between you and him."

"I know," she said, "I have this strange feeling that he is mine. I don't know why, but it's just a force that overtakes me whenever I'm with him."

"I know, Trout, I've seen it. He sure has brought out the mother in you."

"It's not only that," she said, turning to stare out the window, "I'm beginning to feel like his mother, and I have this overpowering feeling that Kinlin really is mine. Do you think that's crazy?"

"No," I said, not wanting to tell her too much of how I was feeling. If a thing like reincarnation did exist, then an example of it walked in the door four days ago holding hands with Jose, "but if you aren't his mother," I added, "you should be."

We embraced, and holding each other close thought of futures that included a sweet child, hopes and dreams, and redwood replacing pickets in a fence that our parents tried so hard to teach us were supposed to be painted white.

Our serene visions were broken by Jose's truck careening up the drive.

I kissed her softly, and with my hand tenderly touching the side of her face, said. "It looks like the bandits are back. We'd better dry off because it looks like our swim is over."

She looked back with those two gray-green diamonds that someone had mistakenly labeled eyes. "You do love me, don't you?"

"More than you'll ever know Trout," I said, "and if you don't want the whole world to know, then I suggest you go take a shower because that love is smeared all over your body, mixed together with that sweet smelling oil."

Trout headed outside in her robe and towel, and met Don and Sancho on the steps. Kinlin leaped up into her arms, almost hitting her in the face with the black plastic handled fish net that was in his hand. It was full of assorted trinkets that Jose had bought for him as they were waltzing down the aisles of the hardware store.

"Kinlin what do we have here?" Trout said, beaming.

He held up the net full of new fetishes like it was the trophy head of a slain enemy, then like a mystic laying Tarot cards on a silken tablecloth, put them on the steps, one by one.

Jose was busy unloading bags from the car and lugging them into the house. As he was weaving in and out of Kinlin's treasures, he said, "Amigos, I have bought enough food to feed all of Mexico City, and if everybody will leave me alone for the next three hours, I will prepare our dinner. I have in these bags enough hot peppers to raise the temperature in the house 20 degrees."

Trout says to him, as he's juggling the sacks through the screen door, "Jose, where did Kinlin get all of this stuff?"

"Well it is like this," he said. "Me and Little Fish were coming out of the super market and he spots the mechanical horse ride and gets this puzzled look on his face, so I put the bags in the truck and walk over and put him on and stick in 50 cents. After a ride that turned his eyes into the size of hubcaps, he gets off and points to the hardware store, so we walk in. The boy is in heaven, and starts running down the aisles. So I grab a basket and follow him. He points at the basket and says, 'NO!' He then points to the fish net. So I get it for him, and then we proceed to shop. About half an hour later we have it filled up, as you can see."

Jose was right about that. Kinlin had laid on the steps everything from a month's supply of Gummy Bears to a plastic bag full of rubber Glow Worms. He had evidently freaked out in the fishing tackle section, and picked up an assortment of bright colored lures, ones with feathers and shiny metal pieces hanging off them. He had enough lures in the net to outfit an entire bass charter cruise. After unpacking them, he held them up with his tiny hands for Trout to admire.

"Well, my little fisherman, what are we going to do with all of these?" Trout said, staring into the fishnet.

He reaches down and picks up a handful, and starts hooking them to his T-shirt, and says with his little fish voice, "Poems!"

Trout reaches down and picks him up, and with her new mother's eyes, says, "Oh little boy, my God, you are an angel. Come on! I'm going to give you a shower."

Kinlin knew immediately what she meant. He ripped off his shirt and headed at a dead run towards the back of the house.

I watched them both turn the corner and heard the water being turned on. I listened as they both laughed and squealed, and could almost see their love floating in the steam above the wood shed. I was almost tempted to join them, but felt that this was some warm waterfall time they should have alone.

Jose yells from the kitchen, "Amigo, come in and let the fish play alone, let's have a drink!"

I walk into the kitchen and Jose hands me a Dos Equis, and a shot of Cuervo 1800. "Compadre, I want to propose a toast to friendship, Trout, and to the little prophet, and to tell you one more time that no matter where I am in the world, if you ever need me for anything, I'll be there."

Jose was serious; it was something that I could read in his eyes.

"Cheers, amigo," I said, clinking his bottle of beer, "and I'm glad you're here. I'm sure that before summer's over, I'm going to have to take you up on that."

"Yes," he said, pouring another shot, "I think you will."

"Amigo," he said seriously, "have you given any more thought to what we talked about a couple of day's ago?"

"You mean about the boy?"

"Yeah, about the boy."

"Yes I have, and there are some things going on that I'm having trouble explaining to myself."

"My friend," he said, grabbing my shoulder, "just let it be, as I said before it is out of your hands. Destiny will take its course. I have watched the boy and Trout together, and I have observed you and him together too, and I tell you, there is no doubt in my mind about where he came from, and whom he belongs to.

My aunt, the one who lives in Baja, has a sister who is one who 'Knows,' and part of that inner knowledge rubbed off on her as she was growing up. When I was getting in the truck with the boy, getting ready to head up here, I said to her that I hope we find his parents, and she said, 'You will not find his parents, he will find them.' I tell you again, amigo, you are his father."

"I don't know, Jose," I said, "I would like to believe that, but it all seems so farfetched to me."

Jose looked me in the eye and said, "Man, just look at him. He is a cross between you and Trout. He even looks like you both. The boy is Trout and you. I see it every day. There is a magic that fills the air every time the three of you are together. He breathes her tenderness and softness from the pupils of his eyes, and he has your heart. I bet that if the three of you had a doctor listen to your hearts all at the same time, he would hear only one beat. The only thing that I'm worried about is that they don't break all at the same time."

"What do you mean?" I said, taking a drink.

"Trout is a wonderful woman and I hope she stays with you the rest of your life. I hope that when you are 80 years old, lying on the bed of death, she is there to hold your hand and kiss your soul goodbye. Even though I believe that your bond is ancient, and as thick as a Peruvian pyramid, I still see a placenta-thin web holding you together. The boy will be a bond to sanctify your love and to fill your heart, but as I said before, she is troubled, and her back still has room for a lot more stones. I just hope the boy doesn't become one of them."

He was right about her. I couldn't deny it. Trout was troubled, and I had been living with it for weeks now. I always tried to convince myself that love conquered all, but in the end, I knew that fear was tougher.

When I was a kid and boxed at the local club on weekends, my father was always giving me tips that were meant to help me when I finally grew up and hit the streets. One of the things he tried to impress upon me was to always size a man up before you fucked with him, because a good big man could always whip a good little man. Well, my dad fought in the ring under the name of Red Davis in the 30's. He was a tough as nails, carrot-topped middleweight, notoriously well known in the streets and bars of central California. He taught me how to defend myself, and how to throw a good hip-powered left hook;

tools that helped me to move through life without getting my ass kicked too badly. The only problem with Red was that he didn't teach me enough about the Main Event, and that was the eternal match between love and fear. I had been TKO'd so many times by love that I ended up believing that it was the good little guy, and that fear was really Mike Tyson in disguise.

Trout had showed me over the last couple of months that she was afraid of just about everything. That included her past, her future, and all of the emotions she was feeling towards me. Deep in my heart I was hoping that Kinlin and the love he was capable of bringing out in her was really David, the shepherd boy, wrapped up in a 30-pound body.

Jose saw me deep in thought and said, "Compadre, don't think about it too much. We cannot change destiny. It will take you and Trout wherever you are supposed to go. Just try to enjoy the love that is filling this house, and in the end it will make its full circle and come back to you. Here, have another drink."

I took the drink and knew he was right. All I could do was to love her and be honest about it. I knew she was the kind of person that in the end would make a decision that was the easiest for her to live with, and right now this was the life she was choosing.

Jose said, "Hey man, come on, we're supposed to be celebrating tonight, why don't you go check on your two loved ones, maybe they are drowning!"

I grabbed my glass and walked over to the window behind my desk and looked out towards the shower. The steaming, piped-in waterfall behind the shed was drenching them. Kinlin was covered from head-to-toe with lather, while Trout, with alabaster skin glistening, shampooed his hair. They were laughing away the afternoon, and it filled my heart to watch them. My God, I thought, they are both absolutely beautiful. A magical pair that I believed had the power, if they felt like it, to swim up that stream of water and disappear into the pipes.

I looked at Trout and I thought something was definitely different about her. Her attitude had changed and I had already realized that. But it was her body that wasn't the same. She turned to the side and I saw her profile, and immediately I knew what it was. It was her breasts. They had grown tremendously. Over the last month she had buried herself in layers of emotional protecting clothes, and stacks of blankets, and seeing her naked was a thing I wasn't afforded too often. Even when we were in bed that afternoon I was so lost in the ecstasy of the hour that their size didn't register in my head. But seeing her standing out there in the mist at that moment, I realized something important had happened in the growth department. It was a subject I would have to bring up later in the quietness of the bedroom.

Jose yelled from the kitchen, "Amigo, what is with Trout and the fish?"

"They're about as clean as anyone can get," I answered.

"That's too bad," he said, "because after they eat this pot of grease that I'm putting together, they'll need another shower!"

I walked into the kitchen and saw that Jose had turned it into a Francis Bacon still life. There were dismembered chickens and pieces of red pork scattered everywhere. Peppers of all sizes and colors were strewn over the counter, mixed in with masses of chorizo and tripe.

"What the fuck are you making?"

"Amigo, this is the Aztecan stew I was talking about. It is written on the walls of the pyramids and in the scrolls of legend that it is capable of giving even the most impotent of priests an aching, month-long, granite-hard erection. It is something that, after I eat, will make me go out to town and look for a woman."

"Yes, my friend," I said, "you've been here for four days now and haven't had a taste. How are you surviving?"

"It is not easy, amigo. I knew what Trout and you would be doing today after I left with the kid, and I have to tell you, I was very envious."

"Yeah, I wanted to tell you how much I appreciated that move, and that it was what she and I needed."

"I know. I saw it in the eyes of you both. As a matter of fact, I could smell it. It was starting to fill up the room with so much smoke I could swear that your hearts were on fire."

"Well, I'll tell you," I said. "It was the most wonderful two hours we have spent together since she arrived."

"I know amigo," he said, throwing chicken legs in the pot. "I saw it in her eyes while she was on her way to the shower. Even if I had been born blind, I still would have known."

"Why's that?"

"Because I picked up the scent of oil mixed with almonds, and I knew that you didn't use the time to bake sweet rolls. That's why."

Jose and I were laughing as Trout and Kinlin came walking through the back door. He was wrapped in her towel, and she was radiant with her damp hair falling in ringlets down the terry cloth shoulders of her robe.

Trout asked. "Jose, what is this?"

"It is the exact duplication of the kitchen of a Peruvian whore house. What else?" he answered, stirring the pot.

Trout laughed and took Kinlin into his room to dress. He came out wearing one of his new Goodwill T-shirts and a pair of white Mexican peasant pants that Jose had brought. He, of course, was barefooted. It was an act that always occurred immediately after you tried to put shoes on him. He sure looked like little David. All he needed in his hand to make the picture complete was a leather sling with a round stone in it.

Trout, Jose and I, spent the next hour in the kitchen drinking beer and laughing at the bandit's stories. Kinlin had gotten his colored pens and paper and, while lying on top of the table, drew pictures of the three of us standing and talking in the middle of the most colorful mass of food he had ever seen.

We ate that night behind plates of folded tortillas, benzene-powered chili, and a stew that looked like the scrapings of all the streets in Tijuana.

Kinlin, as always, sat next to Trout on a stack of books that included a four-pound volume, titled, *A Dictionary of Art and Artists*, *A Pictorial History Of Georges Braque*, and *The Complete Do-It-Yourself Manual Of Home Repairs*. By the time dinner was finished, he had enough grease on his shirt to qualify him for a member of A. J. Foyt's pit crew.

The night moved on and after the telling of the last Jose adventure, and the cleaning up of the mini mechanic, we decided it was time for bed. Kinlin hugged Jose and me, and clung to Trout like a baby gibbon holding on for dear life to his mother as they swung haphazardly through the trees. She tucked him in, and as she was reading him a story out of *Field and Stream* about the grizzlies of the Yukon, he dozed off under the reflection of the ceiling stars.

Trout and I were undressing for bed as we heard Jose's truck heading out the drive.

Trout said, "Where is Jose going at this hour?"

"To Sebastopol, I imagine. To have a drink at Jasper's."

"At midnight?" she asked with a twisted look on her face.

"Yeah," I said with a sly grin. "I think he had too much of the Aztecan stew."

"Aztecan stew?" she said, pausing, as she pulled back the sheets.

"Yeah, it's reputed to have special powers in the annals of championship hard on's," I said, taking off my pants.

She stood there and looked at my naked crotch, and said, "Well, I saw you eat three bowls, Davis. Does that mean we're in for a long night?"

"Could be Trout, could be." I said, flicking off the switch on the wall that controls the overhead light.

We slid between the sheets, and as I wrapped myself around her, she reached over, and like a magician turning on a translucent bird, switched on the winged lamp.

Trout and I made love that night as wonderfully as we had during the day. After the bed's tides had ebbed, and after the flying fish submerged, I asked her about her breasts.

She told me that after the miscarriage, she had, without wanting to tell me, begun to take the pill, and the largeness of her breasts was the voluptuous outcome, and the change that I was seeing. We both agreed that it had been a good idea. For me it was a sign that during those sex-starved weeks she hadn't given up on us.

CHAPTER 20

The next couple of weeks were ones of newfound family adventures with Jose becoming a charter member. The four of us did everything together, and it looked like Kinlin had found his home. I had put off the idea of going to the authorities, wanting to believe, as Jose had said, that it would have been a fruitless venture anyway.

Kinlin seemed to me that he had found his place, with two parents and an uncle living in it. He was the happiest and gentlest boy I had ever seen, and in the three weeks he had been with us hadn't cried once. The boy was soft and kind. One who I believed had the golden heart of a poet. He was starting to talk like a magpie in a mixture of Spanish and English, and would sit for hours thumbing through his growing collection of *Field and Stream* and assorted magazines about art and photography. The walls of his room were beginning to fill with his drawings of galaxied worlds and portraits of us. He had done a series of the "Poet Warrior Society" crashing through the dark forests of life fighting off purple horned monsters and scaled dragons. Whenever Trout's back was turned he would tattoo himself from head to toe, then run through the house with his silver sword and lightning bolts drawn on his arms yelling, "SAVE THE POEMS! SAVE THE POEMS!"

Trout had finally given up bathing him three or four times a day and decided to let him do his thing, thinking that it was a good way to conserve water.

After taking off all the hooks, she and Kinlin sat down and strung all of his bass lures on a piece of leather thong, which he wore around his neck every minute of his waking hours. The only time I ever saw him upset was when she insisted that he couldn't wear it to bed.

Jose had woven him a headband out of red leather, and had attached silver bells to the front. To witness him standing up in a cart moving down the aisles of the grocery store, tattooed like the "King of Borneo," with his sparkling sword in hand was a sight that would put every other child in the store into a mother-grabbing state of shock.

He was the "Mystic Child," the "Warrior Prince," and acted like the world was his. If there were evil, then he would cut it to pieces with his undying pursuit of the protection of "The Poetry Of Life." Kinlin would paint pictures of castles in a storm always shielded from the rain by a halo of yellow light. His group portraits of us were always accompanied by constellations of stars that circled our heads, often with him flying in the air above wearing a cape with wings drawn on the back.

He had become the self-anointed guardian of the "Holy Grail of Unity," the one who bound us all together. And Kinlin was the elfin soldier who, I believe, would fight to the death to preserve it.

I would see Trout standing on the porch watching him protectively as he ran through the field chasing squirrels and singing to the hawk. She would shake her head in worry as he tried to climb every tree on the place. Like every boy, he brought home snakes and frogs and wounded birds. His collection of feathers grew with every rising of the sun, and Trout was wearing out the staple gun just trying to follow him and his pointing finger around his room.

Jose and I fixed the cracks in the pond outside and repaired the pipes that sent fresh water cascading down the eight-foot rock fall into the basin below. Kinlin would spend hours thrashing around in it with Excalibur in hand fighting sharks and anything else he thought was threatening the secrets that only he knew existed in the depths below.

I bought him a little used bike with training wheels that we allowed him to paint himself. He took one of my spray cans of appliance white and covered every inch of his new stallion with it. I made him a tail of red rags that trailed from the back like flames from a torch whenever he took off on one of his adventures.

The three of us would sit on the porch and watch, as the "King of The World" would take off down the road on his white charger sending squirrels and anything else in his way into hurried flight.

He had gotten hold of some scotch tape and had covered the handlebars with feathers and anything else he thought was deserving of his invincible steed. The boy had turned the bike into a kinetic talisman, and he was the Archangel at the controls, and beware the demon that got in his way, because Kinlin had taken "The Oath." The more I saw him in action, the more I believed that it was a vow that was as inherent to him as the feathers were to the hawk flying above his head.

Jose had a cousin in Eureka and he decided to drive up for a couple of days for a visit. Trout, Kinlin and I watched as he took off down the road, and by the look on the boy's face you would have thought that the red-tail had just fallen out of the sky and died. Trout and I convinced him that Jose would be back in a couple of days. Just to make sure that his compadre wasn't totally gone Kinlin went out to Jose's room and brought back one of his bandanas and hung it on the wall above his bed. It was a tender act of love between one friend and another. One that made me wonder what part of Trout the boy would hang from his heart if she ever left.

The three of us spent the next few days as the family that I was somehow beginning to feel we were destined to be. Trout was becoming mother, and I knew that she had gone beyond the point of ever feeling anything other than that when it came to Kinlin. I wasn't quite sure of my role yet. I loved the boy and that was a fact I couldn't deny. The three of us had become the family I had always wanted to have myself, one full of outward affection and harmonious love, and one I hoped would survive the ravages of time.

My defeats of the past and the heavy stone-filled baggage I carried around with me were still interfering with the dreams that wanted to move in and build that little house on that tree-lined street in the town that was called, "Foreversville." I was 51 years old and 47 years older than that little boy and an evident 32 older than Trout and was being confronted with my emotional and physical mortality on a daily basis. That piece of property with the little house still had a place in my heart, but had over the years been subdivided so many times that I felt it only had enough room left in it for a mobile 14-foot trailer. It was a space that was definitely not big enough, or secure enough, for a young family.

I had been living for the last 20 years with the philosophy of, "Never own more than you can tie to the back of a Harley," and here I was being confronted, just four years away from the title of "Senior Citizen," with a laid-in-my-lap family. One that consisted of a boy who was a lot smarter and wiser than me and a young woman who was dragging around a carved iced anchor that could melt at any minute in the late summer sun.

I felt that fate was up to something and that it had placed the three of us together for a reason, and if we were supposed to be the eternal triangle then I think that I could handle it. But if somewhere along the line it decided to change into some distorted geometric design with a big piece missing, then I'm not sure if I could exist within those borders. I had always been a realist when it came to my art, and had confined myself to staying within the lines, but the minute I started to deal with the abstract it pressed buttons in my senses that would bend and distort any relationship I had with what I thought was real. I knew that if this triangle started to fragment and lines and corners started to fall off, then there wouldn't be any masking tape made that would be able to put back a hardedge of containment around it. The colors and dynamic tension of the composition would spill out and run down the sides of the canvas and turn me into a New York gallery's latest example of their newest piece of blobby, non-objective shit.

We spent those days without Jose basking in the sun of contentment. Kinlin tied the three of us together with the chain of hope, and I saw in his eyes that it would have taken an army to drag him away from it.

He was with us wherever we went, and on the couple of occasions where a kindly woman commented on the "Beautiful grandson I had," beamed with pride when I said, "No, this is my boy!" Kinlin was the kind of child that you just stared at when you first saw him. He would fill a grocery store or a city side walked street with an ethereal presence that you couldn't turn away from. When Trout would get the compliments of, "Beautiful boy," she would react like any proud mother, saying, "Yes, we think so too." Kinlin had moved into our hearts and I knew that he would never allow us to move him out. If anyone would have tried he would have grabbed his silver sword and necklace of charms and looked them straight in the eye, and charging into their masses shouted, "Save the Poems!" and, "You'll never take this prince alive!"

Jose returned a few days later and, after saying hello, went straight to bed and slept for 24 hours. The next morning he staggered into the kitchen and would have drank the coffee right out of the pot if I hadn't stopped him. Kinlin ran up to him and jumped into his arms almost knocking Jose through the screen door.

Holding Kinlin in his arms, he said, "My friends, I have been to war and drank with the devil. I smoked opium with a family of Samurai and made love to a voodoo priestess. As Jesus is my witness, I thought I would never make it back alive!"

I said, smiling, "Jose, it seems like you had a great time!"

"Yes, my friends, I just had a vacation laying on the beaches of hell," he said, while pouring brandy into his coffee.

"Well," I said, "is it an adventure you want to talk about?"

"Yes," he said, "but first I must sit down and give the boy a proper hug and give him the present I have brought for him."

Kinlin became all eyes as Jose reached deep into a paper bag and almost went into ecstatic shock when Jose pulled out a snakeskin belt. It was a beautiful piece of handcrafted work, clasped together with a turquoise-studded bone buckle. Jose had gotten the smallest size available, but it was still about 6 inches too long. Kinlin couldn't care less. He ran into his room and put on his faded jeans, then charged back out standing in front of us like one of the "Three Musketeers." He was a "Musketeer," who, at that moment, was waiting impatiently for one of his servants to tie the sacred sash around his waist.

Trout tenderly fitted it around him and buckled him up. It was the signal for Kinlin to run back into his room and grab his sword and jam it between the belt and his pants. He came out with his headband on, the bass-lure talisman necklace around his neck and, of course, Excalibur tucked into his new snakeskin belt. He was a sight! He had a huge grin on his face and a blue felt tip pin in his hand, which he handed to me. Pointing to his arm he looked up at me, and said, "Tattoo!"

I drew a snake with flames hissing out of its mouth, which uncoiled at his upper arm and ended at his wrist. He stepped back in a way to show us that he was now ready to be admired. As we stood up and applauded, shouting, "Hail to the King," he charged out the back door waving his sword totally prepared to slay any beasts that would be unfortunate enough to get in his way.

Now that Kinlin was gone, Jose thought it OK to tell us about his trip.

I said, "Jose, so tell us about Eureka?"

"Eureka?" he said, with a look on his face that would make one think that he had never heard of it.

"Eureka?" he said again, "I never made it to fucking Eureka! Hell, I got as far as a place called Redding, and that was it!"

"Redding?" I said, turning to look at Trout.

"Yeah, fucking Redding!" he said, glaring into my eyes, "Have you ever been to Redding?"

"Yeah," I answered, "why?"

"Because I want to know what it looks like, that's why! I don't remember a damn thing about it!"

I thought, hell, he could have been in Anchorage Alaska for all he knew.

"What do you mean you don't remember a thing about it? Jesus, you were gone for three days," I said, chuckling.

"Amigos," he said, acting like I had just asked him if he understood the theory of relativity, "three days, fuck! It might as well have been three years by the way I feel."

"How do you feel?" I asked, with a halfway grin on my face.

"Like I was eaten by a rabid dog and thrown back up at the rate of a pound a day," he said, standing up to pour some more brandy in his coffee.

"You can't believe the woman I met," he said, walking back in and sitting down at the table, much like a 400-pound man would after just returning from a five mile run.

"She was the craziest, fucking woman I have ever seen," he continued, "and then there were her three sisters!"

"Oh, oh," I said, "Jose, haven't you done this before?"

"Yes!" he said, rubbing his brow, "but never locked in a two- man tent on the shores of a lake called Shasta for two days and nights. Fuck! I didn't even have time to eat! And I'm not even going to tell you about the drugs!"

Jose stopped and laid his head in his arms and groaned like a bear with a bad tooth.

I said, "Jose, I think we've got the picture. It's a warm day, why don't you take Kinlin and go lay in the pond. I think it might do your head some good."

"OK amigo, by the way, where do you keep the aspirin?" He said that standing up, almost falling backwards over the bench.

"Up there in the cupboard," I said, "in front of the whiskey."

Trout and I watched as he shuffled into the other room and opened the cupboard door. Jose reached in, grabbed the bottle of aspirin, and poured out a handful. Then he stuck his other hand in for the bottle of bourbon and filled his cup. After chasing the pills with the booze he walked out the door. He pulled off his shirt, yelling, "Little fish, come on, you and uncle Jose are going for a swim, but please amigo don't splash and fight sharks today, because I am going to teach you how to float and meditate very quietly."

Trout looked over at me from across the table and while holding my hand smiled and said, "Your friend is the craziest man I have ever seen,"

"My friend?" I said, "Hell! He's your friend too!"

"I know," she said, "he is our friend, and a good one too."

Jose and Kinlin spent a good three hours in the pond, which saved Trout the trouble of having to wash off his tattoos.

The day ended and the night moved in like an ebony blanket covering the house and everyone in it. Trout and I swam in our lamb-skin-covered bed and afterwards fell arm-in-arm, into a deep satisfied sleep.

CHAPTER 21

Weeks passed and took us all into late September. Trout hadn't returned to school, and dealing with her mother over the last couple of weeks had been a draining ordeal. Trout had been adamant about her decision, and her mother in turn, had laid part of the blame on me. The presence of Kinlin was as baffling to her as it was to everyone else who was involved in our lives. Explaining him away as a relative of Jose's was as confusing to them as it was to us. But the truth, (if there was one), would be so far out that they would think Jose had not only brought the kid from Mexico, but a car load of strange mushrooms that had forever altered our minds. We had had a few visitors over the last couple of weeks and the presence of Kinlin mystified them all. Telling them that he was a nephew of Jose's worked pretty well until they saw the boy clamor up Trout's body acting like he wanted to be breast-fed.

Trout's mom came up to talk about the college situation and after seeing how the boy related to the two of us, said over breakfast, "He seems to have taken to the both of you quite well."

"Yes," said Trout, "he certainly has."

Trout's mother was an intelligent woman and I knew would be hard to fool. Even without the PhD she would have still qualified for a life membership in "Mensa."

Trout's mom asked, curiously, "Where are his parents?"

That was a question we had never been asked, and one that would have had led us into a stuttering babble if Jose hadn't have jumped in and said, "They live down in Baja."

"Oh," mom said, "and what is the occasion that allows him to be able to travel all the way up here with Jose?"

Again Trout looks towards me hoping that I will have an answer to the never-before-asked-question.

Jose again saves the moment by saying from the kitchen, "Oh, you see, he is the son of my brother who has gone on a two month trip to Spain with his wife. They didn't want to burden the child with such a long trip so they thought it would be better to leave him with uncle Jose, who he loves very much."

Well, that should do it, I thought.

"But, he doesn't look Mexican," mom countered.

Think again, Davis!

Jose says, "Oh yeah, he comes from a long line of Castilians. You know, light skin and light eyes, and if I was to really grit my teeth and tell you the truth I think somewhere along the family line a gringo climbed the family tree, and the boy is a throw-back from that."

Good, Jose, I thought that ought to end the inquiry.

But mom was persistent, and said, "But Kinlin is not a Mexican name is it?"

Trout stood up. "Excuse me, but I have to pee."

I was getting so nervous that I felt like standing up and saying, "Excuse me, but I have to drive to New York!"

Jose was also getting a little twitchy. So he tried to level himself out by sneaking another shot of Brandy into his French roast.

Jose cleared his throat, and said, "No, that is his nick-name. You see, off the coast of Baja there is a little fish that we call the 'Kinlino,' and on the day that the boy was born his father, who is a fisherman, brought home the biggest catch of 'Kinlino' that he had ever hauled in. So they started to call him 'Kinlino,' which, after awhile, was shortened to 'Kinlin,' and walking in with an Academy Award-winning smile, he added, "and that's the reason!"

Well, I thought, that was one hell of an answer. I almost was starting to believe it myself.

Trout walked out of the bathroom looking to me like she had just had another miscarriage and rolled her eyes up towards the ceiling.

Wanting to change the subject, I said, "Isn't it an interesting name?"

"Yes it is," Mom said.

"Yes it is," Jose said.

"Yes it is," Trout said.

"Yes it is," Kinlin said.

I was waiting for all the neighbors to walk in, and in unison cry out, "YES IT IS!"

I wanted to end the conversation so I ended up by saying something like, "It sure is a nice morning."

"YES IT IS!" Kinlin shouted, with a little chicken-shit smile on his face.

I thought, he knows what's going on here, the damn little prophet.

Mom says, "He certainly is a beautiful boy, and if I didn't know any better I would swear that he belonged to the both of you."

"Why's that?" I said, coughing out the words.

"Well, just look at him," Trout's mom said. "He has Trout's eyes and her skin. He even has the color of your hair Davis, that is when you had some. And look at his features; they're a mixture of both of yours. There is an amazing resemblance. Strange, isn't it?"

"Yes it is," we all said, almost in unison, Kinlin included.

"By the looks of his room," mom said, "it looks like he's going to be staying awhile."

"Oh, just for a few weeks, that's all," I said, lying through my teeth.

"Well, he sure is a bright child," Trout's mom said, "he has something special about him, but I can't quite put my finger on it. What's the reason for all the tattoos?"

At that point, Kinlin pulls off his Budweiser T-shirt, and acting like he was displaying scars from some imaginary battle with the evil forces of the world shows off his latest addition.

Trout's mom asks, "What's that?"

After looking at the map of Baja covering his chest and stomach, Trout and I were wondering the same thing ourselves.

Jose said, "Oh, yeah, I put that on him early this morning. He wanted to know where I was born, so I drew a map for him on a piece of paper. After he saw the shape and design he insisted that I tattoo him with it."

"What's the red circle there in the middle?" mom asked.

I could tell by the look on Trout's face that she and I were wondering the same thing.

Jose got noticeably nervous, and gave much thought to the words that he was about to speak. "Well, you see, as I have told the two of them before, the boy is special and seems to know some things that others don't."

"What do you mean?" mom asked, looking over at Kinlin.

Jose looked intently at Trout and myself. I could see in his eyes that he didn't want to give away too much of the secret that the three of us were beginning to believe was true. The truth that the boy was, indeed, blessed with a third eye. But knowing Jose, he would have to titillate Trout's mother just a little bit. So he continued. "Well, after I drew it on him he looked back at the drawing I made, and with a pen marked that circle on the map. Then he handed me the red pen and told me to mark it on the map that was tattooed on him."

"What does it mean?" mom asked, with a furrowed brow.

Trout and I were thinking the same thing and would have asked the question ourselves if mom hadn't done it first.

"You see," he said, clearing his throat, "my aunt has a sister, and she lives in a little village exactly at the spot that he marked with the pen."

"My, that's strange," mom said, looking around the table, "how did he know?"

"Well, that's the whole point," Jose said, while taking a sip from his laced coffee, "he didn't!"

"Oh, it's probably just a coincidence," she said, smiling.

"Yeah, it probably is," he said, staring into his coffee cup, knowing that he was reading in the grounds the results of a bad score on a polygraph test.

What he didn't tell mom that day, and what he told us later that night after she left, was that Kinlin had marked exactly on the map the location of the village where his aunt lived. That in itself was strange enough and could be explained away as an accident; except there was something that he didn't tell her. That was his aunt was a mystic. Not just a fortune teller, or one that spreads Tarot cards on the table and tells you if you are going to get laid or not, but a person that can look into your soul and tell you about past and future lives. He said that the boy knew where she lived just as easily as he knew where this house was located.

The last statement was a signal for Trout and I to reach out and grab each other's hand and squeeze hard.

Jose said, "Listen, we have all watched the boy everyday for over two months now, and you have to had seen that he is not like others. He is also one who knows, and he has come into our lives for a reason, and that reason is becoming more evident every day."

"And what is that?" I asked.

"To show us who we are!" he said, standing up and walking into the kitchen.

I looked at Trout, and she looked back with an uneasiness in her eyes that I hadn't often seen. I had noticed it a few times when she was in doubt about us, or with the decision about the abortion, but it was now something that filled her eyes with fear, and it was a mood change that made her turn away and stare out the window.

"Trout, what is it?"

"Oh, nothing," she said.

"What do you mean nothing?" I said, standing and walking to where she was.

"I don't know how to say this, and please don't take it wrong, but sometimes Kinlin frightens me."

"What do you mean he frightens you?"

"It's not like I'm afraid of him, or anything like that, it's just that sometimes he looks at me in a way that makes me think he knows more about me than I do myself. It just makes me uneasy, that's all."

"Well, that's not bad," I said, "he's soft, and kind, and if he can see into you like Jose says, then I'm sure he would only do it with the eyes of love."

"I know," she said, still staring out the window, "It's just that sometimes it makes me nervous. I don't know why. Forget it Davis, it's not important."

Forget it? Not important? Here we are talking about a human lie detector, and the very presence of that fact makes her uneasy. It makes her uneasy because she doesn't know who she is and is not ready to find out. Hell! She grew up playing a role that had nothing to do with who she was. She was the boy her father never had, and it was a role she had no hand in choosing. Now, she's suddenly found herself living with a man that's five years younger than the man who taught her how to fish and hunt and a boy that came into her life to show her that, yes, you are indeed female. The boy is saying to her, "Look, you are mother! You are woman!" Now comes the test of whether you're able to face it or not. Maybe Jose was right. Maybe the kid is really here to show us who we are, and it seems like he has tagged Trout to be first in line.

I don't know why, but I turned and walked out of the room. It was an act of anger, or one of frustration. But, whatever it was, it was a move that didn't even faze her. She just continued to look out the window at the early evening fog that was starting to roll in.

CHAPTER 22

Jose saw me head for the car. He had seen that look on my face enough times to know that something was wrong. He followed me out to the drive. "Amigo, where you going?"

"To get a drink," I said, looking straight ahead.

"Want some company?" he asked, already opening the door and sliding in.

"Yeah, sure." I answered.

We headed out the drive and passed Kinlin playing in the field with his sword. He looked our way and waved, and watched as we topped the hill. I kept him in sight in the rear view mirror and saw him take off in a dead run towards the house the minute he saw us pass over the hill. He knows, I thought, as we turned left and headed for town. He's probably in the house right now touching Trout on the leg with his little healing hands.

We cut up the hill through the 450 acres of grapes that grew across the road from the farm not saying a word. Jose lit a cigarette, and watched the workers laboring in the late September fields. I was busy in my head, and looking at it labor through what had just happened in the house. I was trying to tap into my anger and frustration, and having a hell of a time concentrating on one thought at a time. Jose, still staring out the window, said, "Amigo, what's going on with you?"

"I don't know."

"Don't shit me, man, maybe if you put it into words it will be easier to see."

"I don't know Jose, but there is something I haven't told you yet. It's about Trout, and something that messes with my head from time to time."

Jose just sat there staring out the windshield. He wouldn't ask me what it was; it wasn't his way. He knew that I had gotten this far with getting it out, and he also knew that it would be just a matter of time before I would fill the front seat with it.

"Before she was involved with me," I said, lighting a cigarette, "she was involved in a gay life style, and it has threatened the hell out of me ever since I first realized that I was in love with her."

Jose still hadn't said a word, and continued to look straight ahead.

I took a drag, and looking out the window to my left, said, "I'm always afraid that she will either tire of the relationship or become so afraid of it that she will run away back into the safety and comfort of other women, and then I fear I will have lost her forever."

I glanced over in his direction and saw that he was studying the smoke rising from his cigarette, just waiting for me to say what I had to say.

"I have the fear," I continued, "that Kinlin will overload her with a responsibility that she isn't prepared for, and it will just become another bad example of a man/woman relationship."

"She loves that boy, and she loves you," Jose quietly said.

"I know, but I'm afraid that her fear of the commitment that comes with the love will overpower everything else. I feel that the fear will treat her like a wounded rabbit running around outside her burrow in larger and larger confused circles until she gets so far away from home she will be afraid to come back, believing she is safe where she is."

We pulled up into the parking lot behind "Jaspers," and I turned off the key. Jose sat there, thinking deep, not saying a thing. He finally reached down for the door handle, and said, "Amigo, come on, I think you need a drink."

"Yeah, about one every fifteen minutes," I said, slamming the door.

We ordered a couple of beers on tap with a bourbon back. I got up and walked to the phone to call Trout, it was something I had to do, if not for anything else than to tell her where I was. It was the first time I had ever walked out of the house without saying goodbye, or telling her where I was going, and I didn't feel good about it. I had been with other women where that wouldn't have been a problem, but Trout wasn't one of them, and I knew she would never be.

She answered the phone with a depressed voice, and I could tell right away that she wasn't doing well. I offered to come home, but she said no, and felt like it was time that I went out alone with a good friend. She and Kinlin were going to fix some dinner and watch an old western on TV, something that Kinlin became very excited about when she had mentioned it to him. She said that Kinlin had come into the house the minute we drove off and asked with a worried look, "where we had gone?" She felt he knew something wasn't right, and hadn't left her side since. Trout finished by saying that she was sorry for being so distant all of a sudden, that she would be over it by the time I got home, and for is to enjoy ourselves.

We hung up and I felt like hell. It was the way I always felt after doing something impulsive, and without thinking. It was worse that night, because it involved her.

With Trout, I had always sworn to myself that I would always keep her feelings utmost in my thoughts, and would never do anything I felt was unfair. Leaving the house like I did seemed to fall into that category. I knew, too, that if I had stayed the place would have turned into a tomb, and we both would have been uncomfortable. So probably being there with Jose was the best thing for us both.

It was one of my tried and true rationalizations that always allowed me a drink, and one I was going to milk like a hundred proof cow as the night went on.

I sat myself back down at the bar next to Jose, who said, "Everything all right?"

"No, I don't think so," I said, tilting the shot glass.

"Amigo, Trout is young," he said pensively, "We've already talked about the dangers of that, and her loving you isn't going to change that fact. She came up for a summer break and all of a sudden she's found herself in the arms of a man who's got enough baggage to fill a Pullman car, and a child who can call her on every shot. How would you have felt at twenty if you had stepped into that?"

I didn't speak, because the two of us already knew the answer.

"I've known you for over fifteen years," he said, "and I've seen you go through so much shit that I'm surprised you're still alive. I remember that young African princess who twisted your heart out of shape a few years ago. Man, if I hadn't been around I feel like you would have gotten confused and ended up sucking the barrel of a gun instead of the bottle."

"That was different."

"What do you mean it was different? She was a woman, wasn't she?"

"Yeah, but it's not the same. I never entrusted her with my soul. She wasn't capable of understanding what was moving around inside of me."

"And you believe Trout would?"

"Yes."

Jose ordered another round, and asked, "Why is it so important to you that she is the one that has to read that fifty-year-old book that is scrolled on your guts. Fuck! You can't even understand it, how do you expect her to?"

I sat and stared at my beer and pondered the question. "Jose, I don't know. I just think that her coming here and us falling in love was no accident, and it has to have more meaning than just a summer affair. I feel that it is the most important thing that has ever touched my life. I believe it began out of a predestined purpose, not only for my benefit, but for hers too. I'm just afraid that she will cut it off before we know why."

"So what you are telling me is that this has more in it than just loving her?" he said.

"Yeah, something like that," I said, "I think that I have always loved her, even when she was a child. It just took the fingerless touch of her presence this summer to give it life. You might think this is crazy, but I feel she is the woman that I was destined to love, the "eternal wife," for lack of a better term.

162

If she packed up and left today it wouldn't change a thing, and I know that I would walk around the rest of my life with this invisible band stuck to a finger on my left hand."

Jose threw down his drink and signaled for two more.

"My friend, you are in trouble!"

"You're damn right I am."

"So you do believe that things are predestined then?" he said, with a little grin.

"I don't know. I just have always felt that Trout and I always had something special going on. Now that Kinlin has entered our lives, I am becoming more and more, as the days go on, a believer, and that something is going on here which we don't have any control over."

"Amigo," Jose said, with eyes full of concern, "what will you do if she someday leaves?"

"Man, I don't know. I don't even want to think about it," I said, standing up, and walking towards the head.

We had been in the bar a couple of hours, and I noticed that the street outside had grown dark. We had a couple more pops and decided to walk down the street to the only other bar in town, "The Main Street Saloon." It was a place with a few pool tables and a different clientele, and there were always a couple of Harley's parked outside.

We walked in and found the joint noisier than the one we had just left. As we pulled ourselves up to the bar I found myself missing Trout and the boy, and wished I were with them instead of with the creeping state of drunkenness that was starting to occupy my mind. Being with Jose was OK, but we weren't having much fun. It was a space that Jose and I had been in before, and a teeth-grinding state of mind that always had one of us tagging along just to keep the other out of trouble.

Jose ordered a couple of the same that we were drinking before, and we looked around the bar as the drinks were being poured. There were the assorted types playing pool, college kids wearing shorts and tank tops, a few of the older local town drunks who were holding down the bar with their elbows, and some carpenter types down at the other end.

Three bikers had walked in looking like the "Earp" brothers after they had just shot up the "Clantons" at the "OK Corral". The place had a good mixture of types that wore their badges of machismo pinned to their shirts like Medal's of Honor. Ten years ago it would have been a place where Jose and I would have gotten half drunk in, and had a ball shooting pool and chasing women. But tonight it was just a loud reminder of how the years were creeping up on us, and showing us how much booze we could drink without showing it.

I had become sullen as hell, and Jose was unable to do anything about it. We had been in this situation before, and had learned to just let it be. After awhile, we would look at each other, and without a word, know that it was time to go home.

I had a pretty good buzz going, but it wasn't pressing any fun buttons. As a matter of fact it was just sinking me deeper into the depression that I had left the house with. If I wasn't careful, it would start turning into a silent rage that would cover me, and anything within ten feet, into a bad "B" war movie.

I said to Jose, in a tone that was about as serious as a case of the plague, "Jose, do you think she will leave me?"

He didn't answer right away, and I know it was because he didn't want to. One of Jose's best traits was that he was brutally honest. But he was also a good friend and I knew he would have a hard time answering that question without wanting to hurt me.

"I don't know," he said, looking down into his glass.

"Come on amigo," I looked at the side of his face, "what do you think?"

"Like I said, I don't know. Come on, how about a game of pool?" he said.

"Fuck pool!" I said, bent down so he could look me in the eyes. "What do you think?"

"What does it matter what I think? What will happen, will happen, and you sitting here trying to figure it out isn't going to change it, or do you any good."

"She will, won't she?" I said, touching his arm.

Jose looked in the direction of the poolroom, and I knew he wasn't thinking about a game. He rolled the glass in his hands, and like a doctor telling his best friend patient that he only had a month to live, said, "Yes, amigo, I think she will!"

Well, he had said it, and the statement suddenly turned the air around us into stale smelling, crematorium smoke.

"Amigo," he said, leaning over to look at me, "I have just told you something that you already know yourself, and before you asked the question, you already knew the answer I would give. Like I said before, just continue to love her, and bless the stars that brought her to you, because something as powerful as this might never come along again. She will never be able to not love you; it's just that she might never be able to live with you, because you, and what she feels for you frightens her. You see in her gain, and she sees in you loss. It is, again, your theory of love and fear. You are finally learning to let love lead you, and to break down those old walls, but she is still controlled by fear and it might take her another thirty years to let those fears go. By that time, my friend, you won't be around to witness it. I have watched how you have loved her, and she knows the value of it. I'm sure that it will be a long time, if ever, before she feels your kind of love again, but in the end something stronger than that love will keep her away, and it's not something that beats like a heart. It is something dark that runs through the streets afraid of its own shadow. You think the fist of fate is kicking your ass, when in effect it has brought you a love that only comes around once in a life time, and with it, a prince of a boy I believe was sent here to save both of your lives. My friend, you should be thanking the stars, instead of trying to piss on them."

"Jose," I said, downing my fifth drink, "I'm afraid I won't be able to live without her if she leaves, and that scares the shit out of me."

"If she leaves, you will die for awhile, but the boy will bring you back to life and give you purpose. I know this!"

"How in the fuck do you know that?" I said, demanding an answer.

"It's just something that I know, that's all," he said with conviction.

At about that time, someone from down the bar shouts, "Hey Yul!"

I'd heard it before from other drunks who believed that my shaved head was their God given reason to get their aggressions out, and something that I had learned to ignore. But it was still a wake-up call for the butterfly in my guts, and a signal for it to go out and arm itself to the teeth.

Jose and I continued to talk, and hoped that the disease four stools away would cure itself.

"Hey Yul, I thought you died a few years back of lung cancer? What the fuck you doing back?"

I continued to pay the drunk no mind, and didn't even look to see who it was.

Jose said, "It looks like you have a fan, maybe he wants your autograph."

"Yeah," I said, "I've got his autograph!"

Again, from down the bar came the words, "Hey, no shit, it's Yul and one of those peasants that he saved from that village with Steve McQueen. No shit, sittin' right here in this bar!"

I saw Jose's muscles tighten in his jaw, so I turned and said, "Hey man, why don't you just enjoy your drink and let us enjoy ours. I'm not in the mood to sign any autographs tonight." After I said it, I saw that it was one of the bikers, and he was smiling like he hadn't eaten in a week, and Jose and I were the biggest steak dinner that he had ever seen.

Jose hadn't said a thing. He just ordered two more drinks and looked in the direction of the poolroom.

"Hey! No shit, Yul, could you sign my napkin here, and maybe you could let me touch your head. I never met a star before."

I turned again, and felt the butterfly start to piss in my guts. I didn't feel like putting up with a drunk, not in the mood I was in, but this was a drunk that had a couple of friends who looked like they were no strangers in the art of self-defense.

Jose looked straight ahead, and with the shot glass touching his lips, said, "Fuck that punk!"

I said, "Jose, let's get the fuck out of here. I don't feel like putting up with this shit."

"I ain't through with my drink yet," he said, ordering two more.

"Hey Yul, no shit, I thought you were dead," and laughing, the cretin added, "but you do kind of look half dead, maybe you are a ghost!"

I knew the only way to end this was either to leave, or to confront him, and by the looks of Jose, leaving wasn't in the cards. My buttons were being pushed. It was a place I had been before, and if there was ever a candidate for unleashing the anger inside of me it was that asshole at the end the bar. I was definitely old enough to be that punk's father, and I couldn't kid myself about my age, or the fact that if I couldn't rip a guy's head of in the first thirty seconds then I was in deep shit.

The last fight I was in was about five years before, when some French punk rocker, with safety pins stuck in his ears and cheeks confronted me in a German beer hall, with the angry fantasy that I had fucked a friend of his in the ass. When I turned to walk away from him he slapped me in the face. After that point, I don't remember a thing, except that when people were trying to pull me off him after I had knocked him sprawling onto the floor, I was trying, with my foot in his throat, to rip out as many of those clasped pins that were stuck in his face as I could. That was about a fifteen-second number. After it was over I felt like I had just run a four-minute-mile.

Jose tossed down his new drink at the same time that the biker said, "Hey Yul, no shit, what the fuck you and Pancho doing in town, shooting a sequel?"

I turned again, and said as calmly as I could, "Hey man, why don't you do everybody in the place a favor, and shut the fuck up!"

With that, Jose turned to the side and stared in their direction. It was the first time he had seen who it was making all the noise at the other end, but I could tell by his attitude that he didn't care, and it could have been the whole Red Army sitting there for all it mattered to him.

The smiling biker said, "Whoa, watch out! Yul and his fucking gardener are pretty bad dudes," and cracking up at his own feeble attempt at humor, added, "If we don't watch out, they might go out to their truck and bring back their rakes and beat us to death."

The kid was turning to his buddies and laughing, when Jose said in a tone that if you ignored it, would demand that you be banned from the "Club del Macho" forever.

"HEY, MOTHERFUCKER! I don't need a rake to whip your ass. I'll just rip off one of your arms and beat you to death with it! NOW, WHY DON'T YOU JUST SHUT THE FUCK UP?"

Oh, oh, I thought, that was it. Jose and I had been here many times before, and I always knew when we had passed the point of no return, and this was one of them. The comment from Jose took away the biker's good mood, and brought him off the stool, saying, "What'd you say?"

Jose took a drink, and putting his glass down, said, "You heard me, YOU FUCKING MAGGOT! You're starting to fuck up our night, so like I said, either shut the fuck up, or get on that steel hard on outside and ride out of my sight!"

The last comment put the bar into a dead silence because everybody knew that the kid was given two choices and either one of those would involve loss of pride.

My adrenaline was pumping, and I felt the butterfly start to strap on his spurs. Jose took another drink, and said into his glass, "Fuck that asshole!"

The three of them stood up, and the kid walked over to us and said, "Listen, if you weren't such an old motherfucker, I'd spank you and your gardener's ass."

I felt Jose start to rise off his stool, so I said, "Listen 'Tarzan,' I might be old, but I ain't dead. Now, why don't you just get the fuck away from us?"

He screamed, "FUCK YOU! Let's go outside!"

Well, I had learned in the back of a pizza parlor in Fresno California in 1961 the hard way, that you don't step outside with anybody, because his buddies always step out with you. And once you're out of sight, and far from help, three or four guys can put the boot to you pretty bad. I also learned through the years that if you can hit a guy first, and hard enough, it can often put a damper on any plans he had of tearing your head off. So, I yelled, "FUCK OUTSIDE!" and standing up, hit him as hard as I could, just about dead center, in the middle of his nose.

Another thing that I had learned was that a blood-bubbling, broken nose will not only temporarily blind somebody, but also take away most of their desire to continue. The kid's face erupted, splattering the bar and me with crimson snot. He reached back for an imaginary handrail and, finding none, crashed to the floor like a wounded buck.

I had also learned that once you had a man on the ground, you wanted to keep him there, because if you let them get up all in one piece they might rise pissed off and beat the living shit out of you.

I instinctively jumped on him. And with a knee on his chest pounded his nose into a blood red pulp of breathing balloons. Jose had leaped over me, and screaming, said, "COME ON MOTHERFUCKERS, LETS DO IT!" ripping off his shirt, popping off all the buttons with it. I had seen him do that dozens of times. It was intimidating as hell, and if he could have ripped open the skin on his chest exposing the lion's heart inside, he would have done that too. Jose took a barstool and threw it halfway across the room, advancing on the two, looking like a man that you wouldn't want to fuck with even with a gun in your hand.

The two bikers put their hands in front of them, and one of them said, "Hey man, this isn't our fight, he got into this by himself. We don't want any part of this!"

Normally, Jose might not have paid any attention to their pleas and would just walk into them for drill, but my relentless pounding of the poor son of a bitch on the floor diverted him. He turned his back on them, reached down, and tried to hold my arms. I was in a rage, and saw the kid on the floor as that same act of fate that was sooner or later going to rip apart my life. Jose grabbed hard and yelled in my ear, "Amigo, Amigo! Enough, don't kill him!"

Jose was strong as a bull and, in that moment, he had to be because I wasn't going to let up.

He grabbed hard and pulled me off, and seeing the tears in my eyes, said, "ENOUGH MAN! You got him, cool down!"

I was in a sobbing rage, and everything that moved in the room became a target for an anger that I couldn't define. I turned to the biker's two friends and yelled, "How about it MOTHERFUCKERS! You want a piece of this?"

Jose dropped his grip on my arms and stood beside me hoping that they would say yes. They backed up, and said again that it wasn't their fight. So I yelled, "Well you better look after that piece of shit on the floor, and when he comes to, you can tell him that he just got whipped by the 51-year-old ghost of Yul Brynner."

Jose and I headed for the car, and as we turned the corner for the drive home we saw the cops pull up in front of the bar. Jose was driving, knowing by my trembling that I was in no shape to do it myself.

We got about a mile out of town, and he said, "Man, if I hadn't pulled you off, you would have fucked that guy up bad. Amigo, I haven't seen you that angry in a long time."

I didn't respond. My eyes were filled with tears and my heart was beating out of my chest. I don't think I could have talked if I wanted to.

Jose said, "Man, this thing with Trout is moving you someplace where you don't want to be. We have been in these things before, but I've never seen you want to fuck someone up that bad!"

He was right. I had hurt people before, but always knew when to stop. I wasn't beating on that kid on the floor. I was kicking the shit out of something else, and I couldn't kid myself about it. I knew what it was, and Jose did too.

Jose said, "You were trying to whip destiny, but you can't do it. You were pounding Trout's affection for other women and the threat it poses to you, and you were kicking the ass of 32 years difference in age and the factors that go with it. Man, let it go, let it take its course. You cannot beat it. Amigo, you have a great woman that loves you and respects you. You have to give her space, and don't make a mistake and think you can hold her, because that will drive someone like Trout away quicker than anything. Don't do something that will make her lose respect for you, because knowing you like I do, that would kill you faster than a speeding bullet."

Jose was right. Everything he said I already knew. I was so full of threats and the fear of her leaving that if I wasn't careful I could turn myself into something that she wouldn't want to love. Sitting there in the car, driving through the late Sebastopol night, I knew I had to just go on and hope for the best. If this love was meant to survive, then it would. But, like Jose said, if it wasn't, then I couldn't do a damn thing about it.

CHAPTER 23

We pulled into the drive and I saw that the only light on was in the kitchen. Jose hugged me hard, and said softly, "Amigo, don't forget that she loves you, and don't forget that she also doesn't know what to do with it, and that makes her afraid. Just do your best to make her feel safe around you; that is what she will remember. There will be a day in the years to come when she will see the value of it, and it will be like a gift to her, something that might open her eyes and her heart and help her through life. She sees you as father and lover, and it confuses her. When she finally figures out who you are, then maybe it will help her to figure out herself. You will then be able to touch each other with different hands, hands that are not afraid to feel. Now go to bed and hold her. Let her know, in a way, that even if she does leave she will never be alone."

Jose took a few steps towards the studio and stopped, then turned and said, "I love you brother and I'll never leave you alone if you need me, OK? And another thing."

"What's that," I said.

"You still are the craziest motherfucker I have ever seen. It still takes thirty dollars to get you drunk and you can still fight. So life isn't all that bad now, is it?"

"Nah, I guess not my friend," I said, turning and walking towards the house.

I walked up the steps and saw the bats reflecting the light from the back porch as they darted around the tower, and I heard the owl up high in the pine hooting good night as I passed through the back door. The house was still. I moved quietly to peek into Kinlin's room. He wasn't there. I knew he had gone to bed with Trout. Moving softly towards our room I opened the door a crack and looked in. They were cuddled together under the sheepskin holding on to each other gripped in a peaceful sleep. I closed the door, went to the fridge and opened a beer, then sat down at the table. I didn't like myself much for the fight and the way I tore into that kid. I could explain away my anger and rage, but I thought I had ended that form of expressing it years ago. In the last few years I had always ended up hurting myself out of frustration, by breaking my hands on walls, or wounding my liver with drink, but trying to tear that kid's head off was something I had seldom done.

I decided to take a shower and wash away the dirt of the night that was covering me like a scratchy wool shirt. Grabbing a towel and a robe, I went out into the darkness; "a redundant act," I thought.

I lit the candle on the wooden shelf and watched it flicker as it sent dancing shadows on the bushes surrounding the steam starting to fill the night air. The water poured over me, splashing against the redwood boards supporting my feet; a skin-rush-sensation that showed me I could still feel. Drying off, I listened to the quietness of the dying summer night and realized the chill in the air was the messenger telling me that fall was moving in. There was already the smell of burning oak in the air. It would be a constant reminder over the next eight months that I had lived to see another winter.

I dried off and walked in the house and stepped into the bathroom to brush my teeth. I figured I would sleep in Kinlin's room that night. To disturb the sweet scene I had witnessed with the two of them in our bed would almost be a criminal act.

I was standing in front of the mirror when I saw the door open. Standing inside its frame was Trout holding a passed out little boy. She whispered she was going to put him down and come back. She walked back into the bathroom and threw her arms around me, silently burying her face in my chest. Looking into her eyes, I pushed her back carefully, and said, "Trout, sorry I was gone so long, maybe I should have called again."

"No, that's all right," she whispered, "Kinlin and I went to bed halfway through the film. It was one where the Indians always lose, and it made him sad, so he turned on the *Discovery* channel and we watched a film about elephants for a little while. Then he fell asleep in my arms. He was worried about you and Jose, and kept looking down the drive for the headlights of the car. I kept telling him you were just out having some fun alone, because that is what buddies sometimes do. We went to bed, and I lay awake waiting for you to return. It was strange though, he awoke about twelve out of a nightmare, screaming, 'Birdman! Birdman!' I had to calm him down, and held him close until he fell back to sleep."

As she grabbed my hand, bringing it up to her mouth, I thought, strange, that was about the time I was on the floor with the biker.

She drew my hand up to her face, and seeing cut marks on it, said loudly, "WHAT'S THAT?"

"Oh, it's nothing," I answered.

"NOTHING! What happened, did you and Jose get into a fight?"

"Well," I said, not really wanting to get into it, "we had a little difference of opinion with some guys."

She looked down at the floor and saw the blood splattered T-shirt lying on top of the dirty clothesbasket. Looking me dead-in-the-eye, she said, "What happened, it looks like someone died in that shirt?"

"Not quite," I said, "thank God the blood's not mine!"

Grabbing the sides of my face with her warm hands, she asked, "Are you all right? You're not hurt are you?"

"No, I'm OK. It's just that my emotions took a beating. Really, I'm OK!"

"Oh baby, I'm sorry, it was all my fault. I shouldn't have turned my back on you. I'm sorry."

"Listen Trout, don't say you're sorry, remember, you're only allowed to say it twenty times a day, and you just went over the mark."

She looked up at me with sad eyes and a smiling mouth, knowing we had just touched on a subject that always brought out affectionate laughs from us both.

"Trout listen, it's not your fault. It's nobody's fault. I just got overloaded and allowed some punk-ass-kid to pull my switch. The only good thing that came out of it was that maybe next time he'll think twice before fucking with someone over fifty."

Holding my hand next to her face, she said, "I knew that you and Jose were going to get into trouble, and Kinlin felt it too. You two are not a couple of kids anymore. Promise me you'll never get yourself into that situation again. I don't want to have to go out and scrape you off the floor of some bar somewhere. And I don't want to have to worry every time you and that warrior friend of yours go out together. PROMISE?"

"Yeah, I promise," I said, crossing my fingers behind my back.

"Come on," she said, leading me out of the room, "I think you need a back rub."

"Yeah Trout, I think you're right," I said, heading in the direction of the bedroom.

I took off my robe and lay on the bed. Trout took off hers, and sitting on my ass began to cover my back with oil. Her hands slid over me, grasping tenderly at muscles that had tensed up tight during the course of the night. I finally relaxed, and turning over, said, "Now it's your turn."

She said, "No, I was going to give you one, remember?"

"You already have. Now turn over, I'm going to give one to you, you know how much you like them," I said with a glint in my eye.

She looked back, not very successfully hiding the smile on her face. "OK, if you insist."

"I do," I said, covering her back and ass with oil.

I positioned myself straddling her thighs and began to carefully massage every square inch of skin on her back and shoulders. I rubbed her like she was the last piece of dough on earth, and I was the poet/baker in charge of making the bread that would be broken in the last marriage ever allowed.

I moved up on her, still massaging her skin, feeling her soft ass under me. She sighed, and said, "It's so soft. I love it when you move on me like that."

I grew hard and slid with all the tenderness in me into her Garden of Rose. She moaned and grasped the pillow, and with a voice that was almost lost in the cotton sheet, said, "God that feels good."

Those were the same sweet words of contentment that she mouthed every time this happened, and words that gave me as much pleasure as they gave her.

I swayed back and forth on her for what seemed like an hour, then reached down under her silken grass and tenderly massaged the part of her that we both knew I would touch even before the back rub began. She sighed deeply and lifted her hips up to meet me. She moaned, and moved like she was riding a runaway horse, and at the moment when we both fell into a bone-twisting orgasm, screamed to all the ambrosia Gods that inhabited that bed.

I laid on her back with my mouth on hers, not kissing, just breathing in each other's warm breath. I whispered, "Trout, I would die for you."

"No," she said softly, "I would die for you, and as a matter of fact, I think I just did."

"Well, do you want me to bring you back to life? I've still got a good ten minutes left in me! You sure that you don't want to go for two?"

"God no!" she said, half smiling. "I couldn't handle it. I want to be able to walk tomorrow!"

"OK," I said, biting her ear.

She rolled over and held me tight and heard me say, "Trout, that was nice."

She grabbed my hand, and closing her eyes, said, "Baby, it was more than that, it's always more than that. No one has ever made me feel as good as you do. Don't ever forget that, and don't ever forget that I will always love you."

"I won't Trout," I said, thinking that it sounded as much like a goodbye as it did a good night.

I watched her fall asleep as I often did after we made love. It was an observation of affection that I had done since the first time we slept together. A habit of the heart I call things like that, and one that would be hard to break if she ever did say goodbye.

I lay there and tried to imagine what it would be like to live without her, but knew if I thought about it too long I would open the cage and let the beast of fear take over the room. I was feeling too full of love to let it come now and fuck up my night. I had done enough damage to myself earlier in the evening to have to deal with that rabid motherfucker. The only thing I wanted at my throat this night was the soft face of that woman buried in my neck.

CHAPTER 24

Fall began to give way to the cold nights and foggy mornings of a creeping winter. The apples had been picked; their leaves were starting to fill the field. The fruit trees dropped their red brown leaves, which fell like crispy potato chips over the moist, dark ground.

The four of us had survived another month, and because of the love that had filled the house, we became inseparable. Jose had offered to leave, but Trout, Kinlin, and I insisted that he stay. Jose never had any real plans, so four or five months out of his life didn't mean much to him. And in his heart I knew he didn't want to go.

Those months with us were the first in many years where he felt like he had a home. I had gotten a couple of gate commissions, and Jose had helped me put them together. When he arrived I knew he had money, but how much I never knew. Jose was the type that I would never have asked where he had gotten it, and he would never volunteer the information. I just accepted the fact that it was there. He was a man who was generous to the bone, and was always bringing home a truck full of food and anything else he thought the household might need.

Jose was the uncle that every kid dreamed of, and always had something special in his pocket for Kinlin. He brought home everything, from the usefulness of a Swiss Army Knife, (which worried Trout to death), to the bizarre, non-function of an antique-store bought, "French Legion of Honor Medal." A "Crux de Guerre." Jose had brought home so many medals and ribbons that he had Kinlin looking like the most highly decorated dwarf soldier since the word "Honor" was introduced into the language of Man. The decorations and battle ribbons, combined with the sword, tattoos and fetish-adorned headband were beginning to be too much for the mothers shopping with their little kids. They would put them and their screaming-in-fear-children into reverse whenever they saw Jose pushing him down the aisle.

Kinlin was talking like a philosophical machine gun, and could tell you better than a zoologist, the weight, length and number of teeth of your average size Kodiak bear. He was becoming an expert on everything that was ever written in and of the art in the Guggenheim Museum. Trout was teaching him to read, and he would take up to an hour of our time every morning having us go, word for word with him, through the comics in the newspaper.

He fell in love with Calvin and Hobbs, and saw in their mystical relationship much more than the average reader. He would pull out the little scissors on his knife and cut out the strip every day, taping them on any space that wasn't as yet filled on his bedroom walls. He would sit with Trout and have her read the TV section, asking if there were any westerns on that night where the Indians won. If not, he would sit in front of the set, and like a scientist taking notes, watch *PBS*, or *Discovery*.

Kinlin would spend hours in the field constructing stone sculptures. They were huge symbols that would stretch for fifty feet or more. They always made me think that we were living on a Peruvian plateau, and at any moment UFOs would, with after-burners on, fly in formation over the house. He bugged me so much about learning how to weld that I had to ban him from the studio whenever I worked. It didn't deter him much, because he started to collect Scotch Tape and Super Glue, and using it like a sticky plastic torch, would sit in his room and put together his own "Found Object" pieces of gallery quality work.

The kid was indeed a wonder, and if his age was really four, then I couldn't even fathom what he would be capable of doing when he was five.

Trout, over the past few weeks, had been trying to adapt to the life that had been handed her, but had showed from time to time it was something that weighed her down. The love between her and I was always there, and the feelings she had for Kinlin were an indefinable kind of tenderness only she and the boy knew. In her heart she believed Kinlin was really hers, and even though she hadn't bore him, she knew he had arrived as a gift, and in her intuitive heart realized that the boy had found his home. She figured out for herself that Kinlin was found at about the same time as her miscarriage, and not wanting to get into the spiritual technicalities of reincarnation, accepted the theory that he had become the much loved birth that had arisen from that bloody summer day of loss.

Trout had her moments of depression, and were typified by her going to ground, which meant pulling the covers and anything else within arms reach over her body and head. Those were moments when Kinlin would go to his room and shut the door and do things only he understood. He would draw and paint for hours, and cut and paste together collages that were as abstract and mystical in design as any Shaman's sand painting. He would take the little portable radio Jose had given him and listen to Mozart and Brahms from morning till night. And like a monk in holy prayer, would fast until she got out of bed. Trout would usually recover quicker than normal, simply by knowing that she had also involved the boy.

Kinlin sensed her moods, and as he saw her going into them would go out of his way to be as tender to her as he could. He would grab a hairbrush, and using mystical strokes sit behind her on the couch, and with the touch of a painter putting a glaze on a priceless canvas try and comb away all her pain. Kinlin would fill the tub with soapy pink suds, and while holding her hand, lead her into the bathroom and hand her a clean towel. Before letting her step in he would stick his hand in the water making sure it wasn't too hot.

When she was deep in these gloomy states he would put away his sword and hang his headband on a nail. Then he would take his special sacred white sheet and cover up his bike. The minute she would take her mind and go away he would take his and follow her, trying with all of his might to find her and bring her back.

Jose witnessed most of those periods, and would search me out when they happened. He wouldn't say much; he would just stay close and try to read where I was. If I was going to slip away and sleep with the dragons, then he wanted to be near enough to pull me out of their dank musty pit.

Once in Europe he was there when I tore up my entire studio, breaking everything I could get my hands on. I jumped on sculpture and took a steel pipe to my workbench, and even tried to pull the plants out of their pots. He sat in the corner and watched, not interfering, knowing I had to get it out. But knowing too that he didn't want me alone when I finished. After I had literally demolished everything in the room he stood up and walked over to me with a five-pound sledge in his hand, pointed to an undamaged piece of work in the corner, and said, "Amigo, you forgot one!"

That simple act put me into a sobbing, laughing fit, where I looked at him and said, "Jose, you are the strangest motherfucker I have ever seen!"

"No amigo, you are the strangest motherfucker you have ever seen. Now go throw some water on your face and let's go have a drink!"

I knew that Jose was staying around, because he was afraid of what was going to happen, and he sure as hell wanted to make sure he wasn't more than fifty feet from the house if Trout left.

Trout and he were fond of each other, and become fast friends. Jose saw in Trout what I had seen, and told me more than once that he understood why I loved her so much. He said to me no matter what happened between her and I, that I could still consider myself lucky to have been able to experience her presence and to thank the gods that brought her to me. We talked about it a lot, and I always thought that in his own way he was trying to prepare me for the end; an end I felt was creeping closer every day. Trout was giving signs, and in the roller coaster way her emotions were showing, was warning us all of the flight that might lie ahead. She was still tender and caring towards me, and tried her best to hide what was going on in her mind. I could just imagine her contemplating the choices she had to make, and I'm sure that paramount in her mind were the ones that had to do with disappointing me.

From what I had seen in the past, her fear of failing me was at the top of her list, and something she would have a hard time facing if she believed she ever did. I had always tried to impress upon her that my love for her transcended all and that the love was one full of forgiveness and understanding. Whatever she did, I would know it would be something done out of fear, and if anyone was an expert on fear, it was me.

Jose was probably right about his theory of her seeing me as parent and lover. I noticed it most when I would try and talk to her about things I felt I knew more about than she did, and those things were mostly about travels of the heart. Maybe I did come across as father sometimes, and I granted Jose that, but I think mostly I came across as threatening, older man. Someone who like her father was telling her what to do, or what to think, and that was something she didn't want, or wasn't ready to hear. Whenever I came across as too all knowing she would back up, and her barbed wire would be strung between us. She would set up her defenses and prepare to go to war, and feeling threatened, so would I. The mental military maneuvers got us nowhere, with the exception of making me gaze into the mirror and look back at a man who can drop walls faster than an iced guillotine, cutting off any hope of letting her get out her feelings. It had happened enough times over the last couple of months that I knew it was something I had to solve, or it would just be added to the list of reasons for her to leave. It was the Pigeon Man's gift, a coldness, that after 50 years of hiding behind, I was having a hard time changing.

Trout was the first person who was ever able to show it to me as it really was, and because the truth was coming from her, it was something that I desperately wanted to change. I knew if she was ever to teach me anything, it was going to be how to melt down those glacier-like walls.

Over the last month I had been careful, treading water whenever we came close to one of those situations. I chose my words cautiously and gave much thought to my actions and the reaction they might bring in her. I knew there existed in her enough reasons for her to run and hide without me adding another to the pot.

Trout had showed me through her love there was a man in me I liked. Her accepting me for who and what I was allowed me the peace of mind and time to find that out. In the five months that we had been together I hadn't had one adrenaline rush of anger towards her, with the exception of the small one before the fight in the bar. It was a sign she was the only woman I had ever met that was capable of calming the raging beast that moved in me, and I knew that if time would permit, the one to help me put the scaled monster to sleep forever. I was afraid that if she left before I had a chance to blow that soul-eating motherfucker away, then it would just be a matter of time before that beast and all his friends would regroup and, starting at my feet, eat their way up, clawing their way out the top of my head. I had always felt that some form of insanity was in the books for me, and had touched on it briefly before, but since her arrival I felt that maybe I could push those thoughts out of my mind forever. Trout had the inherent ability to call a peace to the war going on in me ever since I could remember, and to enable me to finally sign a truce with that platoon of pain. Until now it seemed to have a knack of winning all the major battles that I fought.

I thought often of what it would be like without her and what I would miss most. Her touches and tender love were right up there at the top. To imagine that I would never again lay with her on the sheepskin-covered bed were thoughts that actually made my heart hurt. The loss of her as mother to the boy that we had begun to believe was ours would be like someone taking an axe and hacking away a piece of my side. It would be a wound that no surgeon would ever be able to sew back.

More than anything else I would miss her standing in my corner giving me support between rounds, pushing me off the stool at the bell, reminding me I was ahead on points. I could see her screaming in my ear, telling me to lead with my left, and while softly touching my swollen eyes, say, "You can do it Davis, you got that bum of a beast in the palm of your hands."

Jose's word's always rang in my ears, and I often thought maybe he was right about me expecting too much of her, and laying on her a task I couldn't understand myself. She was only twenty years old and so involved with trying to win her own fights that me thinking she could help me win mine was maybe too much to ask. The only real truth I knew was that I had let her into a part of me no one else had ever seen, and I wouldn't have done it if I didn't think she was capable of touching it with healing hands. Her being so young did have its down sides as far as I was concerned. But maybe it really wasn't that important, because I always thought she was really a centuries-old spirit trapped in a young woman's skin.

CHAPTER 25

W e were into November, Thanksgiving was just a week away and Kinlin was looking forward to the feast.

Trout's mother had invited her to spend the holidays with her down at Trout's grandmother's place, but she had bowed out, saying that she wanted to have it up here with us.

Kinlin had cut out every picture of turkeys he could find, both wild and domesticated, and taped them to his walls. He knew Thanksgiving was a celebration that had to do with Indians, so he let us know a week beforehand that from that moment on he was going to wear only a loincloth and war paint. He also told us that for the next seven days we were to address him only as Cochise. Jose had made him a bow and arrow and a stone-tipped tomahawk, and without any prior warning Kinlin painted black Pinto spots on his trusty white-steed of a bike.

That week it must have been in the forties, and it was all that Trout could do to chase after him trying to make him wear some clothes so he wouldn't catch cold. Jose and I would sit on the front porch bundled up, watching Trout chase him around the field with a coat and scarf in hand. She would finally trap him against a tree, and with a steamed breath argument try to put it on him. He would tell her that Indians didn't wear coats, and until she could come up with a genuine buffalo robe he would rather freeze.

Jose went down to the local craft store and bought him a brown-dyed sheepskin and cut a hole in the top. Trout dyed his Mexican pants red and sewed leather tassels down the sides, and for the next week the boy we knew as Kinlin moved out and a full-blooded Apache chief moved in.

It was a good week and the four of us felt the season definitely change. The outdoor shower wasn't used much, with the exception of Kinlin standing under it once in a while just to get lost in the steam.

The making of sculpture had come to a halt, and I concentrated on the gates. Money was a factor and I tried my best to bring it in. I thought that selling gates was a whole lot easier than trying to pimp my art. Trout didn't like that much, and saw how the lack of putting together sculpted steel ate at my creative side. I told her I was just taking a break. After twenty-five years of doing it every day I needed to step back and see where I really wanted to go with it. She was concerned about me losing something important just so I could feed her and the boy. She had an inheritance, and always talked about taking some of it out, but I didn't want her to touch it. She would sneak out a hundred or two every now and then, and would bring home some things for Kinlin, or some new clothes for herself. But I did my best, with Jose's help, to pay the rent and buy the food. We weren't starving, and our needs were somehow being met.

Trout's mother had always been a supporter of my art and anything else I tried to do. She let me know that just because I was involved with her daughter didn't change the fact that we were still good friends. She was still unhappy about Trout not going back to school, and had some obvious concerned questions about what was happening at the farm, but she trusted me enough to know I wouldn't do her daughter any harm. As a matter of fact, I believed she felt that if Trout had chosen to be with a man, then she would just as soon it was me. She told me that when Trout had told her about us, it had been a lot easier for her to deal with than when she had told her about her involvement with women. Trout's mother felt, I'm sure, that this was just a short interlude in her daughter's life, and maybe it would do her some good. She didn't know that her daughter was now also a mother. If she found that out, I'm sure it wouldn't do anybody any good.

Thanksgiving came and the day was spent preparing our feast. Jose and Kinlin had shopped hours the day before. Jose came back with wild tales of the boy charging through the store scaring the shit out of everyone with his Apache looks and speaking the new "Mescalero" tongue he had invented. He could talk in his new language for hours, hardly ever repeating himself. Of course nobody had the slightest idea what he was saying, (which he found unbelievable), and a puzzled reaction only made him talk louder and longer until it forced you to say, "Oh, yeah, I got it! Why didn't I get it in the first place?"

The four of us cooked throughout the day, putting together the most traditional meal we could, referring back to the *Fanny Farmer Cookbook* every five minutes. Kinlin was always underfoot, speaking Apache and drawing pictures of the historical event and taping them to the walls and windows of the house. It was strange to look at the Fauve colored depictions of Pilgrims and Indians which he splashed with sweeping strokes of magenta, lime and red-orange. Besides the colors, the only other deviation from the original was that he had drawn the Indians eating and the Pilgrims as waiters. I guess it was his way of getting back at Hollywood for always having the Indians lose.

We sat at the big table with a great brown bird in the middle. Green beans speckled with bacon and mashed potatoes filled out a palette dotted by fresh hot rolls and purple beets. We had bought good wine and some matching grape juice for the Chief, and before we started to eat, Jose said that he wanted to give thanks. He made a short speech about friendship, and how lucky we all were to be together. When he finished we all raised our glasses in the air, all but Kinlin. He yelled, "WAIT!" and ran to his room. He ran back in and sat down with a piece of paper in his hand. We set our untouched glasses down on the table and waited for him to let us know what was going on. He unfolded his sheet of paper and placed it before him, dipping one side in the gravy. Kinlin held his finger to his lips letting us all know that silence was in order, and sitting there in his painted face and Indian garb, said, "I wrote a poem for Thanksgiving."

I shot a glance to Trout. "I didn't know he could write?"

"I've been teaching him. He wanted it to be a surprise, but I had no idea he had done this!"

Jose looked in my direction, shrugged his shoulders, and said, "I told you the kid was a genius!"

Kinlin put his fingers back to his lips and said something in his new language that could only mean one thing, and that was, "silence." He stared at the paper and began to read.

"THE TREES
THE SUN
THE EARTH
TROUT
JOSE AND
BIRDMAN
THANK YOU."

We were stunned! There was no need for any command of silence; it filled the table. I looked at Trout. Her eyes were becoming moist and my throat was starting to lump. I looked at Jose and I saw he too, was overwhelmingly touched.

Kinlin raised his little glass, and looking at all of us, said in his special Apache tongue, "HEWAHTAHA!"

I looked at him and said, "Cochise, could you please translate?"

He held his glass up higher, and said with all the softness that floated within him, "TO US!"

We toasted and clinked our glasses to a magical moment of love and brotherhood. After we set them down, Trout grabbed Kinlin and absorbed him with a hug. I looked at them both. Inside my heart I gave thanks to whoever it was that sent them to me. I then asked with a pleading sigh, don't ever take them back.

The rest of the day and night was a time of joy for all. Trout, Jose and I drank all the wine, while Kinlin killed the grape juice. We played poker and charades. At eight o'clock Kinlin got to watch his much-awaited documentary, "The Headhunters of Borneo." He sat an inch away from the TV and became totally engrossed in the film. He did, from time to time, run back to Trout and jump in her lap whenever they showed something that scared him, but would grab his sword and slowly crawl back to the screen when he felt it was safe to return.

That night we allowed him to fall asleep with us, an offer that soon made me think twice about the choice. Trout had given him a bath, so at least he was clean. He was wearing the new pajamas she had bought for him with her sneaked inheritance fund, but he was still the savage that had been running loose on the farm for the past week. For the two hours it took him to fall asleep, he turned the bed and everyone in it into a scene right out of "Custer's Last Stand." I finally put my foot down and said he had to put his sword back in his room, and, "NO," he couldn't tie his bike to the bed. I also let him know in no uncertain terms that the bass lure necklace had to go because it kept sticking me in the ass. He finally fell asleep, asking us over and over with a pensive look, "Why would anybody want to cut off someone's head?"

Trout and I slept together that night knowing the Gods had been kind to us, and had given us a gift that was as golden and pure as the love we felt for each other. We also knew, lying there together, that it was something that was beginning to overwhelm us both.

CHAPTER 26

Fall was ebbing and the beginning of winter was just a couple of weeks away. In Northern California, it brought with it a wet fog in the mornings, and a wetter one at night. Since the house was set in a grove of trees it always seemed ten degrees colder there than in the field that lay in front.

The Zen garden was often shrouded in a mist giving it an eerie, mystical look. It made you think once you stepped inside you might never return. It wasn't a look of evil, or of a place where demons slept, it just reminded you that maybe lurking inside were creatures that knew more about the goings on of mankind than you. It was still one of Kinlin's favorite places to play. Sometimes during those foggy days I'd watch him disappear and not return for hours. I imagined him sitting amongst the ivy in the middle of a circle of fur-robed elves discussing the past millennium and the mistakes that were made. Or of him sitting alone next to an Indian medicine man passing back and forth a hand-carved pipe talking in a secret language about the future. He would lose himself in the grove and, sword in hand, fight the evil he was sure hid behind every tree, an evil he knew, if given half a chance, would eat up all the poems in the garden. After Thanksgiving he put away his Apache life and decided he was going to spend the winter as a trapper from the Yukon, a friend to the Indians, and a man that was one-third grizzly. We had picked up a fur cap and a pair of leather thonged boots for him. Together with his snakeskin belt and sheepskin robe hanging over a red and black plaid wool shirt he could pass for a young "Jeremiah Johnson." As a matter of fact he thought he was "Jeremiah Johnson."

We had all pooled our money and bought a video recorder. We thought it would be one way to bring some high quality films in the house, some films for Kinlin where the Indians won. He had watched "Dances With Wolves" at least forty times. Trout brought home the film about "Jeremiah Johnson," which he watched seven times in a row. The only things that made him pause were going to the toilet, or being spirited away by Trout to eat and take a nap. It made him sad to see so many Indians die, but in it he saw a purpose. It was one man with honor fighting other men with the same thing.

I had taken one of my prized red-tail wing feathers and wrapped the quill in leather and pinned it to his cap. It was a covering he never took off. Trout would sneak into his room in the middle of the night and carefully remove it and place it on his desk, only to walk in the room in the morning and find him sound asleep with the thing stuck back on his head.

His dream, when he grew up, (which I felt had already happened two hundred years before), was to move to Canada and live off the land. That is, of course, if Trout, Jose and I agreed to go with the little frontiersman. He told us in no uncertain terms that food would never be a problem because he could trap, or shoot all we wanted to eat, and that the bears wouldn't harm us because he could speak their tongue. Unknowing to the boy, Jose had scoured every second-hand and antique store within a radius of a hundred miles and one day returned with an original bear-claw necklace. When Kinlin saw it he turned into a screaming-with-joy Alaskan brown bear cub. It was the only time I ever saw Trout and him argue in raised voices. It was because she insisted that he could not take the new prize to bed and sleep with it. She talked on end about bloody sheets and punctured jugulars and poked-out-in-the-middle-of-the-night eyes. The minute that he heard the conditions of, "If I ever find out that you have taken it to be we will nail it to the wall and put a frame around it!" He decided then that it would be one of those things that only had special powers in the light of day.

The three of us, plus "Yukon Jack" were preparing to settle in for the winter. Jose and I had spent the week hauling in two cords of oak, and with my chain saw, cut up all the dead and fallen apple limbs.

The house was cozy, and we always had some hot cider on the stove. Jose and I had made our own version, which was always in a pot by itself in the back. Kinlin had seen a program about the evils of alcohol abuse on PBS and made Jose and I feel like a couple of winos every time we popped a beer. When it happened Jose would look him dead in the eye and say, "Listen, I already have in the house a boy who I believe is Moses in disguise, and one who also believes he is a bear. I don't need a spokesman for Alcoholics Anonymous putting a mark on the wall every time I take a drink."

He followed that with, "If Trout sees you with that felt tip pen in your hand putting those little X's on the fridge she will tan your hide quicker than any Indian ever would!"

Kinlin looked straight back at him, and said, shaking his head, "OK, it's your liver!"

Jose looked at me, and said, "Amigo, what are we going to do with him? Pretty soon he will have us eating Tofu and drinking Chinese tea. Do you think he was given to us to put an end to the only life I know? One where I can't eat pork, or drink Tequila, or chase women?"

Kinlin looked up at him with eyes full of concern. "No, I just want you and Birdman to live a long life and not get sick, because if you got sick and died then I would be alone."

"What about Trout?" I said, looking down at him with a smile.

He looked back up with two sad eyes and said nothing. He just turned and walked to his room.

I said to Jose, "What the hell was that about?"

Jose said nothing. He turned and walked into the next room and began stoking the fire.

I followed him. "Jose, what the fuck's going on? You and the kid know something I don't?"

"No amigo, I don't, but I think the boy does," he said, poking the coals.

"And what is that?" I asked.

"Haven't you noticed Trout lately?" he said, closing the iron door on the stove.

"What do you mean?" I said, already knowing what he was getting at.

"She has become distant and is somewhere else most of the time. Surely you have seen it."

Yeah, I had seen it, but I turned my back on it whenever it moved in front of my eyes. Since the day after Thanksgiving she had changed. She moved through the house like she was packing a load of bricks on her back. She had spent the last week on the phone talking to friends in Oregon, letting the conversations go on for an hour, and talking to me more and more about school. I felt the drift of the conversations. On a couple of occasions they had turned loose the 300-pound moth in my guts.

One night she wanted to talk. I knew it was about something serious. I saw it careering towards me like a derailing freight and cut her off before she had a chance to open her mouth. She screamed at me, saying she could never talk to me about things important to her and what kind of a relationship is it when you can't even talk to the person you love! I walked away, shut her down, and got into that truck I hadn't stepped into in months. I rolled up the windows and turned on the imaginary heater because I had a freezing chill running rampant through my veins.

Trout closed the bedroom door and I went outside to have a beer with Jose. When I came back in I heard her on the bedroom phone talking in hushed tones. My emotions ran the gamut from jealously to loss to gut-twisting fear, and I knew I hadn't done too well in the part of love that had to do with understanding. The simple fact was I was scared to death. And when fear took over it usually became a one-man show. I didn't want, or wouldn't let anyone say or do anything that would threaten to leave that little boy in me home alone. The biggest fear I had was that the eight-year-old would come back and turn me into something Trout would stop loving. I would then become like a lost child searching for his parents during rush hour in downtown Detroit.

Jose and I walked outside and leaned against his truck. Jose continued the conversation that began in front of the fire. "I have been watching the boy and he has been staying as close to her as possible, and I think he feels more than we do, especially when it comes to her."

"Feels more about what?"

"Her moods and needs. Haven't you seen how he reacts just before she gets into one of her jumping-under-the-cover moods? He is like one of those graphs that predict earthquakes. I've seen him take off at a dead run towards the house in the middle of the day and arrive just as she's pulling the covers over her head. He'll slide in next to her asking if she wants her back rubbed. I told you before, without wanting to hurt your feelings that you have to give her space. If she has to go, let her. Just make sure she is loved by you, and show her through that love that she will never be alone. The only thing I find wrong with her leaving, other than it would hurt you, is that I believe if she would stay the love you and the boy have for her would heal her wounds. But in the act of healing she would have to open up a part of her she isn't ready to see. Because of that she will run blindly into what she believes is safe. It is something we have all done and learned from, but amigo, as I said before, she is young, and even though her mind is old beyond her years there is still a frightened, confused little girl living inside of her, and that is the person who will say goodbye."

"I believe," he continued, "that the boy is aware of her pain, and maybe even feels that she might leave. That is why he acted like he did in the kitchen.

The other day when he and I were at the store he asked me out of the blue that if Trout left would you go with her, and would he then stay with me. I asked, why did he ask such a question? He said that he feels like Trout wants to take a trip and it is without him. I said in the best way I could that if Trout ever wanted to take a trip it was because she would want to be alone for a while. Sometimes grown up people need that, and if she ever did, then you would stay with him. Amigo, I hope I didn't speak for you and assume too much, but I also told him that you would never leave him alone. I think I know what is in your heart, so I just went ahead and told him."

"No, it's all right, because it's true. I never would leave him. I've come to the point where I believe he is a part of me. It's just that if she does leave, then the presence of him would be a constant reminder of her and that would be tough."

"Yes, it would be tough, but it would also be something that would keep your soul close to hers. I believe that is what she would want. I know it is what you want. Just try and put yourself in her place, and know that if the decision that she makes is one to leave, then it will be as hard on her as anyone else. She loves that boy with all her heart, and to abandon him would be like cutting a piece of her flesh away, and knowing Trout like we do, that would be a wound that would bleed the rest of her life. Amigo, love her, give to her, and if she leaves let her know that she still has the key to your soul and that she can come back and open the door anytime. Trout is someone who is often lost, and if she knows that you are never too far away from her heart then she will go through life knowing that there is at least someone there who is able to throw her a rope and pull her out of the pit if she falls. I have seen what she has done to you. She has pulled out all of that poetry that has been locked up tight in your heart, and if she left knowing that you were going to push it back in it would hurt her as much as the saying of goodbye. Be thankful amigo, you have looked all your life for a woman who could do that to you, and in Trout you have found her. She doesn't believe it now, but I guarantee that down the line she will see it and it will give her worth and help to erase all the doubt she has about herself."

"Don't you think that would be a little egotistical of me to believe that?" I asked, thinking for sure that it would.

"No, amigo, it has nothing to do with your ego, it is all about hers, and that is what she is having problems with. She knows that you believe there are only two emotions in life, and they are love and fear. Somewhere in the months, or years to come, she will understand that through the love you have for her you will have conquered your fears and she will see that you could not have done that without her. She will see that the love you both have for each other will be the mirror she will see herself in, and because of the love, and not the fear, she will like the reflection staring back."

I just stood there listening, knowing that Jose was deep into what was on his mind. He was often philosophical, and often right on with his perceptions, and wouldn't be saying this right now unless he had been giving it a lot of thought.

"My friend, I have seen the change in you," he continued. "It is something that has been like a soft hand that touched your soul, and something that no one has ever been able to do to you before. Even if it takes Trout twenty years to realize it, one day she will. You might be seventy years old, a wrinkled, crotchety old fart, and she will look you up and say, 'Thanks'."

"For what?"

"For teaching her what love is, that's what! Maybe she will go through life like a lot of us never finding out, thinking that we missed it. At least she has had that, and because of it will make her stronger and enable her to obtain something that has been your problem all your life."

"And what is that?"

"Hope, my friend, hope. She will still be young enough to know that love does exist, and with it comes hope and the knowledge that maybe she was worth something after all because she was loved by someone who puts so much value in it. There is someone who saw enough value in her to invest all of his love in her without demanding anything back. I wish someone had done that to me when I was twenty, but maybe when you are twenty you can't recognize it and end up confusing it with something else, something that is attached to a chain that prevents ships from moving around in the water."

"Jose," I said, "You are one philosophical Mexican son of a bitch tonight!"

"Yes, amigo I am, and I am also one thirsty Mexican son of a bitch. Let's go inside and have a beer."

Jose and I stepped inside and grabbed a beer. I walked into Kinlin's room to see if he was OK. He had on the classical music station and was sitting at his table trying to copy a picture of a mountain goat from a page in *Field and Stream.*

"Kinlin, what're you doing?"

He looked up, and said, "Drawing."

"What are you drawing?" I said, trying to get his attention.

"Drawing a goat," he said, clasping his pen tight.

I walked over to his table and looked down and saw that he was drawing a near perfect copy of the goat that was on the page, but his had a bunch of sacks tied on the back.

"What are those things on the back?" I asked.

"Sacks," he answered, without looking up.

"Sacks for what?" I asked, seeing that he was deep into one of his solitary moods.

"For a trip."

"What kind of a trip?"

"Just a trip," he said, still drawing.

"Whose trip?" I asked, curious.

"Trout's."

"Trout's?" I asked, wishing I hadn't. "What trip that Trout's taking?" I asked, feeling my stomach turn.

"Her airplane trip," he said, suddenly drawing wings on the side of the goat.

"What airplane trip?" I asked, starting to feel the panic move in.

"The airplane trip she told me she was going to take, just a few minutes ago."

Feeling like an idiot for having to ask him, I continued, "Where is she going?"

"To visit some friends," he said, "somewhere up by Canada."

I walked out of the room and into our bedroom and saw Trout lying on the bed, and immediately asked, "What is this I hear about a trip you're taking?"

She answered, staring up at the ceiling, "I decided to go up to Oregon for a few days to see some friends and just take a little break. I'm sorry it was Kinlin who told you. I was going to tell you tonight when you came to bed."

"Well, when was this decided?" I asked in a baffled voice.

"Tonight."

"Tonight? When tonight?"

"About an hour ago."

"What prompted the sudden decision?"

"I've been thinking about it for a few days now. After talking to Sara tonight, I decided to leave tomorrow out of Oakland."

"Sara?" I tried to put the name together with some meaning.

"Yeah, remember I told you she was my best friend up at school. She was the one I mentioned this summer when I first came, the one I was going to get a house with when I went back to school?"

Yeah, I remember. It didn't have any meaning then, but it had suddenly become as important as the president saying he was going to legalize drugs, because I remember Trout saying Sara was gay. I didn't know what to say, and not wanting to say the wrong thing, said nothing.

She sensed my pensive silence. "Don't worry. I just miss some of my friends and feel like getting away for a couple of days. It'll be all right. I'll be back in a few days. You men probably need a break from me anyway, right?"

No matter what Jose had just told me about giving her space and an understanding love I couldn't keep the gnawing fear away that had just moved in and started to lunch on my guts. Early in the relationship Trout and I had got into a discussion about her involvement with women. It was something that had started out nice enough, until her defenses got in gear and she said that she would always be attracted to women. It was a statement that said I had to accept it, but didn't say I had to like it. I dropped it like I had just picked up the flaming end of my torch and didn't go back to it again.

A few weeks later we had got into another conversation about the same thing in the front seat of my car. Evidently I had said something that pushed her button, because her defenses turned into a counter attack, and she said, "I would choose a woman over a man any day!" Well fuck! Who did she think was sitting there driving the car. It was the guy that she was supposed to be in love with, and who was in love with her, and she knew that I was threatened by her past.

She saw the mistake immediately and apologized in her best Trout fashion, and we dropped it. It had an affect on me, the same as it does on a jury when the witness says something terribly incriminating on the stand and the defense objects, then the judge says that they are supposed to forget everything that was just said.

Yeah, RIGHT! I'll just un-log that little motherfucking statement right out of my head and never think about it again. Shit! I carried those words around with me every day of the week from that moment on, and for some strange reason I felt like I was hearing them again. I knew I had to get myself together on this one, and even if I did feel threatened, couldn't act like it. So that's what I tried to do, and if she recognized my fears, she didn't let on.

We went to bed that night and she was tender and soft, and probably knew what was going through my mind. Maybe her fingers had turned to feathers because of that, and she was trying to sooth away a pain that she knew was inherent in some men: the fear of loss of someone you love to another woman.

The next morning Trout called the airlines and got a ticket for that day. She packed some things and we went to get Kinlin. The night before he had insisted that he ride along. We went to his room to get him, but discovered that he was already sitting in the front seat of the car wearing his headband, bass lure necklace and other powerful fetishes.

We drove to the airport with Trout assuring the little worried boy every ten minutes she would be back.

We stood there for a few minutes waiting for the call to board. They were tender moments for us all, and ones that brought Trout to tears. The announcement came to board and we all hugged like it was the last time we would ever touch each other again. Trout kissed me with warm, tear-stained lips and told me to not forget she loved me, and not to worry. She reached down and touched Kinlin's face like it was made of membrane-thin-crystal glass and kissed his eyes. Trout then said goodbye. We watched her walk down the ramp, not turning back, and at that moment Kinlin reached up showing me that he wanted to be held. I picked him up and he buried his face and fur cap in my neck, and we walked in silence back to the car.

On the way back the boy sat the entire time staring out the side window, not saying a word. Normally he would fall asleep if the trip was more than twenty miles, but this time he was a wide-awake passenger in a car that felt like it had been frozen in time. We pulled up in the drive and he went directly to his room and turned on his radio, and the sound of Bach began to echo through the door. I knew that he wanted his privacy, so I left him alone.

Jose was waiting in the house when we got back, and as soon as Kinlin had retreated to his room, asked, "How was it, amigo?"

"Tough," I answered, grabbing a beer.

"How's the boy?" he asked, with the concern of a man who probably loved him as much as Trout and I.

"You know Kinlin," I said, "he buries it somewhere, and won't be letting us know until he works it out. But he took it hard, that I do know."

"And Trout?"

"Yeah, Jose, she took it hard too. It wasn't easy for her to get on that plane."

"And you, amigo?" he looked me straight in the eye, trying to read in them something I hadn't as yet let him see through my words.

"Me?" I looked into my beer as if I was trying to find an answer. "I don't know. It's kind of like someone took a dull knife and slashed me just below the chest. If I feel like this knowing she will be back, how will I feel if I realize that she never will?"

"Like someone slashed you about four inches higher," he said, obviously not making a joke, "Try to concentrate on the boy while she is away. He will need it, and maybe it will take your mind off the wound."

He was right. Kinlin will need to feel like he isn't alone. I knew how much this had to be affecting him, and after awhile, it would be plain to see.

Kinlin was like Trout in the way he thought things out pretty much before he let you know what was on his mind. I could just see him in his room drawing out his emotions with his beloved felt tips, and in two days all I would have to do was walk in his room and see his hurt plastered all over the walls. After that was done he would say something that would define all that had passed through his mind, and it would be as profound and to the point as you would ever need to understand. Kinlin knew that words were important, that's why he wanted to learn them as quickly as he could so he could use them as a tool to describe things his eyes couldn't. He also knew that they were powerful and could hand out as much pleasure as pain, so he made sure to choose them carefully and honestly, not wanting to inflict any damage to someone he loved.

Jose and I went for a walk around the farm and ended up sitting on a fallen tree in the middle of the field. We didn't say much, just sat there and took in the day. Jose knew that if I wanted to talk, I would, if not, then we would just sit and watch the fog roll in. After a while, I said, "Jose, I've been thinking about all the things you said yesterday, and there's something I'm not sure of."

"What's that, amigo?" he said, throwing rocks at an imaginary target.

"If Trout left, how could I continue to just be her friend, knowing we could never again be lovers? I mean, I would be her friend, but how could I separate the two? I think my love for her would get in the way and in the end push us farther apart."

"That is possible," he said, "what has happened between the two of you is something that doesn't happen to many people, so how you deal with it isn't written in many books. I know the two of you will be bound together forever. The only problem you both will have will be in trying to define that bond, and once you come up with the answer, what to do with it. The mistake that could be made would be to have it overwhelm you both, and then one of you running away from it. That would be a tragedy and something that would injure you both. Just make sure you aren't the one to do it, because that would take away a lot of her strength, and knowing Trout, she will need a lot of that in the years to come. This is all easy to say, I know, but to put it into practice is another thing, but I know that your love will in the end transcend everything else. Through it you will finally find out who you are, and she will be able to see herself through what you have given her. She will hand back the mirror that she has held, the one she allowed you to look into. Trout will look back into it herself, and you stepping out of her life would be to steal a reflection she needs desperately to see. If anything, your purpose is a commitment to the bond and to not shatter the mirror because of your hurt. Like I said yesterday, it might take a long time, but in the end she will find out who she is because of the bond, and being lovers or friends will make no difference. You and she were meant to love each other. It is probably something eternal. The only thing you both have to decide is how you will show it without tearing each other apart."

"But what if I can't separate the two?" I said. "What if I haven't really learned that much and fuck the whole thing up by jealousy or anger?"

"Maybe you will for awhile, who knows? But the bond will always pull you back together because the most important thing you will both learn from this is forgiveness. In that act you will learn to forgive yourselves, and through that, you will both find self love and your worth."

I had heard him philosophize before, and to touch on truth, but had never heard him talk like this. I knew in his heart he was a poet and philosopher, and if he ever slowed down long enough to look at himself, he would see it. But over the last month Jose had blown my mind with his insights and shown me a part of him I seldom saw.

"Jose," I said, "where in the hell did you come up with all this?"

"It's just something I know, that's all, and something you also know. It's just a truth I'm reading back to you from a book being written in your heart. I haven't fallen in love over a thousand times for nothing, Amigo. I too, have learned a few things, believe it or not. You and I are both passionate people. Maybe we show it in different ways, but it still is a brotherhood that allows us to look into each other and see the truth. A brotherhood that obligates each of us to tell the other what we think." Acting like what he just said was a fact that was as clear as the blue of the sky, he ended with, "and that is the truth my friend!"

As we walked back to the house I let his words sink in knowing that what he had said probably was the truth. Acting upon them was something else, however. What we had talked about were things that involved a goodbye, a subject I was doing my best to push out of my mind. I thought maybe I should have tape recorded Jose's talk, because if the end ever did come it would be something I would have to hear every day in order to heal my hurt.

CHAPTER 27

T rout called every night. It was a cabled touch that kept her near, one that Kinlin couldn't wait to feel. Every time the phone rang he would dash for it, blocking anyone else from picking it up. After the first few times, Jose and I just gave up trying, and made him the official answerer; a job that he took to like a professional.

He had stopped calling me Birdman, and shortened it simply to Bird. He wanted to put a message on the new answering machine that we bought. After I got the thing set up, he recorded in his little voice, "Hello, you have reached the home of Trout, Jose, Kinlin and Bird, we are out trapping bears, so if you want to talk, speak after the beep."

Trout always sounded good, and if there was anything wrong she never let on. The first time she called, Kinlin said he forgot at the airport to give her his magic bass-charmed necklace, something he wanted her to wear to keep her safe. She said she had his photo and looked at it at least a hundred times a day. Seeing his beautiful eyes was enough to protect her, and even if she lost it, she still had his face imprinted on her heart; that is all she would ever need. He asked her every time if she had seen any bears. It would be great, he told her, if she could bring one home because he had given it a lot of thought, and the old chicken coop would be a perfect place to keep one. He would go over all the bear etiquette with her, especially the part of never getting close to one if she had a baby, because if you did the mother would turn you into her lunch. A lesson-in-life-statement that every time he said it made him chuckle. He always asked her when she was coming back. When she told him, he would have to go over for the tenth time, what time, where, and was she definitely sure? He said he had to know for sure because we didn't want to miss her at the airport, (an event that, he told me, would be like standing on a sinking island and being the last one left after missing the boat). She assured him she was coming back on Saturday, just two short days away. Two short days for her maybe, but 48 hours of dark fear-ridden foggy nights for me.

The three of us had tried to keep busy, but found that without Trout the farm wasn't the same. It lacked softness, a presence that held the place together. We became three guys that found ourselves constantly stumbling over the fact she wasn't around.

Kinlin spent a lot of time drawing portraits of her. I thought it was his way of telling himself that she hadn't left. He filled his walls with her face and other color filled memories of her appearance, captured poses that reminded him of someone he missed to the bone.

The day she left he went into our closet and got one of her T-shirts and wore it every day. It was a token of hers I didn't have the heart to ask him to change. He ate and slept in it and it became a tug of war when it came time for him to take a bath. I took it once when he was in the tub, washed it quickly, and stuck it in the dryer. He had spilled taco sauce down the front at dinner, and on our last trip to the store had the shoppers reacting like they had seen a little boy who had just been shot in the chest.

I had been letting him sleep with me because he was having horrendous nightmares in his own room, which drove him like a boy being chased by screaming beasts under the covers and into my arms. He had seen Trout surrounded by bright red angry bears, and every time he tried to save her by talking to them in their language, he would open his mouth and no words would come out. He would awaken just before they attacked and be filled with fear. I tried to comfort him by telling him that it was just a bad dream, but he would hold me tight and say the bears were bears, but they weren't really bears, they were bears in disguise. I asked him what he thought the bears really were, and all he could say was they were something really bad, and something he was afraid would take Trout away and he would never see her again, that all his power over them wouldn't do any good.

Kinlin was tapping into the fear of loss, and his dreams were telling him there was something out there more powerful than the love he felt for her. It was something that might eat her up, or take her away before he had a chance to kill it with that love. It was a dream that wasn't too far off from what Jose had told me a few days before, a fear the boy was starting to let live in his heart.

I told Jose about the dreams. He agreed with me that the boy was starting to feel the loss that maybe he knew was around the corner, and also felt he was helpless to alter its course.

He hung closer to me than he ever had; feeling that to touch me was in a way touching her.

The two days passed and at Kinlin's insistence we arrived an hour and a half early at the airport, which meant that for ninety minutes I was in possession of a creature that asked every four minutes how much longer before the plane arrived. The kid had learned how to read time, but flight schedules were a little bit too much for him. Kinlin stood as close to the ramp door as was allowed, and to see him in his trapper costume with a rose in his hand waiting for Trout was a sight that would tear the heart out of even the meanest of souls.

We spotted her, and he ran like a charging bear and leaped into her arms holding the rose under her nose, shouting, "TROUT, TROUT!"

Trout saw me, and we faced each other and embraced. I felt like the part of me that had been ripped out when she left had been tenderly, again, put back into place.

The ride home was one of constant chatter, and it all came from him. Questions that included bears and mountains, and the food she ate. He wanted a blow-by-blow description of everything she had done since she had left. I had some questions of my own, but didn't know when, if ever, I would be able to ask them. If there was anything different about her, I didn't notice. Kinlin had her so occupied that talking to me was impossible.

We walked into the house and saw that Jose had prepared a great meal, Mexican of course. We spent the next couple of hours talking about what had been going on around the place. Trout didn't get too much into her trip, and spoke mostly in generalities of old friends that she had seen. The evening came to an end, and Trout had to spend at least an hour with Kinlin in his room before he went to bed, with him showing her all his new creations, and the twenty or thirty portraits that he had done of her. The boy was happy again, and if he did feel that she was going to leave didn't let on.

Trout and I went to bed, and it felt good to lie next to her in again. We lay close and didn't say much. We just enjoyed the reunion of hearts. A short time later I saw her change, recognizing the look she wore when deep in thought. It was also the look she had when she had something to say, but was afraid to get it out. The second that I saw it the tenderness of the moment walked over and opened the windows and stepped outside. The adrenaline in me immediately blew a valve and started to overflow and cover the bed.

I led her into it because it was the only way I could deal with the situation. I wasn't going to lie there and wait for her to spring something on me that would jump on my chest like a frothing predator.

"How was the trip?"

"Good," she said.

"I bet it was nice to see your friends, huh?"

"Yeah, it was nice," her voice sounded like she meant every word of it.

"How was Sara?" I said, not asking her what I really wanted to.

"Good," she said, not wanting to touch it with detail.

I knew I had to come to the point. I believe that's what she wanted from me, too. Like me, Trout had a hell of a time getting things out that had a lot of weight to them.

I prepared myself for the hammer I intuitively felt was going to drive a 16-penny nail into my chest. "Trout, what's going on?"

She didn't answer. I knew by her delayed reaction she was afraid to. It was a look, a sigh, something as simple as a slight turn of the head, but it was a signal I had learned to read, one that always scared the shit out of me.

"Trout, something's going on. What is it?"

"I've decided to go back to school," she said, with a voice trembling in a vibration that started in her throat and ended at her feet. It passed through my hand that lay on her arm and traveled through my chest, ending up like a fifty-pound, iced rock in my groin.

"When did you decide this?"

"I've been thinking about it for a couple of weeks. It was one of the reasons I went to Oregon, to see if it was possible, and to get away from here so I could think about it."

"When does all of this happen?" I was afraid to hear her answer. One I'm sure would have me marking the days off on some imaginary calendar carried in the mouth of the wailing butterfly that would be flying in my guts until the day she left.

"I registered while I was there. I have to be back before January first."

"Why so early?" I asked the question like it was a plea, instead of one that was supposed to give me information.

"Because Sara and I have to have time to look for an apartment. We wanted to live together anyway last year, so this will work out good for us both."

Fuck! I didn't know what to say. I was afraid to say anything. I had already heard enough; anything else would just drive the nail in deeper. Trout knew what was going through my mind; she could probably smell it. She turned to me and touched my face, looking at me with eyes that still showed they were full of compassion. I was bringing down the walled gate and, sensing it, she reached out to me to stop it from falling. She knew what this meant to me, and having to tell me was probably one of the hardest things she'd ever done.

I said, "What about the boy? How will you tell him? He'll have a hard time understanding."

He'll probably understand it better than me, I thought, he's probably known it since the first day he was here.

"I'll tell him," she said, "I'm not quite sure when, but it will be soon. I hope you know this was the hardest decision I've ever made, and because it involves Kinlin and you, almost impossible."

That, I believed. I'm sure she worked this one around inside her head so long, that she came close to having a cerebral hemorrhage.

"You're sure that this is what you want to do?"

"I don't really know, but it's something I think I have to do. I've given this a lot of thought, and I know I have to do it. I don't want you to worry. I can come down on the weekends. I arranged my schedule so I have Mondays off. That means I can leave Friday night and not go back until Monday night. It will be OK, you'll see."

I had heard about as much as I could handle for one night, anything else she said would just roll off me like the illusion of her coming down every weekend just did. She might try to it for a week or two, but then the weeks would become farther and farther apart until they turned into airplane departures that never got off the ground due to unfavorable conditions. I couldn't even think about the days to come and the rehearsed good-byes that would fill them. She was doing her best to make the situation in bed as comfortable as she could, and would have promised me the moon if it would have made it easier for us both. She was tender and soft, and tried in her sensitive Trout way to show me she still cared. I hope she didn't want to make love, because I knew I wouldn't have been able to get it up even with the help of a crane. I told her we could talk about it again the next day, which relieved us both.

She kissed my eyes and said, "You know I love you, and I always will. No one has ever loved me like you. I believe no one ever will. My leaving doesn't mean it will stop. I don't want you to ever forget that. You and Kinlin have become my whole life, because of that I forgot what it was like to have one of my own. I don't mean to say I don't want a life with you both. It's just that I have to step back a little and see it from a distance. From the minute we fell in love I have been overwhelmed with it, and then adding Kinlin to it is almost too much for me to take sometimes. I love you both as much as you love me, it's just you and he can deal with it easier than I can, and sometimes I think that I'm not worthy of it. Don't ask me why, because I don't want to talk about that, it's just sometimes I don't think I can handle it."

OK. Enough, I thought. I don't want to hear anymore, not tonight anyway. I just want to go to sleep, wake up, and have you tell me tomorrow morning that you had thought about it again and changed your mind. Then I can go outside and start to work on that white picket fence and go buy a station wagon. I'll get a Master Charge card and make Kinlin a sister. We'll have all the other things that are supposed to go with this fucking life.

I felt like standing up on the bed with a megaphone and yelling, "OK, folks, friends and neighbors, what we have here is the ultimate tragedy unfolding. Watch the Princess leave and the old man turn into a drunk. Watch how she runs off and marries another Princess, then watch him as he say's "I do" to the barrel of a gun as the small boy becomes orphaned and leaves with the Bandit of Baja. Here it is folks, get out the cameras because this is surely something to show your kids. The American Dream dying right before your eyes.

We kissed softly, and just before she went to sleep, she said, "Don't worry, it will be all right."

As I fell asleep, those words woke up the eight-year-old in me who tossed all night, and screamed out all of those fears that had moved into his head sometime back in those hot, nightmare-filled valley nights of the 1940's.

The next morning we awoke and I found Trout wrapped around my back. It was unusual because she usually slept next to the bed under a stack of covers in a breathing heap. I think it was her way of telling me in her sleep that she was still close to me in her heart, no matter how far away she was planning to move.

I turned and saw the two gray-green river stones implanted in her head looking back, moist and full of sleep. We lay next to each other for a long time, feeling the sauna-like warmth of each other's skin.

I tried to capture the moment, putting it into the pulsating red Mason jar beating in my chest, warmth I could use after she was gone simply by unscrewing the lid and letting it flow through my insides.

Her skin was soft as ever and with every breath moved in a rhythm that pushed against mine. I smelled her hair, a scent like no other I had ever put my nose to. It was Trout's hair, and if I was to stand blindfolded in front of a line-up of a thousand heads I would be able to pick it out in a second. The fragrance of her womanhood that came from the garden between her legs had gathered during the night, and like ambrosia worked it's way up through the sheets covering my face. I tried to imagine it as a mask I would wear and look through every minute she was away. The morning in bed was, for me, a journey of memory. As I walked along its path I tried to pick every flower of its importance so I could seal it under glass, to be taken out at a later date to be observed.

I didn't want the time we were spending in bed to ever end. I looked at the clock and hoped I would see it stop, that the morning fog outside would freeze and become an eternal reminder that time had ceased. She reached between my legs and gently touched me. After awhile her velvet strokes got me aroused. I turned her over on her back and entered her. The lovemaking was all for me, she became a foam needle tattooing the moment to my heart. Trout took me with her touch and the moist warmth of her mouth on a raft of pleasure that moved me over the stillness of that December morning. It was a floating voyage I would chart forever in the core of my mind.

When it was over we lay side-by-side and talked. The subject of her move again stepped into our lives. I didn't want to touch it because I thought that it would turn into a ravenous monster and devour all of what we had just shared. But it was there in bed when we fell asleep, and somehow woke up and crawled between us after we had made love.

Trout said, "I know you are troubled by my decision, and I wish it could be easier, but I don't know how to make it so."

Trying to be as understanding as I could, I said, "I know you can't, and I know it's something that's been hard for you to do. We'll just have to try and make the best out of it." Which was akin to saying the same thing to a man sitting in a wheel chair trying to come to terms with being cut off at the waist.

"I know you're worried about my attraction for women and my moving in with Sara, but please don't be. I'm still committed to you."

"It's something that has entered my mind," I said, thinking, yes, something like an inoperable tumor in its last stage of head-exploding pain.

I continued by saying, "It's just something I don't want to have to worry about, and I would like to be able to trust what you have just said."

"You can, Sara is just a good friend, and somebody I can talk too and that's all she will ever be. I do have feelings for her, but they aren't anything that would ever be sexual or anything like that. Please don't worry about it."

"OK," I said, "if you mean it, I believe it," and not wanting to carry it on any farther, I added, "how about some breakfast?"

She grabbed my arm as I was getting out of bed, and said, reaching up to kiss me, "Just don't ever forget that I love you."

"I won't Trout, I won't," I said, kissing her back.

We all had breakfast that morning with Kinlin not taking his eyes off Trout. He was looking at her with the eyes of love, but also eyes searching for something else. Sometimes he would turn to me with the same look, trying to find out if there was a secret mixed in with the omelet on our plates. The boy's intuitions were in full gear, and he was trying to tap them for all they had. I knew given enough time they would tell him what he wanted to know.

The day was spent with Kinlin occupying all her time, showing her all he had learned while she was away. Trout couldn't believe how his vocabulary had grown, and that his reading was at a sixth grade level. The kid could grasp in one month what most kids did in a year, and most of it was done on his own. We all read to him and let him try to read back. I was amazed at what he could pick up and never forget.

He read to Trout stories out of *Field and Stream*, which she helped him patiently through, and heard him explain in detail the difference between an elk and a moose. But, he became totally confused when she tried to explain why salmon swam upstream. When he asked for more detail she told him that Bird would tell him when he got a little older, and that was done with a sly, smiling look in my direction.

Trout had been back two days and still hadn't told Kinlin of her plan. I asked her the morning of the second day when she was going to do it and she said nervously, that day. I watched her trying to prepare herself for something that her twenty years hadn't. As a matter of fact, I thought it was a task a ninety-year-old Guru would have had trouble doing. She stood by the front window and watched Kinlin playing with his sword in the field, and at that moment I wished I could do it for her, but at the same time was thankful I didn't have to.

She opened the door and headed for the field walking like she was dragging a 1,000-pound sled. I stood in front of the window watching the scene through the rippled antique glass. She approached him as he was squatting down with his sword peering into a squirrel hole. As soon as he saw her coming he started to gesture and point to the hole. I could see him talking and was sure he was telling her what he believed was going on in that secret little world. She knelt down beside him, and I knew the news was starting to fill his ears. It took about a minute before it registered in his mind, and then I saw him stand up and kick the dirt. He threw his sword on the ground and took off on a sobbing run towards the house. He crashed by the front gate and ran through the front door right by me and into his room, slamming the door.

I continued to look out the window and saw Trout staring at the ground. I felt like comforting them both, but didn't know who to turn to first. I turned in the direction of Kinlin's room, then back towards the field. Trout was walking head down towards the southeast corner. I knew it was better to leave her alone, so I turned to go to Kinlin.

Jose, standing in the kitchen, had witnessed the whole thing. I had talked to him the day after Trout had told me of her decision to leave, but he and I had let it lie knowing I wasn't ready to discuss it.

I opened the door and walked into Kinlin's room. He was face down on his bed, sobbing into his pillow. He had his bass lure talisman clutched in his hand.

"Kinlin, you want to talk?"

"NO!" he shot back, choking on his tears.

I went over and touched his shoulder, and felt him pull away. "Are you sure? Maybe we should talk about it."

"NO, I DON'T WANT TO TALK!" he screamed back.

I didn't know what to do. I just stood there and watched the sobbing boy's body heave up and down, feeling as helpless as I had ever felt in my life. He wanted to be alone. I didn't want to leave him, but standing there doing nothing was not doing either of us any good. At that moment I felt Jose's arm on my back, and turning, saw him motion at me to step out the door. I closed the door and met him in the kitchen. By the look on my face he knew I was lost.

"Amigo let him be for awhile. Let him cry it out."

I looked back towards the room, "I can't! I can't leave him alone."

"There are four people here that are feeling this pain, and we are all alone," he said. "We are feeling it each in our own way. Let the boy feel his for a while, he will let you know when he wants to be touched. I didn't see what happened, but I know what happened out there in that field, and I also know what Trout must be feeling now. That orchard she's walking through has just turned into a burial ground for her. By the way, how are you doing?"

I stood there feeling my eyes water. I looked down at the floor afraid to open my mouth. Jose reached into the cabinet and grabbed two glasses and poured us a drink. I was choking on words that hadn't come out yet. Seeing that, Jose handed me a glass. "Drink it," he ordered.

As I pulled the glass up to my mouth my hands were shaking, Jose noticing it, said, "Amigo drink it, it will slow you down."

I bent down with my head and met the glass halfway. I felt the warm taste of bourbon running down the back of my throat.

Jose reached over with the bottle and poured me another shot. I held it in my hand and stared into it.

Not taking his eyes off my face, he said, "This is the day we have so often spoken of. Don't forget the boy, you have to be strong for him."

"I know," I said, hardly remembering what he said.

"You going to make it?" he asked.

"I don't know, and this isn't the day we talked about," I said, looking back at him.

"What do you mean?" he said, perplexed.

"Because she hasn't left yet. That's the day I'm worried about. Fuck! This is a piece of cake compared to what that will be like, and I'm not sure I can make it through this one!"

"You will make it," he said, "you have too. You know there are two people here that need you. One is out there dying in that field, and the other is lying in that room wishing he were dead. You love those two people more than you have ever loved anything in your life, and today you are going to have to use that love to help save their lives, then use it again to save your own."

"Hell, I don't think I'm strong enough, Jose. I think 'Red' was right, and that good big man, that bad ass motherfucker he told me to watch out for is going to whip my ass!"

"No it ain't, because I'm going to be here to pull him off your back, and you know there's nothing I like better than going toe-to-toe with a big son-of-a-bitch who thinks he's tough."

"Yeah," I forced a smile, "I know that. I've seen it more times than I can remember."

"OK then, it's time to put on the gloves, because if you fall apart then the boy will really be lost."

"Yeah, I know you're right," I started to calm down. "I've just got to get through the day somehow. I'll be OK"

After a while I peeked in Kinlin's room and saw that he was sitting at his desk drawing. I went to him and put my hand on his hair, and looking down, asked how he was.

"Sad," he said, not looking up.

"I know you are," I said. "Me too."

With that, he turned and looked up at me, intensely staring into my eyes. I'm sure, searching for the same hurt that was filling his.

I asked, "What's that you're drawing?" knowing full well what I was seeing.

"Us," he said.

I looked at the group portrait that lay before him on the table. It was of the four of us in a green field. He had drawn a black airplane flying over us with a rope hanging from the bottom, and at the end of the rope was Trout suspended over our heads. I knew what he was saying with the picture so I didn't have to ask him the meaning.

"Kinlin, I think that maybe we should talk about this. Don't you?"

"No Bird, I don't want to talk about it now," he said, working on his picture.

"Why not?"

"Because I'm too sad, that's why, and I don't want to talk about sad things right now."

"OK," I said, knowing that it was better to leave it where it was, and also knowing that Kinlin was going to spend the next few hours working his feelings out at the tip of his pen.

Walking back to the door, I said, "Kinlin, remember, if you want to talk I'll be in the next room."

"I know Bird," he said, not looking up from his desk.

Trout was gone for hours. They were hours that moved through the house like the hands on a clock in one of Dali's paintings. They were twisted and bent, and fell off the clock, and it seemed like it took forever for them to get back up on the face and move again.

Trout finally came back and went into our room. I saw her from the kitchen and after a few minutes went in to see how she was. I found her exactly as I thought I would, buried up to her hair in covers. I sat down next to her and laid my hand on the part of the quilt that covered her back. I didn't know at that moment what to say; I just knew that I had to say something. I reached over close to her head, and asked, "Trout, are you all right?"

She didn't move or respond, so I said again, "Trout, please speak to me."

Still there was no answer. I reached over farther and got close to her face and smelled the hurt and the warm tears covering the pillow. Her body was in the throes of sorrow, and it was a silent weeping that filled the bed. I imagined that I was at a funeral in a land of deaf mutes standing in a crowd of a thousand mourners as they silently cried, while watching their King being lowered into the ground.

I was at a loss. I left the room and walked outside into the Zen garden and sat on the bench. I felt like the world had just fallen apart and I was the man chosen to put it back together. Only I didn't have the slightest idea how. I thought of Jose's words, and that he was right, that I had never loved anything as much as I loved her. It was a love I felt I was born with, one that had walked with me every step I had taken over the last 51 years. It was a love I always wanted to feel, and something I wanted so much in my life to someday obtain. I had finally found it and had opened my heart to it. Just as I was getting use to the miracle it missed a beat and slowly started to gasp out its last dying breath. I knew that she wanted to believe she would be back and that the love would go on forever, but I felt that she would run, and over the course of time would find reasons to keep herself away. One of those reasons would be cloaked in another love, a love that would be easier for her to understand and control, a love that would make her feel safe.

After she left here she would find someone to make sure that she wasn't alone. She couldn't stand to be alone when she was in the throes of pain, and that was most of the time. Trout would use that love as a blanket to cover her needs and to keep her warm, and like a small girl, pull it up tight around her when the dragons came. In the end she would love out of need, pulling the blanket tighter around her neck until she found she could no longer breathe. I was afraid that she would end up going through life confusing love for necessity. Using it as something to fill the void that ran rampant through her soul. I wished that I could help her and show her that what we had here wasn't something that wanted to suffocate her, but was something that in the end would enable her to breathe. I knew that the love Kinlin and I felt for her had become a rope and the longer she stayed, a rope that would grip tighter and tighter around her neck.

I sat on the stone bench, the same flat piece of rock where Trout and I gave in to our love and stared at the half-filled pond. I saw her knee deep, as I had many times with Kinlin, thrashing around, laughing and fighting sharks.

The camellias were bare of flowers and winter had dropped all the leaves of the plum. Rocks around the pond were sucking in the fog and turning into brown-green mounds from where the wren stood and drank. The fern drooped, and the evening wind brushed against the pine needles that lay on the ground. The giant redwood swayed and watched as I sat and developed pictures of the past, looking at sweet memories that appeared in sepia tones before my eyes.

I knew that Trout wouldn't make it until Christmas, but if she did, it wouldn't be about the birth of a king, but the death of her heart.

CHAPTER 28

Trout left two days later. The days before she left were as gray as the thick fog that covered the trees in the field. A mist that had worked itself through the walls and invaded the house accompanied them. She was distant; in a tremendous amount of pain, and in her much used way of smothering it spent a lot of those two days in bed.

Kinlin was confused. He recognized her hurt and did his best to help her make it go away. Whenever he was in her presence he would stare into her eyes, like a doctor trying to diagnose her numbing pain.

I watched it all from a distance, because that is where I had been put. It was an emotional shove that she used to let me know that to touch was to feel, and I knew that she was trying to break away from any feelings that would cause her anymore hurt.

Kinlin would see the tragic theater's curtain being slowly closed and would retreat to his room trying to figure out the meaning of the drama by using the tip of his pen. Jose spent most of his time in his room, or down at the bar trying to numb the thoughts of her escape that, he too felt, couldn't be far off.

The night before she left we made love, but it was an act of tenderness that she used to try and erase the thoughts filling her mind. She had done it before using the act of making love as a passionate ordeal. An act filled with Valium-like screams and the tear-filled anti-climax of being back in the real world. We didn't talk that night, and the bed was empty of the affectionate smiles and jokes that usually followed our making love. She moved close to me and in her own secret way was telling me goodbye. I smelled her tears and the warm breath of sorrowed, unspoken words. Words that, unbeknownst to me, were saying, "I have to go."

Before she turned over to sleep she reached up and set the alarm, and I knew from the sound of my own alarm deep in my guts that this was going to be our last night together.

I watched her fall asleep trying to remember every sound and breath she took, unscrewing that jar in my heart and sticking them inside. I felt her body twitch, which was always the sign that she had reached the place where she felt safest. She was deep in a world where, with the exception of her bad dreams, offered her no harm.

I got up and went in the kitchen to have a beer and found Jose had just gotten home and was doing the same.

"Amigo, is Trout asleep?"

"Yeah," I answered, breathing the word out instead of speaking them.

"You all right?" he asked, a voice full of concern.

"I don't think so Jose."

"What's going on?"

"She's going to leave tomorrow, early."

"Oh," he said sadly, "how do you know?"

"I feel it," I said, tipping my beer.

"I knew it was coming," he said, "and that it was just a matter of time."

"Yeah, me too."

"She has too much pain, amigo," he said, reaching out and touching my shoulder, "If she stayed any longer she would just fold up and die."

"I know, Jose," I said, looking back in the direction of our room. "I would rather have her leave than to go through this. I love her too much to see the hurt filling her eyes. If leaving is what will take it away, then I guess that is what has to happen. But knowing that doesn't make it any easier."

"Does the boy know?" he asked.

"No, but I'm sure he feels something is going to happen that he has no control over, but you know him, he's just working it through his head trying to find some reason in all of this."

"It will be hard on him amigo. You know that!"

"Yeah, it will," I said, hearing the words echo like a rifle shot in my ears.

"You are going to have to reach in and pull out every bit of love and gentleness that you have in you to help him pull through, and he will have to do the same for you."

"I know," I said, "and what about you?"

"Me? I'm going to hurt too, my friend. Trout has become like a sister to me, and the woman who is deeply loved by a man who I consider my brother. I feel like the family that I always wanted to have is going to fall apart, and it is a loss that is making my heart hurt. I will miss her."

He reached up and grabbed the bottle and poured us a shot. Raising his drink towards me, said, "We are going to drink to Trout and to all the love that she has brought to our hearts, and pray that she finds the peace she so desperately needs."

With that, we drank, and as I saw Jose say good night he reached up, and with the knuckle of the first finger of his right hand wiped away something that showed me how deeply he cared.

The alarm went off. At first the sound moved Trout just a bit, but suddenly had her sitting on the edge of the bed with her head in her hands. She leapt up and went to the bathroom. I lay there not knowing what to do, and waited for her to come back. She returned in her robe with all the things that were hers; sweet smelling jars and bottles that for six months had lived on the bathroom shelf. She turned on the closet light just as I looked through the window and saw the first light of day turn the orchard a cold orange.

She was busy, putting things in her bags that she had prepared the night before. Trout came out wearing a pair of baggy jeans, a dark blue turtleneck sweater and her Elmer Fudd shoes.

I looked up at her, and said, "You're sure this is what you want to do?"

"I don't want to talk about it now," she said stuffing something in a bag. What she meant was, "I can't talk about it now!"

I didn't say anything more because to continue would have probably brought her sobbing to her knees. I knew, too, that there was nothing to say. Silence was the best thing for us both. I got up and put on my clothes and looked into those beautiful eyes staring back. Those two precious stones were filled half with sadness, half with fear.

She was in a hurry and had no emotional time to look back. I followed her and her bags to the kitchen where she paused and looked into Kinlin's room. I felt that if she would falter, it would be there. She sighed deeply, bit her bottom lip, and then walked out the back door. She popped the trunk and threw her things in the back while I waited at the driver side door.

Trout walked up to me, trembling in the morning cold. She threw herself around my neck, and as I felt my skin become wet from what was falling from her eyes, I heard her say in a shaking voice, "I love you, and always will. Please don't ever forget that."

Doubting that I could even get the words past the growing barrier in my throat, I said, "I love you too, Trout."

She opened the door. As she was getting in she said, "I'm sorry, but I just couldn't say goodbye to Kinlin, it would have just been too hard. Tell him I'll call him in a couple of days."

She was almost sobbing, and I knew we weren't going to be able to say anymore. There was nothing more to say.

Trout put the car in gear and blasted up the drive into a morning day free of fog. She just had passed the eucalyptus when I heard the back door swing open and bounce off the back porch wall. It was Kinlin leaping down the stairs wearing his pajamas running as fast as he could, following her dust. I watched him, and heard him scream her name over and over, once tripping, but getting up again to continue his pursuit.

I knew not to chase him. He would tire before he got to the top of the first hill. I turned in the direction of the studio. Jose was standing behind a window that mirrored the morning light. He stood with his hands in his pockets looking back at me like a man lost in a surrealistic painting filled with distorted pines, splashed in orange, reflecting back on a glass-covered canvas.

I started up the drive. By the time I got to the boy I would have to somehow bury my hurt and prepare to deal with his. As I got closer I saw him standing at the top of the hill looking at a cloud of dust drifting over the highway, and the three mailboxes to its right. When I was about ten feet away I saw him drop down in the dirt and rocks on the road staring at the brown cloud that was slowly starting to disappear. I reached him and stood by his side. Looking down, I saw the streaks of abandonment staining his cheeks.

"Kinlin, come on, I'm going to take you back to the house."

He said something, but it was so soft and quiet I couldn't make it out.

"What did you say?"

"She promised," he said, in a voice I could hardly hear.

"I know, Kinlin," I said, feeling like I had just said the words myself.

"She promised, Bird. She promised she would stay until Christmas." He said it with words reeking of betrayal hidden in his voice.

"I know Kinlin, she promised, but sometimes there are things more powerful than promises, and that powerful thing is so strong that it makes them hard to keep."

"But Bird," he said, looking up at me with confused tear-filled eyes, "don't you remember when we talked about promises and lies, and you and Trout said never go back on a promise, to never lie?"

"Yes, I remember," recalling the day perfectly in my mind.

"Well, why did she leave then? She promised she wouldn't!"

I knew this was something I was going to have to solve, explaining an act I was having trouble accepting myself. I knew why she left. I understood it, but she had left the boy and me, and that hurt, and hurt always had a way of interfering with anything logical. Kinlin wasn't in the mood to deal with logic today, but I knew if it weren't dealt with in a way he could understand and believe, then this feeling of betrayal that had moved into him would affect him the rest of his life.

I reached down and grabbed his hand and gently pulled him to his feet. We started back towards the house and heard the red-tail scream overhead on its first morning flight over the field. Trying to change the subject, I said, "Look! It's our friend, can you here it scream?"

"It's not screaming," he said, beckoning me to pick him up to be held.

"Sure it is," I said, "I just heard it!"

"No," he said, laying his head on my shoulder. "It's crying because it saw Trout leave too."

As we approached the house, I thought that the boy was probably right, and the hawk had witnessed the whole thing from his perch in the Monterey pine. He was probably sent here to watch over me as a duty and payback for saving one of his kind back in '52. The bird was screaming that, if he could, he would follow her down High Way 116, grab the car and bring it back. In doing so he would be returning the favor he owed, but his talons couldn't pierce steel so he would have to wait for another day, and return the debt in another way.

The hawk wanted to tell me that he could see the car about three miles away. It had pulled off to the side of the road. The woman inside was sitting with her face in her hands weeping like she would never stop. The bird saw her start to turn around and come back, but halfway through the turn straighten it out and punch the gas to the floor and head 80 miles an hour for highway 101. He then would say she hit the freeway and headed north crying all the way to Grant's Pass. He saw her pull over at a rest stop and try to sleep away the hurt. The last he saw of her she was going in the direction of Portland, breaking into tears every ten miles.

Kinlin and I got back to the house and I carried him into his room so he could get out of his pajamas. On the way to his room we passed the kitchen. Jose was washing the dishes while staring out the window into the garden. He didn't say a thing, just kept working the sponge in circles on the same plate, a constant circled movement that reminded me of a soaped, porcelain sounding 'Ohm' he was using as a prayer to bless Trout on her hard road ahead.

Kinlin changed into his jeans and baggy sweatshirt, and with boots and coat on he and I proceeded to the front porch. We sat on the edge of the step and heard the crackle of dried oak leaves under our feet. With the eyes of the father I had become, I observed him starting the painful process of grief. We had to talk about her leaving, and it had to be in terms he could understand. I started with the question he had in his mind about promises. "Kinlin, do you want to talk about promises some more?"

Staring down at his feet as he kicked the leaves, sticking out his lower lip, he said, "Yes."

"Are you confused why she broke hers?"

"Yes," he said quietly, still kicking the ground.

"Remember out on the road when I told you sometimes there our things stronger than a promise and it makes somebody break that promise?"

"Yes," he said, softly.

"Well, that's what happened to Trout. It was so strong it even made her break a promise to you, the person she loves more than anything in the world. The thing that made her do it was fear."

"Fear?" he said, looking up at me with his little, puzzled, identical Trout eyes.

"Yes, fear. You know all of those monsters we fight in the Zen garden, the one's that want to eat our poems? Well, Trout has some of those inside of her."

With that, he moved over, making sure his leg was touching mine and looked up into my eyes with his own that had doubled in size.

I continued, "Now, they aren't monsters with big sharp teeth or purple skin. As a matter of fact, they are invisible; they live in your heart and in your head. Those monsters are called fear."

He looked up at me trying to figure this one out. I explained further. "Remember when you have those bad dreams and you come running into our room? You know how you get afraid and have this terrible feeling something bad is going to happen, then you get this squishy feeling in your stomach and you want to run away and hide?"

He shook his head up and down. I saw by the look in his eyes that he wanted me to continue.

"Well, that is fear, and fear comes in all kinds of shapes and sizes, invisible shapes and sizes, that is. When fear moves into your head and your heart, we become afraid, that's where the word afraid comes from, understand?"

Shaking his head up and down, he said in a whisper, "Yes."

"People can be afraid of anything. For instance they can be afraid to get in the car and drive to the store because they fear something bad will happen on the way, or afraid to go out in the dark alone because they fear what might be hiding in the blackness."

"Not me," he said, acting like what I had just said was something his little warrior heart had never felt, "because I've got my sword and necklace."

"I know," I said, "but some people don't have a sword and necklace, so they don't have any protection against their fears. After awhile the fear grows and grows, and pretty soon it fills them up until they feel like they are going to explode, then they run away because they can't stand to be around it any more. It's just like you running into our room to escape that terrible thing you were dreaming about. You couldn't stand to be in the same room with it anymore, but after you got into bed with us you realized it was just a fear that was in your head. Am I right?"

"Right!" he said, not taking his eyes off me.

"OK." I said, "Trout has fears too, and the fear that made her run is love."

"LOVE?" he said, sticking out his little neck closer to my face. "LOVE? But love is a good thing Bird, she shouldn't be afraid of love."

"I know, but Trout loves you and me more than anything she ever loved before, and since that was a new feeling to her she didn't understand it. Because she didn't understand it, it made her afraid."

212

"Afraid of what. Bird?" he said, grabbing my hand.

"She was afraid that if she gave all of that new love away there wouldn't be any left over for herself, and if she didn't love herself she would feel alone. The new love confused her. She didn't know how to split it up. If you don't love yourself then you don't know who you really are. Trout loved you and me so much she forgot who she was. She felt that if she didn't understand who she was then she might do, or say things she didn't mean and it might us. Trout loved us so much that she didn't want to ever hurt our feelings."

"Is that why she left Bird, because she didn't want to hurt our feelings?" he said, wanting to find some good out of all this.

"Yes, she left so she could think about all these things we're talking about. If she stayed the fear would turn the love into something bad, and she loved us too much to have that happen."

"Does she still love us Bird?" he asked, looking back towards the ground.

"Oh yes, she still loves us as much as ever, that's why she was so sad the last few days. The thought of leaving us was almost too much for her."

"But, Bird," he said, looking back up at me, "if she would have stayed I would have shown her how to split it up. I don't need all of it, we could have split it in half."

"I know you would Kinlin," I said, loving that little boy with all my heart, "but it was too late, the fear was too strong and it won the fight."

He stood up and looked me dead-in-the-eye, and said, "If I would have known that then I would have got my sword and chased it away and it would have been afraid to come back!"

"I know son," I said. It was the first time I had ever called him that. "I know you would, but maybe you still can. The way we can help her is to continue to love her with all our hearts, and that love will be so strong it will chase away all her fears. It might take some time, but in the end it will win. Tomorrow I'll have Jose carve the word 'love' on your sword, and that's what you'll think about every time you think of Trout."

"Bird," he said, deep in thought, "how long will she have to be away to win her fight over this fear?"

"I don't know, Kinlin. Trout has to learn to love herself, and sometimes that is a long hard fight, but it is something she has to do alone. When she has won she will let us know."

"How will she do that?"

"We will see it in her eyes and know. It will be as simple as that. What we have to do is to continue to love her no matter what, no matter how far away she is. She will feel it. It will give her strength and keep her from feeling alone."

"But Bird," he said, looking at me, "why didn't she say goodbye?"

"Because she was too sad, and the sadness was so strong she felt it would make you sad too, even sadder than you are right now. Kinlin, she loves you so much she didn't want you to feel that awful sadness."

"Yeah," he said, staring off into space, "that really would have been sad. I would have tried to hold on to her and keep her here."

"She knew that," I said, picturing him with a death grip on her leg as she tried to walk out the door. "It would have been the saddest thing ever to have happened to you both. She loves you too much to have to see you go through that."

Deep in thought, Kinlin stared off into the field. I wondered if I had said anything right. I felt as sad and abandoned as he did. I might as well have been talking to myself. The things I told him about Trout were true enough, I just didn't know if he was able, in his small boy way, to understand them. Knowing Kinlin, he would give it concentrated thought. In the end I hoped he would see it clearly.

He interrupted my thoughts by turning to me and saying, "Bird, I have just decided that love is the strongest thing in the world. It is stronger than fear, and the next time I see Trout I am going to tell her that. And every time I see her I will show her, and after awhile she won't be afraid anymore. Fear is going to try and eat all of her poems, and I won't let it. I will take my sword and fight them off, then she will see how strong love can be."

He looked at me with a furrowed brow, "Don't you think that's a good idea, Bird?"

"That's a good idea, Kinlin." I felt my love for him grow stronger by the second. "As a matter of fact, that's the best idea I've ever heard."

He looked up at me, still sad, but with a faint smile on his face. "Bird, I think I want to go to my room for awhile and be alone." Then, asking in a tone of voice that showed he wasn't in this alone, said, "Bird, are you as sad as me?"

"Yes Kinlin," I said, speaking a heart tearing truth, "I am."

"Do you want to be alone, or should we talk some more," he said, changing rolls.

"No, you go ahead. I think I will sit here awhile and think nice thoughts about Trout, maybe she will feel them, wherever she is."

"That's what I'm going to do too. Bird, I think I will draw some pictures of her, pictures where she is smiling. Maybe she will feel my pen drawing her mouth and her eyes and she will smile too and not feel so sad."

"That's a good idea. Draw some pictures with a lot of smiles in them, I'm sure she will feel it and smile too."

Kinlin stood up and hugged me tight. "Bird, you aren't afraid of love are you. It won't make you run away, will it?"

"No, Kinlin," I said. "I used to be, but you and Trout took away my fear. I promise I won't run from love, don't worry."

He drew back from his hug and stared into my eyes looking for the truth. "Really promise?"

"Yes," I said, "I promise, I never will."

He smiled and hugged me again and walked through the door. I hoped what I had just said was a promise I could keep. For some reason I knew that if I ever broke it to him it would shatter us both, and probably be the only reason he would ever have to break his sacred sword in two over his knee.

After awhile Jose came out and sat next to me. "Amigo, how is the boy?"

"I don't know, trying to cope. We talked for a long time. I hope it did some good."

"And you, my friend?" he asked, touching my arm.

"I don't know Jose, I honestly don't know." I spoke the words like they were written in stone.

We sat there for a long time and talked. We watched the sun reach noon, and I wondered where Trout was. I worried about her and the thoughts that must have been going through her mind. I wanted to believe everything she had said, that everything would be all right, and that she loved me and not to worry. But hope and me were archenemies. I tried my best to believe it hadn't disappeared with that cloud of dust that followed her car down the road.

That night I gave Kinlin his bath, with him telling me every ten seconds that Trout didn't do it that way, and this was how she did this and did that. I knew he was missing her like crazy and correcting me was a way to tell himself she was there in the room with him.

We went into his room to get him ready for bed. "Kinlin, if you want to sleep in my bed tonight, it's OK with me."

He sat on the edge of his bed with his sword in his hand and looked up at me with a little doubt in his eyes. "No, Bird, I'm going to sleep here tonight and see if fear comes. If it does I'm going to make a test and try to fight it. That way when I see Trout I can tell her I did it and it was easy."

"OK, Kinlin." I watched him get into bed and tuck his sword under the covers. "Don't feel bad if you can't do it the first time, sometimes it takes awhile to learn how to do it. I'll leave the door open, just in case."

Looking back at me with eyes doing their best to be brave, he said, "Good idea, Bird."

I knelt down and touched his face and said good night and not to worry. In the end everything would turn out OK.

He looked up. "Bird, I miss Trout. I never missed anybody before. I don't like the word miss. It makes something in me very sad. Does it make you sad too?"

Thinking that I was going to see the words "Miss You" written in neon letters on a three-story billboard outside my bedroom window blinking on and off all night, I said, "Yeah, I don't like that word either. Maybe we shouldn't use it any more. What do you think?"

"Yeah, let's not use it anymore."

"OK, Kinlin, good night," I said, turning off the light.

"Bird," he said, "are you ever afraid?"

I thought about answering, "Every fucking minute of every fucking day." but didn't, saying instead, "Sometimes I am, but as long as I know you are here with your sword, I feel better."

Smiling, and looking under the covers to make sure his sword was still there, he said, "Good night Bird."

I went to bed feeling like I had just been cast adrift at sea. I missed Trout so much I wasn't sure if I was going to make it through the night. I thought of the phrase, "feeling it to my bones," and knew whoever came up with it must have felt it at one time. At that moment I knew exactly what they must have gone through. My body was hurting to the core. I felt like my blood was filled with driftwood banging against my arterial walls. I thought of life without her, and would the boy be enough to erase my pain?

The fear I had so knowingly talked about to Kinlin was moving in on me. I knew that it was going to sleep with me that night. All the wonderful things Trout and I had shared were not powerful enough to chase it away.

The eight-year-old had visited, and was telling me that maybe Trout was my last chance, that I would never find another like her. The worst fear was maybe I would never want to find any one else. If she really was the eternal wife I had talked to Jose about, then I knew the life of monogamy that lay ahead was going to be a lonely one. I had learned over the years that my heart had only enough room for one person at a time, and to stick someone else in it would be a lie, a betrayal I wouldn't be able to live with.

I laid there trying to let sleep take me away, imagining myself in some rundown hotel watching the sign outside blink on and off sending a strobe-light message bouncing off the room inside. It was orange and yellow, and ran down the walls rhythmically covering the bed. I fought the beating rays and covered my eyes, but the words kept bouncing off my mind. As I fell into the darkness of sleep I was illuminated head to toe with the 12 foot high neon words "Miss You" tattooed across my back, words that would color the walls of that room every second she was away.

CHAPTER 29

Trout called the next evening and told me that she was OK. I could tell by the sound of her voice she wasn't, but went along with her just to not have to talk about the pain that she and I were both suffering. Before asking to speak to Kinlin, she told me again she loved me and not to worry, she just needed time to think things out. I watched Kinlin as he spoke to her. In his caring way he tried to reach through that 650 miles of cable and show her he understood what had happened. The call was short. I knew Trout wasn't strong enough to stay on the line too long. I heard Kinlin say that Jose had carved the word "LOVE" on his sword, and the next time he saw her he was going to chase away all the monsters that were trying to eat her poems. They hung up and he somberly went to his room.

Later on in the day he told me that Trout said she would see him soon, and she was sorry she didn't say goodbye, but she was too sad to do it. He seemed to understand her explanation, but never told me he had accepted it. I could tell by his actions after the call that it had been a traumatic communication for him, something that had put him at his desk all day drawing out his feelings.

The three of us toughed out the next few days, but found it was pretty much like the first trip she had taken. Her absence put us all in a sullen mood. Jose did his best to pick things up, but even he couldn't kid us. We knew his loss was as big as ours was.

She hadn't called again, and the few times the phone did ring put Kinlin on a dead run in its direction. The look of disappointment on his face began to show in his drawings, and Jose and I were at a loss of how to try and wipe it off. He had spent that first night alone in bed and I was proud of his effort, and of the apparent success with his triumph over the forces of fear. He was doing a lot better than me. I thought about asking Jose to make me a sacred sword, thinking maybe it would help me through those fear-ridden sleepless nights I was having.

No matter how much I believed what I had been telling Kinlin about defeating the demons of the night, they still crawled in bed with me after the lights were out. I had too much time to think and the thoughts entering my mind were ones I couldn't chase out of my head. Anger was starting to fill me. It was an emotion I had never felt for Trout before. I watched Kinlin suffer the loss every day and saw how he hurt. I was beginning to blame her for it, but at the same time knew he was just a mirror I was looking into. I was in a growing rage for her abandoning me too.

The eight-year-old had returned taking the place of Trout in bed with me at night, constantly reminding me that we had been betrayed. He kept trying to reach back into our past and demanded I find instances where it had happened before, but I couldn't. Instead I said, "We had the perfect childhood, didn't he remember playing underneath that big willow in the back yard next to the pigeon pen? There were ball games every weekend with the folks. And what about the boxing matches twice a month at the fair grounds? Small town gladiatorial events where I would get up in front of hundreds of people and fight other seven-year-olds during intermission. Didn't he recall the cheers and applause as I tried reluctantly to tear the head off of the other little boy in front of me? Hell! We were never alone," I told him, "and never abandoned."

He said, *"Remember when you were afraid to stay home alone, even in the daytime? And feeling ashamed, you would set on the front steps until your parents got home from work? When your folks played poker with their friends and all the other kids went out and slept in the family cars when it got late, why were you the only one who didn't? It was because you were afraid. You thought you'd wake up in the car and everybody would be gone and, shit, you couldn't even drive! Then you would have to stay there forever, or until the monsters came and ate out your guts.*

You were abandoned all right; you just can't remember when it happened. It was probably so subtle you didn't even log it where normal pain is stuck. You took that betrayal and buried it in a place where it is so dark and forbidding even Red Davis, as tough and fearless as he was, wouldn't dare to venture in. I'll tell you, old man, it's not The Trout's leaving that's pushing your buttons, it's a gray executioner's day somewhere back in the forties that's putting you through all this pain. You better solve this, or you will never have a peaceful night's sleep again. She hasn't even left you yet. As a matter of fact, she's still trying to hang on. What the fuck are you going to do if she actually does say goodbye forever? You think that car was lonely! You will end up turning this bedroom into the biggest, blackest, locked-door 48 dodge that ever rolled off the line. Then all you have do is take a garden hose and hook it to the tail pipe and turn the key and we will have solved this problem of being afraid to be alone forever. I can tell you right now what's going to happen. All that booze you are using to try and numb the pain is going to catch up with you and torque out your mind. That anger is going to fester and drip pus all over your common sense and you are going to do something that will make you hate yourself.

You've seen it before. Remember that time in Germany when those months of fear and anger ate at your soul and you ripped that cigarette machine off the wall in that bar, sobbing and in tears? Fuck! The thing was bolted three inches in the wall and must have weighed a hundred pounds.

Don't you remember throwing it over the bar and fucking up the shelf full of glasses in back? Hell, man! That anger ate you up and you scared the shit out of everybody that night.

Then that friend of yours, the poet psychiatrist, slapped you in the face to try and straighten you up and you proceeded to tear his head off. OK, so he was a drunk and thought he was tough, but he was no match for you even if you weren't the angriest man in the world that night. You hated yourself for that. I bet you apologized to him a thousand times. To this day you still feel bad about it. What are you going to do now, knock the shit out of Jose and the kid? Then drive up to Oregon and beat the hell out of The Trout? You're a sick motherfucker, old man, and you better lay off the booze because if you think those demons fucking with your mind right now are unbearable, just wait till they get on the phone and call up their buddies. Ripping a cigarette machine off the wall isn't going to impress them in the least. They would just stand back and laugh and one-up you by going over and tearing the whole fucking wall out, then eat the concrete and spit back the pieces in your face!"

The little eight-year-old son of a bitch was back. Trout had pretty much kept him at bay, but her leaving was the signal for him and all of his insecurities to return. Since the little warrior with the magic sword wasn't going to bed down with me, he felt like he had all the right in the world to take his place.

It had been a week and she hadn't called. Kinlin had quit answering the phone. I hurt for us both when I answered it and found it wasn't her on the other end.

One night Jose took him to the movies and a pizza afterwards. It was the first time in months I had been alone. I had been drinking all day, but was holding it well. Jose had noticed my more-than-normal-intake over the last few days and had even mentioned it to me once. I told him I was all right, that I would cut down soon. He said he had seen it fuck up my mind a few times before, and just wanted to make sure I knew what I was doing.

The phone rang when I was in the kitchen pouring myself a drink. I was so depressed I almost didn't answer it, but walked in and picked it up anyway. It was Trout. Her voice was shaking so much I imagined it moving the lines on the pole outside.

"Trout, what's going on?"

"Nothing," she answered in a trembling voice.

There was no, "How you doing?" or "How's Kinlin?" or "How's the weather?" There was only one thing on her mind, and it had nothing to do with small talk.

"What do you mean nothing? I can hear it in your voice. What's happening?" I already knew what was coming.

"Oh, I don't know, it's just, I don't know. It's just that I've been thinking a lot," she said faintly.

"Thinking a lot, about what?" I felt like I could probably end the conversation for her, by the way my guts were feeling

"About us," she said.

Boom! The fucking butterfly took off and exploded in my chest disintegrating into a million little ones who worked their way into my muscles and fettered in my veins. When I asked, "What about us?" I knew what was coming.

"I've just been thinking that maybe it would be better if we ended the relationship," she said nervously.

"What are you talking about, end the relationship? You mean it's over?"

"Yes," she said, starting to cry.

"It's Sara!" I said. "Hell, I knew this was going to happen. Damn it, Trout! You told me not to worry about it, that it was going to be OK. How in the hell can you do this?" I was sounding like Kinlin, the same betrayal he felt had just moved into my camp.

"Sara's part of it," she said, her voice shaking more and more, "but it's not the whole reason. I do have feelings for her, that's true. But it's not just that, it's everything! It was just too much for me, and I know I have to get away from it."

I yelled, angrily, "I CAN'T HEAR THIS RIGHT NOW!" and hung up the phone, cutting her off like I had done so many times before.

It rang back immediately, and I picked it up. Crying, she said, "Don't do this, please don't do this!"

She was openly crying now, full of hurt. I was starting to break down myself, becoming angrier by the second.

"Please, I don't want it to end like this. Please try and understand. It's not you or Kinlin. It's me. I just can't continue with it. I'll always love you. I know you are hurt, but so am I. It's just that it has to end."

Feeling the anger and hurt well up inside me, I countered, "You've been lying to yourself, and in lying to yourself you've been lying to the boy and me. This thing with Sara has been going on in your mind for weeks, and now you are telling me? You're just running and you don't even know what to. Sara can't fill your needs. As a matter of fact it's the best way to lose a friend. You take a good friend and turn them into a lover just because you are needy and before you know it you've lost the new lover and the friend forever. Think about it Trout."

I was seething with an emotion I couldn't define. It was a mixture of every hurt I had ever had, and it was overpowering every bit of love and understanding I had for her. The anger and pain I was feeling was controlling the show, drowning out any hope she had of telling me anymore.

With a voice full of despair and empty of any hope of repairing the damage of what had just filled the wire, she said tearfully, "I can't talk anymore. I have to go, but please remember that I do love you, and try to remember the good times." Her voice trailing off said, "I have to go."

I stood there; phone in hand staring at the wall, thinking, it's over! It can't be. Not like this. But I knew Trout well enough to know that she had worked this one over in her mind before making the call. If she said it was over, it was over.

I hung up the phone and went into the kitchen and poured my glass full of bourbon, then went back and sat on the couch.

She can't do this. How could she leave after saying I was the best lover she ever had, and nobody had ever loved her as much as I did? She told me more than once it was the happiest that she had ever been, and that she loved the boy with all her heart. She couldn't leave us, not with all those wonderful things that had passed between the three of us. Hell! Mothers just don't walk out on their kids and the man they love. I don't care if they are only twenty and scared to death.

The child in me poured himself a drink too. He came back in the room, sat next to me on the couch and said with a chicken-shit smile on his face, *"See, I told you so. Feeling a little abandoned are we? I told you it was going to fuck you up, but you didn't listen, did you? You've got get rid of those walls old man and take a good look at yourself. Who the fuck you trying to kid? You knew this was going to happen, so what's with the theater? You and that little poet friend of yours needed her so much it scared the living shit out of her. What the hell did you expect? You think she wants to hang around with you and the kid, watching him grow up knowing her like a book and watching you grow old and die. Get real! She's young with her whole life ahead of her, and yours is coming to an end. Fuck! You scared her to death. I don't blame her for running. You've been running all your life, so what's the big deal? You'd better get your own shit together before you start demanding it of someone else."*

I sat on the couch for a couple of hours dealing with that little son-of-a-bitch, wishing he would materialize so I could beat the shit out of him.

I kept trying to understand what had just happened. The feeling of loss was running the spectrum of every fear I'd ever had, and everything I had told Kinlin about love and fear had just been thrown in the trash.

I was getting drunk, but it was a drunk I could do real well. It wasn't a falling down sloppy obnoxious drunk, but one I took all inside and let apathy and deep depression take over. I was fucked up, but to the innocent bystander I was a morose, extremely depressed man they didn't want to fuck with.

I had been this deep into sullen helplessness a couple of times before and had actually toyed with the idea of suicide. I even picked up my pistol once, holding it in my hand trying to figure out the best spot on the head to put the barrel. It was so bad I called the "Crisis Hotline," and they told me to get in the car and come right down. I did, and it took away the desire, but that night on the couch I was right back there again. Getting up and dialing the phone hadn't crossed my mind. I stared down into my drink and saw the words "Fuck it!" stamped on the ice. At that moment I didn't give a shit if I lived or died.

I always knew that if I ever did off myself it wouldn't be a premeditated act. One where I would spend all day writing goodbye letters to loved ones saying how sorry I was for leaving them and to please forgive me. Instead, it would be an act of rage where I would blindly grab a pistol and screaming to the beasts in the room that they had won, stick it to my temple and squeeze the trigger.

I got off the couch and poured more bourbon in my glass. On the way out into the December cold that was lying heavy on the front porch, I stepped into my room and picked up the gun behind the bed.

An hour had passed, and I spent that time intermittently crying and refilling my glass. The pistol lay on the railing next to me. From time to time I picked it up and held it in my hand. I knew I had been there before but never this far in, and the thoughts of not caring about a damn thing had taken on gigantic proportions, almost crowding me off the porch.

I saw the truck pull in and heard Jose and Kinlin get out. They sounded happy. I could hear Kinlin excitedly talking about the movie. I heard him in the kitchen yelling my name, "BIRD, BIRD! You should have seen the movie. It was great! Bird, where are you?"

He saw me standing on the porch and came running out the door with a big grin on his face and a piece of pizza in his hand, "Bird, we brought some pizza for you!"

He saw me leaning against the column at the front step, and right away saw that I wasn't doing well. With a small voice filled with concern, he asked, "Bird, what's the matter?"

"Nothing," I said, turning my face away from him.

"Bird, look, I got some pizza for you. You want some?"

"No, I don't want any right now." I moved myself in front of the gun so he couldn't see it.

He walked around trying to look into my face. Finally succeeding, he said, "Bird, you're crying! Bird, what's wrong? You're sad," he said, trying to look deeper into my eyes.

"I'll be all right. It's late. Maybe you should get ready for bed. I'll be OK."

He turned in protest and went into the kitchen and said something to Jose. Jose came out to the porch. "Amigo, are you OK?"

"No, I'm not," I answered, trying my best to hold back the tears.

"Trout?" he asked, already knowing.

"Fuck it!" was my answer, and by that reaction I knew exactly where I was, and so did he because he had been there with me before.

He said, "Let me put the boy to bed. I'll be right back!"

I heard him talking to Kinlin, and above the boy's protests, took him to his room. After five minutes, I heard him close the door and come to the porch and step outside.

"What's going on amigo, what's happened?"

"It's over," I said, my voice trembling.

"How do you know?"

"She called and told me, that's how!"

"What did she say?"

"Fuck it! It doesn't matter what she said. She just said it was over; try to remember the fucking good times. That shouldn't be too tough now, should it? Hell! They were all good times, at least for me."

"How much you had to drink?" he asked, looking me in the eyes.

"Not enough, amigo," I said.

He reached over and grabbed my arm, "Come on, come in the house and we can talk. It's cold out here. You should sit down for a while. It looks like you've been out here too long."

"Fuck no," I said, pulling away from his grip, "I don't give a shit. It'll be the same in the house. You go. I'll be all right."

"Amigo, you're drunk, and for me to see that means you've had a lot, come on in." The last words were tender, and if I had stood back and watched it with someone else's eyes I would have been able to see the caring and friendship in them.

"Fuck it man, she's gone. Don't you get it? It doesn't matter anymore. Don't you understand? She's not coming back! She isn't ever coming back. It's fucking over!"

He was standing three feet away trying to figure out what to do next, when he looked down and saw the pistol. He looked back up at me and got an intense, angry look in his eyes. "Man, what the hell do you think you're doing? You have to think about the boy."

"Fuck the boy!" I said, turning my face away from him.

Jose took one step and caught me on the side of my face with his open palm. I saw him slap a guy in a bar one time and break his jaw, and I felt like that just happened to me.

I fell back and feebly tried to grab the column behind me. I just brushed it with my fingers and toppled sideways off the porch into the wet oak leaves on the ground. I ended up on my hands and knees, my forehead bent down touching the damp earth.

Jose stood there waiting. As he watched, it all came out. I wept, and that little boy in me sobbed too. I was letting out all the pain and hurt of my 51 years. My body rocked and heaved, and the sobs turned into a wail that echoed through the field. I had never cried so long and so hard. Clutching at the leaves, I tried to crush them in my hands, pressing them with all my strength into the ground.

Jose put his hand on my back. "Come on my friend, let me help you up."

I didn't move. I couldn't. I was sobbing so hard it seemed impossible. He put his arms under my chest and picked me up, turned me around and hugged me hard, supporting my sagging weight. I laid my head on his chest, still trying to get it all out. He said with moist eyes, "Amigo, you know I love you like a brother. To hit you is, to me, like a sin. I would rather cut off my arm than have to do it. I know that you didn't mean what you said."

"I didn't," I said, still crying.

"I know you didn't. I hit you because I don't ever want you to forget this night, and to ever forget those words said in anger about someone you dearly love."

"I know, Jose," I said, whimpering, my head still buried in his chest, "I'm sorry."

"I know you are, my friend, and I also know you didn't mean it. Just never forget this night and the words that fell out of your mouth. I know you feel like you want to die, and I understand. But don't forget the boy, he is your life and he needs you, and you need him. Trout is in pain too. It doesn't matter where she is or who she is with, she is still suffering. Remember what you told Kinlin about love. Love her and understand her, and that love will give you life. Even though she is far away, still hold her in your hands and blame her for nothing because no one is at fault. Time will teach us the entire lesson we have learned here. We will all become stronger because of it. Come, my friend, let's go into the house. Go see the boy. You should have seen his eyes when he saw you were in pain. I have never seen so much worry in the eyes of anyone in my life."

Jose reached over and picked up the pistol. "What in the fuck were you going to do with this?"

Looking down at the weapon he was sticking into his back pocket, I answered with a sheepish look. "Ah, I don't know. Hunting maybe?"

"What?"

"I don't know," I said, wiping my eyes, "Dragons, I guess."

"Dragons? Hey man, that's Kinlin's job. You think that little peashooter would slay dragon? Fuck! That would either piss them off, or put them into a laughing fit. Man, you need a sword for that. One made by the blessed magical hands of a Mexican."

We looked at each other and smiled. Jose was always good at lightening things up, and he had just done it again.

"You always said you owed me a life. Are we even now?"

"Yeah," Jose said, hugging me hard, "I believe the debt is now paid."

We walked with our arms around each other into the house. As we stepped into the kitchen, he said, "Forgive me for hitting you, you know it broke my heart."

"It's OK, I deserved it, but I thought you could hit harder than that?"

"I can amigo," he laughed, "but I didn't want to mess up that beautiful old face, besides I don't want to have to ride in the same car all the way to Baja with a beat up bruised ugly man."

"BAJA?"

"Yes, Baja. When I saw you on the ground I decided we have to get out of here for a while. So we are going to Baja to visit my uncle and aunt, and to have Christmas with them. Don't say no because it won't do any good. We are going!"

"When?" I said, knowing I had no choice.

"Tomorrow, amigo, now go talk to the boy. I know he's waiting for you."

I walked into the bathroom to wash my face. When I looked in the mirror I saw a reflection looking back I didn't like. At least Jose's hard right hand had sobered me up a bit, and brought me back to reality.

How could I have said that about the boy? It was a sign of how low I had driven myself, and Jose's knocking me to my knees out there in the yard was his way of reminding me. The words I spoke towards Kinlin were blasphemous, and far removed from the two words Trout and I had so often spoken. To even think them about someone I loved so much made me nauseous.

I was angry at Trout, but angrier with myself for not trying to understand her, and pissed off for allowing jealously and hurt to overpower the love I had for her. Everything I had told the boy the day she left I believed and thought I could practice, but the power I gave that love turned against me, almost destroying the sacredness of the feelings I had for her and Kinlin. I would use the night as a guide, something to keep me from ever sinking that low again.

I walked into Kinlin's room. He was in bed wide-awake. He was lying on his back with his bass-lure necklace on one side and his sword on the other. He didn't say anything, his eyes just locked on mine, full of concern. I sat on the side of the bed, and said, "Kinlin don't worry, I'm OK."

"Bird, I was worried, I knew that something was trying to eat your poems. What was it?"

"It was the same beast I told you about, the one Trout ran from," I said grabbing his hand.

"FEAR?" he said, with big eyes.

"Yes, Kinlin, it caught me at a weak moment and decided to creep into my heart, and the worst thing was, I almost let it."

"Why, Bird?" he said, shaking his little head back and forth.

"Because at that moment I didn't care about my poems, as a matter of fact, I didn't care about anything" How could I have gotten to the point with my anger and hurt where I didn't care about something as wonderful as this boy lying in front of me?

"But, Bird," he said, sitting up, "you always told me to never forget about the poems. You said they were stuck in a special place in our hearts to always remind us of goodness and love, and to always fight anything that tried to take them away."

"I know, Kinlin, but the monster tried to take them away, and he almost succeeded."

"Bird," he said, moving closer to me, "I can help you fight them. I love my poems. I would never let anything take them away. I would never let anything take yours either."

He looked up at the photo of Trout next to his bed. "When I see Trout, I'm going to tell her that too. Every night when I go to bed I think about her. I know something is trying to chew up her poems. I think real hard and try to chase them away." He grabbed his sword and held it up high over his head. I saw the eyes of Trout in his face, the way his mouth was starting to take on the form of hers. It felt good knowing part of her was still here in the house with us.

"Bird, do you love Trout?"

"Yes, Kinlin, very much," I answered.

"Me too," he said, looking up at the ceiling, staring at the constellation above his bed.

"Kinlin," I moved over and put my arm around his shoulders, "we always have to think good thoughts about Trout. Pretty soon those thoughts will help chase away her fears. I bet she feels it tonight, don't you?"

"Yes, Bird," he said, looking back at her photo.

"Kinlin, I've got a surprise for you."

"What's that?" he said, with eyes full of anticipation.

"You and me and Jose are going to take a trip tomorrow. We're going down to Baja!"

"Baja? I've been to Baja!" he said, excitedly.

"Yeah, I know. We're going to visit the nice old man and woman you stayed with. Remember them?"

"Yeah, they live by the ocean, and he's a fisherman. Bird, that's going to be fun. We can go fishing and camp on the beach!" he said, squeezing my hand hard.

"I thought you might like the idea. So tonight you better think about what you want to take."

"My sword," he said matter-of-factly, "my pens and paper and my fish net." Looking around the room excitedly for other sacred things a boy like him would take on a trip, he glanced up at the photo of Trout above his head. "I have to take the picture of Trout, Bird."

"I know you do, maybe I'll take one too," I said, knowing that I would like to take half a dozen. "What about your bass necklace?"

"Bird, I was thinking," he said, looking at the holy piece of jewelry, "I want to give it to Trout, I think she needs it. Do you think before we go we could put it in a box and send it to her?"

"Sure, Kinlin," I said, knowing how important it was for him to give away something he cherished so much, "We'll get a box and drop it off at the post office on the way out of town."

"Bird, when we get to Baja I'll make myself another one out of shells and feathers and pieces of wood. I will touch it with my sword and it will become just as powerful as this one." Pausing a moment, deep in thought, he said, "I'll make one for Jose and you too, then all the poet soldiers will have one!"

"Good idea," I said, "then nothing will ever be able to eat our poems, right?"

"Right, Bird!" he said, gazing off, thinking of the great battles the three of us were going to fight, and all of life's dragons we were going to slay.

"Kinlin, I think we had better get some sleep now, it's going to be a busy day tomorrow."

"Bird," he said with a concerned look, "you want me to sleep in your room tonight?"

Good question, I thought. It's going to be a tough night. There's going to be one boy or the other in bed with me tonight. If it isn't Kinlin then it's going to be the little insecure son-of-a-bitch that's been pitching his tent inside me since 1942. After mulling it over, I decided. "No, it's a good offer, but I think I will try and follow your example and see if I can fight those monsters on my own."

"You sure, Bird?"

"Yeah," I said, unsure of myself, thinking I could probably use all the help I could get.

"OK," he said, reaching down and grabbing his necklace, "I think you should take this just in case. It works for me, and I have the sword."

I took the talisman from his hand, remembering the day Trout strung it for him. She had used a pair of wire snips and cut away all the hooks and anything else sharp, not wanting anything to puncture the skin she once told me felt like new down on a baby owl.

I took the charm, gave him a hug, and said good night. As I was walking out the door he said loudly, with sword in hand, "Bird, don't forget, SAVE THE POEMS!"

"I won't forget, Kinlin, sleep tight."

It was a long walk back to my room, one I dreaded. The reality of spending untold nights in there alone gave the room the feel of an eight by ten maximum-security cell.

I slid between the sheets trying to recover her smell. I stared at the falling arrows and the mystical, leather-covered chair. I reached over and switched on the winged lamp. Its shadowed flight covered the wall to my left. The screened relief hung above my head. The unfolding flower with the brilliant blue feather in the middle had become the soft secret place between her legs I had so often touched. The room came alive with the memory of her and all that had taken place within its walls. The altar-pond I was floating on pressed against my back and rippled against my loins. It had become an ebbing reminder that I probably would never swim with her again.

I looked at the necklace lying on the pillow she had used and hoped it could magically bring her back. My intuition told me that even its power's weren't capable of that. The feelings of loss and abandonment were the strongest I had ever experienced. If I could visualize them, they would turn into cement clouds hanging above the bed, threatening to drop on me at any moment.

I recalled Jose's words about her leaving, and the fact I couldn't do a damn thing about it when she did. Nothing we had shared together, or the boy coming into her life would change the fact that she was running. I knew she wouldn't stop until she became exhausted, trying to out distance the dark shadows of her past. I wanted to be there when she tripped and fell, but it was now something I could only do after a 12-hour trip in a fast car. I thought about our trip the next day, wishing she were going along. Kinlin's presence in the back of the van would mean that at least part of her would be with us.

That night I dreamt continuously of abstract births and slow motion, near deaths. I was the groom in a monotone-colored marriage to someone I couldn't recognize, and a pallbearer at a funeral where the casket was so laden with stones it couldn't be carried. I saw gazelles being chased, leaping ahead of charging lions, falling to their knees with horrified eyes. Crows covered my prone body, fighting each other for possession of my eyes. And then I became a Peregrine, flying so high that the ground down below was nothing but a cataract blur.

The eight-year-old visited me, and stood at the foot of the bed with a glowing Duncan yo-yo in hand doing loop-the-loop's and world-class rock the cradles. He reminded me of fear filled, California nights in Merced and the panic that used to sleep with me in bed, of the shame I felt for not being able to tough it out.

"Even The Pigeon Man couldn't make you feel safe," he told me, *"Then when you wanted someone stronger to beat the piss out of those demons you would hand the job over to Red Davis, (Who, in the end, himself was no match for those screaming, 15-round heavyweights). Red wasn't afraid, so what the fuck is wrong with you? Hell, he taught you how to box, you were born with his natural strength, so what are you afraid of? The Trout's leaving is one of those monsters. It isn't one with jagged teeth or a long tail, but it is still a wailing serpent that's going to have you leaving scraping fingernail marks on the wall.*

You'll never make it through this one. The fear is too ingrained, and no matter what you tell the boy, you don't stand a chance of kicking the ass of this moonless night horror.

Trout was the 'ultimate female breast nipple,' and now that she's gone, the only thing you are going to be able to suck is sweet memory, and in the end you will turn that into the flat, milk-less breast of a starving African mother. She has abandoned you, you sick son of a bitch and left you home alone while going to the store. Your ultimate fear of mom forgetting to ever come back again is going to come true. You are 51-years-old, this was your chance to get healed, probably you're last chance too. But your nurse has left and you will end up rotting in that bed, the same bed that used to be filled with her skin. You'll come here every night trying to recover her smell, and end up like a frustrated dog with his nose to the ground sucking in dust, not realizing she's covered her tracks by leaping from rock to rock. You'd better take Wonder Boy and head down to Baja old man, because this place is going to turn into a morgue with you the one laying on the slab with your guts cut open."

"And another thing," he said, with a relentless tongue, "quit telling the boy all of that philosophical shit about love and the power of the heart, because an emotionally blind motherfucker like you is going to have to live up to those words. The kid is so sharp he will see soon enough that you don't know what the hell you're talking about, and go find himself another dad. The Pigeon Man you are not, and you certainly don't have the courage of Red, and that's what the boy needs. Cash it in dummy, grab that gun from behind the bed and get it over with. Do everybody a favor, because you'll never get out of this one alive. This was 'The Big One,' and you watched it slip away. Someone like her will never come again. So put another mark on the wall in your column of failures, that is, if there's any room left."

CHAPTER 30

I awoke in the morning with the hard reality of the night before curled up in bed beside me. The talisman pressing against my leg was a reminder that something else other than Trout's soft touch was under the covers. My jaw felt like I had been hit in the face with a two-by-four, and my mouth tasted like the scum that collects under the wooden slats of a bar room floor.

I strained to look out the window to see if it was day or night. The fog made the visibility just ten feet beyond the porch. I could see the tips of the spiked century plant shrouded in heavy mist, and the young Eucalyptus next to it weighed down by moisture. Nature had moved in with its critical touch to show me what was going on in my mind. I thought, thank God the windows are closed or I would have trouble finding my pants seeing through all the grayness.

I guessed it was about six-thirty, and figured everybody would still be asleep, so decided to lay there gathering strength for the task of raising myself out of the floating coffin that had been cast adrift.

The noise I was hearing from the kitchen and Kinlin's room showed me I actually was the last to awake. The smell of coffee was the sign Jose was up, and the sudden appearance of Kinlin at my bedroom door showed me he was almost ready to hit the road. He stepped in quietly, not knowing if I was awake. Seeing that I had one eye open, he smiled, forcing the other to reluctantly unglue itself so I could see in the third dimension.

What I saw was the guardian of the sanctity of the house standing with sword in hand. He looked around the room trying to find evidence of any night battles that had been fought. Seeing no blood stains, or moldy scales on the floor, he covered the five feet in two steps and a leap, landing with sword in hand on my chest. He sat on my stomach looking around the bed for the necklace. Suddenly, he saw the tip of one of the metal strikers sneaking out from under a sheet, and grabbing it held it high above his head, saying, "Bird, you OK?"

"Yes," I said, lying.

"Bird, get up, we've got to eat breakfast and pack and clean out the car and go to the post office, and do a hundred other things!"

He was talking so fast my clouded mind could only pick up every third word. "Slow down, can't you see I'm recovering from a near-death experience? If you want to do something, go look in the closet to see if any of those giant snakes are still in there, and while you're at it, grab me that blue sweatshirt on the shelf."

Giggling, he got off me, with the sword stuck out in front of him and stepped into the closet. "Bird, there's nothing in here but a full grown Kodiak bear and a pack of white timber wolves. Want me to ask them to leave?"

Well, the kid had a sense of humor, I thought.

"Just tell them to hang out in there until I leave the room, then they can do what they want."

I heard some gibberish that sounded like one of Kinlin's secret tongues. I knew the closet was probably full of beasts, and that he was soothing them with the voice and touch of Daniel.

He walked back out with a smile and said, "It's OK, Bird, they're asleep, but it's a good thing you didn't go in. The bear has a cub, and instead of you having breakfast this morning, you would have been breakfast!"

Laughing at his own attempt to pick up my spirits, he grabbed my arm and tried to pull me out of bed. I didn't fight it, and struggled to my feet and let him lead me to the bathroom. He said I had better brush my teeth, because I smelled like something had died in my mouth. The little prophet's wisecrack made Jose drop whatever he was doing in the kitchen and say (while cracking up), "Little Fish, don't stand close unless you have a gas- mask."

I answered loudly in the direction of the kitchen, "Uncle Jose has fixed it so I can't open my mouth to fit in a tooth brush, and we'll probably need a hydraulic jack to pry it apart."

Kinlin gave me a puzzled look, and figured what I had just said was something private, only understood by old horses like Jose and me. After giving me a, "boy are you guys weird look," he ran into his room to pack.

I staggered out of the bathroom into the kitchen and saw Jose preparing huevos rancheros. I felt like turning around, walking back and sticking my head in the toilet.

"Amigo, you are alive!" Jose said.

"Barely, I'm thinking about going to the emergency room to have these claw marks on my back stitched up."

"No, you look good," he said, "last night, before you went to bed, you looked like a hard-ridden 65. This morning you look like a hard-ridden 51. See, my friend, there is still hope. After you eat this breakfast you will feel like a new man. Would you like a little hair of the dog with tomato juice?"

"Yeah, not a bad idea. Hairy dogs have been biting me all night; maybe this will help heal the wounds."

"Don't worry," Jose said, "I am going to drive today. I feel like a man reborn and can already smell the ocean beating against the Baja shores and the touch of a good glass of tequila in my hand. Amigo, it will be a much needed rebirth for you too."

"And how do you know that, old enlightened one?"

"Because I know, that's all. We will swim and fish and eat healthy food from the table of my aunt. You will see my friend, you will come back a new man."

I hope so, because I sure was tired of living with the one wearing these clothes. Fuck! Anything would have to be an improvement over the haggard son-of-a-bitch drinking that red beer.

I heard Kinlin calling from his room and went in to see what he wanted. I walked in and saw everything he owned on the bed and floor. It looked like a merchant from twelfth century Persia had walked into the room and spread his wares out. There were feathered and belled fetishes, tomahawks and stone-tipped arrows. Stacks of bright drawings and tattooed T-shirts covered the floor like a collaged carpet. *Field and Stream* magazines tied together in bundles and his favorite prints of old Masters he had cut out of art magazines were rolled together and bound with rubber bands. A photo of Trout was lying on his pillow staring out from a sealed zip-lock bag, well away from anything that could damage it. He was reaching into a brown shopping bag in the corner pulling out things that looked familiar to me.

I mentioned that they looked like a pair of Trout's socks and a T-shirt. He admitted that he had taken them the day before she left and put them in the bag. I asked him why. He shrugged his shoulders. Something just told him to do it and he was glad he did, because if he hadn't, she would have left before he had a chance. He explained that as long as he had Trout's things in his room he knew she would always be close by, and he could still smell her skin on the cotton.

A boy after my own heart, I thought, wishing I had had the same idea. I almost asked him if I could have one of the items so I could tie it around my neck. Maybe I should have had her breathe into a jar before she left, then quickly sealed the top. Then I could, forever have something that had passed close to her heart.

I watched Kinlin jump around the room trying to decide what to take. He finally gave up, saying he wanted to take it all. Telling him it was too much was hard for me to do. After I told him the van only had so much room, and that it couldn't pull a trailer, he carefully started choosing his favorites and putting them in a pile by themselves.

After he had sorted things out, he grabbed the bass lure necklace and said we had to find a box, and would I help him pack it. We went into the woodshed where we kept things like that, and found one small enough to fit the necklace in.

We filled it with tissue. When I wasn't looking he disappeared outside. Just as I was going to go look for him he returned with a small paper bag full of leaves and pine needles, small stones, sticks and assorted wild flowers. He said he wanted to include some important things from the farm, things he and Trout had stepped over on their many walks around the fields. He told me it was stuff she would recognize. Things that would help her remember the nice times they had when they were together, and if she would put them in a glass jar she would always have a piece of happiness with her. He said he didn't know what Oregon looked like, and it probably wasn't as pretty as the farm, so maybe it would make up for her being away. It was a wonderful idea, I told him, at the same time thinking that maybe we should have gotten a bigger box and crawled inside ourselves.

We packed the box and before sealing it I asked if he wanted to write a note. He said he didn't because a note wasn't needed. She would understand without words after she saw what was inside.

I knew he was right, and was amazed at his tremendous little mind, and of how much he understood the importance of the "fingerless touch." He wasn't into sentimental overkill. A trait he had that I would do well to observe.

We ate breakfast and talked about the trip, deciding to play it by ear, three words Kinlin logged in his memory bank and would use whenever Jose and I were undecided where to spend the night.

Jose and Kinlin washed the van and cleaned out the inside. While Jose was changing the oil and making it roadworthy, Kinlin filled a tray with red paint. After placing the flat of his hand into it, he put a sacred, war-pony-palm and fingerprint on both doors.

We put a foam mattress in the back and packed the two-man tent. After double-checking our belongings and making sure that the house was secure, climbed in.

As Jose started the car I looked at both side mirrors and saw that the young poet-warrior had tied feathers to them. As we pulled out the drive he stood in the space between the seats with his sword touching the dashboard. He said something in Mescalero that could have only meant, "Clear the way because the 'Warrior Society of Poets' is coming through, and those who stand in our way will be trampled by the white charger that is, at this moment, heading out the drive!"

Jose stopped at the last hill and we looked back at the house in the grove. Kinlin said to be still, and couldn't we hear it? Yes, we could, we acknowledged. As we continued towards the main road the unmistakable sound of the red-tail screaming overhead filled the car. The scream lifted and curled and dived back into all that lay within the fourteen acres, disappearing in a cloud of dust behind us.

CHAPTER 31

We headed south on highway one, stopping every now and then to get out and look at the Pacific whittle away at the sheer cliffs falling off to our right.

The first night we camped at Morro Bay. Since it was the first time Kinlin had ever camped out, it was a night of initiation and celebration.

We cooked hot dogs on an open grill, and sat around the fire seeing who could tell the best ghost stories.

Jose's stories were of Mexican vampires sucking the blood of hard working peasants. Mine were about night creatures creeping their way through your toes, slowly working their way into your brain, eating everything in their path.

When it came to Kinlin's turn, he stared at the fire and thought hard before speaking, a trait he had gotten from Trout. It was a trait I knew would help him to stay away from the impulsive, headlong mistakes of the future. He told us a story of "The Invisible." Of the evil armies we couldn't see. They were the ones that, without words, condemned the Indians to death. The boy talked of the quiet hate he had seen on the History Channel that had sent the Jews to their death. He spoke of the dead buffalo and the silence of the men as they fired their guns. He described, in gory detail, the helicopters he had seen in Field and Stream, swooping in and laying waste to packs of Timber Wolves.

It was a horror story about the silent monster of fear and destruction, a story he knew well. It was one that included Trout and the demons that forced her to run; the ones we couldn't see. His eyes got wide telling the tale, and his descriptions of what they must look like. They were dark and sinister things, without shape or smell, entities that appeared in day or night when you least expected them.

The fire flickered against his youthful face as he spoke of the demon that invaded Trout and made her run. He said he knew it was still with her, and that it was up to us to chase it away. Fear was the scaled beast that had taken her away and it was our first duty as poet warriors to save her.

After the last statement, he grabbed his sword, and doing what he had seen in a King Arthur movie, reached over the fire and touched Jose and I on each of our shoulders. He passed the magic wand to me so I could touch him. He then told us to wait a minute, and ran to the car and brought back a piece of paper. He sat back down between us, and said, "I wrote a poem for Trout, and I want to read it now."

Jose and I looked at each other. With our eyes we said, "Why not? You've already blown our minds with the horror story you just told. Go ahead kid finish us off!"

Kinlin took a breath and started to speak,

"Trout is a white bird
with wings on fire,
falling.
We are water
us three.
A storm full of
rainbows and rain
touching,
then holding in
our hands
a wet ocean
full of love.
Catching her
and putting out
the flames."

There was no more to be said. We sat in awe of Kinlin and the words he had written. I had been around enough poets and had written enough myself to know that Kinlin was gifted when it came to writing down, "The Words." Words that wanted to fill the air with a healing touch, and words that were spoken with so much love they left Jose and I speechless.

Jose broke the silence. Filling Kinlin's glass with 7- Up. He told me to raise my bottle of beer. He then repeated what he had once said to me in the kitchen, saying, "To Trout, and to the brotherhood of us three, and to the love we feel for her tonight. We bless her with all the poems that have ever been written and all the comets that have ever filled the skies. Tonight we take 'The Oath,' and that is the oath to never forget her, and of how she has filled our hearts!"

Kinlin stood up and threw his arms around us. He looked us both in the eyes, and said, "You promise?"

Jose and I looked at each other, knowing the importance of the moment, and said in unison, "WE PROMISE!"

Kinlin smiled and sighed, then said all of a sudden, "I'm tired, can I go in the tent and go to sleep?"

I took him in and stuffed him into a sleeping bag, and told him we would just be outside.

"It's OK, Bird, I'm not afraid, I know you won't leave me alone."

"I never will," I said, betting my life on it, "but just for my own information, how do you know that so definitely?"

"Because you know that night Trout left and you came into my room and we talked?"

"Yes."

"I saw it in your eyes, and Bird, eyes don't lie. The mouth lies, and touching lies, but not the eyes. Bird, I knew Trout was going to leave. I saw it in her eyes a long time before she left. Bird, I knew."

"Me too, Kinlin, but I didn't want to believe it. I still had the hope she would stay."

"Bird, I had a dream about Trout the night she left. After the dream, I understood more."

"What did you dream?" His answer would probably help me to understand too.

"I saw her looking through a book full of photographs of herself. They were pictures of her that were taken from the time she was a baby up until the time she left. There were hundreds of them, Bird. She was sitting out on the stone bench by the pond. She kept turning the pages and was getting more and more confused. Trout didn't know which one was really her. She started to cry and threw the book in the water. It wouldn't sink, so she dropped rocks on it, trying to push it down. The book finally went to the bottom. Then another picture floated to the top, a photo of her father. Then she ran away."

"What do you think the dream meant?" I asked.

"After she ran away the dream still went on and I looked closer. I saw the picture had your eyes, then I knew why she had run."

"Why?" I asked, afraid to hear the answer.

"Because she was your wife, and she knew she couldn't be married to you because she didn't know who you really were. Then she got really confused because she didn't know who she was. So she ran away, afraid."

Jesus, I thought, the kid's trying to tell me something, something I've been afraid to look at for weeks.

"Bird," he said, asking like he wanted an honest answer, "is Trout really your wife?"

I didn't know if I could answer that, but knowing somehow that I had too, I said, "Kinlin, Trout is my wife, but it's not the kind of wife we see in the films, or the wives we see down town with their husbands and kids. She is the kind of wife that's there because it was supposed to be. It's a marriage without all the ceremony and tradition we usually think of as a marriage. It's a partnership of the heart and soul, something that has always been there and always will be."

"Bird, is that why sometimes after I went to bed I would hear you and her say, do you want to get married?"

"Yes," I said, "those were times when we both knew the importance of the love we were sharing, and for us to say it only meant that we both believed it was true. You see, the words we were saying to each other were like the most beautiful poem ever written. It was a poem that showed us how much love we had for each other. When we went to bed we would say the words 'I do.' Words that meant we understood the importance of what we were feeling. As you have said, the truth could be seen in our eyes."

"But, Bird, if she was your wife, and she also saw you with the face of her father, didn't it make her afraid? You know, like in my dream?"

"Yes, I think it did. What you saw in your dream was probably true."

"But, Bird," he stared down at the red checkered flannel of the bag that engulfed him, "if it's true, how does she understand that you aren't her father, and just your wife?"

"That's a question I don't know I can answer. She first has to understand what her father meant to her and what she meant to him. After that is solved, then she can understand who I am. It's not easy for her, Kinlin, she was given a task she didn't ask for."

"What's that Bird?"

"Trout grew up trying to please her father by being the boy he never had. It was a job she wasn't prepared for and it ended up confusing her. That's why in your dream you saw her looking through all of those pictures, and becoming frustrated with the faces she saw staring back."

"But Bird!" he said adamantly, "Boys can't be mothers!"

"I know, Kinlin, and they can't be wives either. That's one of the things that scared her. Trout still has a lot of that little boy her father wanted in her and it confused her and made her angry. You and I were asking her to be something she wasn't prepared for, to be wife and mother. In the end, she saw me as a father who was putting her in a role she didn't understand."

"You see," I continued, "she is still trying to please her father, but it's a task she will never finish, not until she looks deep into herself and loves herself for who she really is, not who she thinks her parents wanted her to be. When she has that solved, she will know who I am, that I am not one of her parents demanding she be something she is not. Understand?"

"I think so, Bird. But what if she never understands who she is?"

"Then she will grow up always being the little boy her father wanted. But every time she looks in the mirror, she sees a woman, and it only confuses her more. She will feel like she hasn't totally completed the job that she has let him down. The secret of her womanhood buried deep inside her will always eat at her."

Kinlin was deep in thought, processing all I had told him. Telling him that Trout was bi-sexual would have been too much for him, but putting it into terms of her not understanding herself, trying to be the boy her father wanted and disliking herself for biologically not succeeding was something he could possibly grasp.

"Is that why she left, too, Bird?"

"Yes, Kinlin, that's one of the big reasons."

"Will she ever feel like my mother?"

"She already does, Kinlin, but that is scaring her because she still isn't through being her father's little boy. When she solves that she will understand what it's like to be your mother. Then, as you have already said once tonight, you will be able to see the truth in her eyes."

"Will we all be together again?"

"I don't know Kinlin. I really don't know," I said, not wanting to lie to him. "Hey, it's time you fell asleep. Tomorrow will be a long day. Who knows, maybe by this time tomorrow night we'll be in Mexico."

His mind was on other things, Trout and the three of us, and of what I had just told him.

Closing his eyes, he said, "Bird, are you happy being a man? Is that what your father wanted you to be?"

"Yeah, he wanted a boy. Thank God I didn't disappoint him," I said, feeling for Trout.

"Would you and Trout have been unhappy if I was a girl?"

"We wouldn't care what you were, you could have been a little Kodiak cub and we'd love you just the same."

He smiled and as his eyes slid shut, said, "Bird, I don't care if Trout is having trouble finding out who she is, I'll always love her the same as I do tonight."

"I know you will, me too."

"Night, Bird," he said, grabbing Trout's picture in his hand.

"Good night, Kinlin."

Knowing that it was going to be a cold coastal night I pulled the red flannel up close to his chin and walked out to the fire.

Jose was stirring the coals with a stick. "I heard the talk, amigo. Think he understood?"

"I don't know. It's tough enough for me to understand."

"It sounded like you had a pretty good grasp for a man who wasn't there to watch her grow up."

"Maybe I'm wrong, but knowing her like I do, it all seems possible."

"Not only possible, but probable. Maybe her father didn't know what kind of a message he was sending her, and no matter how subtle it was she probably grew up trying to please him. Now she's faced with loving a man his age and being mother to a boy; a boy she never was. It's a pretty tough situation for a person with her sensitivities. It would scare the shit out of me if I was her."

"Yeah," I looked down at the fire, thinking of all the times I did things that reminded her of her father, and how she fought the urge to tell me. Once she hugged me and rubbed her velvet skin against my unshaven face and told me it reminded her of times when she had done the same thing with her father. She later came out to my studio to talk about the feeling. I reacted with fear and guilt, not wanting her to identify me with him. She turned to tears when I said that wasn't how I wanted our relationship to be. I didn't want her to see me as father. Every time she hinted at it I overreacted. It was one of the many things I would look at in the weeks to come, actions I took because I was afraid to lose her. Those very actions helped drive her away.

"Amigo," Jose said, "how are you doing? Where are you, and how in the hell is your heart?"

"Jose," I said, "all the things I tell Kinlin about healing yourself through the power of love are a truth I believe, but one I don't think I'm strong enough to practice. He will probably grow up strong with a healthy heart, ending up pushing me around in a wheelchair. He'll end up dragging me around by the shirt begging me to get up and walk, telling me not to be afraid, and to use the sword he carved for me. Maybe this isn't the lifetime I was given to work this one out."

"Yes it is, and you are going to work it out even if Kinlin and I have to kick your ass every day to make you do it. It is in you; just stop being afraid to open it up. You are so full of Trout's leaving that you are starting to rot. The only thing stopping the decay is your love for the boy. That's not enough, my friend. You'd better start caring for yourself. In the end even Kinlin won't be strong enough to hold your fragile ass together. You have to find purpose with the thoughts going through your head, thoughts you are giving the boy. They are ideas that have meaning and truth. If you can convince Kinlin, you sure as hell can talk yourself into the same truth!"

"I know you're right, Jose. I just have to unlearn a lot of things, things it took me 50 years to bury deep in my guts. They won't be easy to rip out. So maybe we should have some patience and hope I get rid of them before they get rid of me."

Jose slept in the van and I crawled in the tent next to Kinlin. It was the first night of a long journey, one that would draw the three of us closer, and maybe one that would push Trout farther away. I settled in hoping that it would become a magical voyage. As I fell into sleep I couldn't deny the illusion that filled my head that Trout would be waiting on the front steps when we returned.

CHAPTER 32

We reached Jose's uncle's place two days later. They were two days of running with Kinlin on white sand beaches, of combing those same beaches for anything he felt worthy of sticking into his fishnet bag.

He collected earthen jewelry, driftwood gems and gray emerald stones. He held each item up to the sky, looking at them intently. He was either studying it for its quality, or blessing it to the gods. We had to get a cardboard box to hold it all. After a couple of days the carton was filled. He had brought his scotch tape and stuck his favorite pieces wherever there was space. The back of the van looked like a mystic's temple.

The van looked like something out of a "Road Warrior" movie. Cars full of people would pass us gawking at the threesome inside. There was Jose with his bandana with the pelican feather sticking out the back that Kinlin had found, and me with shaved head and a gray four-day growth on my face. Kinlin was in the back in war paint and headband, with a sacred weapon in hand, stringing newfound fetishes on leather thongs. He looked like the dwarf king of some secret sect, the two insane men in front, his bodyguards.

We hit the Mexican line and the border guards just stood there and shook their heads, trying to recall if there was a "Grateful Dead" concert somewhere they hadn't heard about.

Jose was in heaven and began singing Mexican songs the minute we crossed the line. Kinlin stopped speaking Apache and started talking in his own version of Yaqui, with something that sounded like Hindu thrown in. All that, plus the sounds of John Coltrane blasting from the tape deck was too much for the normal mind to fathom, but we weren't normal. By the looks the Mexican locals were giving us, they didn't think so either.

We pulled into Jose's uncle's place with feathers flying and were greeted like three lost sons returning from some foreign war.

Jose's uncle Pedro was a short man with a face that looked like it had weathered seventy years of salt-water storms. He was stout with forearms that looked like four-by-fours. His stomach told me it was fond of beer and tacos. His hair, and long drooping mustache were thin and gray, flecked with black strands. His eyebrows were almost as long as the hair over his lip, and his two eyes looked like black marbles set deep in his head. I imagined him with a sombrero and serape, and figured he looked just like Pancho Villa in retirement.

His wife's name was Teresa. She looked like the mother of all mothers. Short like Pedro; she had a beautiful face with a touch of Aztec in it. Her skin was the color of a mahogany table that had never felt wax, and her snow-white hair tied in a braid looked like a color she'd had since birth. Her eyes were the twin of her husband's, and when she smiled I saw straight teeth whiter than her hair.

The two had the look of people who had worked hard all their lives, never wearing gloves. Hands that were strong reached out to us, touching Kinlin and I like we were family. They smothered Jose with a love that showed he was their favorite nephew, and could have easily been their own son. They asked us into their weathered, white adobe house that was set about a hundred yards from the beach. Hand-hewn timbers that looked like they could withstand the strongest of hurricanes supported the inside of the house. Wooden furniture standing on the red tile floor appeared to have the same strength.

The kitchen was the room used the most, and was full of the same colors that Jose had filled our kitchen with when he cooked. Red and green peppers mixed with strings of bound garlic hung from the walls. Dried corn in every red and orange earthen tone was bundled together, filling all the spaces the peppers didn't. Terra cotta bowls and jars were stacked on a hand-oiled wooden sink filled with various sizes and colors of beans and rice. It was a Mexican cultural still life that should have been framed and hung on a wall. In the corner was an open baking oven fueled by wood. It gave out a manzanita perfume that permeated the walls.

It was a home I had stepped into, one that defied the changes of time. It was an environment I could have walked into a hundred years past.

Jose was rambling on in Spanish, telling them both of his latest adventures of the life the three of us had been sharing. Every now and then Teresa would look down at Kinlin with eyes of caring and concern. It made me wish I could read her thoughts because I felt she knew something I didn't.

Pedro brought out tequila and we drank a toast to the safe arrival of their guests, and of the future happiness of us all, a phrase that made Teresa look at Kinlin and me, then turn back to the window towards the breakers rolling in on the beach.

Jose had told me that Teresa was the sister of the one who "Knows", and that some of that insight had rubbed off on her. It was that insight I was seeing as she stared at the gulls outside. She obviously knew something I didn't. As we sat at the kitchen table I saw her remove herself from a conversation that had nothing to do with the thoughts filling her mind.

She turned to Jose and said something in Spanish. It made him turn in the direction of Kinlin and me. They were words that furrowed his brow. I saw him begin to talk with his eyes instead of his mouth. Jose could say more with one look than the normal person could with a thousand words. That was exactly what was happening at the table.

Pedro picked up on it and beckoned Kinlin and I to come outside and look at his boat. They both spoke broken English and when we talked I felt like I was in the middle of a late night movie featuring "The Treasure of The Sierra Madre." As Pedro spoke in great detail of the prowess of the 30-foot diesel powered wooden ark that lay tied to a pier; I looked back towards the house. I wondered what details of the past six months they were discussing.

Kinlin jumped around the boat. After Pedro told him he was going to take him fishing the next day, he looked in the direction of the open sea. I could only imagine what great battles he was going to have with serpents and giant octopus.

I watched as Pedro and Kinlin discussed the fine art of fishing and the intricacies of net tying. Kinlin fingered the twine looped together and let it fall through his hands like hemped water. He carefully touched the pointed hooks tied to the thick, nylon line. I know, in doing so, he felt the same pain the fish must have felt as the hooks pierced the tender flesh of their mouths. Kinlin knew the value of life, but also the necessity of food on the table. If he could live without having to cut into the flesh of another living thing he would have reached another goal into preserving the sanctity of life.

We were called to lunch and sat down at a table overflowing with red-sauced chicken and brown rice. Steamed tortillas at least a foot high were stacked in the middle, and the smell of barbecued pork drifted over the stove. A pitcher of beer sat on the table next to glasses of lemonade. As I sat there I thought it was a feast fit for Cortez.

The rest of the day was spent in siesta and cool beer. The family talked for hours about Jose's adventures. Kinlin and I slept side-by-side in the sun. Upon awakening, we went for a swim. We fought invisible sharks and sea monsters and dove deep for shells, treasures Kinlin would carry to shore and add to his collection.

Kinlin was in a place he had been before but it was an experience we hadn't talked about. I waited for him to bring it up, knowing him well enough to know he would when the time was right. Whatever this place meant, and the secret of Jose's uncle finding him on the beach was stuck somewhere deep in his mind. It was an area so fragile I felt if I tried to pry it out it might shatter into a million confused pieces. He had never mentioned it to Trout and me. Even though she and I had talked about it, we never got up enough nerve to talk to him about the secrets of his past. The thought that he had been dropped from the heavens and landed in Baja naked was an Immaculate Conception even the most devout religious scholars would have trouble believing. But any other explanation was frightening to me. That he had other parents out there somewhere made me think that if I had to ever give him back, it would put me in a class with the guy who kidnapped the Lindberg kid.

Kinlin fished with Pedro, but wanted to throw everything back. Pedro finally convinced him of the cycle of life, and of the financial responsibilities of bringing home the catch. It was a fact Kinlin accepted, but not without first trying to get Pedro to change his profession to an artist. Pedro told him that the only art he knew was how to weave a good net. Kinlin told the old man that is what he should do, be a net weaver, and let other people catch the fish. The two went out every day. As the boat left with Kinlin on the bow, sword in hand, I knew he wasn't praying for a good catch, but rather a boat full of nets with gaping holes in them.

While they were out fishing Jose and I sat around trying to relax. For Jose it wasn't hard, he was Mexican to the bone. When the sun told him it was time to nap he fell into a coma as inherent as the color of his skin. I spent my time thinking of the past six months trying my best to find meaning in it. I sat for hours staring at the horizon where the dark blue water cut a fine line between itself and the powder blue sky.

Everything I did involved Trout, she was in my shoes and the pockets of my pants, and immersed in the warm sand I constantly ran through my fingers. I tried to rid my mind of thoughts of her with someone else. It didn't matter if it was man or woman. My anger at the thought of her being tender to another person in the same way she had been tender to me ran against the grain of all the things I had told the boy. I had convinced myself that the philosophy of selfless love I wanted him to grasp was true, but also an act of utopian ego-less giving, one my 51 years of fear-filled losses wouldn't let me practice.

I sat there in the Baja sun fighting jealously and sense of abandonment and rejection. I knew one of the purposes of our falling in love was to teach us both the value of giving yourself unconditionally. The anger I felt at the thought of her falling into the arms of another person put a coat of opaque paint on any poetry I felt as the result of her pulling into my drive at the beginning of summer. I fought the feelings and punished myself for my anger. I wished all I had told Kinlin was something I could really feel; that we had to love Trout no matter what happened. There was no doubt in my mind that I loved her, it was the most intense feeling for another person I had ever felt, but the eight-year-old in me was always there to remind me she had run away. Along with her leaving, hope had also slammed the door.

In the act of trying to teach him the value of understanding, of giving without wanting anything back, I failed the lesson myself. I knew that my past was going to dictate the actions of my future when it came to understanding her. I was suffocating the love I had for her with all the betrayals of my past.

It was a choking of the heart I knew would stand in the way of forgiveness, a heart that would always blame myself for what had happened.

We had been there a week. A week where clouds never covered the sun and one that saw Kinlin and me turn "Gringo" brown. Jose was in heaven, speaking his native tongue non-stop. Pedro and Teresa were good hosts, talking to us in English, constantly asking Jose for help with difficult words. When they spoke alone, far from us, the conversations were always ones of seriousness. I knew they were speaking about the boy and me. Teresa, between cleaning fish and preparing meals, always had a moment to look in our direction.

She was meshed in the life Kinlin and I had been handed, and in the memory of finding him on the beach. Her eyes showed the concern of wanting to help us, but also showed the frustration of not knowing how to guide us along the path of understanding.

On the eighth day I saw her take Jose aside. Sitting on a bench at the beach she grabbed his arm and spoke to him four inches from his face. I watched from the kitchen window knowing the talk was serious. I knew, too, it was about us. That night Jose took me outside. We leaned against Pedro's boat. He told me his aunt thought we should go the next day and visit her sister. It was a thirty-mile drive up into the hills. She lived alone in a settlement of farmers and goat herders. She was the one who lived at the place on the map drawn on Kinlin's stomach. It was the red dot Kinlin had marked, the spot of the woman who can see things others can't.

I asked him why. He said over the last week his aunt had come to realize there were questions that had to be answered about the boy and me. They were so important she believed her sister was the only one who could answer them. Jose believed also, that Kinlin and Trout and I had issues that needed to be resolved. He knew I couldn't exist in peace with what was going through my mind, and if the woman could help, then it was a thirty-mile trip that should be taken. I agreed, but felt the actions Trout took two weeks before had no solution, and nothing less than a life-long prescription of Valium would have any affect.

The next morning the three of us climbed into the van and headed out the gravel drive. As we turned into the main road I looked into the rear view mirror. I saw Teresa crossing herself. I had the uncanny feeling the three of us were heading off in a cloud of Baja dust to some great, unknown, bloody war.

It was the longest, dustiest thirty miles that I had ever driven, with a stretch of rocks, lizards and vultures that kept Kinlin's sword in a tight grip all the way. The country looked like some giant scientific experiment where a bunch of frizzy-haired scientists had taken a piece of the earth's surface and planted iron vegetation that could exist on absolutely no water. I imagined the buzzards as vegetarians waiting a half-mile up, watching for the last gasp of a cactus before swooping down and ripping at its skin. Even the lizards looked thirsty. I visualized them in the heat of the day lying around hallucinating, sucking on rocks.

Kinlin acted like we were in another world, and kept telling Jose and me how much he loved fog and promised he would never again complain about the Northern California rain, even if it did keep him indoors when he wanted to play outside.

It was the hardest ride that Vanna ever made. I thanked God her clearance was a foot and a half off the ground because if she had been any lower she wouldn't have cleared most of the rocks on the road.

We arrived at the top of a hill two hours later and looked down at a small village with the population of about thirty. Seven or eight adobe shacks were spread out amongst stick-wood corrals, full of haggard looking goats and burros. There were enough chickens running around to supply all the Kentucky Fried restaurants in L.A. for a month, but what they ate remains a mystery to me to this day. Kinlin figured out it must have been dirt, because that's where their heads were most of the time. It was too hot for a bug to survive, he said, and there isn't much nutrition in a rock, so dirt was the only thing he could come up with. Kinlin told us that he would never eat another chicken, saying anything that frazzled and ugly would have to make you sick. I think he was on the tenth step of the twelve-step program swearing off meat. We tried to tell him that the chickens at home were a lot healthier, but he fired back that we probably had better dirt. He also said he was real glad that the goat of Picasso was only a picture on the wall because if it had of been a real one, and it smelled as bad as the ones in the road, he would move into the Zen garden and sleep in a tent. Kinlin wasn't a happy camper. He kept saying he wished we were back at the beach swimming and repairing nets.

The place obviously bothered him. As we approached the house of Jose's aunt he suddenly pointed his finger and without anyone telling him, said, "She lives there!"

Jose looked at him and asked him how he knew. He said that he just did, it was as clear to him as the cloudless sky behind the dry hills that surrounded us.

We pulled up to the front and scattered chickens the same way a bird dog flushes quail, except these birds tripped and fell over each other as they tried to fly, instead of blurring away at the speed of sound. The old adobe looked like it had been there as long as the mountains in back. It was in need of repair. The right side of the porch's roof was falling at a forty-five degree angle. There were three goats and a thousand chickens hanging around the yard.

With the exception of them, and a turkey tied to a stake, there was no one to be seen. A stack of firewood leaned on the side of the house, grayed and dry from the sun. A straw chair and old couch slumped on the porch. I looked for electrical lines, and seeing none, realized the old woman wasn't into radios or toasters. Parked in the back was an old Dodge pickup that hadn't been moved since Kennedy was shot. It was now the home for a dozen roosting chickens.

The place looked deserted. When I mentioned that to Jose he told me she was there, and would show herself soon enough.

The house and surrounding grounds had an ominous feeling about them. I kept waiting for a flock of ravens to land on the roof and a tall woman with a warty nose draped in black to step out. I wondered how a woman out here could survive alone. I spotted a small sparse garden in back, and a well. Other than that pickings were pretty slim. The nearest grocery store had to be 400 miles away.

I was wondering what kind of hell I had gotten myself into. I had a hard time believing in mystics. I wanted to, but it was like the perception of God to me, if He's there, great, put me on the list, if not, I haven't been disappointed. I always felt God was a brand new Harley and a platinum American Express Card in your back pocket.

I asked Jose how Teresa's sister existed. He said the people in the surrounding area took care of her. They dropped by from time to time and left baskets of food or portions of a slaughtered hog. They were tributes, offerings to someone they felt they were fortunate to have living among them. The peasants knew that she was blessed, capable of seeing things from the "Other World." They came to her from time to time to seek advice or counsel. Once, many years ago, one of the children from the village became lost in the hills and was gone for three days. Everyone thought the small girl was dead. His aunt stayed up all night seeking help from whomever it is she speaks with. The next morning she drew a map pinpointing the exact location of the lost child. The villagers found her and ever since have treated his aunt like a saint. Over the years she has performed other feats of vision, which have convinced everyone that she is, indeed, a person who is blessed.

"She seeks no rewards," Jose said, "and stays out of the public eye. The only one she is close to is her sister, Teresa. Teresa and Pedro drive up a couple of times a month and bring her fresh or smoked fish. Other than that her contact with the outside world is limited. As a small boy, she favored me. Instead of getting hugs like other kids, she simply touched me between the eyes with her fingers. Every time she did that I felt as though a warm stone had been glued to my forehead."

CHAPTER 33

The sun was sinking slowly to the west. Just as I was thinking we had better leave because I didn't want to be there when it got dark, the front door opened. She stepped out unto the porch. After what I had just heard of her healing people with her hands, to see her with her feet touching the ground was a disappointment.

She saw Jose behind the wheel and immediately smiled. That was a good sign because I was thinking maybe she was going to come out after having a bad night, point to the car, and make it disappear.

We all got out. Kinlin made sure that he had a tight grip on my hand, and a vice-grip on his sword. She walked up to Jose, and like he was still that little boy thirty-five years before, touched his forehead. He said something in Spanish and she turned to Kinlin and I. She nodded to me with smiling eyes, then turned to the boy. The woman had given me about a second of recognition, and Kinlin half a minute, which seemed like an eternity. It seemed like she was looking through, and not at him. She turned to Jose and asked something. He nodded his head yes. She knelt down on one knee and placed the palm of her hand on Kinlin's face. She said something again to Jose.

As politely as I could, I said, "Jose, what did she say?"

"She asked if that was the boy her sister had spoken of. The second thing she said was that she knows him."

Knows him? Does that mean she knows whom he belongs to, and that I was going to lose him? I panicked inside. "What does she mean, she knows him?"

Jose turned, and asked her a question. After her answer, he turned back to me. "She said she knows his soul, not the skin covering it."

She spoke something again to Jose. He said, "She say's he's the oldest person she has ever seen."

Kinlin turned to me with a totally confused look. "Bird, what does that mean? Am I older than you?"

He looked so worried I expected him to go over to the car mirror and check his face for wrinkles.

"I don't know, Kinlin. I always thought you were going on five. Maybe five hundred would be more like it."

Kinlin looked at his uncle Jose. "Jose, you always said I'm a hundred and fifty, and Bird say's I'm four. HOW OLD AM I?"

Jose's aunt asked Jose what we had said. After he explained, she looked back at Kinlin and smiled. She turned towards the hills and pointed towards them and said something to Jose.

"What was that about?" I asked.

Jose smiled. "She said he was as old as the mountains."

Kinlin jumped into my arms. He looked at the skin on the back of his hands, and said with a frightened look on his face, "Bird! What does that mean?"

"I don't know son. I'm sure it isn't bad, but I'm sure we're going to find out soon enough."

"Bird, I'm getting a funny feeling inside," he lay his head on my shoulder. "You know that squishy feeling we talked about when Trout left? It's kind of like that."

"Are you afraid?"

"A little."

"What are you afraid of?"

"I don't know," he turned to look me in the eyes. "You know that red dot I put on the map of Baja on my stomach?"

"Yes."

He pointed to the house and said, "I think this is it." He inched up higher on my chest and buried his head against my chest.

Jose had picked up on the conversation. He said something to her that made her place her hand, again, on Kinlin's face. She had the look Trout sometimes gave me when she knew I was in the throes of emotional pain. It was a look that said, "It's OK. I'm here. Don't be afraid."

Kinlin suddenly calmed. It was a change I immediately felt by the release of his grip on my neck. He turned and looked at her staring into her face. She smiled at him. The little boy that seconds before believed he was going to be eaten alive, smiled back.

Jose said, "I've not introduced you. This is Isabella" In Spanish, he said, "Isabella this is my good friend Bird, the boy's name is Kinlin."

Isabella tipped her head and said something in Spanish that Jose translated, "If you are a friend of Jose's then you are a friend of mine. You are welcome." With a gentle sweep of her arm, she invited us in.

Inside the humble clay dwelling I was overtaken by the simplicity. There were no fetishes hanging from the walls as I had expected, or a cloudy crystal ball on the table. It was a house that looked and smelled like it belonged to a woman living alone. It was feminine, but Spartan, void of any luxuries. Incense I couldn't recognize permeated the interior. It was a scent that didn't offend, but seemed to belong. A sweet earthy aroma that smelled like it had been there since the first brick of clay had been laid.

There were two rooms; the largest was the living area, separated from the kitchen by an open wall. Her bedroom was off the living room facing the hills. The bedroom had the look of a place she sought comfort in. There was one window set deep into twelve-inch-thick walls, and on its sill sat the horn of a large male mountain goat. Covering the wall, behind the old oak dresser, were several bunches of dried flowers hanging upside down, their stems bundled together in white silk. The floor was the same wood as those in the rest of the house, except this one looked like it was hand-oiled every week. In the middle of the floor was a large red Persian rug on which sat a hand-wrought Spanish iron bed. The bed was covered with layers of ivory white lace overlapping in waves, crashing against salmon colored satin pillows.

The kitchen was much like Teresa's. It was basic, full of color, with an open oven in the corner. In the middle of the room four chairs circled a thick wooden table with a large bowl of fruit in the center.

In the living room were a couple of worn, overstuffed chairs and a comfortable couch overflowing with suede pillows. All of this surrounded a flat slab of oak, supported by brass pots. There were no crucifixes or pictures of the Holy Virgin on the walls, something I found odd in a house belonging to a woman whom I imagined deeply religious.

The four of us sat in the kitchen. Isabella brought out bowls and a big clay crock filled with some kind of stew. She set a bottle of red sweet wine on the table, some limes and tequila, and a glass of juice for Kinlin.

As we ate and drank, Jose and his aunt talked. The conversation was periodically spotted with laughter. I imagined Jose telling her of the adventures he has had since he had last seen her. The mood changed and the talk became serious. It was one that had them both, from time to time, glancing at Kinlin and me. It made me uneasy thinking there was a person sitting that close to me who might be able to read my mind.

Jose nodded to her in agreement, then looked to me. "Amigo, my aunt would like us to spend the night. She said she has been getting overwhelming impressions from the two of you ever since we stepped out of the car. She would like to look into them tonight and talk to you about it tomorrow."

Kinlin asked if he could go to the car and get his pens and paper because he wanted to draw some pictures of the goats. After he left, Jose said there were a few things Isabella had to say to me. As she began, Jose translated. "There are things that you must know. There are spiritual answers that will help to heal the pain I see in the eyes of you and the boy. The echoes I am hearing from the other side are some of the strongest I have ever felt, and crucial in your quest to find peace within yourself."

I interrupted, and said, "Jose, does she only see Kinlin and me?"

Jose turned to her and asked the question.

She said, "No, I see three people, but it is not a triangle like you might imagine. There are two circles, one larger on the outside and a smaller one in the middle. The big circle is the swirling of your soul mingled with someone else's. The small one in the middle is the boy. It is much like an egg with the outer circle being the shell, and the smaller one is the life-force embryo beating inside."

"Jose, ask her if Trout is part of the circle?"

"I do see a woman," she answered, "I also see the circle is beginning to break, but it is not time, because the nucleus isn't prepared to step out of the circle." Then, looking at me and through me, she said, "You have come to me to learn how to keep that from happening."

I turned to Jose, and said nothing, but he read the words, "How do I do that?" written all over my face. So did she.

She continued, "You have to listen to what the spirits say. It is no accident you are here. You are here because it is the most important journey you will ever make."

With that last statement Jose read my mind and slid a glass over to me, pouring me three fingers of tequila and four for him.

She ended by saying, "Enjoy your day. Tonight I want you and the boy to sleep in the house. Jose should sleep outside." With that, she stood up and went to her room and closed the door.

Jose stared into his glass, catching me with a sideways glance. "Well, amigo, what do you think?"

"Pretty scary," I said, taking a drink.

"Amigo, she is a good woman and I know she cares about you and the boy. She feels maybe she can help you both and be a guide in a quest that has been chosen by destiny to find out who you both are."

"And Trout?"

"Yes, her too. She told me that she feels Trout's presence strongly in connection with you and the boy, but to see one of you clearly she has to look at all three of you together. That is the meaning of the circles."

"What is the purpose of Kinlin and I sleeping in the house without you?"

"I think she wants to be alone with the two of you so she can feel what is floating between you both without the interference of any of my drunken ghosts filling the room," he said, with a big grin.

"Yeah," I said, appreciating his attempt at trying to lighten things up, "if she wanted to look deep into you she'd have a tough time sorting through all the women hanging onto your heart and the noise of the ten-piece blues band in the background. Fuck, she'd have to join the party just to be able to cope!"

"It would be hard for a mystic to handle," amigo, "unless she was drunk too."

We went outside and joined Kinlin and his sketchpad. He had drawn every goat in the neighborhood. On each of their backs he had put a garden full of brilliant flowers. It was, no doubt, his way of dealing with their stench. He had drawn a field full of chickens buried up to their necks in dirt, dotted here and there with giant bugs threatening them with fanged teeth. He was dealing with the situation at hand. It was one where I'm sure would have him taking Picasso's goat poster down when he got home. From that moment on, Kinlin would be looking at Chicken McNuggets whenever he saw them advertised, like they were little dusty earthen cubes.

The three of us took a walk and sat on a boulder and watched the sun brilliantly melting behind the hills to the west. It was one of many sights I knew I was going to see here, sights I wished Trout was experiencing with us. But the thought that she was sitting with the three of us on that rock didn't seem to work. It would have been nice to see things as Isabella did, and to be able to feel Trout's spirit, but I knew Trout was over a thousand miles away and probably having someone else feeling it. I had spent days trying to understand what was going on with her, but found that the realities of my past, and the hard lessons it had taught me were interfering with any rational opening of my heart.

The eight-year-old was sticking me with voodoo pins, and jealousy and anger were beginning to bleed from their holes. I felt that this was "The Test," and if I failed at coming to terms with my emotions, and loving her unconditionally, then everything I wanted the boy to learn would have to be taught by someone else.

That little boy in me said, in no uncertain terms, *"You haven't done too well with tests in your life, and this is an entrance exam you're not prepared for. You can cheat your way through it, and lie like a dog, but in the end Kinlin will see it and stop believing in you; something that would fit in perfectly with your philosophy of not believing in yourself. There are so many questions involved there isn't enough room on your palms for the ballpoint, cribbed answers. Quit the class and run. That's how you've handled all the heavies in the past, so why spoil a good record by getting your shit together now?"*

Jose saw I was somewhere else, and said, "Amigo, where are you?"

"Somewhere in the San Joaquin valley after the war," I said, "someplace where those hot summer nights used to fill my room with blast furnace-born beasts. Nights that made the sheets stick to you like napalm."

"That bad, huh?" he said, looking at the sun do its best to catch the hills on fire.

Kinlin was off in the distance chasing lizards into their holes, and throwing rocks at mutated-armed cactus. Jose said, "What was it like in that den of your youth?"

"I don't know Jose, I wish I did. It seems like it was all so perfect, but I'm getting strong messages that tell me it wasn't. The pictures I'm getting are ones of the ideal youth, but somehow I feel more powerful forces than me are censoring them. Forces that are trying to keep me from viewing the atrocities of a childhood war that I'm afraid to look at."

"Walking wounded, amigo?"

"Something like that."

"Well, maybe you can get a little healed while we are here, because I'm getting tired of watching you bleed!" he said, watching Kinlin peer down a snake hole.

"Jose, I'm sorry for involving you in this, it wasn't my wish, and if you want to split, I'll understand."

"Hey man, shut the fuck up!" he said, watching the sun burn the top of the last hill. "If I wouldn't want to be here, I wouldn't hang around. Besides, who's going to rip your heart out as it beats its last beat on your pyre if I'm not here to do it? Fuck, I've got to be around just to make sure that Kinlin doesn't jump in after you!"

"Good thought, amigo," I said, "now that we've got my funeral arrangements figured out, how about us going and getting a drink?"

"Best idea I've heard in an hour," he said.

We called to Kinlin, and heard him yell back that he was just learning how to speak lizard, and that if he just had a couple more hours he would have it down pat. I told him he could finish tomorrow, and the three of us headed back to the house.

Isabella fixed a wonderful meal, and afterwards we sat and talked and laughed at Jose's jokes. As it grew late, we decided to go to bed. Jose said good night, and went to sleep in the van. Kinlin and I bedded down with our sleeping bags on the living room floor and watched Isabella, after saying good night, go to her room and quietly shut the door.

It had been a long day, and the two of us were beat. I was glad Kinlin was tired, because having to sleep in the house with Jose outside confused him, and made him nervous. I explained to him that was the way his aunt wanted it. He tried to understand it and wanted to act like he didn't care, but his insistence of sleeping in my bag with me, with his sword poking me in the ribs, was a sign that he wasn't going to be taken in the middle of the night without a fight.

We finally dozed off. I woke up in the middle of the night, not by any loud noise, or demon-filled dream, but of the feeling of a presence in the room. Lying with my head on the pillow and opening one eye, I looked in the direction of the two overstuffed chairs. I saw a presence that alarmed me. It was Isabella sitting in the room staring at Kinlin and me. She was sitting there, not moving, or making a sound, just filling the area we were sleeping in with her eyes. I figured it must have been at least three in the morning, and had no idea how long she had been there. There were one or two candles lit in her room, which cast dried flower shadows on her walls, bouncing wispy reflections off her hair. It began to feel like a dream. The longer I looked at her and the candle lit background, the more I felt she was in the bag with us. It was either hypnosis, or the sheer weight of the feeling in the room that put me back to sleep. I awoke to the smell of coffee, barely remembering a thing.

Kinlin crawled out of the depths of the red flannel, and stuck me in the chin with the tip of Excalibur. It was a wake up call that would have brought someone out of a six-month coma. Kinlin inched up to my eyes, and said, with sleep-filled ones himself, "Bird sorry, are you hurt?"

"No, I just won't have to shave today, that's all!"

He smiled and whispered, "Bird, did you see her last night?"

"See who?" I said, knowing full well what he meant.

"The lady!"

"Why are you asking?"

"Because I dreamt that she was floating over our bed watching us. Are you sure she didn't leave her room, because I think I saw her flying around in this one," he said, rolling his eyes up at the ceiling.

"Nah," I said, not wanting to tell him that my vision was no dream.

"Are you sure?"

"Sure, I'm sure," I said, "if you think I would have seen her doing figure-eight's above our heads, and not screamed like a roomful of jackals, then you don't know the Bird very well. You would have wet the bed, scared more of me than of the flying woman!"

He chuckled, and hugged my neck, and said he was starving to death, and like so many times in the past tried physically to drag me out of bed. I always got up just to keep him from hurting himself, or of seeing him succeed, and hurting me in the process.

We went into the kitchen and watched Jose preparing us a meal. Isabella was outside gathering eggs for an omelet, which made Kinlin say he would prefer something else. When asked why, he stated that he was watching his cholesterol. Jose and I looked at each other and slyly smiled. Jose agreed, and said he would fix him a bacon and tomato, tortilla sandwich, something that Kinlin liked after Jose said that pigs didn't eat dirt. But a statement that made him stick out his tongue after I told him they lived in it.

Isabella came in, and Jose threw together the eggs, chorizo, and peppers, and we all sat and watched the Baja day begin. Nothing was said about the experience I had of seeing her sitting up all night, or of Kinlin's vision-filled dream.

After breakfast she spoke seriously to Jose for a while. He looked at me, and said that she wanted to spend some time with the boy and him alone. After she had talked to Kinlin, she wanted to sit with me. I agreed, and got up and walked to the front door. Suddenly I found Kinlin at my leg. He looked up with worried eyes, and asked me where I was going. I said I would just be outside, and not to worry because Jose was going to be here with him to translate. I assured him that he was going to learn something. Those were words that always sparked his interest, and probably chased away any fears he might have had. Before turning back to Isabella and Jose, he reached up and asked for a hug. It was a sign he wanted the act of touching; an act he knew comforted us both.

CHAPTER 34

I spent the next couple of hours sitting in the sun wondering what was going on inside the house. I knew intuitively that it was going to be a communication between Isabella and Kinlin that wasn't going to do him any harm. I had seen the kindness and peace in her face, and believed that doing anyone harm wasn't a part of her being.

When the door opened Kinlin and Jose came into the yard. Kinlin crawled up my arms and laid his head in my face. I looked through his hair at Jose for some confirmation that he was OK. Jose looked back and smiled, telling me with his eyes that Kinlin was all right.

I asked Kinlin anyway, wanting him to know I was aware of something that was going on with him. "How's my little poet doing?"

"OK, Bird," he said, "I got a little dizzy in there sometimes while she was talking. It kind of made me feel like I was in a dream."

"But, you feel all right?" I asked.

"Yeah, I feel OK. She's a nice lady, Bird. She's kind of like those grandmothers I see on those old movies on TV, except she's like a magician. She can see things that are invisible." He went on to say, "Maybe after you talk to her, you will see what I mean."

"I'm sure I will Kinlin," I said. "I'm going in with Jose now. Will you be all right out here by yourself?"

"Sure, Bird," he said, "I'm going to study the chickens and try to find out what they really eat. When I do, I'll tell you and Jose."

"Good," I said putting him down. I reached out to him and touched the side of his face as Jose and I walked into the house.

Isabella was sitting at the kitchen table drinking a cup of tea. Jose and I sat across from her. Jose immediately shoved a glass of tequila in front of me, saying with a smile on his face that I would probably need it. By the way she was looking at me I felt like asking for the whole bottle.

Jose started out by saying, "Amigo, last night she didn't sleep. She stayed awake in the room with you and the boy."

"I know. I saw her."

"Yes, she told me you did."

"How did she know that?" I asked, nervously.

"Amigo, something like that is a piece of cake for her. What she's dealing with now is something a lot harder."

"What's going on, Jose?"

"Last night in this room, she felt the presence of the spirits of you and the boy and Trout so strongly that she had to stay. Sleep was out of the question for her. First, she wants to tell you about Kinlin. Then she wants to talk about you and of your bond with Trout. It is all for your good, my friend, so don't run from it. She sees many things. The energy she felt in this room last night was among the strongest she has ever had."

Isabella reached out and gently touched my hand, and through Jose, said softly, and with conviction, "The boy is yours and the woman's. It is clear. The day that Pedro found him on the beach was no accident. He was placed there to be handed over to you by Jose. The only mystery is who placed him there. To think that he just dropped out of the heavens is something all of us would have a hard time believing. He is the birth-son of two people of this earth. I know he was abandoned."

I interrupted by saying, "Does Kinlin know this?"

"No," Jose said, "she didn't tell him."

Isabella went on, saying, "He was either left on the beach by his parents, or was the only survivor of a catastrophe at sea. I don't have the answer for that. It doesn't matter how he was left, or what has happened to his birth parents. The reasons he was abandoned were written before he was born. The purpose of it was to bring him to you."

She continued, "He is the rebirth of the child that was lost to you and your woman months ago. The child was lost because she wasn't strong enough to carry it, strong in her heart, that is. Her soul wanted the child, but her mind didn't, so she threw it out of her body. But destiny had already given birth to her child four years before, knowing she was going to rid herself of the one she had growing in her."

Jose said, "Listen amigo. It is all good to hear."

Isabella said, "I see the bond so powerful between you and the woman that last night I saw her spirit in the bed with you and the boy. The boy was given to you two to complete the bond because fate sees the two of you are capable, because of your fears, of breaking it. The boy is here to help you erase those fears, and to help you to not destroy something that is eternal. To break it would damage something so important to you both that it would take another lifetime to repair it."

"Does the boy remember any of his life before Jose's uncle found him?" I asked.

"No," she said, "he has blocked it out. I could have brought it out of him with time, but it is a memory he has to recall himself. Maybe he never will. If he does, he will just see fragments of it, and possibly see his birth parents as two friends he had in the past. What I told the boy is that you and Trout are his parents. They were words I didn't need to say because he believes in his heart that you and she are that, anyway. It is a knowledge that is inherent to him, something he felt the moment he laid eyes on you both. The boy is gifted and I'm sure you have seen it. He will grow up with the same gift that was given me. Don't ever try and suffocate it. Let it grow in him. As he gets older you will see it blossom."

"What do I have to look forward to with him? Will I be strong enough to allow him to grow and fulfill his destiny?" I said, doubting that I was the right choice to be his parent.

"Kinlin's gift is that of 'healer,' and one of his main tasks is to heal you and his mother. He will make sure you are strong enough. The spirit world wouldn't have chosen you for his parents if they had thought you would fail at the job of letting him be who he is destined to be."

"But what if I fail?" I said, with eyes full of doubt.

"You will falter, and struggle with your own life, but the love you feel for him will be there to catch you. Through the love you and his mother share for him, you both will learn to love yourselves. As I see you both, that is the hardship you now face. It is buried deep within you and her, an anchor you both have had tied to you since you were small children."

I said, "The bond I have always felt for her even when she was a child is a union I cannot explain. I have spoken to Jose about it, and have asked myself over and over for reasons why it exists. If you can help me with that, then a big question that has occupied my mind ever since she drove up last summer would be answered. It would help me to understand the meaning of the intense love I feel for her."

"Yes," she said, "what I tell you now will be the most difficult thing for you to understand. You only have to trust me, and believe in what I say. I've already told you that last night as I sat and watched you and the boy, I felt her presence floating in the room with you. I sought answers that would help me to define the bond I knew existed between you and her. The answers I received were ones that define destiny as well as mortals like us can understand it." She turned to Jose, and then to me. As he translated, she kept her eyes glued to mine. After he was through, she continued. "You and the woman have had an intense relationship in a past life. The bond you have been feeling with her is a continuation of that past life experience."

I stared at her trying to fathom what she had just said. They were words that went against the grain of everything my western mind was taught to believe. It wasn't that I didn't want to believe it. It was just that I didn't know if I was capable of it.

Jose turned to me, and said, "Amigo, I know it is difficult for you to accept this, but just look into all of the things we have spoken of. Open yourself up to what she is saying, maybe it will help to set you free."

She waited for him to finish. "The woman came to you this summer to try and re-tie the bond, and to complete something that was never finished in a past life, but this life interfered with that process. The pains you both have suffered since your births have placed walls between you, walls that have kept you both from finding out what the bond means."

She touched my hand again, and continued, "When she came to you this summer, she was unconsciously looking for her father, or someone to replace him."

Jose looked at me. I knew what he was thinking. They were the same thoughts he and I had spoken of before. Hearing it from the old woman only confirmed my deepest fears.

"But," she said, "in her search she also found a love that had nothing to do with father. It was the love she had felt for you a lifetime before. It was a love that frightened her because what she wanted was acceptance from you as parent, and not as lover. She was raised in a role of trying to please her father. It was a role she wasn't prepared for. I saw that her father is no longer close to her. He is either dead, or gone,"

"Dead," I said.

"Then it is even clearer to me now. He died before she could please him ultimately, and that was to be the child he wanted her to be. She transferred that obligation to you, but in doing so she also transferred her anger at herself, and anger towards you of being the critical parent. I see her in torment. It is a pain that is controlling her life. She feels like she has failed her father."

"But Isabella," I said, "she has led a homosexual lifestyle. It is part of what drove her away from me. She was going to finally tell her father about her sexual preference, but he died before she had a chance."

"Of course she was," she said, "it was the final step of her becoming what he wanted. She was going to go up to him and show him with her sexuality that she was the boy he wanted. Maybe she didn't have a boy's physical characteristics, but she could fulfill his wish by acting like a boy when it came to the ultimate act of sexual preference. I also see her in her relationships with other women as the dominant partner, again, taking the role of the man and pleasing her father. I'm sure the decision to tell him was a difficult one for her to make, but in her eyes it was the only one she had. From her birth on she wasn't allowed another choice. Deep in her soul she is angry with that. The suffocation her father put on her was probably very subtle, but it was one she was raised with. It has affected everything she has done since. She never loved herself for who she was, she only tried to please people who loved her for who they wanted her to be. To this day I see her thinking that she will fail at everything because of her loss of identity, and self love."

I reached over and poured Jose and myself another drink. I thought what Isabella had just said were the same things I had tried to explain to Kinlin. It was a truth that had powered Trout into her headlong dives of self-loathing.

Isabella said, "In seeing you as critical parent, she is also trying to please you. But the bind that destiny has put her in, as your lover, only compounds the anger she feels against a father who put demands on her. She is also angry with you, because you demand that she be a woman. She ran from you because she was frightened, and terribly confused. Until she stops seeing you as critical father, fear and anger will control any relationship you want to have. She feels she can do nothing right in your presence, and misinterprets many of your reactions as criticism."

"How do I continue the bond without breaking it, by running away in fear?" I asked.

"That is the hardest thing you are facing, and are going to face. You and her are alike in so many ways. The most crucial is that you have no self-love either. Yours also began early in life. You were so busy pleasing your parents that you never learned how to please yourself. After awhile it turns into anger. It is anger directed at yourself and not the ones who forced you into a behavior that you had no control over choosing. You have failed at every relationship you have ever had. You have chosen partners that only support your lack of self-worth, either though ridicule or trying to change you into something that you are not, much like your parents did."

Isabella paused, deep in thought, and said, "Something happened to you when you were a small child. There were a series of events that you experienced that had a negative effect on your development. I believe there was some abuse. There is one traumatic event that happened to you. It involves your mother, someone you loved and trusted. It is about betrayal. I don't know what happened, but from that moment on it has had an effect on how you view women. You have never trusted them. In your relationships you expect to be betrayed, and you always are. It is a self-fulfilling prophecy. Trout came into your life to heal that pain and to rid yourself of the anger you have always felt towards women.

You chose her because she was someone you knew before, in another lifetime, someone you trusted. As a matter of fact she is the only person you trust. Because of that you have let her into your soul. I see that you will try to destroy the privilege you have given her because you feel she has betrayed you. You think you are not worthy of any love she might feel for you. I see you doing things that will push her from you. If you continue like you are, you will succeed. If you fail with her, then it will be your ultimate failure and prove to you that you are not capable of loving or receiving love. You chose her to show yourself who you really are; to test that frightened inner voice that has always told you to run away. If you succeed in chasing her away it will be a rejection you will have trouble living with. It is not the wish of fate for you to do that. But sometimes we can alter the course of destiny. If we do, we will only be confronted with the same challenge in the next lifetime. So my advice to you is to not run from her and the abandonment you feel. Embrace the love that exists between the two of you. It is a love that has always been there."

Praying that she would have the ultimate answer, I asked, "What will happen now?"

"That I cannot answer," she said. "I can only tell you what will happen if you or her run from the bond before it has time to clarify itself."

"And?" I asked.

"The both of you will feel like you have failed at the most important task that this life has given you."

"And what is that?"

"To find yourselves through each other's eyes. The opportunity has been given to you, and believe me, it is a gift. The boy will be your messenger, but in the end the choice will be yours and hers. The only thing that will stop it will be the fears of your pasts. If your commitment to the bond is broken, it will be a loss and a tragedy that will affect both of your lives forever."

"How do I survive the loss I'm feeling now?" I asked.

"By not forgetting the reasons for the bond in the first place," she said.

"And what are those?"

"A love that is eternal; one that was born a long time ago. Your commitment to the bond is to love her for what and who she is, not for who you want her to be. If she feels that your love is critical, she will continue to see you as parent. It will become a wall you will not be able to break down, not in this lifetime anyway."

I looked down at the table, trying to let it all sink in. She said, "Follow your heart, not your head. Remember the first time you touched her with the hands of a man, a touch that told you she wasn't a child anymore. A touch that sent a message to your heart telling it that it was in love. Remember how it felt. Remember the tenderness and unselfishness of it, and what it did to her. Touch her with it every day. In doing so remember the feeling. It will be that touch of purity and love you have searched for all your life. In touching her soul you will have also touched your own. It will free you of your pain. Believe me, with the bond you both have, she will feel it. It will also help her to rid herself of the pain she's carried with her for years."

"Isabella," I said, "will we ever be lovers again?"

"You will always be lovers. Whether you will ever make love again, I don't know. I see her as someone who will fall in love many times, believing it will satisfy the needs of her soul. She will be very unhappy in her search. She will begin each one with the knowledge that she will fail. She feels she has failed you by not being what you needed. It has made her angry, not only at herself, but at you for giving her a responsibility she wasn't prepared for."

The more she spoke, the more I saw the truth and the mistakes Trout and I had both made, both of us expecting too much from each other.

"Last night I saw that she is afraid of you and of your intensity. She doesn't feel safe around you. Don't mistake what I say; she knows you won't do her harm. She feels you are capable of taking something from her that she is not ready to give up."

"What is that?"

"If she gave in to her feelings and gave herself to you, she would have to give away something she feels the safest with. It is the safety of that little androgynous child that is locked away in her heart. She still is unsure of how to enter this life, as man or woman. Committing herself to you is forcing her to choose. It is a choice that offers her no safety, and sometimes you will feel her anger. But the anger is not towards you. It is what you represent, and that is parent."

"And the boy, how will all this affect him?"

"She doesn't feel safe with the boy either. He forces her to become something she is afraid of, adult and mother. If she fully accepts the role of mother she has to deny the existence of that little boy in her and that is for her to deny the wish of her father. It would be a very painful self-betrayal for her. It would just be more proof that she has failed him. When she finally accepts Kinlin as her son, and finally accepts you for what you are not, her father, then she will be on her way to becoming healed. But you have to help her by not acting like her father."

"How do I do that?"

"By continuing to be what you have always been in this lifetime, and in lifetimes past. You must be a lover that doesn't demand to be touched, a partner of the soul that will always be there. There are a lot of ways to make love, and you and her are on the verge of finding the ultimate touching act. It has nothing to do with the sexual act. It is the dropping of all your walls, and the opening of your souls to each other. It is something that very few people obtain." She looked at me with eyes that hoped I would grasp what she was about to say. "That is the reason you two have met again, and the true meaning of the bond. It is the fulfillment of destiny. The boy was given to you to help re-tie the knot that was broken a lifetime before."

She was exhausted. So was I. Jose poured us another drink. As I sipped mine she spoke to him. When she was finished he turned to me and said, "It's time to go. Amigo, she has emptied herself and must lie down. She wants to see you and Kinlin again, in a year or so. She also said if you have more questions, or feel like you have come to a rock wall in your search, to come back anytime. You are always welcome. She is very fond of you and the boy. Isabella knows of the importance of the relationship between the three of you. She doesn't want to see it fail."

She gently took my hand, and said one more thing to Jose. He looked at me, and said, "She told me to tell you one last thing."

"What's that?"

"You and Trout have to forgive each other."

"For what?" I asked with a puzzled look.

"She has to forgive you for not being her father, and of you forcing her into choices she's not prepared to make."

"And me?"

"You have to forgive her for the feeling of abandonment you blame her for. Once that is done then you both can go on with forgiving yourselves. In that, the healing begins."

Isabella walked outside and softly kissed Kinlin on the forehead. She said goodbye to me by placing her palm on my cheek. She approached Jose, and treating him like the little boy she has always known, took one finger and pressed it between his eyes, leaving a warm glow.

We drove off scattering chickens into a warm December day. Kinlin fell asleep amongst his pens and drawings of goats and chickens, his trusty saber at his side.

Jose and I sat in the front and drove for twenty miles without saying a word. It was a silence that wasn't uncomfortable or forced, but one that was needed by both. When we finally did talk, it was about the last two days and what they meant. We both realized that a lot of what Isabella had said we had already talked about, and knew. Her story of the finding of Kinlin blew our minds. The revelation that Trout and I were lovers in a past life did the same. Her perceptions of Trout's sexuality were ones I had given thought to before, and her seeing it only helped to confirm them for me. I didn't know how Trout looked at it. I only knew that it was an explanation I could deal with. If it was correct, then it was just another tool to help me open the box of understanding I knew I had to have for her. I felt there were many parallels in our relationship that Trout had placed between her father and me. Looking back, I realized that she only brought them up in negative situations. In the past I took them personal. I reacted to them like they were an assault on my behavior, and let her know that I didn't like it. I see now, after the eye-opening talks with Isabella, that I should have handled it differently by pushing my ego aside and allowing her to get out her feelings.

Trout's father I never wanted to be. Over the years I had gotten to care for the man and knew there were shoes in his closet that would have been hard for me to fill. There were issues with her father she had to deal with, and the fear controlling my reactions whenever the comparisons came up didn't help her much in that quest. I knew, too, that it was going to take me weeks, or months, to grasp all that Isabella had said. In the end, I hoped that it would lead me back to the unconditional love I had, early on, preached to Kinlin about.

About two miles from Jose's uncle's house I said that I wanted to spend Christmas at home. The holiday was still five days away, but if we left tomorrow we could still get there in plenty of time.

I wanted to enjoy the time with Kinlin, and I missed the fog and chill of a Christmas day in Northern California. Jose agreed, and looked forward to a celebration with Kinlin, also. He said instead of the "Three Amigos," we would be the "Three Wise Men." Five minutes into the conversation he had already planned on how big the tree would be, and asked if they sold those outdoor lights in strings of a thousand feet. It was going to be Kinlin's first Christmas, he told me. One he had to remember. In the next half mile he had already figured out the menu and what kind of rum to put in the punch. Jose asked if I thought Kinlin was sharp enough to drive a car, because he thought a '68 Mustang would make the perfect gift.

The rest of the ride was filled with talk of sombrero-wearing Santa Clauses and topless Santa's helpers. It was good to laugh again. Jose recognized the need for it, doing his best to help me along with it.

It was a good night with Pedro and Teresa, with a fish barbecue on the beach I shall long remember. The next morning we packed up and left. It was a farewell that moved us all. The two of them had become attached to us, and we had seemed to fill a void that replaced children they never had.

Pedro and Teresa both cried as they passed Kinlin back and forth before handing him to me in the car. Jose's aunt saw beauty in the miracle of Kinlin, and the memories of finding him on the beach. Pedro had lost a fishing buddy with no equal. He demanded that we come back in a couple of months so he could finish with Kinlin's deep-sea education, promising him a job as his partner whenever he wanted. The affection was so strong, that on the day we left, Pedro painted over the old name on his boat, replacing it in bold letters with, "LITTLE FISH."

CHAPTER 35

We headed north planning to make the drive in two days, that is, if Vanna held up. We drove straight through to Big Sur and spent the night in a campground, again, telling ghost stories. Kinlin's were, this time, about monster chickens that lived off the fresh liver of stinking goats and any other warm-blooded creature they could get their dirty mouths on. They were ravenous, scraggly creatures that squawked in Mexican and crept into the tents of unwary campers. Their favorite livers were those of poets. The only way you could keep the monster chickens at bay was to recite poems all night. Something he proceeded to do until Jose and I got so tired of it that we grabbed him and stuck him head first into the nearest sleeping bag. It didn't stop him, but it put a muffler on the endless string of rhymes coming from his mouth. He finally tired and I put him sound asleep into his bag.

Jose and I stayed up and drank cold beer and talked of the past three weeks, of the effect that they had had on all three of us. In going through it with him, I didn't realize how much he had been affected by it too. He told me of how much he missed Trout and of how the absence of her in the house when we got back was going to change all of our lives.

The conversation got back to me, and he asked, "How are you feeling, my friend, any better?"

"Yeah, a little. The talk with Isabella helped me tap into some important feelings, and moved me away from the anger I was having towards Trout."

"Good, amigo. I hope as the days go by it will get even better for you." Then he said, voice full of empathy, "Do you expect her to be there when we get back?"

"No," I said, staring into my beer, "I've had my fantasies, but they are just illusions." Continuing with a sorrow-filled conviction, I said, "I know she won't be there."

"Amigo, I know you are still deep in pain. If I were in your place I would be too. I don't have an answer for you on how to deal with that."

"I know, Jose, it's just an emotion I will have to learn to live with. It's kind of like a man with an amputated leg that can still feel its presence and phantom pain after being without it for ten years. Except I feel that this loss I feel inside will be around a lot longer than that."

Seeing that the direction of our talk was taking me someplace he knew I didn't want to go, and wanting to change the subject, said, "I noticed at my aunt's that you had done some writing during those long days alone on the beach."

"Yeah, I've gotten back into scribbling down some poetry. It's been awhile since I've had the urge."

"I told you amigo, that Trout had brought it out of you again. She will build a fire under you. It will be a rekindling of your creative spirit."

"Something has to be rekindled," I said back, smiling.

"No," he went on, "you write good, you just have to believe in yourself. Trout will be the one to give you that belief. I know what I'm talking about. Wait and see. What was it that you were writing?"

"Just a poem I thought I would send her when I got back. You know, one of those lengthy numbers full of 19th-Century sentimentalities and rabid, 20th-century-filled metaphors. Lines full of beating hearts and heart-eating beasts."

"I know that it is probably good amigo. Don't be so hard on yourself."

"You want to read it?" I said, knowing that the closet poet I was only allowed a selected few to read the secret words I had been putting down for the last twenty years.

"Yes, I would."

I reached in my backpack and pulled out the dog-eared, lined paper tablet and handed it to him. Entrusting Jose with words that came from deep in my soul and were meant only for Trout was another sign that I trusted him as someone who wouldn't tear the six pages apart with criticism.

I watched him read through the pages, filled with everything I had been going through over the last few months. It was a symphonic graph. The poem was filled with mountains and valleys of hope, loss of the same, and the desperate demon-filled dreams of my past. It was a testament of love to a woman I knew I had lost, and the pained metaphors of the memories that still held her close to me.

I described her as a woman/child, lost in a Cézanne landscape. As I tried to reach out and embrace the colors it turned into a slow-motion dream of never grasping her in my hands. It was a poem of reality. I knew if I was ever going to embrace anything, it was going to have to be the truth that I would never again lay with her in that lily-filled bed.

Jose finished the poem, and waited a minute before saying anything.

I asked nervously, "Well, what do you think?"

"It is good, it moved me," he said, still holding the pages. "Trout will think so too. It is just another of the many ways you show how much you love her, but also an example of the tremendous heartbreak that has unfolded between you two."

"Yeah," I said, somberly.

"Amigo, I never told you this before, but I am sorry for what has happened to you, and her. If I had the power to make it right, I would."

"I know you would, Jose." I said, "Instead of fucking your life away, sailing boats all over the world and chasing women, you should have learned to be a magician. Maybe then she would be waiting for us when we got home." Holding my bottle up to his I said, smiling, "and I'll never forgive you for it!"

As I tried to sleep that night I thought of the boy laying next to me and of Trout and all the profound realities of what had happened over the past six months. Never in all my travels and the fantasies that accompanied me in the last 51 years did I ever imagine something like this moving into my life. As I lay there grieving, I heard lamentations pounding in my ears. I knew I wouldn't have traded those last six months for anything, because I had obtained a love that would have taken me six lifetimes to find.

I watched Kinlin sleep, and reached over and touched his soft face. I followed Isabella's instructions, reaching out to Trout and touching her with the same hands I had used the first night we had kissed. It was a touch I carried with me into a sleep that was filled with those same Cézanne landscapes and lily filled Renoir ponds. Dreams of a woman/child in a silken white dress surrounded by white gulls carried me through the night, a night of peace filled sleep.

CHAPTER 36

We arrived home three days before Christmas. The last fifty miles were driven with Kinlin transforming into a dancing elf in the back. He drove us both crazy with that deadly, neck-poking sword of his. Jose had threatened more than once to rip that headband off his head and bind his hands with it. If that didn't work, he said he would take the saber out of Kinlin's hands, and cut his tongue out and feed it to the crows. They were words that only made the poet warrior stab him more, and dare him to try. It got so bad that Jose said we should stop at a bar and get the kid drunk, and then maybe he would pass out and leave us alone. Kinlin heard the remark and fired back at him, saying that he liked his liver just the way it was. He said that to be the leader of the poet warriors he had to remain sober!

Kinlin was excited to be going home, and couldn't wait to get back on his sacred white Schwinn charger. As we pulled off the main road and headed through the orchard, I hoped he didn't have the same fantasies I had going through my mind of Trout sitting on the back steps waiting for our return.

We parked in the drive and got our bags, opened the back door and walked into the house. The same quietness that had filled the rooms when we left was still there, waiting for us when we walked in.

I watched Kinlin, knowing what he would be looking for. Jose feeling the same thing I did watched him too. The boy first went to my room and peered inside, then back to his own and did the same. He walked out into the kitchen where Jose and I were standing, and trying to be hide his emotions, said, "I thought maybe she would be here."

"I know you did, Kinlin," I said, sadly.

"I'm going to walk around outside," he said, with disappointment.

"Why don't you go tell your squirrel friends that you are back, and say hello to the red-tail while you're at it? I know he missed us."

He grabbed his sword and went to the wood shed for his bike. Jose and I looked out the window. We watched him ride to every place he thought Trout might be.

Jose said, "I knew he hoped she would be here. I dreaded to see the look of disappointment on his face when he found that she wasn't."

"Jose, I had the same fears that you did. Now what do we do?"

"Let him search, that's all we can do. When he's through, love the hell out of him."

"Yeah, I guess that's all we can do," I watched Kinlin peering through the windows in the studio.

"Amigo," Jose said, "I have to be honest with you. I had the hope that she would be here too. I couldn't share it with you, but believe me, it was a fantasy that entered my head and wouldn't leave."

"Hey, man, you might be tough and hard as nails, but you don't fool me. You still are a sentimental bleeding heart son of a bitch, and don't ever try and tell me different," I said, trying to put a smile on his face.

He looked back and smiled. Opening the fridge he said, "Amigo, look! The beers I left are still here waiting for us. They are very lonely and need to be opened. What you say we have a drink on our safe return?"

"Jose, that is the best idea I've heard from you since the time you talked me into going on that crazy midnight trip to Paris, ten years ago, drunker than skunks."

He looked at me and laughed. "Fuck! Don't even talk about that week of my life!"

"I won't, because that was the 'ugliest' woman I have ever seen!"

"Amigo, amigo, please. I just got home and don't want to remember things I have tried so hard to forget. It wasn't so much the woman, but the penicillin shots I had to endure for a week after we got back. Please! Let us enjoy our first day home!"

Jose and I tried to lighten up the situation with some laughter, but in the end it was hard to lift the heaviness off the fact that we had returned to a house void of Trout. We walked over to the front window and looked for Kinlin. He was in the field with his sword raised in the air screaming at the hawk flying over his head. We were sure he was telling the great bird of his travels, and asking him if he had seen Trout anywhere in his searches with his powerful eyes.

Jose continued to watch Kinlin. I went over to check the answering machine for messages. The light was blinking, so I punched "Message," and waited for the usual small talk of friends who didn't know where we were, and the hang-ups of people who hated the machines as much as I did.

I wasn't paying much attention until I heard the unmistakable voice of Trout. It was a message that made me rewind and turn the volume up to five, then hover over the machine so I wouldn't miss a word. It was simple and to the point. She said she had called a few times. And where were we? And to call her when we got back from wherever it was.

Jose heard the message and walked into the room and asked me what I was going to do. At the same time he was talking, we heard Kinlin pounding on the front door.

Jose let him in. Kinlin stepped into the living room with a brown wrapped package in hand, screaming, "Look, it's for me! See, it say's Kinlin on the front, and it has Trout's name in the corner. WHAT IS IT?"

It was all a little bit too much for me, first the message, then the package. So I said, honestly, "Hell! I DON"T KNOW!"

"Well, let's open it," he and Jose said in unison.

"OK," I said, giving in to a situation that I wasn't sure I was prepared to handle.

Kinlin ripped off the brown paper and inside saw another package wrapped in Christmas paper with a card tied to the ribbon that said, "For Kinlin, my little fish. From Trout."

Kinlin looked at me and while holding the present in front of him, asked, "What is it?"

"It's a Christmas present."

"What do I do with it?" he asked, totally confused. "I've never had a Christmas present before!"

"Well, inside," I told him, "is a gift Trout has sent to you. You are supposed to wait until Christmas to open it. Inside you will find a surprise."

"Well, when is Christmas?" he asked.

"It's in three days you know that. We've been talking about it now for days."

"Oh, Yeah," he said, blinking his eyes three or four times, "I forgot. But Bird, I can't wait for three days. I want to open it, now!"

"Slow down," I said, "let's just think about this for a minute." Actually, I needed about an hour because I was still trying to deal with the message I had just heard.

"Kinlin, first things first," I said. "Trout called and left a message, and I'm supposed to call her back. After that is done, we can deal with the package. OK?"

He didn't even answer. He took off with the package in hand and ran to the desk and put the phone in my hands. He grabbed the address book in the process, and sticking it in my face, said, "Here, her number is in the part where the T's are."

He leaped up unto the desk and would have dialed the number himself if I wouldn't have stopped him.

I hesitated, knowing that if she answered I was going to hear a voice on the other end that was going to push buttons of longing I wasn't quite sure I could deal with. But with Kinlin hanging onto the moment, I didn't have much of a choice.

Jose had discreetly gone into the kitchen, leaving the two of us alone with the task at hand. A task I heard him handling by pushing aside the aspirin and grabbing a glass.

Kinlin kept saying, "Dial the number! Dial the number!" until I finally said, "Calm down and I will!"

He eventually did calm down but not without first moving as close to me, and the phone as possible. He was poised, and stared at the phone with such an intensity I thought he was trying to will it into dialing itself. With his little finger pointing out the telephone number, I reluctantly dialed. It was a three-ring-eternity lasting six seconds and about a hundred heartbeats. The phone was picked up. On the other end I heard a voice that had the accumulative effect of the sound of every bird's wing I had ever heard.

Trout said, "Hello?"

"Trout, it's me," I said, hoping she would remember the sound of my voice.

"You're finally home," she said, "where have you guys been? I've been calling all week."

"Baja!"

"BAJA?" she said, surprised. "What were you doing in Baja?"

"Jose, Kinlin and I went down for a couple of weeks and stayed with his aunt and uncle. It was a nice trip." I wanted to add that I wished she could have made it with us.

"How's Kinlin?" she asked, concerned.

"Toughing it out," I said, not wanting to overload her with the bloody details.

After a long pause she asked, "And you?"

"Just like Kinlin," I said, "hanging in there."

I didn't know what to say to her, it was either everything or nothing. It was a mood over the phone she was picking up, and I knew she felt the same.

There were more pauses than words. It was an uncomfortable silence of wanting to say more that began to frazzle the cable. It was putting an unbearable static into a connection of two people who weren't ready to talk about what had happened between them.

Trout and I were both runners, and the heaviness of the moment was starting to tell us both that it was time to bale. Kinlin's face, four inches from mine, wasn't helping much. When she asked to speak to him it was a relief for us both.

I gave him the phone and walked into the kitchen where Jose was standing. He was lurched over the sink, looking into the garden. He didn't say anything, just turned to acknowledge I was there.

I opened the fridge and got a beer, then he and I stood there picking up fragments of their conversation. After awhile, Kinlin yelled to me to come back on the phone. I walked up to him and saw the excitement on his face as he stuck the phone into my hand, telling me to talk to Trout, at the same time saying she wanted to see him.

I grabbed the receiver and asked, "Trout, what's going on?"

She said, in a pleading tone, "I wanted to ask you if it was all right if Kinlin came up here for Christmas?"

I paused, trying to let the request find a space in a head already overloaded by just hearing her voice. After a few seconds, I said, "Well, it's kind of sudden, as a matter of fact we just walked in the door. I mean, you know, boom! All of a sudden you are on the line, and you know how difficult that is."

"Yes, I know," she said, softly.

"And then the idea with Kinlin. It's just a little much all of a sudden."

"I know, but I really want to see him. If you already have plans, then I understand," she said, with sadness only Trout could exhale.

At that moment I found Kinlin at my leg, tugging on my pants, looking up at me with eyes full of hope, whispering, "Bird, please, please let me go."

I looked down at him and then through 650 miles of cable at Trout and without any more thought, agreed. "OK, how about tomorrow?"

Kinlin screamed, "REALLY?" at the same time Trout did. He dashed into the kitchen telling Jose in his loudest Kinlin voice that he was going to get to see Trout.

I said into the phone, "Trout, let me try and call for a ticket for him, then I will get back to you."

"OK. Thanks," she said, and after a short, silent pause, said goodbye.

I walked into the kitchen and suddenly felt the forty pounds of Kinlin leap into my arms. With his face pressing against mine, he said, "Bird, do I get to go?"

"Yes, if I can arrange a ticket at such a late date. Let me get on the phone and see." Excitement erupted on his face.

He jumped back onto the floor and ran to his room. As Jose and I stared at each other,

We heard him pack.

"Jose, what do you think?"

"Well, amigo, it would have been nice to have Christmas with him," he said, with some disappointment, "but I think this is more important for him. It's probably the best Christmas present he could possibly get."

"I agree, I'll miss him, but Christmas is the day of giving. Maybe this will put the true meaning to that word, I'll call and try to get a ticket."

After failing a few times trying to get him a flight, I finally got him a seat on Alaska Air for 3 p.m. the next day.

I called Trout back, and after the first ring, she picked it up. "Trout, everything's OK. I got him on a flight tomorrow afternoon with Alaska Air, at three, it gets into Portland at four-forty."

"Thanks Bird," she said.

"What are your plans with him?"

"I want to take him camping, and thought we would fish too. I made a reservation at an old hotel in the woods just over the border in Canada. It's over a hundred years old and there are stuffed grizzlies in the lobby. It's one of those stone and redwood monoliths with a huge fireplace down stairs. I thought it would be a good place for him to spend Christmas Eve and Christmas day. You know how much he dreams of Canada, so I thought it would be a great present for him."

"Yeah, it will," I said, knowing how much he was going to love it.

"Trout, I think I'd better go now," I said, knowing I wouldn't be able to hear the sound of her voice much longer.

"OK," she said, with a touch of sadness. "Can you put him back on the line?"

"Sure."

"Bird," she said softly, "I miss you and I think of you often."

"Me too, Trout, more than you'll ever know." I felt like I was going to break down.

I set the receiver down on the desk and called for Kinlin. He ran into the room and grabbed it, smashing it against his ear. As I walked back into the kitchen I heard him yell back at me, "BIRD, I'm going to CANADA!"

"I know, Kinlin," I said, feeling happy for him, but trying to fight the emotion of feeling sorry for myself.

He finally got off the phone, and as he ran into the kitchen I thought if there was ever a definition for hope reborn, it was written all over his face.

He talked like a magpie about the trip and about bears and the stone castle he was going to sleep in. He said that Trout said it was OK for him to open his present now, and she had some more for him to open up there. He told us Trout got his package with the necklace inside and has it hanging on the wall above her bed. She said having it in the room with her was like having him there too. Kinlin was ecstatic, and his mood was doing wonders for Jose's and mine.

I thought that the two old dogs standing there in the kitchen with him were going to have a pretty lonely Christmas, but it wouldn't be the first time. Seeing the joy in Kinlin's face told me it would be worth it.

Kinlin grabbed his present saying he had to open it now. We agreed, and sat at the redwood table with him. We watched him take his Swiss Army Knife and carefully unfold the scissors. He wasn't going to rip anything apart on his first Christmas present. As a matter of fact, he touched it with such gentleness that one would have thought the "Holy Grail" was inside.

He cut the tape and ribbon and after taking off the paper, placed them all carefully in a neat stack next to him on the table. He stared at the white box in front of him, probably thinking that whatever was inside was so magical the lid would rise by itself, and the celestial storm inside would erupt before his eyes and fill the room.

Jose and I were getting impatient. Jose said, "Little fish, go ahead, let's see what Trout has given you."

"I know, but this is the first Christmas present I've ever got, and I want to remember what it felt like opening it."

After logging the moment in his head he took a deep breath and tenderly lifted off the lid. By the look in his eyes one would have thought Trout was in there herself.

"Bird, Jose, look!"

We bent over the table. Inside was the most beautiful deerskin jacket we had ever seen.

Kinlin acted like he was afraid to touch it, thinking maybe it might dissolve in his hands. I reached over and pulled it out of the box for him and held it up in front of his face. His eyes get as big as Kennedy half-dollars.

The jacket was magnificent. It was hand-sewn from the softest leather and had fringes hanging from the arms. From each shoulder, running down each lapel was a patchwork of hand-sewn beadwork in blues, reds, blacks and yellows. Clasping the two pockets together were the same antler buttons that ran down the front. The jacket was just his size. I knew Trout probably had it made special.

I told him to stand up and slipped it on him. He looked like a young Kit Carson. Jose said Jeremiah Johnson would have sold his mother for such a coat. He was probably right.

Kinlin ran into his room and stood in front of the mirror studying every square inch of a coat I knew he would wear until he grew out of it. Kinlin spent the rest of the day either staring at the buttons and holding them in his little fingers, or preening before his bedroom mirror. His hair had grown down to his shoulders, and Jose had fixed him a ponytail wrapped in a leather band. Being the proud father that I was, thought a more beautiful boy didn't exist. I knew Trout would think the same thing when she watched him step off the plane.

The next day I helped him pack, making sure he had a bag big enough for his sword. It was getting time to leave, and he insisted that Jose come with us.

He made one more final check to make sure he had his pens and papers, and then satisfied he had everything he needed, jumped into the van with us.

At his insistence we arrived an hour early, and like the time we waited for Trout, bugged me every five minutes about departure time. We walked up to the check-in counter to confirm his flight and to get him a boarding pass. I had told him before that he had to be at least five-years-old to be able to fly alone, which meant that we were going to have to tell a little off-white lie to get him on board.

The woman behind the counter looked at me, then bent over to see the little buffalo hunter grabbing onto my leg.

She said, "My, what a beautiful coat!"

"Thank you," Kinlin said, and then proudly added, "Trout gave it to me."

"Trout?" she asked.

"Yes," he said again, full of pride, "she's my mother!"

The last line threw me because I had never heard him put her in those terms before. At that moment I knew that the Baja trip had not only opened my eyes, but the talk Isabella had with him had confirmed a belief in him too.

The woman studied his ticket, and asked, "Are you his father?"

"Yes," Kinlin said, from down under. Another statement I thought was the nicest Christmas present I would ever have.

"How old is the boy?" she said, with a little skepticism in her voice.

"150!" Came the words from the young Kit Carson down below. He wasn't messing around, I thought, and not wanting to lie, told her the truth.

His last statement had her leaning over again, staring at the oldest person in the world.

"My," she said, "150, that makes you more than five, doesn't it?"

"I'm really older than the mountains in Baja," he said, confidently, "but Jose believes I'm 150. I thought you wouldn't believe that I was as old as a mountain, so I said 150 instead."

"Well, you are a bright boy," she said.

"Yes, I am!"

"I bet you watch Sesame Street don't you?" she said, in a patronizing tone.

"No!" he answered, adamantly; "I watch *History Channel* and *Discovery* and sometimes *American Movie Classics* if there's a worthwhile film on."

She wasn't about to give up, wanting to convince herself that the boy down there in the deerskin jacket really was five, and not smarter than her. I felt like telling her to save her breath, because the kids IQ was probably about three figures higher than hers.

She continued, by saying, "Well, I bet you can't wait until you can read, can you?"

"I already do!" he said, like it was common knowledge.

"Oh, really?" she said, in a patronizing tone. "What do you read?"

"*Field and Stream*, and *Art Forum*."

She looked at me and decided not get into it any further, fearing that the boy was smarter than she was. "Here's his boarding pass, have a nice flight," and adding, as we turned to walk away, "the other passengers are going to feel a lot safer knowing he is on board."

"Why's that?" I asked, turning around towards her.

"Because if the pilot has a heart attack, at least they know there is someone on the plane that will be able to take over the controls," she said, staring at Kinlin as we walked away.

We watched as his plane taxied up to the gangplank. He saw that it was a white one, with the big face of an Indian painted on the tail. He told us Trout probably had them paint that Indian on the tail just for him so he could recognize it as it pulled up, that way we wouldn't miss it. I agreed with him, knowing that if it had been in her power to do so, she would have.

It came time to board, and the three amigos, with Kinlin in the middle, hugged each other hard. I picked him up, and with him seeing the sadness and worry in my eyes, said, "Don't worry Bird, I'll be OK. Trout will take care of me."

"I know," I said, "I'm just going to miss you, that's all."

"I thought we weren't going to say that anymore."

"Sometimes we have to break the rules and tell it like it is."

He thought about what I had just said and said, "I'll miss you too, Bird. But I'll be back!"

And knowing what he would say next was a pledge he would keep, said, "I promise!"

Jose and I walked him to the boarding door. I watched as a stewardess held his hand. Just before turning the corner he turned and waved goodbye. The fringes on his new coat swayed on his arms like a young bird's feathers on its first flight. I watched as he disappeared into the plane and thought of Isabella's words that he was the one that would keep the bond together. I knew the steps that he was now taking getting on the plane were his first steps on that journey.

CHAPTER 37

Jose and I spent the rest of the day and night moping around like two lost souls, realizing how much the boy was part of our lives. The next day was Christmas Eve and spending it without Kinlin or Trout meant we were going to have to tough this one out together. We had spent a couple of Christmas's together before and they had turned into emotional disasters of gigantic proportions.

Jose wasn't going to let this one get us down, so he spent the next day buying a turkey and picking up a small tree. He went to the hardware store and bought a small strand of lights, tinsel, and a few colored bulbs. He then stuck the tree he had bought in a pot, then began, with a margarita in hand, to decorate it.

He made his famous holiday punch and set it in the middle of the table, saying, "Amigo, we are not going to let this get us down. I remember that Christmas Eve you and I spent in Greece. It was a good thing I was thrown in jail, because at least there I had company. You were the sorriest partner I had ever partied with."

"Yeah," I said, "that was a lonely night. You socking that sailor didn't help matters much. You sure fucked up his plans of celebrating the birth of baby Jesus. It was going good until you tried to convince him that Jesus was a Mexican. When he said that Jesus was never a greaser, you should have dropped it right there. But no, you had to knock out his front teeth. Do you think spending Christmas Eve trying to bail you out was fun?"

"Sorry amigo," he said, a big smile on his face, "I think we should stay home tonight and celebrate. I'd hate to have to put you through the same thing again."

"Yeah," I said, "let's stay here and finish the punch. I'm not in the mood to go out and watch you punch someone else."

With that he laughed and continued to decorate a tree that was starting to look like the ugliest evergreen I'd ever seen. About every five minutes he would step back and say, "Isn't that the most beautiful tree you have ever seen?"

"Yeah," I answered, "If there was ever a more blasphemous expression of Christmas, than that scraggly ass bush, I've yet to see it."

We joked our way through the day doing everything we could to keep us from falling into the depths of depression. Jose was good at it, doing his best to keep up our spirits.

The sun had fallen and the fog moved in. Jose and I sat at the table staring at the punch bowl, watching its level get lower and lower. Around eight o'clock the phone rang. Picking it up and hearing Kinlin's voice on the other end did wonders for my tarnished spirit.

"Hello, Kinlin?"

"Bird, it's me. Guess where I am?" he said, excitedly.

"Ah, I don't know?" I said, "Mars?"

"No," he said, chuckling, "in Canada!"

"Canada? Have you been doing any trapping?"

"Nah," he said, chuckling again.

I could tell by the tone of his voice that he was happier than hell. "What're you doing?"

"Bird, I'm in this huge hotel, the one made of rocks. And Bird, you won't believe it, but there is a full grown Kodiak bear standing about ten feet away from me."

"Well, you better start talking to it or you just might end up being his dinner tonight," I said, giving him back the same line he had always given us.

Laughing again, he said, "No, it's not alive. It's dead, sort of. What I mean is, it's stuffed full of sawdust or something, but it has its mouth open and its teeth are showing and its claws are sticking out. Bird, it's the biggest thing I have ever seen. Scary too!"

"You having a good time?" I asked, wanting to be there too.

"Yeah, Bird, Trout and I are having fun. Tonight is a big Christmas party here with food and presents and some guy running around dressed like Santa Claus. The only thing is his breath smells like Jose's after drinking a six-pack of Tecate. I hope the little kids don't notice it and believe from that point on that Santa has an alcohol problem."

The last line brought a smile to my face and he heard me laugh. "Bird, are you and Jose all right? Are you guys going to do something fun?"

"We're trying," I said, turning to Jose, "but you know uncle Jose and what an old stick-in-the-mud he is. He bought something that kind of looks like a Christmas tree and stuck it in the corner with a couple of lights on it. I'm going to leave it up until you get back so you can tell him just like I did, that it is the ugliest thing we have ever seen."

Kinlin giggled, and said, "Bird, the day after tomorrow we are going camping. It's a good thing I brought my sword, huh?"

"Yeah, maybe you can protect Trout from bears and wolves," I said, not letting on how worried I was about the two of them in the wilderness.

"Bird, I have to get off now, but Trout wants to speak to you. Say merry Christmas to Jose for me, OK? Bye Bird."

Trout got on the phone and the adrenaline started to move in me. The phone symbolized an invention I equated with pain when it came to her. I didn't know if I was emotionally prepared to deal with her. After I heard her say, "Hello?" I didn't have much choice.

"Trout," I said.

"Merry Christmas," she said, softly.

"Merry Christmas, Trout."

It was another conversation of pauses and unsaid words. The feeling on the phone was so heavy I was sure it was weighing down the cable between here and Canada, making it bend and bow, touching the ground.

"Kinlin's wonderful," she said.

"Yeah, takes after his mother."

"He reminds me of you," she said, tenderly.

"Really? It's nice of you to say that Trout."

Feeling the importance of our words starting to pull her away, she said, "I think of you often, you are in so many of the things I look at, and feel."

"Yeah," I said, wanting to crawl through the line and hold her. "I think of you too. As a matter of fact, I don't think of much else."

"I've got to go now," she said, after a long pause, letting me know she wasn't prepared to end up where the conversation might take us.

"Have a nice Christmas with Jose," she said, fading.

"Thanks Trout, we'll try," I said, dreading the word goodbye I knew would follow.

"Bye," she said, in a trembling voice that sounded like it really was a thousand miles away. "Bird, I miss you."

"I miss you too." I heard her hang up.

I would have stood there all night staring out the window if Jose hadn't said, "Amigo, come over and sit down."

"Yeah," I said, the words startling me back into a place far removed from where I wanted to be.

"Amigo, have a drink and tell me about Kinlin," he said, wanting to take me away from where he knew I was.

We sat, and I told him of the conversation with Kinlin and how happy he sounded. We both agreed it had been a good idea to send him up there, and that it was going to be a good experience for them both.

Jose and I talked and watched the punch disappear. He brought out the bottle of tequila, a plate of limes, and two beers. I knew then what had been occupying my mind ever since we left Baja was going to be laid out on the table.

"Jose, there is something important I have to talk about. It has been on my mind ever since we left your uncle's."

"OK, amigo," he knew by the look of my face that it was important.

"Jose, I have a confession to make. It might not sound like that to you, but to me that's exactly what it is. It's been eating a hole in my guts ever since I realized it."

Pouring us both another drink, he looked at me, letting me know with the look to go ahead, he was there to understand.

"Jose, I have found out the reason for the suffocation she felt from me, and of her feeling that she was not safe around me."

"And what is that?"

"I will tell you," I said, "but first I have to say that in realizing it I have also found the grounds for what I have to really forgive myself for, and in the end, why Trout has to forgive me."

I put the glass to my mouth, and finishing my drink, continued. "I sought in her my immortality, and in that I thought I had also found the ultimate witness."

Jose looked at me. Trying to understand what I meant, said, "What do you mean your immortality, and a witness for what?"

"Everyone wants an immortality of sorts, and a witness to document their life. Whether it is children or a piece of art. They want something to carry on the legacy. With me it wasn't the thousands of pieces of sculpture I have made, or the poems I have stacked in a cardboard box, it was Trout. I didn't know it until a few days ago. In realizing that, it was a revelation that explained many things to me, it also filled me full of guilt. Knowing what I now feel kept her from seeing me as she should have. It deprived her of truly seeing herself. I see now that I mistakenly defined part of the bond as a role for her to be that witness, to carry on my legacy."

"How was she to do that?"

"Through her youth and that eternal love I thought the bond had given us. It was no wonder she could never communicate with me. The relationship wasn't about her; it was all about me. Because it was about me, it stopped her at every emotional turn. It was about my ego and the need for someone I trusted so much to be able to look inside of me and document every poetic thought I ever had. But in doing so she would have to also document all the pain. I was blind to the fact that it was contagious. In the end she would become infected too. I cheated her Jose, and in doing so, cheated myself."

"Don't be so hard on yourself. It has nothing to do with the love you both felt for each other," he said.

"Not the love, that is for sure, but it might end up destroying that love if it hasn't already. In my search for a pure love I let myself get in the way and allowed selfishness to replace that selflessness I so desperately wanted to find, that I knew existed."

"And what did you want her to witness, my friend?"

"The struggle, and to hang around for the triumph of finding that selfless love. But my intensity frightened her. Intuitively she recognized that it was my search, not hers. In the end she saw that whatever was moving in me kept her from moving. I wanted the love to never die and at the end, for her to testify at my grave. I wanted her to say things that would erase all the fears that have been growing in me all my life. I wanted her to give worth to my existence, by telling the world, 'OK, he had his weak points, but he was a good man and he was worth something. If he hadn't of been I wouldn't have loved him all these years."

I looked at him and he saw my eyes well up with moisture. "You see, Jose, I have to forgive myself for that. I hope she can forgive me for it too. But I am afraid if I would ever tell her what I have just told you, she would only find it another reason to run, discovering that I'm not the man she thought I was."

"Amigo, you are a sensitive man," he said, reaching out to me. "Sometimes too sensitive for your own good. If you feel like you need forgiveness, she would be the first one to do it. If Trout was here right now and heard what I just did, she would see that you are the man she fell in love with. Trout would never fall in love with a man who couldn't look into himself and search for the truth of who he was. Maybe you did demand too much of her, but amigo, you both did. Trout doesn't have to wait for you to die and then stand at your grave to tell the world how much you are worth. Hell, if I were to call her right now and tell her what we have just talked about, she'd run out on the street and yell it to the world! Amigo, you and Trout are both dreamers. You both want the unobtainable. Yours was immortality through her."

"And hers?"

"The unobtainable she wanted was you, and all you represented, but after she fell in love with you and felt the power of it, she realized she wasn't prepared to obtain it. By the time she would be, time and all the factors that go with it wouldn't allow her to have it. Amigo, it is the tragedy of dreamers like you and Trout. It is their unobtainable dreams that we must mourn, not you thinking you have been dishonest with her."

"Jose, I realized all of this when were in the car somewhere between Baja and here. At that moment I felt like I was back at step one, that the search had to begin all over again."

"That realization didn't put you back a step, my friend, it put you ahead a thousand. I told you, and so did Isabella, that Trout was your mirror. What you saw in the car was the biggest reflection she could have given you. She opened the way for you to honestly look at the rest of yourself. It can only profit you, and along with it, profit her too."

I was staring out at the garden trying to find reason in what he had just said when I heard him say, "Trout knows what your search is, it is not much different from her own. You hoped that you would both find the answer together, you probably won't, but that doesn't mean that whoever finds it first can't share it with the other. Amigo, that is what the bond really means, never forgetting what you both mean to each other."

Grabbing my arm, he said, "Amigo, the pain of the loss is still young, give it some time, in the end you will see it as the same as Trout's loss of her child last summer. It wasn't a death, but a rebirth of something beautiful. Amigo, Trout has given you the best Christmas gift possible."

"And what is that?" I asked.

"She has given you back your life, and with it all the poetry you have lost along the way. She has shown you that you can feel for someone in the deepest way possible. I tell you, she will always be there for you. I know that!"

He refilled our glasses, and while touching the glasses together, said, "If it is really a witness that you want, then I drink to the one that is up there in Canada at this moment laying next to Trout and dreaming of Kodiak bears and white timber wolves."

Realizing that he was right, the toast brought a smile to my face. I knew that through the love we will always share, Trout had given me immortality. Along with it she had given it to herself. The little boy curled up next to her was a legacy I couldn't deny.

It was midnight. Jose drank a toast to the birth of a king and I drank the same to a possible rebirth of myself. I walked alone out unto the porch and looked at the same stars Trout and I had seen on the first night we gave in to our love. I remembered the field on fire and the inferno that had burned inside of us both. The field lying in front of me, covered in a holy late night glow, brought back memories and my mind began to wander.

I saw the red-tail circling, catching wind, and as a blurred shadow floated over the field, I heard it scream. The shadow became a dark umbra dancer gliding through December gray Gravensteins, passing over eucalyptus and brushing the pine. It transformed into black water, rippling across freshly tilled earth, splashing against stone and fallen tree. Like lava, it moved unobstructed, crushing the rusty steel plow and coiled barbed wire, touched the white poppy, then dipped quickly to smell the wild onion. I watched as it fell back to the soil and gently filled the fresh tracks of last night's deer. It was being blown by the wind, and like a shaman, I saw it fade and disappear into the oak.

I envisioned myself alone, standing in the orchard with a silent wind touching my face. Looking up, I saw the sky a black abyss, swallowing all shape and winged form. I felt desolate and alone. My eyes searched the grove, and became blinded by the winter light. I found myself hungering for the scream, but instead heard Scottish pipes play a silent dirge echoing through the fields. I felt the loss and wandering, began to mourn.

The quiet was suddenly broken by the screeching sound of a thousand diving falcons. I looked down and saw a warm shadow at my feet. I watched it crawl up my leg and cover my loins, then like a butterfly swim through my gut. It made its way into my chest where I felt it fluttering, like a feathered heart.

It flew through muscle and bone and fell from my shoulder, becoming an eclipse on my arm. The dark amulet burned my skin. I saw the wailing metamorphosis grow and change into ebony, winged raven, its talons digging deep into my flesh drawing blood of my past. It feasted on memory and savagely ripped at the tendons and veined tributaries of the dried riverbeds of my soul.

The raven commanded packs of plumed jackals and black crested dogs that hovered and tore at my skin, feasting on my marrow and devouring all hope.

My right arm that was once strong, connected to a hand that was once tender became a lion's kill weighted down by the skeletons and bones of my past lives and of all the loves I had lost.

I was visited by ex-lovers with magic wands, hatchets in hand, and saw how we wept together for dreams destroyed and castles not built. I envisioned Walter lying by my side and heard us talk of the Black Death, and watched as we cut off each other's ears. I went deep into my past and saw a boy on his first bike on a hot valley day, his back bloody and punctured with arrows fired by the demons of his future.

Alone on the porch on that Christmas Eve I found my mind was taking me places I didn't want to be, that my search for peace was again being eaten by my past. I felt a gray moss begin to grow and hang from my eyes, becoming a widow's veil through which I saw the bleached white ribs of dead peregrine dreams.

Realizing that I was alone, I wanted to escape the parasoled banshee that had invaded my mind. I saw myself running, stumbling and falling, becoming immersed in the thorned catacombs of blackberry and wild rose. Watching, I felt old wounds never healed, open again. As my spirit bled I saw it cut deep paths of crimson visions that flowed slowly and melted into Zen garden memories. Through eyes clouded and moist, I saw fingers of emerald green ivy caressing red barked trees. Lying there, I looked at the pink camellia petals, falling and sticking to the dew-covered fern.

I stood on the porch trying to fight the vision and the memories that came with it, but in looking towards the garden I knew it had overpowered me and I couldn't fight it. I stared into the black vegetation and let the vision take me farther. I gave into it and saw myself lying on the ground surrounded by granite walls and spiked palm.

I stared at the gray stone altar and remembered a warm summer day where sacred words like family and father were whispered, and concealed affections tenderly shared. They fell from the heart like crystal stars, and with hands touching were spread out on the warm July rock as gently as one would lay precious stones on velvet cloth.

Witnessing myself weary, I laid down on soft needles of pine. Looking at my ravaged arm, I saw it healed, and felt my hand again, muscled and strong.

Drifting into sleep, I eyed the pond and saw that it was filled with blue heron and white swans. They were swimming in a silken down, floating amongst Renoir lilies. Scenting leather, I felt my face being pressed down into the soft, pillowed, open hand of the falconer's glove, with its suede fingers touching, closing my eyes.

I slept deeply, falling into visions of silver crane and snow geese, calling Van Gogh crows, witnessing the porcelain wings of albatross arms unfolding.

Finally feeling safe and unafraid, I saw myself being pulled into the warm fleeced breast of mother, then of woman, and I dreamt and remembered, as the red-tail circled, caught wind again, and screamed.

I was brought back to reality by the voice of Jose calling to me from the house. As I turned to open the screen door I saw Trout dancing through the field with smiling eyes, and knew at that moment in that bag she carried with her the first day she arrived was a needle of quill, and silken thread that she used to sew wings to my heart, and in doing so fulfilled The Pigeon Man's dream. In that summer of '93, she taught me how to fly.

I returned to the house and saw Jose take a book off the shelf and lay down in front of the fire, reading through the pages. I looked out again at the Zen garden and thought of Trout and Kinlin cuddled together, and of the peace that must be flowing through them at that moment. I heard Jose say, "Amigo, I have never read this one, this, 'Fishing With Trout In America.' I like it!"

"No Jose, that one is called, 'Trout Fishing In America'."

"Oh," he said, perplexed, looking back at the cover.

"'Fishing With Trout,' is another book in itself," I said.

"Oh," he propped himself up on one elbow and said, "amigo, maybe someday you write that one, huh?"

"Maybe I will Jose."

"Hey amigo, you going to put me in it?"

Looking back at the stone bench in the garden I said, "You already are Jose. You already are."

EPILOGUE

Bird died on a fall day, 14 years after Trout first pulled into his drive way. It was sudden and painless. He was sitting on the stone bench by the pond when a clot imbedded in his leg broke loose and exploded in his chest with the force of a rocket-propelled grenade.

Kinlin, who was then 19, was out in the orchard trimming apple trees when he looked down and spotted the wing feather of a red-tailed hawk; its quill encrusted with blood. The feather told him that something terrible had happened to Bird. He picked it up and took off in a dead run towards the pond. His father was lying motionless on the rock slab. Nobody had to tell him that Bird was dead. He knew the moment he looked at him.

Trout had come for a visit 3 months after her vacation in Canada with Kinlin, a decade and a half before, and never left. It seemed like Trout and Bird's karmic bond had finally defined itself, binding the two of them and Kinlin into an alliance of harmony and hope.

The farm had been put up for sale and Trout and Bird purchased it with the help of Trout's mother. They told Jose that he could live there rent free for the rest of his days on the condition he cut down the 20 marijuana plants growing in the patch of poison oak behind the water tower.

Trout finished her college years at a local university and went on to complete her Masters and a PhD in English literature. Later she would teach and in the years that followed, write a novel that was published and did quite well. A month after receiving her Masters degree she gave birth to a boy who was the spit and image of Bird. They named him Aaron. It was the Pigeon Man's name and a tribute to a man Bird dearly loved. Jose was upset that they didn't name him after Pancho Villa, so he protested and said he would call him Pancho. Kinlin said he would call him Young Bird until the boy got old enough to name himself.

Kinlin grew up to become a visionary and healer, exactly what Isabella had predicted. Trout schooled him at home and she taught him all he needed to know. He was a published poet at the age of 12 and had his paintings exhibited in a major San Francisco gallery when he was 16. At the time of Bird's death he was writing a thesis on the existence of the first poem ever written. He was, indeed special, and like Isabella could see things others couldn't. He became his little brother's teacher and mentor. It was a duty he was destined for, much like the one he used to bring Trout and Bird together.

Jose had stayed too. He built a small adobe house on a wooded corner of the property. It had to be adobe, he said, because it reminded him of Mexico, and besides, how could a "Real Mexican" live in anything else? Over the years Jose still took his journeys, but always had a home to return to. As he grew older his feelings to be closer to a family that had become his own halted his wanderings. He was the best uncle two boys could ask for and he loved them like they were his own.

Bird's creative energy had been rekindled and he had become reasonably successful with his art. He started a small pigeon farm on the property. When he wanted to be alone he would retreat there and sit on a chair facing the pens, just as his father had done years before. Those were moments when Bird was in his own private world, and everyone knew not to disturb him. His life had finally become one of tranquility. Bird quit feeding the beasts within him, so they left, never to return.

Five years after the death of Bird, Trout received a letter. It was postmarked from Tibet. She opened it and found a photograph and a note. In the photo two young men with backpacks stood on a fog-shrouded mountaintop. One had a long ponytail and headband. Trout could barely make out the bass lure tied to a leather thong hanging from the man's neck. Next to him was a younger man with a shaved head and mustache. Her heart bounded. It was her boys. She opened the folded piece of paper and slowly read the note.

Dearest mother,

As you can see by the postmark, we are in Tibet. Our search for the first poem ever written has been long and arduous. Our trip through Africa and Egypt was so disappointing I felt like turning back. But I felt a need to come here and look through some ancient archives. Young Bird keeps telling me that we are wasting our time; all we have to do is return to the farm and set on the stone bench in front of the pond. He says if we stare into the water long enough the poem will rise to the surface.

Love, Kinlin

Trout held the letter in her hand and stared out the window at the stone bench in front of the pond. She whispered to herself, "Yes, Kinlin, listen to your little brother. It's time to come home."

ACKNOWLEDGEMENTS

To Pam Noli, a true friend, for the undying support she has given me over the years in my creative endeavors. Jerry Kamstra, my friend and teacher who does his best to show me what the written word is all about. Julia Grove Benkofsky, daughter of my mentor Walter Grove, who with her sensitive, kind help enabled me to finish this book. My dear friend Bob Beer, one of the first to read the unedited mess that this book was, and told me it was worthwhile, that it was good. Jay Miller, for his advice and his expertise and graphic work on the front cover. Chrystal Durgans for patiently taking my picture, and also for jump-starting my heart. Gary Czychi, the spiritual Mac master, who took my old worn out floppy disc and re-formatted it into something readable. Rex Miller of Author House, who was always there when I needed him. Cathy McDowell, who, during our once a week sessions, helped me to quiet the beast, which allowed me the peace of mind to publish this book. To my ex-wife and life long friend Kim Morgan, who, twenty years ago, allowed me to build a small cabin on her property. It's a place where I have often sought refuge from the chaos of the outside world; a fortress that I locked myself in when I wrote this book. But, most of all to my father, "The Pigeon Man," who did his best to teach me all he knew, all that was good.

Printed in the United States
83051LV00005B/103-150/A